NEVER TOO LATE

MICALEA SMELTZER

- A WILLOW CREEK NOVEL -

Ashli,
ever give up
on true love!

Never Too Late
Copyright © 2015 Micalea Smeltzer

Cover design and photography by Regina Wamba, Mae I Design

Interior design by Angela McLaurin, Fictional Formats

BOOKS BY MICALEA SMELTZER

TRACE + OLIVIA SERIES
FINDING OLIVIA
CHASING OLIVIA
TEMPTING ROWAN
SAVING TATUM

SECOND CHANCES SERIES
UNRAVELING
UNDENIABLE

WILLOW CREEK SERIES
LAST TO KNOW
NEVER TOO LATE

STANDALONES
BEAUTY IN THE ASHES
RAE OF SUNSHINE

"Music washes away from the soul the dust of everyday life."
—BERTHOLD AUERBACH

CHAPTER ONE

I NEVER THOUGHT I'd end up back here.

Back in the place where my whole life blew up into a million tiny pieces.

When we drove away with the moving truck in tow I thought I was saying goodbye to this part of my life forever.

I'd been wrong.

Anger simmered inside my veins—anger at the boy I'd loved and lost here. He'd discarded me like I was a piece of trash, just when I needed him most. I was nothing to him.

Back when we were sixteen he'd been nothing but a bad boy with a scowl on his face.

Now, Mathias Wade was the lead singer of Willow Creek—one of the most popular bands in the world.

I couldn't escape him.

Everywhere I looked his face was on a magazine, or one of their songs played on the radio.

At twenty-three years old I should've been over him.

I guess to an extent I was, but the pain and anger had never gone away.

Now I was back home, and according to the copy of *People*

magazine clutched in my hand so was Mathias.

The pages of the magazine began to crinkle where I gripped it tightly.

I wanted to throw it down and stomp all over it—on *him*, just like he had done to me.

I wanted him to feel even a smidge of the pain I'd felt when he broke my heart into a million pieces.

I was convinced that once you fell in love with a Wade you could never stop loving them.

He should've been nothing more than the boy I loved as a teenager, but he wasn't.

He was everything.

And I was nothing to him.

"Ma'am?"

I startled at the sound of the cashier's voice.

"Do you want the magazine too?" She asked.

I'd basically mauled the poor magazine into oblivion so it would've been rude to put it back on the shelf. "Yeah." I handed it over. The way I figured it, I could burn it and chant some kind of spell that would turn him into a toad.

I swiped my credit card and she handed over the bag full of cat food, and the magazine.

I'd only gotten back into town last night and realized I didn't have cat food.

Percy was not pleased.

I made up for it by giving him too many treats.

He still wasn't happy with me, but at least I felt better.

I made the short drive home—still fuming over Mathias.

I couldn't believe that he was back in town. Although, I guess he never really left—according to the tabloids anyway. All the Willow Creek boys kept places in their hometown of Winchester, Virginia, even if they did spend a lot of time in L.A.

I pulled into the driveway, staring over at the plastic bag on the passenger seat.

I'd never finished reading the article, and now I was desperate to know everything it said.

I warred with myself, but finally I ripped the magazine from the bag and flipped through the pages.

Basically, the gist was that the guys were home for the holidays before their Coming Home Tour kicked off in the New Year.

I ran my finger over the picture of the four of them. I didn't know the blonde one, but I knew Maddox—Mathias' twin brother—and their best friend Ezra. While I'd mostly hung out with Mathias the other guys had been nice to me.

Even with the anger simmering in my veins I couldn't hate Mathias' success. I'd always wanted that for him. When we were young he'd never seen his own self-worth, but I'd always known he was remarkable. I hoped he saw that now too.

I still hated his fucking guts though.

I startled at a noise and realized I'd ripped apart the magazine.

Oh well. There goes another one.

Sadly, it wasn't the first time I'd torn apart a magazine because of Mathias.

I gathered up the torn shreds and put them in the plastic bag. I climbed out of the car, drawing my coat closer around me. After living in Arizona the last seven years I'd forgotten how cold it got here.

I stepped into the older home—inhaling the scent of freshly baked chocolate chip cookies.

"Grandma!" I called as I locked the door. "You're supposed to be in bed!"

"I wanted some cookies," she called back, "so I'm making

some God damn cookies and no one can stop me."

It was safe to say I got my fiery personality from my grandma.

I stepped into the kitchen and set the grocery bag down on the granite countertop—my parents had paid for the whole house to be remodeled a few years ago.

I kissed my grandma's cheek. "Here, let me help." I took the bowl from her so I could mix it. "Go sit down and I'll finish this."

She glared and yanked the bowl from my hands with surprising strength for someone as small and frail.

"Grandma!" I admonished. "You're supposed to be resting. You had a heart attack."

"And yet I'm still here. It's going to take a whole lot more than a faulty heart to knock me down," she huffed.

"Like what?" I asked, hiding a smile.

She thought for a minute, turning her head to the side. Her white hair was fluffed around her head and her duster hung limply on her frail frame. "Hmm, that chick that's always sticking her tongue out on a wrecking ball. *That's* what will knock me down."

I busted out in laughter—not only at the visual that had formed in my head, but also at the fact that my nearly eighty-year-old grandma knew who Miley Cyrus was.

"Grandma, how do you even know that?" I asked, leaning a hip against the counter. Percy—my black cat—rubbed against my legs.

"I watch MTV. It's the most entertainment I get during the day," she frowned. Looking up at me she said, "I saw that young man you used to hang around on there one day. He was a bad influence on you."

I rolled my eyes. "I think we were an equally bad influence on each other."

She stared at me in disbelief and finally shrugged her thin shoulders. "You go finish unpacking your room while I do this."

"Grandma," I groaned, "if I do that then I'm already failing at taking care of you."

"And like I told your over protective father, *I'm fine*. I don't need a babysitter." She grabbed a spoon from the drawer and waved it around. "Besides, something is going to kill me eventually. I can't live forever."

"Aw, grandma, and here I thought you were invincible."

"The wrecking ball will get me one day," she winked. She began to spoon out the cookie dough onto a pan. "It's nice that you and your parents are worried, but I've been getting by fine on my own for years and I'll continue to do so." She glanced up at me. "You're young, Remy. You need to live your life, not take care of me. Go get a job, meet a guy, and have some fun."

I frowned.

"And give me some great grandbaby's before I die," I flinched at the mention of babies. "That's an order." She flicked the spoon at me and a glob of cookie dough landed on my shirt. I grabbed it and popped it into my mouth.

"You know my dad will kill me if I don't keep an eye on you." I warned her.

"Your dad is all the way in Arizona, what he doesn't know won't kill him."

I wasn't really into the idea of dating (or babies) but a job would be nice. I'd already been groaning about how boring it would be lazing around here day in and day out.

Back home I'd been working as a receptionist. I hated it. I wasn't a desk job kind of girl. I wanted to be moving.

I had a degree in marketing, but I'd never done anything with it—much to the irritation of my parent's. I'd only gone to college and studied that because I knew it was what they wanted and I'd been trying to please them. They'd never really understood me. They both had high paying jobs—my dad a doctor and my mom a lawyer—and then my big brother was an attorney. They never made me feel like I wasn't loved, but I knew they never really got me.

I was wild and spontaneous.

I was loud and obnoxious.

I was the girl that wasn't afraid to be crazy.

I'm sure my dad would bust a vein in his forehead if he knew some of the craziest things I'd done.

Like that one time I road tripped to California by myself and went diving with sharks.

Or the time I was riding in the back of a friend's truck and ripped my top off, letting my boobs fly free for the whole world to see.

Yeah... it was a good thing my dad didn't know these things. *He'd* be the one headed to the grave, and not grandma.

"Alright, I'll go finish unpacking and see if I can find any jobs online."

"I'll just be here, baking cookies, and not dying," she cackled.

I shook my head and clucked my tongue for Percy to follow me.

Grandma had long ago moved into the bedroom downstairs so she didn't have to use the stairs.

Fortunately for me this left the whole upstairs as my domain.

When I arrived yesterday afternoon she'd been quick to tell me I could do whatever I wanted with the whole space.

I was definitely considering painting my room a dark purple. Right now the walls were a pale green and everything was light and pretty in the room. My mother had clearly decorated it. While there was nothing wrong with her taste, it just wasn't me. I preferred darker colors.

Percy jumped up on the pale yellow quilt, his black fur already covering the thing. Percy shed on everything. I might find it more of an annoyance if I didn't usually dress in black.

I hadn't brought a lot with me from Arizona, just clothes, some towels, and necessities. Unfortunately, I didn't own much else, since I'd been living with my parents.

I was kind of a failure like that.

I frowned.

I hated feeling like a disappointment, but I did. When I was sixteen years old I lost all the trust my parents had in me, and I never really got it back. It didn't really bother me, in the sense that I still always did my own thing, but sometimes I wanted them to look at me the way they did Robert—my brother. I wanted them to be proud of me, but the fact of the matter was I never really did anything worthwhile.

All I did was fuck up.

Time and time again.

It was my specialty.

I sighed, yanking clothes out of my suitcase and dumping them on the floor. I wasn't a very organized person—but since grandma didn't come up here I didn't have to worry about anyone seeing my mess.

I leaned my head against the bed and heard a soft meow when Percy jumped down and climbed into my lap.

I scratched him under his chin and looked down at him. He opened one amber colored eye to peek up at me.

"Well, Perce, what kind of trouble do you think I can get into here?"

He closed his eyes and laid his head back down on my lap.

I answered for him.

Lots.

CHAPTER TWO

I WALKED INTO the restaurant, heading straight for the bar with my red four-inch heels clicking against the concrete floors. I pretended to be oblivious to the stares of the men in the room, but I wasn't. I felt the way their eyes perused my body, admiring my curves. I didn't mind them looking. It was when they got touchy that I got pissed.

I strode right up to the bartender and leaned against the counter.

He turned to look at me, doing a double take. He couldn't have been more than two years older than me. He was good-looking with sandy brown hair, enough scruff to almost be considered a beard, and searing green eyes. Unfortunately for him I was only attracted to danger, and this guy seemed too normal for me.

"What can I help you with darlin'?"

Darlin'. Really?

I raised one pale blonde brow and leveled him with a glare. "I'm not your darlin' or hun or whatever else you might come up with."

He swallowed thickly and took a step back.

Yeah, that's right.

Be afraid.

Most people were.

Except for Mathias.

He embraced my prickly personality.

I closed my eyes momentarily dismissing all thoughts of the moody singer from my mind.

"Can I get you a drink?" He asked.

"No." I pouted my red lips. "But you can get me a job."

His eyes widened in surprise.

"You are hiring, correct? That's what the website said." I'd spent the afternoon browsing local online job ads and this was the only one that sounded mildly appealing.

I purposely leaned just a bit closer so he'd see a flash of my cleavage. Like all men his eyes dipped to my top. So fucking predictable.

"Yeah." He answered and his voice was surprisingly steady.

"So...?" I tapped my nails against the top of the bar. They were painted a shiny black and topped off with silver glitter.

"Hire her man, she's fucking gorgeous."

I leaned over to look at the man that had spoken from across the bar. He was probably in his forties, with a beer gut and balding, but I still sent a wink his way and with the way he sputtered you would've thought I kissed him.

"Well..." The bartender spoke. "I am the manager..."

"Great!" I chimed in before he could say anything else. "When do I start?"

"Tomorrow night too soon?" He asked.

"That would be perfect." I flashed him a flirtatious smile.

He seemed stunned for a moment, shaking his head. "I'm Tanner."

"Remy."

"Have you ever done bartending?" He asked.

I let out a twinkling laugh, drawing even more attention to myself. "Oh, Tanner, don't you think you should've asked me that before you hired me?"

He appeared sheepish.

"No, I haven't... well not officially." I flashed a smile and turned around. "See you tomorrow."

I heard one of the men at the bar say, "I'll be here every night you're working sweetheart!"

"No fucking nicknames!" I yelled and the men erupted into laughter.

Oh, this was going to be fun.

I DRESSED IN a pair of black ripped skinny jeans, and a white V-neck tee that dipped low enough to show a bit of cleavage, but not enough to be obscene. I shrugged into a leather jacket and pulled on a pair of heeled black boots, fluffing my straight light blonde hair to give it some body. This wasn't exactly proper work attire, but it was a bar, and I had to dress a certain way to get bigger tips. Plus, these jeans made my ass look amazing, so bonus points for that.

"See you later, Perce." I scratched the cat behind his ears for a moment. He began to purr and leaned into my touch.

I'd found Percy on the side of the road. He'd been in a nasty shape from a fight with another cat. I'd taken him home and tended to his wounds, even though he clawed up both of my arms while I tried to help him. I wasn't normally a caring person, but I saw something in Percy that reminded me of myself. He was lost and hurt, and needed someone to love him. So I did and he never left.

I headed downstairs and said goodbye to my grandma,

kissing her on the cheek.

Before we moved I'd always been close to my grandma. Our old house was in this very same neighborhood and when I was little I used to ride my bike over. We'd bake muffins and other treats together.

She'd ask me about school and boys, and let me gossip.

She never judged me the way my parent's did.

Well, not until...

I wasn't going to go there.

Not today.

Not ever.

I'd buried those memories for a reason.

I unlocked my car and slid inside.

I grasped the steering wheel in my hands so tightly that my knuckles turned white.

I leaned my head back and took a deep breath, in and out.

I wasn't going to start crying now.

Not about this.

I sat there, doing my breathing exercises, for as long as it took for the feelings to go away.

I'd started doing yoga a few years ago. I found that it helped soothe me. There was something so comforting about it.

I'd have to find a new studio to attend here. I didn't think I'd make it without my yoga.

Once I was composed I backed out of the driveway and headed to the bar.

I turned on some rock music and flailed about in my car.

I needed to prepare for my new job, and that meant getting myself pumped.

Most people turned to energy drinks, or drugs, for that.

Me? My drug was music.

That was another thing that Mathias and I had in common.

Fuck.

I was thinking about him again.

In Arizona I'd done a better job at pretending he didn't exist.

But here, where we grew up, it was impossible to escape his presence and the memories.

Oh, the memories.

I parked my car in the parking lot of the bar and leaned back; closing my eyes as I remembered the first time I ever met Mathias Wade.

"YOU KNOW THOSE will kill you, right?"

I looked up to see the good-looking guy from my biology class standing in front of me. His messy dark brown hair fell into his eyes and he gave me that blinding smile that had most girls spreading their legs for him.

"Do I look like a care?" I puffed out some smoke right in his face.

He didn't cough or flinch away.

"Give me one." He said.

I raised a brow. "They'll kill you, you know?" I mimicked his voice.

He smiled slowly and straightened. "Something's going to kill me one day," he shrugged. Something dark flashed in his unique gray eyes. "I might as well do the killing. I'm already screwed."

I handed him a cigarette and lit the tip.

"Enjoy, because you're not getting anymore freebies from me."

His lips twitched with the threat of a smile before he settled with a brooding stare and leaned against the brick exterior wall of the school.

"How'd you find me out here?" I asked.

He pushed his hair out of his eyes. "I followed you," he admitted, not ashamed.

I stared at him. "Why?"

"Why do you think?" His eyes were serious and his mouth was a straight line. I found myself staring at his lips. They were slightly plump and pouty, but not in a girly way. They tempered the sharp cut of his jaw and I wondered if they were as soft as they looked.

I shook my head free of those thoughts, focusing on what he had said.

"I'm not sucking your dick," I sneered. "That's a vicious rumor Jake started because he's an asshole."

His eyes glinted dangerously and my stomach stirred with something I'd never felt before. Not lust, I'd felt that plenty. It was something else that made no sense.

"That's not what I wanted, but now that you mention it..." He reached for his zipper. "Ow!" He yelped when the tip of my cigarette burned the skin between his thumb and forefinger. "I was only joking. Fuck."

He waved his hand through the air.

"That's not something to joke about." I squared my shoulders. "And for the record, I'm not against blowjobs, I just don't want to be forced to give one."

He stared at me like I was the most mysterious creature he'd ever seen.

"I don't want to have sex with you... well I'd like to," he admitted sheepishly, "but that's not why I followed you out here."

"It's not?"

"No." He stared at me intensely. "I've been watching you,

and I've realized that you're a lot like me."

"I am?" I looked at him like he was crazy.

He nodded and leaned close to me. "You're not like the other girls here who piss their pants if they see a fucking spider. You're wild. You don't care what people think of you. You're the bad girl they scoff at, but all secretly want to be."

"And you are?" I asked, lighting a new cigarette.

"I'm the fucked up bad boy everyone wants to save," his voice lowered, "but you wouldn't try to save me, would you, Remy? Because you're just like me."

My breath stuttered and he grinned at having made me react.

"I don't understand what you want." I stood tall and my voice never quavered.

"You."

He started to walk away, but promptly turned back around. He dug something out of his back pocket and I realized it was a pack of cigarettes. He handed me one of the slender white sticks and grinned. "No freebies, right?"

And then I jumped on his back and tackled him to the ground.

The rest is, as they say, history.

I DIDN'T KNOW it then, but looking back I could see just how much Mathias changed the course of my life with only one meeting—and not for the better.

He'd screwed me up even more than I was—stirring up a fucking tornado in my life and leaving me behind to clean up the mess while he lived his life.

I hated him for that.

I hated him for leaving me.

I hated him for hurting me.

But most of all I hated him because I loved him.

And I didn't think I could ever stop.

CHAPTER THREE

"You did good." Tanner commented, leaning against the bar with his arms crossed over his chest as I cleaned the glasses.

I arched a brow. "I think I did a little better than good. Have you seen my tips?"

"That's only because the guys that come in here are horny old men and if you shake your ass a bit they'll throw a hundred dollar bill at you."

I rolled my eyes. "Maybe you should shake your ass more then." I glanced up at him and smiled evilly. "You know, if you helped me with these we could get out of here sooner."

"I'm good." He sat on one of the barstools. "I like watching you work."

I rolled my eyes yet again. I did that a lot around Tanner. I grabbed a rag and threw it at him. "Help me, don't be a dick."

He chuckled and stepped behind the bar. "Okay, okay."

Tanner actually wasn't that bad to work with. He could be annoying, but that was only because he thought he was funny when he wasn't.

Working together we managed to finish in no time. Tanner locked up and we walked across the street to the parking lot.

"See you later, Red," he called, unlocking some small Dodge car.

I saluted him, making him chuckle.

Somewhere during the course of the evening he'd started calling me Red thanks to my signature red lipstick. Normally something like that would piss me off, but I found myself not caring. Maybe I was finally growing up—ha, not likely. I'd still sucker punch him if he tried to call me darlin' again.

I got in my car and sat there for a moment. It was well after three in the morning, so if I was smart I would head home and go to bed.

But I'd never been smart.

Instead, I found myself driving around town, reacquainting myself with my old haunts.

Somehow I ended up at my old high school.

Despite the chilly November air I slipped from the car and strode across the lot and around the building.

There.

Right fucking there, was where I met Mathias.

Where he forever changed the course of my life and fucked me up for anybody else.

My breath fogged the air as I stood there in the dark, staring at a damn brick wall like it held the answers to the universe.

Mathias and I had, had a... strange relationship.

We were friends.

We were lovers.

We were everything.

But in the end it wasn't enough.

We might've broken up and ended our relationship because of me moving—and because Mathias is an asshole—but I know in my heart we would've never worked anyway.

We were too much alike.

Both of us were like fire—loud, all-consuming, and willing to burn anything that got in our way.

I let out a sigh and crouched down, pulling up some of the dry brown grass.

Maybe there was something wrong with me, because even though I knew Mathias had been bad for me, I never wished I could take back everything that happened between us. The fact of the matter was I never felt more alive than I did when I was with him.

It was all so stupid.

I stood up again, kicking at the dirt.

It had been seven fucking years and I still couldn't seem to let go of the past.

I wondered if Mathias ever thought of me.

Probably not.

According to those celebrity news shows on TV he had a new plaything every day of the week.

I was nothing but a blip in his past. I didn't matter to him. I never had.

He told me he loved me once.

But if you love someone you don't destroy them.

CHAPTER FOUR

"YOU LOOK TIRED." My grandma commented, taking in the dark circles beneath my eyes.

"The night shift will do that to you." I took a sip of my too hot black coffee. "My body hasn't adjusted yet." I yawned.

It was well after ten in the morning, but I'd only gotten five hours of sleep.

"Let me make you some breakfast." She was already bustling about the kitchen, grabbing a pan.

"I'm supposed to be making *you* breakfast." I yawned again and laid my head on the table.

"I don't think you could lift a finger right now. Besides," I heard the refrigerator door open, "it does me good to take care of someone else."

I lifted my head up and propped it in my hand. "Why do I feel like I moved here to take care of you, but *you're* going to end up taking care of me?"

"Because I'm your grandma and I'm supposed to tend to you. I might be old, but I'm not completely useless." She rolled her eyes, scrambling some eggs. "I swear, your father thinks I just lay around and don't move or do anything." She waved a hand at me. "I'll have you know that I have a boyfriend."

I snorted. "A boyfriend?"

"Yes," she nodded rapidly. "I met him at the senior center during dance night—the way he moved his hips..." She licked her lips and made a noise in the back of her throat.

"Oh! Ew! Grandma!" I covered my eyes.

I might've seen and done a lot of crap in my life, but I did *not* need the visual of my grandma getting it on.

She snickered at me and said, "Oh, Remy."

She finished making the eggs and slid a plate in front of me along with some orange juice.

"Thanks," I smiled at her. "Now go lay down."

She glared at me, but I glared right back.

"Fine," she relinquished, "but only because Kathy Lee and Hoda are on the *Today Show* right now, and they crack me up." She started to waddle out of the room, but stopped. "How about you come back with me, we'll open a bottle of wine, and every time they laugh we'll drink."

I gaped at her. "We'd be drunk in no time."

"Exactly."

Only my grandma.

"You just had a heart attack. Let's lay off the alcohol for a while, okay?"

She sighed and mumbled, "Fun sucker," under her breath as she went back to her room.

I finished my breakfast and cleaned up before heading upstairs in the hopes of getting some more sleep.

Percy was curled up on my pillow and I scooted him over only for him to promptly move back to my pillow.

Cats.

I relinquished my pillow to him and lay down on the other side of the bed.

I'd been working at the bar for a full week now. I actually

liked it. The people I worked with were nice and the patrons might've been rowdy, but they weren't rude. Yet.

I crooked my arm across my face—blocking out the sunlight that still streamed into the bedroom despite the closed blinds.

It didn't seem to matter how tired I was my brain didn't want to shut off.

I kept thinking about what a failure I was.

That at twenty-three years old all I had to show for my life was a degree I would never use, a job at a bar, and I was living with my grandma whom I was supposed to be taking care of, but really she was looking after me.

I was pathetic.

I covered my face with my hands and let out a small scream of pent up rage.

I had to get out of here.

I jumped out of bed and changed into yoga pants and a tank top. Since it was cold out I shrugged into a sweatshirt before putting on my tennis shoes.

Yoga would help calm and center me, then all would be well again.

I hoped.

I bound down the steps, said goodbye to my grandma, and headed to the nearby gym that had a yoga studio. I'd found it earlier in the week. Surely they'd have a class right now and I could join in.

I got there and hurried inside to escape the windy weather.

When I reached the room that housed the yoga studio it was closed.

"Fuck!" I screamed, kicking the door.

"Hey," a guy approached me slowly, "are you okay?"

"Do I look like I'm okay?" I glared, ready to kick him too if he pissed me off.

He held up his hands in a placating manner. "Sorry," he chuckled, flicking his head to the side so that his sweaty blond hair didn't hang in his eyes. "Is there something I can help you with? I own the gym."

I eyed him up and down. He seemed pretty young—definitely not in his thirties yet—with a lean athletic body.

"Yeah," I huffed, "I'd like to do some yoga." I tossed my thumb over my shoulder at the closed studio.

"Sorry," he shrugged. "I can't do that."

"But you're the owner!" I snapped.

He merely chuckled at my outburst. "I'm teaching a boxing class, why don't you check it out. You might find that it's more to your liking than yoga. That was one mean kick."

I frowned. I didn't want to do boxing, but I didn't see what choice I had. I needed to work off some of this pent up rage and at least boxing would allow me to hit something and pretend it was Mathias' face.

"Fine." I agreed reluctantly, lifting one of my shoulders in a half shrug.

"I'm Drew," he introduced himself.

"Remy," I replied.

His brows rose. "That's a unique name."

"So I'm told," I sighed.

I followed him through the building and into a room similar to the yoga studio. People were just beginning to arrive, standing in front of the punching bags. I was surprised to see that all the people were women.

"There's an empty one back there." Drew pointed and I detached myself from his side.

It was kind of surprising that I'd never tried boxing before. I guess maybe I'd been afraid it would only make my aggression worse, whereas yoga calmed me.

Drew came to my side with a wrap for my hands. He waited for me to hold my hands out so he could do it but I refused.

"I can do it myself." I wasn't helpless.

He raised a brow and leveled me with a look. "You haven't been taught the proper way. I'm doing it this time and next time you can do it on your own."

"Who said I'd be back here?" I challenged.

He smiled, ducking his head. "Trust me, you will be."

"You're very full of yourself."

He snorted. "I wasn't meaning you'd be back because of me, besides I'm married." He waved his left hand in front of my face. "I meant that boxing can be addicting. Sometimes it's nice to hit something."

"And kick something," I added, finally holding my hands out for him.

I watched what he did, careful to memorize the movements so I could replicate them the next time. *If* there was a next time.

He finished and flashed me a smile. "You're not going to kick me?"

"The day is young."

He chuckled and took a step back. "I like you."

"You might be the only one." I mumbled the words under my breath and he walked off, not having heard me.

He turned on some really loud rock music and I twisted my neck from side to side, smiling.

I listened to Drew's instructions on how we should position our feet and hips. Then he moved on to explaining what our fists should look like.

After that he basically let us have at it.

And I punched the shit out of that bag, wishing I could make it as broken as me.

AN HOUR LATER I left the gym dripping with sweat, but feeling a hundred times better.

After the class I'd approached Drew and signed up to return to the classes.

Goodbye yoga and hello boxing.

I stopped off at Starbucks on my way back to the house, ordering an iced Caramel Macchiato.

I was waiting by the bar for them to make my drink when I heard a shriek of, "Remy Parker, is that really you?!"

I turned to look over my shoulder and my jaw dropped at the sight of one of my only high school friends.

"Lana?" I asked, my eyes zeroing in on her *very* round stomach.

"It is you!" She screamed again, drawing the attention of everyone in Starbucks. She threw her arms around me and I was reluctant to return the gesture. I couldn't remember Lana ever being this bubbly in high school. She'd been a lot like me, angry at the world. "You look so pretty!"

I took a step back. "You look... large."

She let out a giggle and rubbed her stomach. "It's twins!"

That explained it.

"So much has changed since I last saw you," she continued, forcibly pulling me over to a table.

"Yeah," I agreed. "I thought you hated kids."

"I hated everything when we were friends." She laughed, scooting the chair back to accommodate her stomach. She flipped her brown hair over her shoulder. In high school it had been dyed black with hot pink tips. "A lot changes in seven years."

"It sure does," I muttered, my eyes shifting around as I tried to formulate a plan of escape.

"So, how are you?" She asked.

"Good," I nodded.

"What are you doing back in town? I figured you were gone for good. You were always better than this place."

"My grandma needed someone to take care of her, so I volunteered for the job," I sighed, looking towards the bar and hoping my drink was ready.

"Oh, is she okay?" Lana frowned.

"It would take a lot to knock her down, trust me." I laughed. My drink order was called and I stood up. "That's mine," I pointed.

"Oh, okay," she smiled. "Would you want to meet up for lunch one day?"

I hesitated. I'd cut off contact with everyone I knew from here after I moved to Arizona. It had been easier that way. A clean break.

Looking at Lana now, she seemed like a stranger.

But I found myself saying, "Yeah, that would be fine."

Fuck, what had I just agreed to?

We exchanged phone numbers and I grabbed my drink, waving goodbye.

So far, moving back here wasn't going anything like I expected.

I thought it would be hard being back here—that the memories would overwhelm me.

And I guess in a way they were.

I was certainly thinking about Mathias more than I had in Arizona—and let's face it, I thought about him plenty there.

But it didn't *hurt* like I expected it to.

I didn't feel like my insides had been ripped apart and

splayed open to be picked apart by vultures.

Maybe coming back here was actually a good thing and I'd finally be able to move on and let go.

Then again, maybe I was wrong.

CHAPTER FIVE

"NO MORE MTV!" I called over my shoulder as I left.

"I'm older, you can't boss me around young lady," my grandma yelled back.

I laughed at her response, shutting and locking the door behind me.

I was working another late night at the bar. The money was excellent, but I wasn't sure if I liked how many hours Tanner had me working. I was quickly becoming exhausted. I wasn't a night owl like I used to be. I kept hoping my body would adjust, but so far it hadn't.

I parked my car, grabbed my purse, and scurried inside and away from the cold.

"Hey, Tanner!" I called, heading to the back.

I tucked my purse away, reapplied a coat of red lipstick, and put on my game face.

When I worked I put on a show.

I strode back out into the bar, swaying my hips and smiling as I felt the men's eyes zero in on my ass.

You can look, but you can't touch.

"Evening, Red." Tanner nodded when I slid behind the bar.

"Todd needs a refill." He nodded to the end of the bar where one of the regulars sat.

I might've only been here a week, but I'd already memorized what most of these guys ordered.

I grabbed a Bud Light, popped the cap off, and handed it over to Todd with a wink.

I swore the poor guy blushed.

Bless his heart.

I quickly picked up where Tanner needed help.

When the bar and restaurant area were packed it became insane trying to keep up with all the orders.

Not to toot my own horn, but I honestly didn't know what Tanner did before I came along.

Hours passed and I never got a break—and someone spilled their beer and it splashed on my shirt, so that kinda sucked. The good news was I was wearing a black shirt, the bad new was that despite that I still looked like I was competing in a wet t-shirt contest. At least I got bigger tips.

The bar began to empty out as closing time approached.

I was ready to collapse with exhaustion. Tonight had been one of the times where there never seemed to be a moment to catch your breath.

I wiped down the bar and got the lone guy there another drink.

I had my back turned when I heard another stool pull out behind me. "I'll have the usual."

Ice.

My body was a frozen block of ice.

Seriously, give me a tap and I'd go crumbling to the floor.

There was no fucking way.

It couldn't be possible.

I had to be imagining that voice.

"Hello? Did you hear me? I said I'd have the usual. If you don't know what that is, maybe you should find a new job."

Nope, I definitely didn't imagine it.

I turned around, facing a ghost.

I watched all the color drain from his face and he reared back, nearly falling off the stool.

"Remy?" His voice was nothing more than a whisper, but it still managed to affect me.

"The usual?" I asked. "Let me guess, that?" I pointed at the most expensive bottle of scotch the bar had—something that no one else had ordered at this point.

He nodded woodenly, still stunned.

I grinned evilly and reached for the bottle.

I took the cap off and acted like I was reaching for a glass, but instead I lunged forward and tilted the bottle, dumping all of the contents on top of his head.

I let the bottle drop to the ground where it shattered at my feet.

I didn't care if I got fired.

I'd wanted to do that—or something like it—for a long time.

The lone man at the bar looked like a deer caught in headlights. He probably thought he was next. He pulled his wallet from his back pocket, slapped some bills down, and grabbed his coat before hauling ass out of there.

Mathias looked at me with a sneer on his lips and anger in the depths of his eyes. The amber colored liquid stained his crisp button down white shirt and dripped from his hair onto his face.

He barred his teeth, a growl rumbling in his chest. He slammed his palms against the top of the bar. "You always did know how to piss me off. Would you like a fucking medal?"

I smiled, batting my eyes innocently. "What did I do?"

"Why are you back here?" He seethed, leaning forward. His look was menacing, and most people probably would have been shied away from him, but I'd never been scared of Mathias. Then again, I wasn't very smart, so maybe I *should've* been afraid. "You shouldn't be here."

I widened my eyes. "Really? It's a free country. I'm pretty sure there's no rule against me being here. Although with all the money you have now you can probably pay to have someone kick me out of the state."

His eyes flashed with danger. He opened his mouth to speak, but was cut off by Tanner.

"Did I hear something break?" Tanner asked, returning from the bathrooms. "Oh." He frowned when he took in the drenched Mathias. He turned to me and said simply, "You're fired."

"What?" I gasped. I mean, I'd been expecting it, but still.

"You can't pour drinks on customers," he flailed his arms. "Especially not that one." He pointed a finger at Mathias.

I rolled my eyes. "Whatever," I sighed.

I wasn't going to argue with him. I knew it had been a dumb move, but I didn't regret it. I marched around the bar, leaving behind the broken glass, and pushed open the door to the backroom.

Since I was fired I wasn't going to stay there a second longer and be subjected to Mathias' presence. I wasn't a masochist.

I let out a startled scream when a heavy body grabbed me from behind and pushed me against the wall.

Mathias pinned my hands above my head and pressed his hips into mine so that there was no way I could move. I couldn't see much of him like this, but I could take in the broadness of his shoulders and the way the wet shirt stuck to his sculpted chest. Mathias had always had a nice body, but now? Oh my God, the guy was built, and feeling him pressed up against me like this was doing all kinds of crazy things to me.

Fuck.

I bit down on my tongue until I tasted blood—the pain burning away my treacherous thoughts.

"What are you doing here?" He asked through gritted teeth.

"I'm not here for you, if that's what you're getting at. You always were such a pretentious asshole. I don't know why I ever liked you."

His anger seemed to disappear momentarily and he leaned in close. He glided his nose along my neck, like he was inhaling my scent, and my pulse jumped.

"You loved me Remy."

I jerked in his grasp. "The love of a sixteen year old doesn't count," I spat.

He grinned. "Jumpy?"

"Let me go." I bucked against him, trying to twist away.

"No." His eyes darkened again as his anger returned.

He pressed into me further so that our chests were pressed together.

"How'd you get back here?" I asked.

"I know, Tanner," he shrugged. "You're not fired by the way." He grinned like he was so fucking wonderful.

"I don't need help from you." I wiggled again, testing his grip to see if I could slip away or knee him in the groin.

He clucked his tongue. "You always were so unwilling to take help from anybody."

"Don't act like you know me." I was seething, a cobra coiled and ready to strike.

His voice lowered and rumbled against my body. "I know you very well, Remy."

"Sex doesn't count."

He chuckled, his breath fanning against my neck. "Oh, Remy.

We both know it was so much more than that."

"Let me go." I bucked against him again.

"That's not allowed." He growled.

"What are you going to do?" I taunted. "Tie me up?"

"I'm considering it." His gray eyes were serious.

"What do you want with me?" I asked, my voice sounded breathless—not with want or desire, but with pain and suffering.

He leaned close and his delectable lips touched my ear. "I want you to stop haunting my fucking dreams."

And then he let me go and walked away, like nothing ever happened.

Just like the last time.

I LAY IN bed, with Percy hogging my pillow, convinced the whole thing had been a hallucination.

There was no way that had happened, right?

I mean, I didn't really pour a bottle of scotch on his head and then have him pin me to a wall?

The tender spots on my wrists where he'd held me disagreed with my thoughts.

When I saw the article saying that Willow Creek was back in town for the holidays I'd known there was the *possibility* of bumping into Mathias. I just never expected it to be like that.

So... explosive.

But that was our way.

It always had been.

People had never understood our relationship.

We spent most of our time arguing and the rest fucking each other's brains out.

It was how we functioned.

32

Despite all that, we still knew each other better than anyone else did. Within each other we found someone we could confide all our deepest, darkest secrets in.

After that first day where he approached me for a cigarette our strange friendship bloomed, and then blossomed into something more.

Were we ever boyfriend and girlfriend?

I suppose we were together in the only way two fucked up sixteen year olds knew how to be together.

He'd been my everything.

And I'd been his... I don't know.

Sometimes I wondered if I ever really mattered to him.

I rolled onto my back, squishing my eyes closed and wishing for sleep, but it was futile.

I'd always been a strong girl who didn't take any shit.

But Mathias was my weakness.

With him I turned into someone I didn't recognize.

And it was all because I'd given him my heart and never gotten it back.

It was time to turn the tables.

I was going to make him fall in love with me, and when he didn't see it coming I'd break his heart just like he'd done mine.

I smiled up at the darkened ceiling.

Let the games begin.

CHAPTER SIX

"I NEED YOUR help with something." I leaned against the bar, giving Tanner the most sincere look I could muster. I really hoped it didn't look like I was constipated. That would be tragic.

He eyed me, tucking the rag he'd been using to wipe down the bar into his back pocket. "My help, Red? Why would you need my help?" He scratched at his beard.

"You're friends with Mathias, right?"

He straightened. "I'm not getting you his autograph, if that's what you're asking for."

I snorted. "You do recall the fact that I poured a five-hundred dollar bottle of scotch on his head, right? Do you *really* think I would've done that if I wanted his autograph?"

"Good point." He shrugged his wide lumberjack shoulders. "We're not really friends. More like acquaintances. He likes it here because no one bothers him and I always keep his drink of choice on hand."

"Whatever." I sighed, not interested in the details of his relationship with Mathias. "I just wanted to know if you knew some way I could contact him to apologize?"

Step One of my plan was to ambush him—preferably wearing

a slinky dress and killer heels. I knew Mathias' tastes and there was no way he'd be able to resist that. Once I had his attention I'd seduce him, drag him almost to the edge, and then leave him hanging and begging for more.

I hadn't really thought of a Step Two yet.

I figured it would come to me when the time was right.

"Sorry," Tanner turned his back on me, drying off the clean glasses, "it's not like I have his phone number or anything."

Dammit.

This was not going according to plan.

Think, Remy. Think!

I came up with nothing.

"He lives in the penthouse of that fancy shmancy hotel around the corner. That historical one or whatever."

I perked up with interest. I couldn't believe Tanner was actually giving me some details after the stunt I pulled. Maybe he was high or something. It honestly wouldn't surprise me.

"The George Washington Hotel?" I asked.

"Yeah," he glanced at me over his shoulder and nodded. "That one."

If I was a hugger I would've hugged Tanner in that moment.

It might take a few tries, but if I started hanging around the hotel—which was coincidently on the same block as the bar—I was bound to run into him.

I resisted the urge to rub my hands together like some evil mastermind and cackle insanely.

"But I didn't tell you this!" Tanner leveled me with a glare. He seemed to have come to the sudden realization that he probably shouldn't have extended this kind of information to me.

Too late now buddy-boy.

"No, you didn't." I agreed.

I hopped up on the counter and pointed at the glass Tanner was currently trying to dry. "You missed a spot."

He looked up at me and glared. "Get off the bar, Red. And if you think you can do better, maybe you should take over."

I climbed down and took the glass and cloth from him.

"I will." I bumped his hip with mine.

He had me working an earlier shift today and the bar was relatively dead. Even the waitresses didn't have many tables to tend to. I decided then, that even though it was exhausting, I'd rather work late. Not only did I earn a hell of a lot in tips, but it was a lot more fun.

Right now I was bored, and cleaning this glass was the most fun I'd had in an hour.

Pathetic, I know.

Once I'd dried all the glasses and put them away Tanner found me and told me to head on home since it was so dead.

On my way to my car my phone buzzed in my back pocket. An unfamiliar number flashed on the screen.

"Hello?" I answered hesitantly.

"Remy!"

"Oh hi, Lana." For a moment I'd thought it might be Mathias. How stupid of me.

"I'm free and was wondering if you might want to meet for dinner? How about Toulouse?"

"Where is that?" I asked with a small laugh. "It's been so long since I've lived here."

"It's the new French restaurant at the George Washington hotel."

I stopped in my tracks in the middle of the road, causing cars to honk at me. I hurried to the other side, internally doing a cha-cha at the perfectness of the situation.

"Sounds good. What time are you thinking? I just got off

from work and smell like a bar."

"Is two hours from now too soon?"

I slid in my car and cranked the engine, looking at the time that flashed on the dashboard. "That'll be perfect."

"See you then!" She chimed cheerily, completely oblivious that she'd just given me the perfect excuse to run into Mathias.

But first, I had to buy a new dress.

And shoes.

Yes, definitely shoes.

I CURLED MY blonde hair, running my fingers through it to make it more loose and natural looking. I sprayed it with enough hairspray that it was probably a miracle I didn't pass out. But my naturally straight hair had never held a curl for long and I needed these to last.

Not that I was planning to stay the night if I ran into Mathias.

I needed to leave him wanting more and not show all my cards up front.

Once my hair was finished I moved on to makeup.

I used smoky grays around my icy blue eyes, layering on the mascara to make them pop even more. I coated my lips with my favorite red lipstick and stepped back to appraise my appearance.

Perfect.

I padded down the hall and into my room, so I could slip on the new black dress I got.

The dress fit me like it was tailored specifically to my body. It had random triangular cutouts that showed bits and pieces of my skin.

I slipped on a pair of red heels and grabbed a clutch.

"See you later, Perce."

I gave the cat a quick belly rub before going downstairs to say goodbye to my grandma. She was in bed watching recorded episodes of *Arrow* and drooling over Stephen Amell's abs. My grandma was one of a kind.

"I'm going out," I told her, poking my head in the doorway.

She shushed me for interrupting her show.

That woman.

"There's a pause button," I commented with a grin.

She grabbed a pillow to throw at me, so I hurried away.

I'd made dinner for her earlier when I got home, even though she insisted she could do it herself. The woman was so God damn stubborn.

But then so was I.

My heart raced as I drove to the restaurant to meet Lana. The possibility of running into Mathias again had my body humming.

I was a bit afraid that the humming had nothing to do with my plan for revenge and everything to do with the way he affected me.

I turned up the music, hoping it would help center me and give me the strength I needed to do what I had to do. I could not forget the mission.

I parked my car across the street and deposited some change in the meter.

I wrapped my knee length black coat tighter around my body and ran across the street to the hotel—well, ran as fast as I could in the heels I was wearing.

I stepped into the warmth of the hotel and let it wash over me for a moment.

The hotel was surprisingly fancy—but I should've expected as much with a rock star supposedly living in the penthouse suite. It's not like he would live in a dump.

The floors were a shiny marble and the walls were painted a buttery gold color accented with dark wood tones.

It was beautiful and looked like something you'd see in New York City—or so I assumed, since I'd never actually been there.

In front of me sat a round table with the largest vase of flowers I'd ever seen. I stepped closer, reaching out to touch one of the delicate petals and gasped when I realized it was real.

The bar was to my left, and I knew that would most likely be the best place to search for Mathias, but I was supposed to be meeting Lana at the restaurant. Which sat to my right. So close, and yet so far away.

I started over to the restaurant and immediately spotted Lana sitting at a table waving at me like she was trying to land a plane.

I was going to need Vodka if I was going to make it through this dinner without gagging.

I couldn't believe this was the girl I'd been friends with in high school.

Back then she'd been just like me and even had her eyebrow and tongue pierced. Now she was like a fucking Stepford wife. It was scary.

I pulled out a chair and sat down. "Thanks for calling me." I smiled, smoothing my hands down my dress.

"I wasn't sure you'd be able to join me." She admitted with a shrug, taking a dainty sip of her glass of ice water. Jesus Christ. Had she been to some kind of etiquette class? She held her glass like she was the Queen and sat perfectly straight.

"Normally I wouldn't be able to. I usually work at night." I picked up my own glass of water that had already been filled before I arrived.

Lana set her glass back down and I got an eyeful of a very large engagement ring on her finger. The thing was massive and looked like it needed a crane to lift it. Her wedding band was just as flashy, with diamonds going all the way around. She was only twenty-three like me and that seemed so young to be married with a baby on the way. *Babies*, I corrected myself.

"So, who's the guy?" I asked, nodding at her hand and glancing down at the menu.

"Uh... you remember Clayton Jamison?"

My head shot up. "That asshole football player who's the Mayor's son?"

She nodded.

"You married *him*?" I scoffed, feeling like I was choking on something sour. "*Why?*"

"People change, Remy." She huffed, fiddling with the cloth napkin already placed in her lap.

"I guess they do," I agreed, taking a sip of water to have something to do.

I didn't feel like I had changed at all from the girl I was in high school. I guess I knew more now, and was therefore a little wiser, but I was still a bitch. I didn't care what people thought of me. I was always going to do my own thing.

A waiter appeared to take our order and I told him to bring me whatever their specialty was. I didn't really care what I ate at this point.

"This place is nice," I commented, trying to steer the conversation in a different direction.

"It's one of Clayton's favorite's," she smiled.

I arched a brow. "And what's Lana's favorite?"

She frowned, mulling over my words. "I'm not sure."

"Are you happy?" I asked her suddenly.

Her nose crinkled. "Yeah?" She framed it as a question. "I

mean, not all the time, but usually."

"Good," I nodded, sitting back. "That's nice to hear."

I might've thought it was weird that Lana grew up to marry one of the biggest jerks we went to school with, but if she was genuinely happy then I was happy too. She deserved the fairytale ending.

Bitches like me?

We didn't get the fairytale or the romance.

We got the raw and the real, and then we got dumped on in the end.

It was the way of the world.

We spent the rest of the dinner catching up and trying to get to know each other again. It was weird and definitely awkward at times, but while talking to Lana I discovered how starved I'd been for a friend.

A real friend.

Someone you talked to.

And not someone that constantly got you into trouble.

I walked with Lana to her car—frankly I was afraid if I left her alone her water might break and she'd end up being one of those people you heard about on the news that had their kid in the back of a car.

I watched her taillights disappear around the corner and I headed back into the hotel and to the bar.

It was nearing ten and the place wasn't packed like where I worked.

It was mostly lone businessmen sitting around nursing a drink.

I sat down on one of the barstools and ordered an ice water.

I needed to keep my head right now, not end up drunk.

Time trickled by slowly and Mathias made no appearance.

Maybe he didn't drink as often as he used to—where he

drank himself into oblivion every night so he didn't have to relive the horrors of his past.

Or maybe tonight he was drinking alone in his penthouse.

Or he could even be at the bar I worked at.

My throat closed up at the fourth possibility—the one that said he might be on a date.

I wasn't supposed to *care* about him.

He broke my heart and didn't bat an eye.

This was about revenge, not about being in his arms again.

The stool beside me slid back and my body sparked with hope, but when I looked the man sitting down next to me wasn't Mathias.

Of course not.

The man eyed me, unashamed in his perusal of my body.

I wasn't vain, but I knew men admired my body and I used it to my advantage.

"Here on business?" I asked.

"You could say that," he replied, his dark eyes flickering over the tops of my breasts. He turned away briefly to signal the bartender. Once he had the man's attention he placed his order and turned to me once more. "I'm Gavin."

"Remy," I replied, taking a sip of my water.

His eyes zeroed in on the way my lips wrapped around the straw, and I was sure he was picturing my lips around something else.

"Why are you alone here, Remy?"

I shrugged, counting the bottles behind the bar. Gavin was boring me and he was also distracting me from my mission. "Because I want to be."

His hand landed on my knee, snaking up my thigh and I stiffened.

"How much?" He asked me.

I reared back. "Excuse me?" He couldn't be asking me what I thought he was.

"How much?" He repeated. "For the night."

Before I could respond—and my response probably would've been to slap him—a heavy hand descended on Gavin's shoulder.

"I suggest you leave," the new arrival growled lowly.

Gavin glanced up and smiled cockily. "Sorry, I didn't know she was already taken for the night."

"She's not a fucking prostitute."

I closed my eyes. I didn't know what to make of Mathias showing up and defending me. This was not how I'd planned this.

"I couldn't tell the difference," Gavin spoke.

Mathias growled unintelligibly and cocked his arm back, ramming his fist into Gavin's face.

Gavin fell out of the chair and onto the ground.

Mathias dove after him, punching him again.

When Mathias got like this I knew to get the hell out of dodge.

I grabbed my clutch and hurried away—the bartender already rushing to break up the fight.

My heels clacked against the marble floors as I hurried for the bathrooms to compose myself.

The door swung closed behind me and I grasped the nearest porcelain sink in my hands, trying to slow my breathing.

I couldn't believe that had happened.

Shockingly, the most unbelievable part of the situation had been Mathias coming to my defense.

My hands shook like I was coming down from an adrenaline rush.

I hadn't been scared of the man, though. I'd handled plenty of guys like him before.

No, this reaction was only caused by one person.

He stirred up my insides, shaking me around until I couldn't make sense of anything—and he hadn't even said a single word to me.

The door opened and I grabbed my clutch to leave, not wanting another woman to be a witness to my breakdown. Or whatever this was.

But it wasn't a woman.

Mathias stood in front of me, his pressed white button down shirt now wrinkled. The suspenders he wore were slightly crooked and I itched to straighten them.

Instead, I said, "You've really changed, Mathias. What is this? Nerd chic?" I waved a hand at his clothes that probably cost more than I made in a month.

"Shut up." He sneered, crowding into my space.

"Make. Me."

With a growl he grasped my hips and pushed me into the wall. His hands moved down to my thighs, lifting my legs so I was forced to wrap them around his waist.

His lips descended on mine before I could take a breath, and then he seemed to become my air.

His touch sparked an electric current in my body.

His hips pressed into mine and I moaned into his mouth, pulling at his hair.

When his lips tore from mine for a moment, I panted, "I could've handled that guy myself."

He didn't reply, he just kissed me again.

Our hands seemed to be everywhere at once.

I wanted to weep at how good his hands and lips felt on me. No one had ever compared to Mathias and what he could do to me. A spark like the flow of an electrical current seemed to flow through my veins anytime he touched me. Hell, sometimes I felt it with a single glance from him.

Suddenly my plan to seduce him seemed so stupid, because here he was seducing me. Or at least it felt that way.

I was in over my head when it came to this guy.

I always had been.

Yet here I was, once again, unable to let him go.

He was like my drug—an intoxicating high but the crash left me defeated, alone, and searching frantically for the next hit.

He ripped his body away from me and I dropped to the ground, barely catching myself.

Without a backwards glance he was out the door.

I would've thought I imagined the whole thing if it wasn't for the swinging door.

Instead of standing there I stormed after him and jumped on his back, much the way I had the first day we ever talked.

This time he didn't fall to the ground.

It was like he expected me to jump on him.

I wrapped my arms around his neck and my legs around his waist, holding on for dear life.

"You don't get to do *that* and just *leave*." I hissed the words in his ear. "You're always walking away from me, but not anymore."

"Get the fuck off me," he growled, swatting at my limbs like I was pesky fly.

"No!" I shouted not caring who heard me.

"Remy—"

I dropped from his body, the fight leaving me—for now at least—and he swiveled around to face me.

"I really don't know why I ever liked you," I spat. "You kiss me like I'm everything to you—after all the shit you said to me—and then you just walk off! You're so fucking confusing!"

45

"I didn't like him touching you." Darkness flashed in his gaze.

"So, what? You had to kiss me to get rid of his hands being on me? That makes a whole lot of sense." I laughed manically.

Tonight was not going at all how I had planned. I had no idea how to rein this in and put my plan in motion. I wasn't sure my plan even mattered, because the way that kiss made me feel proved to me that I wasn't over him. I thought I'd stopped loving him—that all I felt for him was this searing hate and anger—but I'd been wrong. I wasn't sure I could do this without getting hurt again. If I was smart I'd shut my mouth, walk out of here, and be done with this.

He looked away, not giving me an answer.

Once upon a time we might've known everything about the other person, but right now I felt like we were strangers. I guess we were. We had seven years of mistakes and experiences to change us from the people we knew.

"I'm going back to the bar, finding Gavin, and seeing if he wants to have a little fun."

I started to saunter away but his hand snapped out to grasp my wrist.

"You'll do no such thing." He pulled me against his chest. "I will fucking handcuff you to me if that's what I have to do to keep you from spending the night with that guy."

"Let me go." I tried to pull away. "You have no say over what I do."

His eyes flashed with silver fire. "No say?"

I nodded.

He leaned in close, rubbing his lips against my ear before he whispered, "I fucking *own* you."

I ripped away from him and rushed out of the hotel as fast as I could manage with my heels.

I heard his heavy footsteps behind me.

He wasn't running, but he was keeping a quick pace.

I reached my car and I wasn't surprised when he stepped up behind me, pinning me to the door.

His chin rested on my shoulder, his stubble tickling my bare skin—because I'd been stupid and left my coat in the bar.

"Why can't things be like they used to be?"

His question surprised me, and I opened my mouth to say, *because you destroyed it*, but stopped myself.

This.

Right here.

This was the moment I'd been waiting for in order to put my plan into motion.

It was the perfect opening and I jumped on it.

"It can be," I whispered.

His body pressed more firmly into me. "I hated you for leaving," he admitted, his voice sounding pained in my ear. "But seeing you again..."

"I know what you mean," I panted.

My body seemed to be humming at the way he was pressed up against me.

"I want you." His lips ghosted against my cheek and then he turned me around so we were face to face. "Come inside."

"Yes."

CHAPTER SEVEN

"MATHIAS!" I SCREAMED—and not from ecstasy might I add. "If you do not unlock this right now I swear to God I will *kill* you when I finally get my hands on you."

He stood at the end of his massive bed, grinning with his hands shoved into the pockets of his dark colored pants. His dress shirt was gone, leaving him in only a thin sleeveless t-shirt with the suspenders dangling below his waist.

My dress was gone as well, leaving me in my lacey bra and underwear.

"Unlock it now!" I yelled, shaking my wrist that was handcuffed to the elaborate wrought iron bed.

"No."

"Mathias!"

"I had to make sure you didn't try to go find that guy." He said simply, like that explained everything.

"I'm with *you*, not him!" I roared, trying to shake free of the handcuffs. I was going to end up rubbing my wrist raw, but I didn't care. I also didn't want to think about who else he might've handcuffed to his bed.

He shrugged. "I know you, Remy." He leaned forward,

bracing his hands on the end of the bed. The movement did incredible things for his chest muscles. "And I know you like to play games."

"This isn't a game." I groaned, my arm starting to hurt the more I pulled at the handcuffs. I guess it *was* kind of a game to me, but not in the sense that I would've fucked that other guy just to mess with Mathias. I wasn't *that* crazy.

He clucked his tongue like he didn't believe me. "Get some sleep."

He started for the door of his bedroom.

"Where are you going?" I practically shrieked in panic. Was he seriously going to leave me alone handcuffed to his bed?

"Out."

The door closed behind him, and I started screaming, cursing his name and threatening him in every way I knew how.

But the door never opened again and eventually I fell asleep.

I WOKE UP when someone touched my arm. I jerked away, barring my teeth like I was about to hiss.

"Don't be so damn skittish." Mathias growled, holding me still so he could undo the handcuffs.

My shoulder and arm were numb from being in that position all night, but that didn't stop me from launching myself at him like a crazy person—a scream tearing out of my throat.

I tried to scratch at him, but it was useless. He was so much bigger and stronger than me.

He slammed me down onto the bed, wrapping his hands around my wrists, and pushed his whole body into mine. He was so heavy I felt like I couldn't breathe.

"Let me go, you stick twisted bastard."

He smiled slowly. "I like it when you call me names."

"Ugh! You are impossible!" I bucked my hips against his, trying to throw him off, but it was futile.

"Why are you here?"

"In your bed?" I sneered. "Because you tricked me and then fucking handcuffed me!"

He rolled his gray eyes. "I know why you're in my bed, I didn't forget. I want to know why you're *here*, back in town."

"How is that any of your business?"

He glared down at me, pressing me harder into the bed so my back rubbed against the smooth sheets. "Anything to do with you is my fucking business."

"Oh, really?" I snorted. "I'm pretty sure you gave up any right to know anything about me when you walked away from me."

He winced, no doubt remembering the day he cut me open with words and left me alone in a parking lot feeling like I was bleeding out.

"That was a long time ago," he sneered. "We were both kids then, let's act like fucking adults."

"Says the man that handcuffed me to his bed all night for no good reason!"

His lips threatened to turn up into a smile but he schooled his features. "Just tell me why you're here, Remy. Why did you come back?" There was an almost reverent look on his face.

Now it was my turn to cut him. "I didn't come back for you if that's what you're thinking."

His face fell slightly, but then his gaze heated and I knew I was in trouble.

"You mean," he lowered his head, pressing his lips to my neck where my pulse jumped, "you haven't thought about me at all over the years?" He pressed another kiss to the spot behind my ear. "Not about how we used to talk for hours about anything and everything? Not how my lips felt on yours?" He ghosted his lips over mine in a teasing touch. "Not how I felt inside you?" His voice dropped to a husky whisper and his eyes had deepened with lust.

"Stop." My voice came out weak sounding.

"Tell me," he growled, "tell me you haven't thought about me, about *us*, at all, and I'll stop."

I swallowed thickly. I couldn't say anything.

"Just say the words, Remy, and I'll let you go. I'll let you walk out of here and that'll be the end." His dark brown hair brushed against my forehead.

He grasped my chin, forcing me to look at him. "Say it!" He roared. "Tell me you don't want me the way I want you! Fucking say it!"

My chest heaved, and if I'd been a weaker woman I would've started crying. "I *can't*."

With my admission his lips crashed into mine. We collided angrily, clawing at each other like wild animals.

He kissed me until my toes curled, and my skin felt like it was on fire, but then pulled away roughly before things went too far.

He backed away from the bed like my touch had electrocuted him.

I sat up slowly, trying to catch my breath and calm my racing heart.

"You can't kiss me like that and then not do anything about it." I glared, looking around the room for my dress. When I found it I grabbed it up and slipped into it.

He sat down on a high-backed chair in the corner, resting his elbows on his knees and his head in his hands. "You confuse me like nobody else can."

"Back at ya." I nodded, heading for the door to his bedroom.

"Don't leave," he called.

"Why shouldn't I?" I stopped, not looking over my shoulder at him. Instead I stared straight ahead with my shoulders squared. "It's what we do best, right?"

"WHAT THE ACTUAL fuck?" I whispered to myself, pacing my bedroom. Percy cracked one amber eye open to watch me from where he snoozed peacefully on my pillow.

I kept replaying everything that transpired last night and this morning and I was no less confused each time I analyzed it. Mathias was so hot and cold. One minute he was all over me and the next he acted like my touch was going to poison him.

He wanted me, that much was clear, but he was fighting it.

Why?

He was the one that broke up with *me*.

He was the one that hurt *me*.

This should've been easy—but it wasn't.

I needed to continue with my plan. I knew that for sure. He was clearly still attracted to me—despite the fact that he was always photographed with a brunette on his arm—so I needed to turn up the seduction a notch and work on my acting skills. I couldn't let him realize this was a game. It had to look real.

And that's where it would get difficult, because in the hands of Mathias Wade what was left of my heart just might be obliterated all together.

Then I'd be left with nothing.

CHAPTER EIGHT

I FINISHED MY workout and sweat dripped off my body.

I grabbed a clean towel as I headed towards the locker room and used it to dry myself off some.

A hand clamped down on my shoulder and I turned to find Drew, the boxing instructor and gym owner, standing behind me.

Once he had my attention he released me and took a step back. "I just wanted to tell you that you're doing an excellent job."

"Oh, thanks." I spared him a smile.

"It's better than yoga, right?" He joked.

"Only a smidge." I held my thumb and forefinger up with a tiny bit of space between them.

He chuckled. "And yet, I don't think I've seen you attend a yoga class since you started boxing."

"Touché."

"Anyway, that was it," he smiled. "I'll see you soon."

"See you," I replied as he walked away.

When I started towards the locker rooms I stopped in my tracks.

Mathias.

Oh, fuck.

I hadn't seen him in over a week. I hadn't sought him out and he hadn't come by the bar.

I was unprepared for this encounter, so I darted around a pillar out of his sight and into the locker room. I showered and changed into clean clothes. I had to head straight into work from here so I took extra time in front of the mirror applying my makeup.

When I left the locker room I looked left and right and didn't see any sign of Mathias—thank God.

With Mathias' celebrity status he probably had his own fucking room to workout in.

Sometimes it still surprised me that he was actually famous. To me, he would always be Mathias. I didn't look at him and see dollar signs. Instead I saw a guy that was lonely and begging for someone to understand him.

There was so much more to him than what he showed to the world. All everyone else saw was a brooding lead singer going through more booze and women than should be allowed. But I saw past that. I saw the pain he was trying to hide. He might've been a bad boy through and through, but I believed wholeheartedly that there was *good* in him. He just chose to hide those bits and pieces from the world so they couldn't be held against him.

I shook my head free of my thoughts. I needed to focus and get to work, not think about Mathias.

The drive was short and inside the bar was dead but the restaurant area was packed. Before I could get behind the bar Tanner threw an apron and notepad at me. I caught both easily. "We need you out there today."

Waitressing would be harder for me than manning the bar

54

since the customers were more diverse. But since the bar was dead this would give me more tips.

I tied the apron around my waist and grabbed the notepad. A pen was already clipped to the end.

I spoke with the other waitress, Amy, and she told me which tables to take—flashing me a relieved smile in the process.

Hours passed and we finally began to slow down. I was getting tired though. Being a waitress was hard, carrying the heavy trays and running here and there. I wanted nothing more than to go home and take a long hot bubble bath.

When Tanner said I was free to go I couldn't get out of there fast enough. I grabbed my bag and twisted my hair up on top of my head in a messy bun. My neck was damp with sweat from all the running around I'd been doing.

I grabbed my purse and headed out, waving goodbye to Tanner and the other waitress that had come in.

I hurried outside and immediately encountered a wall of smoke.

I coughed, waving it away.

I hadn't smoked since I was sixteen and now the smell made me ill.

The guy sitting on the steps with a cigarette dangling between his lips looked up at me, his gray eyes stopping me cold.

He dropped the cigarette on the ground, snuffing it with the toe of his shoe, and stood up blocking my way before I could even process the fact that he was sitting there.

"What are you doing here?" I asked when it became obvious that he wasn't going to move.

"Waiting for you." He shrugged, running his fingers through his hair in a nervous gesture.

"Why?"

"I think that's pretty obvious," he looked at me like I was stupid. "I wanted to see you."

"I'm tired," I stood up straight, "and I'm going home to take a long hot bath. I don't have time to get into it with you again." He got under my skin so bad that I couldn't even think about trying to implement my plan.

I went to brush past him, but he grabbed my wrist and said something that very rarely passed through his lips. "Please?"

"What do you want?" I stopped, looking at him sadly.

He rubbed at his now clean-shaven jaw. "Dinner. That's what I want." He nodded, like he was agreeing with his words. "Come back to my place and we'll have dinner."

"Okay," I agreed, "dinner would be nice." And maybe it would give me enough time to get my shit together and actually go in for the kill.

I *had* to make him fall in love with me again.

I *had* to break his heart.

And I *had* to stop getting so mad and flustered around him, so that I could actually do it.

I'm sure that sounded twisted, especially since I'd loved him once, but after the hell I went through he deserved to hurt too. Right?

"Good, come on." He placed a hand on my waist, guiding me forward.

"I have my own car, you know." I looked up at him through my lashes.

"I know," he replied. "But we're going in mine."

He led me to a brand new shiny red Corvette. When I knew him, he didn't even own a car, he had a skateboard.

I slid into the car and he got behind the wheel. "Why did you drive here if your penthouse is around the block?" I asked.

He chuckled huskily. "Because I didn't come here from the penthouse."

"Oh, right." I mumbled, looking out the tinted windows. From the outside the windows were so dark that no one could see in. I'm sure Mathias enjoyed the privacy. It had to be hard having practically the whole world watch your every move. When the band was in L.A. the paparazzi relished in following their every move. Right now, Mathias and Maddox seemed to draw the most attention—Maddox, because the paparazzi expected him to propose to his girlfriend Emma any day, and Mathias because he was always getting into trouble. I'd lost count of all the articles I'd read where Mathias had been kicked out of a bar or restaurant for being drunk and causing a problem. Not to mention, the paparazzi loved how he went through women. Mathias was gorgeous, and despite the fact that he was a very obvious player, women flocked to him. Even me. After all, I was here wasn't I?

But this was different.

This wasn't him batting his eyes at me and making me lose all sense.

This was *me* going after *him*.

Right?

Fuck. My brain was all kinds of rattled where Mathias was involved.

This was never going to work.

But I had to try.

Even if I broke myself in the end, it would be worth it if he experienced even the tiniest bit of heartbreak I'd felt.

Mathias was quiet when he parked the car in the underground garage attached to the hotel.

He climbed out of the car and I knew I was expected to follow.

We stepped into an elevator and he inserted a key, pushing the PH button.

"It must be nice," I said, leaning against the wall of the elevator, "being here and not having to deal with the paparazzi."

He shrugged. "Yeah, that's nice, but that doesn't stop random people from stopping me on the street for pictures or taking one from afar and trying to sell it online." He ruffled his hair and his brows furrowed, wrinkling his forehead. "But this place... it's home. It always has been and it always will be."

The elevator dinged and opened into the penthouse. He grabbed the key and pocketed it, pressing his arm against the door so it wouldn't close and I could exit first.

"You hate it... don't you?" I asked hesitantly. I wasn't sure if my question might piss him off, because with Mathias the stupidest things could make him explode. But I also knew I was one of the few people to know everything about him—at least, I used to. Like I knew that he was dyslexic. It was something that had always bothered him and made him feel like he was worthless and stupid. But that was the farthest thing from the truth.

"Hate what?" He asked, striding past me and into the open concept kitchen.

I followed, looking around the space. The last time I'd been here I'd been otherwise occupied thanks to Mathias' heated kisses—but then the fucker had to go and trick me and handcuff me to his bed. Jerk.

The kitchen boasted white cabinets and white marble countertops. The floors were a gray hardwood looking tile that extended through the whole living area, but turned into a plush carpet in the bedrooms.

"The fame." I shrugged.

He braced his hands on the countertop, tilting his head to

study me as if weighing his options. Finally, he nodded. "I do hate it. I mean, this is what we always dreamed of, but now... sometimes I wonder if getting to live our dream is worth all the other things we've had to give up." He looked down at the countertop, his knuckles turning white. "I love the music. I love feeling it. But having people judge me for being human? It fucking sucks. We all mess up and make mistakes, but when you live in the spotlight people act like you're supposed to be a fucking saint," he shook his head, "and that's not fair."

I couldn't believe he'd said all that and been so honest.

I jumped up on the counter and he moved to stand in front of me, bracing his hands beside my hips. I kicked my legs against the cabinets like a little kid as he stared down at me intensely. I wasn't sure what he was looking for in my eyes, but he must have found it, because he cupped my cheek and leaned in.

"This feels like when we were younger," he whispered. "Like no time at all has passed."

I closed my eyes, feeling his breath fan across my lips.

God, I'd missed him.

It didn't seem possible to miss someone I'd grown to hate, but I did.

I was pretty sure that when someone like Mathias came into your life they were impossible to forget.

He was like the sun, burning so bright that even once he was gone I was still blinded.

"Did you ever miss me?" I asked. "Even once?" I held my breath, waiting for him to explode—because that was Mathias. He could be nice one minute and an asshole the next. I wouldn't put it past him to kick me out for my question.

Instead he surprised me by leaning in impossibly closer and nuzzling my neck. "Always."

I opened my mouth to say something back, or maybe to kiss

him, but a high-pitched whimpering cut me off.

"What was that?" I asked, jumping against him and grasping his shoulders like his body alone would protect me from whatever the beast was.

He chuckled, unhooking my arms. "Stay here. I'll show you."

He sauntered off to a back part of the penthouse suite. I watched him go, my eyes glued to his ass. His dark gray pants hugged it perfectly and his navy sweater pulled taut against his wide shoulders.

He returned a moment later with the cutest gray and white pit-bull puppy in his arms.

I jumped off the counter, my mouth hanging open. "Mathias Wade has a puppy? You realize you have to feed it right? And give it love and affection?"

He rolled his eyes at me. "No, Remy. I thought she lived off of the air."

"She?" I asked, raising a brow.

"She," he repeated. "Her name is Shiloh. I... I rescued her." He shrugged. "I stopped by the shelter and she just looked at me and..." He looked away from the puppy, glowering at me now. "I had to have her."

"Do you go to the shelter often?" I asked reluctantly, fearing his wrath.

He shrugged, putting the puppy on the ground. She promptly made her way over to me, sniffed my feet, and must have deemed me okay, because she licked my toes.

"Hey," his eyes narrowed, "I'm not a heartless bastard you know? I went in to donate some money and they were showing me around the place and..." He trailed off.

"And?" I prompted, bending down to pet the puppy. I swore Shiloh smiled at me.

"And she chose me," he mumbled, looking away.

"She chose you." I repeated, fighting a laugh.

"Well it sounds stupid and improbable when you say it that way." He crossed his arms over his chest and leaned against the wall.

"She's very sweet." I gathered her into my arms and she licked my face. "And for the record, my cat is going to be livid when he smells her on me."

"You have a cat?" He asked, looking adorably confused.

"Yes," I nodded. "Percy chose me, the way you say Shiloh chose you... okay, that's probably a lie," I laughed. "I found him in a really bad shape and took care of him, tending to his wounds, that kind of thing. He scratched the shit out of me, but then he never left and became mine."

Mathias nodded, looking distracted. "I better take her out." He mumbled, taking the puppy from my arms. He grabbed a leash and fastened it onto her collar. I bit down on my bottom lip to keep from laughing at the sight of Mathias walking a dog with a hot pink leash.

While he was gone I snooped around—because why wouldn't I?

I didn't find anything of merit though. The place was pretty empty and there was nothing personal around. Not even a picture of his friends and twin brother.

I didn't understand how he could possibly like this starkness.

It made the otherwise lovely penthouse seem cold and depressing.

I vacantly wondered if his home was as empty as his heart.

When Mathias returned he was like a whole new person, he smiled when he entered, Shiloh right on his heels. "I'm going to order room service. Why don't you go take that hot bath you talked about wanting?"

My eyes widened. "Are you serious?"

"Of course." He stepped closer to me but left an appropriate amount of space between us. If Mathias Wade had a theme song it would be 'Hot n Cold' by Katy Perry. Mathias would hate the cheesiness of that, but it was true. I guess I was the same way with him, though. We were quite a pair. It was like neither of us could ever decide what we wanted.

"I don't have any clean clothes to change into," I argued.

He laughed but there was no humor in the tone. "Remy, with my money I'm pretty sure I can get you some clean clothes delivered."

I bristled at that. "You don't need to flaunt your wealth in my face," I spat. "I'm not some model or actress you need to impress. I'm *me*. I'm the girl that knew you when you were nobody."

"It's not flaunting when it's the truth," he countered easily.

I narrowed my eyes on him. "What do you want with me?" I finally asked.

His eyes flooded with confusion. "I don't know," he answered. At least he was honest. His fists clenched at his sides. "You infuriate me like nobody else," he continued. "But you also make me feel better than anyone else. You've always been able to get under my skin. And I've *never* stopped thinking about you, Remy. Every day I wondered about you. But I was never man enough to find you." I closed my eyes at his words, biting my tongue so I didn't tell him he wasn't man enough even now to apologize for what he did. "You scared me when we were teenagers. What I felt for you scared the shit out of me, because it shouldn't have been possible. I thought then that the feeling would go away once you were gone, but it only got worse. I *ached* for you." I don't know when he moved, but suddenly he was right in front of me. "I still do." There was a pain in his eyes I'd never seen before. "When you left I was a scared teenage boy that had no idea what he was doing. I pushed you away, because I thought that was easier. I felt like you were abandoning me. But it was all me. I was the one that abandoned *us*." Years of pain and torment echoed in his words.

Was it possible that Mathias was as torn up about what went down between us as I was?

"I still don't know what I want with you." He leaned his forehead against mine, his Adam's apple bobbing. "I don't know if I'm even *right* for you, but God dammit I want you so fucking bad right now. I want you in my arms, in my bed. I want a chance to make this right between us." His voice lowered and his lips brushed against my jaw. "Give me a second chance. Please tell me it's not too late for us."

I wasn't used to this Mathias—a pleading one.

"But-but," I stuttered, "you seemed so angry that I was back in town."

"I was," he admitted, one of his hands cupping the side of my neck. I was sure he could feel how fast my heart was racing. "I thought you were here to destroy me all over again. But then I decided I didn't give a fuck, because I only feel like I'm alive when I'm with you."

I leaned forward, pressing my face into his chest. I didn't want him to see my face right now and all the emotions raging across it. I needed a moment to think.

This was exactly what I had wanted to happen. *This* was my in to destroy his heart the way he had mine, but suddenly that didn't feel right. I felt dirty and ashamed to have wanted to hurt him, but I couldn't get my feet to move—to walk away and end this.

"What do you want to happen between us?" I lifted my head and peered into his eyes.

"I want you to be mine," he growled lowly, "and only mine."

"Does that mean you'll be mine and only mine?" I twisted his words around. My heart clenched painfully as I recalled all the photos I'd seen of him with different women. Mathias got around, that much was obvious.

"I've only ever been yours." He ghosted his lips against my neck. "I might not be a hearts and flowers kind of guy, but it's the fucking truth."

"The-the women?" I panted as his lips explored further and my eyes fluttered closed.

He pulled away, glaring down at me. "Are you telling me you haven't been with anybody since me?" His look said *not likely*.

"I've been with other guys." Of course I had. It had been seven fucking years, and I thought I'd never see him again.

"And I've been with other women." He shrugged. "But right now, here we are, just the two of us." His voice lowered to a husky murmur. "Tell me that you want me as much as I want you."

"I do." I gasped the words, a small cry accompanying them. I wanted Mathias more than I wanted my next breath. We were made for each other. They might say opposites attract and never to fight fire with fire, but neither of those things applied to us. We defied the laws of the universe.

"Just like old times?" He asked. "You and me against the world?"

I nodded, afraid that if I opened my mouth the truth would spill out and I'd tell him he was playing into my plan exactly as I wanted.

"Just like old times."

CHAPTER NINE

I SAT IN the bathtub with bubbles up to my chin.

Mathias was somewhere in the penthouse ordering our dinner.

His open vulnerability had me worried.

I was playing games, and Mathias... what if he really did want me?

That should've been a good thing for my 'love him and leave him' plan, but suddenly I felt sick to my stomach and I wasn't sure I could go through this. It felt wrong.

I drew my knees up to my chest, water sloshing over the sides.

Mathias had always been able to wrap me around his finger better than everybody else. He was so fucking charming and I fell for it every time. He could just as easily be playing games with me.

But what if he's being honest? What if he really does want you? A little voice in my head spoke up.

It doesn't matter. I lied to myself.

I'd barely been around the guy and he already had my thoughts all kinds of messed up.

It was like a storm was roaring through my mind, kicking up dust and overturning everything in its path to the point that I was lost and confused.

I climbed out of the bathtub, wrapping a towel around my body.

I stared at my reflection in the mirror. "You can do this, Remy." I whispered. "Revenge, remember?" I nodded to myself. "You have to destroy him like he did you. He ruined your life and he's not good for you. Do *not* let him into your heart again. Do *not* let him trick you into thinking he's changed. He doesn't care about you. He didn't care about you then and he definitely doesn't care about you now."

I probably looked like a crazy person standing there talking to myself, but let's face it, I lost my mind a long time ago.

I closed my eyes, remembering my last conversation with Mathias before I left for Arizona.

The stifling humidity of the summer heat made my clothes stick to my body. I was tempted to take my tank top off and leave myself in my bra and jeans, but I was still on school property and I wouldn't put it past one of the teachers to report me even though it was the last day of school—and after school hours.

Mathias' hand was clasped in mine as we walked together.

My heart beat irregularly in my chest.

I had to tell him that I was leaving.

I'd been putting this talk off—and another—for weeks.

But time had caught up to me and now I was left with no choice but to break the news.

"Mathias?" I spoke, stopping in my tracks.

He stopped too and looked at me questioningly. "What is it? You're not sick are you? You've been looking a little pale."

"I'm fine, but there's something I have to tell you..."

He stopped and crossed his arms over his chest like he knew whatever was going to come out of my mouth was going to be bad.

"What's going on, Remy?" He asked. "Is this some sort of intervention? I didn't drink that much at that party, I swear."

"No, it's not about that," I mumbled.

I shook my head, tears clinging to my lashes. I never cried, so Mathias knew this was bad.

"Rem?" He prompted.

"We're moving." I choked on the words like they were something physical lodged in my throat. "We leave in a week."

"Moving? Where?" He asked, his dark brows furrowing into a straight line.

"Arizona." I squeaked.

"Arizona?!" He roared. "Next week?! That might as well be all the way across the world!" He threw his arms in the air.

"Mathias," I said his name calmly, "we can do the long distance thing."

He shook his head roughly back and forth, his shaggy brown hair falling into his eyes. He pushed it back and slapped his baseball cap on backwards.

"No. No. No." He seemed to be in a state of disbelief. "You can't fucking leave me."

I closed my eyes. He'd once told me he had abandonment issues. His dad had driven his car into a tree on a drunken binge and his mom was in jail. Even though his foster parents were great people, I knew he feared they'd grow tired of him and kick him out.

"I'm not leaving you by choice," I reached for him and he flinched away from my touch. "This is my dad's job, I have to go."

A look of hatred settled over his face. "Just go then."

"Mathias—"

"GO!" He yelled right in my face. "I always knew you would! I knew you were too good for me and that's why I fucked Josie!"

"What?" I gasped, taking a step back and clenched my heart like I'd been shot. Josie? Josie Miller? That girl that was always batting her eyes at him in our biology class? How? What? When? Why? We spent so much time together, I didn't see how...

"You heard me," he seethed. "I fucked her, because you'll never be enough for me."

Tears coursed down my cheeks at his cruel words. "You cheated on me?"

I'd fallen in love with Mathias in a way I didn't know you could at sixteen years old. I'd given him parts of myself I never shared with anyone. He knew everything about me, and right now he was destroying me.

He nodded, his teeth clenched together. "Did you really think I'd settle for you?"

I flinched. Those words were like a slap to my face. "I don't know what I thought." My voice came out as no more than a whisper. I was normally a strong girl, but right now all my strength had left me. I felt like a piece of me was dying.

"She wasn't the only one. There've been more."

He continued to drill holes in my heart.

"How many?" I asked, gasping for air.

"More than you want to know," he spat.

"I hate you!" I shouted, a sob cutting through my throat.

"Good, because I hate you too!" He yelled back.

"You're nothing but a lying, cheating, filthy bastard and I'm sorry for thinking there was more to you than that." And then my hand reared back and connected with his cheek. My hand *left behind a red imprint on his cheek.*

He nodded once, like he was agreeing that he deserved that, and then he turned and walked away.

He left me standing there crying in the school parking lot as my entire world blew up in my face.

When his body was nothing but a speck in the distance, I whispered, "You're going to be a dad."

And then I fell to the ground in the fetal position and cried until a teacher found me.

CHAPTER TEN

I ATE DINNER with Mathias last night and then had him drive me back to my car with the excuse that I had to check on my grandma. It was the truth too. I'd been gone all day. I was really sucking at the whole Babysit Grandma thing. I should be fired.

The sunlight streamed in through the kitchen windows as I made breakfast. I felt like shit today, and I knew it had everything to do with remembering that day in the parking lot. I purposely tried not to think about it, because every time I did it filled me with the same feelings of loss and emptiness.

Grandma came out of her bedroom, hobbling with her cane. I set the plates of poached eggs down on the table and hurried to her side to help her to the table.

"Are you okay?" I asked her.

She waved away my concern with an age-spotted hand and said, "It's this damn arthritis getting to me. Nasty stuff makes me ache like I've been run over by a car."

"You've been run over by a car?" I joked.

She narrowed her eyes. "You know what I mean."

I laughed at her and got each of us a glass of orange juice before sitting down.

"Do you have to work today?" She asked me.

"Not today." I took a bite of my breakfast.

"Good, you can drive me to bingo. Normally Charlene picks me up and takes me," she said, referring to one of her elderly friends, "but she drives like this is the Indy 500. The last time I swore my false teeth were going to come flying out."

I laughed, choking on a bite of egg. She reached over and beat my back with a surprising amount of strength. I coughed up the lodged eggs and spit it into a napkin.

"Can you try not to make me laugh when I have food or drink in my mouth?" I asked, reaching for my glass of orange juice.

"What's funny about my dentures falling out? That's a tragedy, Remy."

I shook my head. "It was funny, trust me. Anyway," I continued, "I can definitely take you to bingo."

"You better stay in the car when you drop me off, though. If you come inside the old farts might try to flirt with you, and the women there get jealous easily."

"Grandma," I laughed. "I think I'm a little young for those men."

She eyed me. "They don't know that. Men are men, and they think anything with two legs and a pussy is fair game."

"Grandma!" I exclaimed, stifling a laugh. "Stop it!"

"It's the truth." She nodded her head, finishing off her breakfast. "You stay here with me for very long and I'll teach you everything I've learned over the years, like the fact that men think their penis is a gift to womankind. It's not."

At this point I was laughing so hard at her that tears were streaming down my face and I could barely breathe.

She soon joined in with my giggles.

Living here with my grandma actually wasn't that bad. I mean, I did get free comedic entertainment with breakfast.

Once I had composed myself I cleaned our plates and glasses before guiding my grandma into the living room and getting her situated on the couch with the TV on.

"You know," I said to her as I plopped in the rocking chair, "if there's ever any place you want to go to I'd be happy to take you."

She turned to look at me. "Do I look like I want to go anywhere?"

"Well, you did say you wanted to go to bingo," I laughed. Sobering, I added, "I hate you being cooped up in this house all the time. If it was warm outside I'd try to get you out for a short walk. I could always take you to the mall," I suggested.

"No," she growled. "No malls. Annoying teenagers frequent that place. The last time I was there I had to hit one with my cane to get him out of my way."

"Grandma!" I felt like I was shouting that a lot, but she kept surprising me.

"What?" She looked at me innocently. "He kept standing in my way and wouldn't move, not even when I asked politely. A little tap to his knee and he was out of my way."

"If you keep this up I'm going to pee my pants," I warned her.

"I honestly don't see what's so funny," she huffed, "it wasn't a joke."

I shook my head and stood up, stretching my arms above my head. "I'm going to head to the gym for a while. I won't be gone long."

"Can you pick up Chinese for lunch?" She asked, perking up. "I haven't had that in forever."

"Of course," I replied. "Let me get you a notepad to write down what you want."

I left her with the pen and paper and went upstairs to change.

Percy was sitting on top of the dresser. His tail swished lazily back and forth as he watched me.

I grabbed my gym bag and headed downstairs. She handed me the piece of paper as I passed her on the way to the kitchen. I grabbed a water bottle from the refrigerator and put it in my bag.

I stopped and kissed her wrinkled cheek. "Bye," I called over my shoulder.

She mumbled something under her breath that I didn't catch as I locked the door.

There wasn't a boxing class today, so I planned to run a few miles on the treadmill in order to feel like I had accomplished something.

I was halfway through my run, and damp with sweat, when a dark form strolled over beside me.

When I looked over and saw that it was Mathias my feet stumbled and I would've face-planted if it weren't for his quick reflexes. He reached out and grabbed me around the waist and yanked me off the treadmill into his arms. I stumbled against his hold, feeling slightly dizzy.

"Are you okay?" He asked, reaching up with his free hand to turn off the treadmill.

I nodded weakly, struggling for air. My legs seemed wobbly and I was glad he hadn't let me go yet.

"What are you doing here?" I panted, my chest rising and falling with each breath.

"Exercising." He gave me a 'duh' look.

"Obviously," I huffed, "I meant here scaring me half to death."

He chuckled. "That was an accident. I saw you and I

couldn't resist coming over."

"Uh huh," I nodded, finally letting him go since my limbs no longer felt like Jell-O. "Next time give me a warning."

"Are you finished?" He asked, nodding his head at the treadmill.

"I am now," I grumbled, crossing my arms over my chest. The movement pushed my boobs up and his eyes zeroed in. He quickly looked away though, clenching his jaw. It wasn't like Mathias to be this way. In the past he'd never tried to hide his ogling.

"Go to lunch with me."

I was startled by his words. I hadn't been expecting that. His gray eyes narrowed on me, as if daring me to say no. "I can't," I replied. He opened his mouth to argue with me, but I cut him off by holding my hand up. "I promised my grandma I'd bring Chinese home for lunch. I'm taking care of her, remember?"

He leaned against the side of treadmill. "No, I think you conveniently forgot that bit of information."

"Oh, right," I mumbled. Squaring my shoulders I jutted out my chin defiantly. "Well, that's why I'm here. To take care of her."

His eyes flashed a dark gray and he glowered at me. "Does that mean you're leaving again? You're just here to check on her and then you'll be gone?" He turned away, shaking his head, and mumbled something under his breath. It sounded a lot like, "I knew you'd never stay."

Mathias being, well, *Mathias*, he started to leave.

I grabbed his arm and he turned around sharply to glare at me. He shook my hand off and spat, "Forget it, Remy. Forget everything I said last night. I don't want to see you." He stalked off once more, towards the exit.

"Hey!" I yelled after him and he stopped. He didn't turn

around though. "What the fuck is your problem?" I seethed. "I'm not going anywhere. I don't know what the future holds for me, but I like it here."

He continued to stand there, not looking at me.

"You know what, you're a fucking coward. That's all you are." I let out an exasperated sigh and stormed away to the locker room. I didn't care if I looked like a five year old. Mathias was so damn confusing. He was giving me whiplash. One minute he was coming on to me and the next he was pushing me away. At this point I was starting to not give a fuck about trying to break his heart, because he was exhausting me so damn much.

I opened my locker to grab my things—I'd shower at home—and a hand slammed into the metal door closing it.

I whipped around and came face to face with Mathias.

"Stop doing that!" I yelled.

His body caged me in against the lockers. The room was empty except for the two of us. In the corner a leaky faucet dripped, the quiet splashing the only other sound save for our breaths.

"Stop doing what?" He tilted his head, leaning so close that his nose touched mine.

"You know what," I snapped, spitting the words through my teeth. "One minute you're nice to me and the next you push me away. It's unfair!"

He shook his head, his face darkened with shadows. "You don't know what you do to me, do you?" He asked.

I shook my head, my breasts brushing his chest every time I took a breath.

"You've done nothing but haunt me since you left. No one and nothing compares to you," he nuzzled his face against my neck and I arched against him. "One taste of you and I was fucking ruined." I squished my eyes closed and winced in pain.

Hadn't I said basically the same thing about him? "What I feel for you scares me," he breathed, his lips brushing over mine. I whimpered at the feel of them. "When we were teenagers I thought for sure it would go away, that I'd grow sick and tired of you, but I was wrong," he growled lowly, "I only ever wanted you more."

I couldn't seem to stop myself from saying, "But Josie?"

He shook his head, his hair brushing against my forehead. "I don't want to talk about that."

"You never want to talk about anything!" I roared, struggling against him.

"That's how I am." His eyes seared into me, his nostrils flaring with anger. "It's in the past. Let it go."

I squished my eyes closed, anger boiling my blood. Anger was good though. That's what I wanted to feel for him. It made it all the easier to play the game.

"Fine," I panted. "We'll forget the past," I agreed. "It'll be like it never existed."

"I want this to be a second chance for us," he whispered, brushing his lips over my cheek. My anger began to dissipate and lust filled its place with one simple touch. Mathias was the only guy that had ever been able to make me go weak in the knees, and I hated him for it. "But I keep fucking it up." He bit my earlobe, tugging it gently between his teeth. "And I'm sure I won't be able to stop, because that's what I always do... ruin everything." His lips grazed my chin. "But I'm not strong enough to walk away from you. You're my fucking addiction. Always have been. Always will be."

He grasped my chin and tilted my head back, capturing my lips with his. He tugged on my bottom lip with his teeth and let it go with an audible pop. My blood heated with want and desire. I grasped his hair, pulling sharply and a hiss escaped between his teeth.

"You want it rough?" He growled, his eyes flashing with heat.

"Don't I always?" I panted, my eyes flaring with desire. Just because I was playing a game, didn't mean I couldn't reap the benefits. I needed him to ease the ache inside me.

He chuckled huskily in approval, grasping my thighs and lifting me up so my legs were wrapped around his lean waist. The cold metal lockers dug into my back, but I didn't mind.

I took his face in my hands, angling my mouth over his. I normally wouldn't be able to kiss him like this, but since he was holding me it put me higher up than him.

While I kissed him he tore away from the lockers and moved through the room. I didn't care where he was going as long as he didn't stop touching me.

One of his hands left my body as he tore open one of the shower curtains and carried us inside the stall. He closed the curtain and reached over to turn on the water, dousing the both of us and drenching our clothes.

I didn't care and neither did he.

He tore off my wet tank top and palmed my breasts that heaved against the confines of my sports bra.

"It's been too fucking long since I've had you like this," he growled, kissing my neck.

"Since when did you become such a talker," I groaned, bucking my hips against his as the shower streamed down us. "Just shut up and fuck me."

He chuckled in a way that let me know I was in trouble.

Oh, how I loved being in trouble.

The shower beat down on us, scalding our skin—or maybe that heat was from our touch.

He ripped my sports bra off and then his mouth was on me

and I let out a long moan—not caring if someone walked in and heard us.

I tugged at his white t-shirt and he pulled away just long enough to discard it.

One by one our clothes landed in a wet heap on the tiled floor of the shower.

Our hands and lips seemed to be everywhere at once. I couldn't get enough of him. For seven fucking years I'd been missing this. It didn't seem possible that I had survived that long without this... this... whatever this was.

With a groan he pinned my hands above my head and a look of anguish stole over his face.

"Condom," he ground out, "I forgot a fucking condom."

"Don't need one." I nearly cried the words. I needed him inside me and he was taking too damn long.

"Are you sure?"

"Mathias!"

He laughed, taking my lips between his and thrusting into me instead of responding with words.

I clenched around him, nearly weeping with joy at how fucking good he felt inside me.

My head fell back, soft pants passing through my lips as he fucked me just the way I liked.

It seemed he'd never forgotten my body and the way it responded to him. He still knew the exact right things to do to get to me.

His tongue swirled over one of my swollen nipples and I cried out from the sensation, clenching around him.

"You feel so fucking good," he growled, biting down on my shoulder and I knew a mark would be left behind.

He rolled his hips against mine and I let out a small scream. "Do that again." I pleaded. He did. "Oh God."

"No, my name's Mathias." He smiled. The arrogant bastard.

"Harder, please." I begged.

Normally he would go against my requests because he liked to drive me fucking insane, but this time he obliged.

He let go of my hands, holding my hips, and I grasped his wet shoulders.

I flicked a wet piece of hair out of my eyes, fighting to gain control of my breaths.

"Fuck, right there," I urged. "Oh, God." I fell over the edge with a small cry that he covered with his mouth and I panted his name against his lips.

He growled low in his throat and rested his head in the crook of my neck as he found his release.

He stayed there for a moment, letting his breath even out. The water was turning cold but neither of us moved to turn it off.

Finally he raised his head and kissed me deeply before murmuring, "Fuck I missed this."

"Me too," I agreed, clinging to his shoulders as he lowered my legs to the ground. When I was sure I wouldn't fall I released my hold on him.

He shut off the water and poked his head out of the shower so he could look around.

"No one's in here." He reported. "Wait here, I'll grab us some towels."

I did as he asked, shivering slightly from the cold water that still clung to my body. He returned only seconds later with a fluffy white towel for me—one already tied around his lean waist. I wiped myself off and then wrapped it around me.

"I might have a change of clothes here," I told him, eyeing the pile of soaking wet clothes, "but I'm guessing you don't." I laughed. "I mean, this is the women's locker room," I joked, winking at him.

He leaned against the tiled wall and my eyes zeroed in on a water droplet that dripped from his chin onto his collarbone, slid down his abs, and disappeared beneath the towel.

He shrugged, not caring. "What's the worst that can happen? Someone snaps a picture and sells it to a magazine? They've printed plenty of shit about me, so I really don't give a fuck at this point."

"Aren't you supposed to care about your public image?" I asked. It was pretty obvious that he didn't when you bothered to look at most of the headlines sporting his name or image. He was always being photographed in some compromising position—the last one I'd seen had been when he attacked a paparazzi for tailgating him. I couldn't say I blamed him for getting pissed about that. I would too.

"Does it look like I care?" He raised a single dark brow. "I'm sure you've seen the headlines."

"I have," I confirmed, "I've also seen all the women."

He smiled at that. Not even the slightest bit embarrassed. "I like women," he replied. His eyes darkening he added, "But I don't like any of them the way I do you."

"Good to know," I huffed. "I also noticed most of them were brunettes."

He chuckled, shaking his head, a playful smile on his face. "You noticed that, huh?"

I nodded. "I've got news for you, Mathias. I'm not a brunette." I grabbed a piece of my wet hair and waved it in his face. "Never have been."

"I know." He closed the space between us. He placed his hands on either side of my head and leaned in so he could whisper in my ear. "But there's only ever been one blonde I wanted. No one else compared to her."

I closed my eyes, breathing in his words.

And when I opened them he was gone.

CHAPTER ELEVEN

MATHIAS WAS WAITING for me in the parking lot when I stepped outside the gym. He was leaning against the back of his red Corvette, smoking a cigarette. He'd changed into a pair of nice jeans and... was that a cardigan? Normally I would make some dig about him turning preppy, but he looked too hot in it for me to complain.

"I can't believe you still smoke," I sighed.

"You don't?" He asked, a brow rising in interest. "You used to smoke more than me."

That was true. "I quit." I stopped smoking after I found out I was pregnant and never picked up the habit again.

"Shame." He let out a puff of smoke and we both watched it circle the air. He reached up, ruffling his now dry hair. Looking at him standing there so calm and composed you would have never guessed that not too long ago he had me pinned to a wall in a shower fucking me senseless.

"So, I was thinking," he started, putting the cigarette out, "you and I should go get lunch and then you can take your grandma whatever it was she wanted."

I looked down at my watch. "I have an hour."

"Good," he nodded, not smiling, "now get in."

I STARED AT the pile of pasta in front of me. "How is one person supposed to eat all this?"

Mathias lifted a single brow and looked at me like I was crazy. "It's family portions, or whatever. That means you have to share with me." He smiled like the cat that ate the canary.

"I forgot you can never get enough to eat," I laughed.

"It's my superpower."

"A bottomless stomach?" I asked.

He nodded, dipping a piece of bread in olive oil. "Yes, that and my ability to get you to scream my name."

I rolled my eyes. "I can make you scream my name too. Or have you forgotten?" I winked, kicking his shin lightly with my foot beneath the table.

He grinned and when he smiled it transformed his whole face. Normally he looked so angry at the world, but when he smiled... it was magical. "I haven't forgotten anything about you." He let out a sudden laugh and leaned forward, lowering his voice. "Do you remember Mr. Johnson?"

"That really mean history teacher?" I asked, racking my brain.

He nodded. "We glued all his stuff to his desk after he gave you an F on that one paper."

"Oh yeah." I laughed with fondness at the memory.

"I ran into him the other day in town," Mathias snickered, "and he asked me for my fucking autograph."

"Oh God." I laughed, hiding my face behind my hands. "What did you do?"

"I pretended to give him an autograph, but instead I drew a penis and said SUCK THIS."

"Mathias!" I giggled. "What are you? Twelve?"

He chuckled. "Well that's what I used to put instead of my name on all those stupid worksheets he gave us, so I thought it was fitting."

"And that'll probably end up in the news next week," I told him. I could see the headline now: *Mathias Wade gives former teacher penis drawing.*

"Probably," he agreed. "I fucking hate the media," he speared a piece of pasta, "but I'm learning to ignore it. It's easier that way. I went out of my way to purposely piss them off and look like an asshole."

"Why?" I asked, confused.

"It's what I do," he answered simply. "They don't know me, but they think they do, so I just give them what they want. It's easier than letting them see the truth." He stared down at his plate of food, his brows furrowed together.

"Why are you so intent on making people hate you?" I asked, even though I already knew what the answer was.

Mathias always pushed people away. If they didn't care about him, then they couldn't get close enough for *him* to care, and ultimately end up hurt. I'd been one of his only exceptions—and I didn't think I'd ever know what it was that drew him to me in the first place—and look how we ended up? We crashed and fucking burned down the entire forest.

"You know why," he grumbled.

"I wish," I took a deep breath, twisting the wrapper from my straw around my finger, "that you would let people see the real you."

"That is the real me, Remy," he growled, glaring at me. "I'm harsh and a jerk. I'm the alcoholic womanizer everybody loves to hate. I hurt people because it makes me feel good. I like to make other people as miserable as I am, so that maybe, for one fucking second, I won't be alone in my suffering."

I remained steady, looking right at him. "I know you think that's all you are, but you're wrong. You can't lie to me."

He grabbed his glass of wine and took a sip—that sip turning into him downing the entire thing. "I am what I am."

I sighed. This was going nowhere.

Finally I changed the subject. "You've never really explained to me what we are?" I questioned.

He glowered at me and spat, "I think I've been pretty fucking clear."

"Nope," I shook my head, "with you there are a lot of gray areas."

He rolled his eyes. "You're mine and I'm yours. End of fucking discussion."

"Yes," I started, "but are we like a couple? Or fuck buddies? I'd like to know upfront before I see a photo of you in some magazine with some other woman and it catches me off guard."

"We're Mathias and Remy—that's all that matters. The rest will fall into place."

Ha! If only he knew.

"Ah, yes. I'm sure it will just be that easy." I laughed, taking a sip of wine.

He glared at me, anger simmering off of him. "Why is it so fucking hard for you to believe me?"

"Because," I sat back, the picture of ease, "I've seen photos of all the women you go through, and I doubt I'll be enough for you." I laughed. "And on top of that, I've only been in town all of three seconds and you've been nothing but hot and cold. It's so hard to read you."

"Just because I don't profess my fucking feelings by shouting them from the rooftop, doesn't mean I don't have them," he snapped, his irritation with me leaking into his words. "It's not like I'm sitting here telling you I love you, we both know how that ended up the last time. I'm just..." He looked away for a moment. "I don't really know what the fuck I'm asking for." He shrugged. "I told you I wanted this to be a second chance for us," he whispered, "and I meant that, but I..."

"But you're not going to promise me forever," I supplied.

"Yeah, I guess that's what I'm saying." He sat back in the booth, glaring at his food like it had offended him somehow.

I smiled slowly and lifted my glass of wine. "Lucky for you, that's fine with me."

His eyes closed and he looked almost pained.

Shouldn't he have been relieved that I was agreeing with him?

Instead he seemed tortured. It made no sense.

Mathias wiped his hands on a napkin and set it on the table. "I'm not very hungry anymore."

I looked down at my food and realized I'd only been pushing it around. "Me either."

He motioned for the waiter and asked for the check and boxes.

After paying we headed out to his car and he drove me back to the gym so I could get mine.

He parked beside it and I glanced at him.

He stared moodily out the window, not looking at me.

I had no idea what he was pissed about, but with Mathias it was always something.

I wore a challenging smile and undid my seatbelt. Instead of getting out of the car like he expected I climbed onto his lap. Up until this point Mathias had been playing into the game better than me, and he didn't even know it.

He looked at me, startled.

I took his face in my hands, kissing him deeply with every

ounce of passion I had left in my body.

The goal was to leave him aching and begging for more.

He let out a low, pleased growl, and his fingers tangled into my hair, tugging lightly.

When we were both panting for air, I pulled away and slid off his lap.

I was out of his car before he knew what happened.

I sauntered over to my car, swaying my hips more than necessary.

When I heard his car door open I smiled with satisfaction and looked at him over my shoulder.

"Come by tonight?" He asked, rubbing his fingers over his lips.

I let out a soft laugh and shrugged. "Maybe."

He narrowed his eyes on me as I got in my car.

God, I loved playing with him—and it was only just beginning.

CHAPTER TWELVE

"YOU DIDN'T COME over."

I looked up from the glass I was drying to see Mathias standing in front of the bar with his hands flat on the shiny wood top.

"Was I supposed to?" I asked, raising a brow.

"Um, I'm pretty sure I asked you to come by last night." He slid onto one of the barstools.

"I'm sure you were heartbroken by my absence." I put a hand over my chest.

"I was hoping for a repeat of the shower." His eyes raked over my body, and it felt like he was undressing me. Some of the other guys sitting around the bar perked up with interest and started watching the two of us. Apparently we were more entertaining than whatever football game was playing.

"I was busy." I gave him a look that said, what-was-I-supposed-to-do, and shrugged my shoulders while lifting my hands innocently in the air.

"Busy?" He repeated, making a face like the word tasted sour on his tongue. "What could possibly be more important than me?"

I rolled my eyes at his arrogance. "Bingo." I said in an even voice.

"Bingo?" He snorted.

"You betcha," I nodded, grabbing another beer for Melvin and sitting it on the bar before he could ask. "I won a hundred bucks. Most fun I've had in a while."

He narrowed his eyes until they were nothing but thin slits. "You're such a fucking liar."

I propped my elbows on the bar in front of him and leaned forward. "Should I come over tonight?"

He nodded eagerly, his eyes dipping to the swell of my breasts as his tongue slid out to moisten his lips. "And I'm going to sit here until your shift ends to make sure you don't flake again."

"I didn't flake," I leveled him with a glare, "I was playing bingo, remember?"

"Uh-huh," he nodded, scratching his slightly stubbled jaw. "Now get me my scotch."

Now it was my turn to narrow my eyes. "Are you really going to wait here until my shift ends?"

He nodded, looking up at the TV screen.

"I'm here until midnight." I warned him.

"And I'll be right fucking here," he said, never taking his eyes off the screen. "Put in an order of cheese fries while you're at it."

"Scotch and cheese fries," I mumbled, "that sounds delightful."

He still didn't look at me, but I saw his lips twitch and knew he was fighting a smile.

I put the order in first and then poured his drink. I set it on the bar and his eyes flickered to me. "You know," he said, his voice serious, "I like that when I'm here no one tries to take my fucking picture."

One of the guys sitting at the bar—a regular named Jason—piped in with, "That's because we don't like you pretty boy and your music sucks."

Mathias grinned. "See? This place is wonderful."

I shook my head. "I think you forget that it's also a restaurant." I pointed over his shoulder to a table of giggling high school girls who were pointing at him—a few tearing apart their purses, probably in search for something for him to sign.

"Fuck," he groaned, not even turning around.

"Be nice," I warned, "their money makes your life nice and cozy."

"It was never about the money," he told me, "just the music."

"Then prove it," I challenged. "Go say hi to them."

"Fine, I will." He finished off his scotch and stood up. He sauntered towards the girls, but suddenly turned and changed course.

My mouth fell open when I saw him stop at a different table—this one occupied by a mom, dad, and their daughter—who couldn't have been more than thirteen and her head was bald from chemo treatments, concealed behind a bandana. The girl looked up at him with an awed expression as he spoke, waving his hands through the air. He must've asked to join them because suddenly the little girl was sliding over and he sat down beside her.

"Remy!" He called to me where I stood open mouthed behind the bar. "You can bring my cheese fries to this table and whatever they ordered make sure it gets put on my tab."

I nodded woodenly, watching in surprise as he interacted with the parents and daughter. The little girl seemed enamored with him and I was shocked that he'd managed to bury his usual asshole attitude for a moment.

Mathias stayed at their table until they had desert and then moved back to the bar—but not before giving the girl a hug and posing for pictures.

My icy heart might've melted a teeny tiny bit. A miniscule amount really.

I wiped down the bar and said, "That was quite a show you put on."

He snorted. "It wasn't a show. I'm not quite the asshole the world believes."

I crossed my arms over my chest. "Why wouldn't you want the world to see that part of you?" I nodded my chin at the family walking out the door.

"Because," he replied, "it's the only good part of myself I have left, and if the media found out that I'm actually a softy when it comes to kids then they'd twist that somehow and taint it." He stared at me, his forehead wrinkling as he thought. "No matter how much I might wish it so, moments like that don't make me a good person. I'm still a piece of shit."

Mathias used to say that about himself all the time when we were teenagers. Nothing I said to the contrary could prove him wrong, and it seemed with the media's scrutiny his self-hatred had only become worse. That should probably please me since I was hell bent on seeing him suffer, but it didn't. I felt bad for him. He shouldn't have hated himself the way he did.

"I hate that you think that," I whispered, almost hoping he didn't hear the words.

"Why?" He asked, truly curious.

I shrugged, busying myself by rearranging some glasses. "Because you're not a bad person. You're good, Mathias, you've just... you've made some bad choices." I flinched, thinking about the pain I felt when he told me he'd cheated on me. Despite how much I worked to *not* be like every other girl, once I got with Mathias that's exactly what I became. I went from the girl who wanted to rule the world, to the one that dreamed of marriage and a happy life for our baby. But all of that was ripped away from me, because of the choices we made.

"Bad choices?" He laughed. "I've fucked up at every turn."

I opened my mouth to reply, but was cut off by Tanner scolding me to get back to work.

"Later," I warned Mathias.

THE MINUTE WE walked into his penthouse suite I started in again. "For someone that thinks they've fucked everything up, you've done mighty good for yourself." I twirled around, my arms lifted in the air.

He stood with his hands in his pockets watching me. "Trust me, I've fucked up everything that matters." He glowered at a wall. "Luck is what got me all of this." He waved his hand to the fancy furnishings.

I shook my head in disagreement. "Talent is different than luck."

"So what? I can *sing*, yeah that's such an amazing talent." He sat down on the couch while I stood by one of the windows, looking down at the empty street below us.

"But it is," I replied.

"You call it a talent," he mumbled, leaning his head back to look up at the ceiling, "I call it a curse."

"Why are you such a pessimist?" I marched toward him, sitting on the coffee table in front of him.

"It's not pessimism, it's realism. I don't deserve this," he waved his arms around. "Not any of it."

"*Why?*" I pestered.

He scrubbed his hands over his face. "I don't want

to talk about this."

"You always used to say that," I sighed, "but you know what?" He looked at me, not saying a word, so I continued, "You would tell me anyway."

"Things are different now. I might want you just as much now as I did then, but it doesn't change the fact that we're strangers now."

"Do you really believe that?" I asked.

He looked away and I knew I had my answer.

"You trusted me then, why can't you trust me now?" I asked. Even if I had ulterior motives for being with him, I would *never* betray his trust in the sense that I'd run to the media and sell a story.

"I don't know." He growled.

"Think about all the things you told me then, and I've never told another soul."

He closed his eyes, and I wondered if he was reliving one of the countless memories we shared. I knew I was.

Tap. Tap. Tap.

I slid out of the warmth of my bed and over to the window. I pushed the curtains aside and found Mathias looking at me through the window, perched on the roof outside. I opened the window, and muttered, "What the hell are you doing here?"

"I needed to see you," he said, reaching for my hand.

I slipped outside and sat beside him on the roof.

Now that I was closer to him and the light from the moon was shining on his face I could see the bruise covering his cheek. "What happened?" I asked, reaching out to tenderly stroke the side of his face. He relaxed into my touch and let out a content sounding sigh.

"I got into a fight with some older guys. They outnumbered me."

"Over what?" I gasped.

"I started it," he whispered, drawing up his knees and draping his arms overtop, "I wanted to fight them."

"Why?" I couldn't understand.

"I wanted to feel something," he admitted.

"Why can't you feel something without punching someone?" I spat. It wasn't the first time I'd seen bruises on him, he'd just never told me where he'd gotten them from before.

"I'm fucked up," he whispered.

I shook my head. "Only because you let yourself be. Maybe you should try being a man and stop looking for trouble."

Mathias sought out pain like it was a drug, the way I way I found things to get my adrenaline pumping.

"What if those guys beat you unconscious and left you for dead?" I asked him. "Have you even thought about that?"

His jaw clenched together. "It's what I deserve."

"No, it's not." I shook my head.

He nodded. "It is. You don't understand..."

"Then explain it to me!" I raised my voice and quickly put a hand over my mouth, afraid I might wake up my mom and dad. Or worse, my brother.

"You can't tell anyone," he warned, glaring at me.

"Who am I going to tell? Lana? She's barely my friend," I snorted. "You know you're like my best friend, and that's only because you're so fucking stubborn that you won't leave me alone."

"It's only because you're hot." He cracked a smile.

I rolled my eyes. "I'm still not sleeping with you. So nice try."

He chuckled, but quickly sobered. "My real mom's in jail," he whispered. I knew he was a foster kid—everybody did—but no one knew anything about his real parents. "For prostitution.

Awesome, huh?" He laughed humorlessly, ducking his head. "And my dad's dead, but he wasn't a fucking saint either. He was nothing but an alcoholic with anger issues."

"So?" I asked, missing the point.

"With parents as fucked up as that it's only inevitable that I follow in their path." He sighed, looking up at the stars.

I put a hand on his shoulder and he tilted his head down to look at me. "We might be made up of our parent's DNA but it doesn't mean that we're them. We make our own choices and become our own people. There's not some predetermined future for us at birth. We have the choice to be anyone we want to be."

His jaw ticked. "It doesn't feel that way." He winced as if he was in pain. "...I can still hear her yelling in my head about how I was worthless, and stupid, and nothing but a fuck up..."

"Your mom said that about you? Your mom that's in jail?"

He nodded.

"Um..." I started, "I think those things apply to her. She's the one that's in jail for making bad choices."

"But I'm her kid. Cut from the same cloth."

"But not the same person," I countered.

"She was right though... I am stupid," he mumbled.

"No, you're not. Hating school is different than being dumb."

He shook his head. "I can't read."

"What?" I asked.

"I. Can't. Read." He said each word slowly. "I'm dyslexic. Anytime I look at a piece of paper all the words get all jumbled and I can't read it."

"So what?" I asked. "There are plenty of people with dyslexia. I'm sure there's some kind of exercises for your mind or something."

"You have an answer for everything," he chuckled,

glaring out at the night.

"Maybe you should shut up and accept my help," I snapped, "instead of being so fucking stubborn."

He glanced at me, smiling slowly. "I love it when your sass comes out."

"You're so weird," I rolled my eyes.

"I'm surprised you're not looking at me like I'm a piece of trash," he said suddenly, startling me with the turn of conversation. "I told you the kind of parents I had, and here you are living in this nice house with your doctor dad and lawyer mom."

"So? Having successful parents doesn't make me better than you. We're all just people in this world," I leaned back, resting my elbows on the roof, "and that's it."

That was the first night Mathias ever appeared on the roof outside my window. But it soon became a nightly routine where we'd sit outside for hours, talking about anything and everything. Sometimes we discussed something that happened at school, and other times our conversations got deeper as he opened up more about his childhood. He told me some horrible things, but none of it made me love him any less, and love him I did.

"Why didn't you ever tell anybody?" He asked, looking at me with a perplexed expression. "There were so many things you could've told on me. You could've ruined my career if you wanted to."

"I didn't want to," I shrugged. "Things between us might've ended on a sour note, but I loved you once and how could I possibly hurt someone I used to love?" My voice cracked, and I frowned. Wasn't that what I was trying to do now? Arguably, breaking his heart wasn't the same as destroying his career, but it was still bad, wasn't it?

I drew my knees up to my chest and hugged my arms around them.

Mathias stared at me for a moment before shaking his head. "You were always too good for me."

I shook my head, smiling sadly. "You're wrong."

He chuckled, leaning forward and prying my arms from around my knees and yanked me onto his lap. I straddled him, wrapping my arms around his waist.

"Okay," he smoothed a hand down my back, resting it at my waist, "then you're the less fucked up one."

Wrong again.

Mathias had no idea how messed up I was and I hoped he never found out. Better to break his heart on purpose than to shatter it with the truth.

CHAPTER THIRTEEN

HE HELD ME in his arms for a few minutes and then placed me on the couch in a manner that was far too gentle for the Mathias I was used to.

"Do you remember all the movies we used to watch?" He asked suddenly, reaching for the remote.

"You mean when we'd watch those old kid's movies and recite all the lines?" My nose crinkled as I thought.

He nodded. "Yeah. Let's do that." He reached for the remote and brought up Netflix. Our weekly movie night had been one of the few things we did together that was actually relatively normal. Most everything else we did involved some kind of trouble—a lot of it illegal.

He typed something in and I turned to look at him, stifling a laugh.

"Little Rascals?"

"Wasn't that always your favorite?" His pouty lips turned down in a frown.

"It is," I nodded, "I can't believe you remembered."

He looked at me strangely. "I remember everything about you, but that doesn't change the fact that I don't feel like I know you now." He got up abruptly and headed to the kitchen, opening and closing drawers. A moment later I heard the telltale pinging of popcorn popping.

The movie began to play, but I was too busy looking behind me waiting for him to return.

He strolled back into the room, shoving a handful of popcorn into his mouth. He sat down right beside me, so that his thigh touched mine, and put the bowl in his lap. "It has extra butter and that powdered cheese you always liked."

I shook my head at his thoughtfulness. He was hurting me with his kindness and he didn't even know it. I reached over and grabbed a handful of popcorn, popping one into my mouth.

Looking around the spacious penthouse, I ignored the movie and asked, "Why did you decide to live here? In a hotel?"

He chuckled. "The penthouse might be attached to the hotel, but it's still my place. I mean, look around," he waved a hand, "does it *look* like a hotel to you?"

"No," I agreed, taking in the sparse white decorations that hardly matched the rest of the hotel, "but isn't it a part of it?"

"It's attached to the hotel, obviously, but the top floor was originally divided up into two apartments for sale. I bought both so I could turn it into one large apartment. So, it's not a fucking hotel room, m'kay?"

I rolled my eyes. "You didn't need to get nasty. It was just a question."

"I have a home in L.A. and I guess I wanted something different while I'm here. I mean, I could've stayed at my mom and dad's place, but that felt weird. Besides, Maddox and his girlfriend have taken over the fucking guesthouse, so I didn't really want to stay there anymore. This place is all mine," he waved a hand to encompass the space. "Plus, I can still order room service, and have access to the indoor swimming pool. I wouldn't have had that in a house."

"Yeah, but you could've built a huge mansion to be whatever you wanted it to be," I argued.

He shrugged. "I don't want a mansion, besides..." He trailed off, letting out a sigh. "I didn't want a house, because being in a big space like that makes me realize how alone I am and then that makes me feel fucking depressed. That's why I hate my house in L.A. It's not even that big, but when I'm there it's... it's so quiet. I don't like it. At least here," he shrugged, "I can look out the windows and see the town and I can walk down the street to a restaurant or bar if I want to. I'm not isolated, and I don't have to worry about being bombarded by paparazzi."

"And now you have Shiloh," I added.

As if she heard her name the little puppy began to whine.

Mathias chuckled and stood up, pausing the movie. "I better walk her, do you want to come?"

"Sure," I agreed, surprised he asked.

I followed him back to a laundry room and he let her out of her crate. "I have to keep her in here when I'm gone," he glanced up at me, "she chewed through five pairs of my shoes and then started in on a belt."

"At least the suspenders weren't harmed," I joked.

"You love my suspenders." He grinned, holding Shiloh in his arms and standing up to leash her.

"I do," I agreed, because it was true. He definitely made those suspenders look hot.

I followed him to the elevator and out onto the street. The hotel didn't have a grassy area so poor Shiloh was forced to do her business on the sidewalk. Once she was done we headed back inside and sat down on the couch with Shiloh. She sat in Mathias' lap and kissed his chin, then tried to steal the popcorn every time he took a bite.

I finally took pity on her and gave her a piece.

Mathias narrowed his eyes at me. "Did you just give my dog popcorn?"

"I did," I smiled innocently. "I felt bad for her."

"She's not supposed to eat people food," he glared, now holding the bowl in the air so Shiloh couldn't get into it.

"Aw, come on," I pouted, "I hardly think one piece of popcorn is going to hurt her."

His eyes darkened for a moment as he stared at me and then before I knew what was happening, the bowl clattered to the ground, popcorn going everywhere with Shiloh running after it. But Mathias paid no attention to that. Instead, he pounced on top of me, pinning me to the couch.

His lips devoured me, biting and nibbling and staking his claim.

My heart beat madly behind my ribs as my fingers wound around his neck.

His touch scorched my skin, burning me from the outside in.

He cupped my face in his large hands, angling my head back and sweeping his tongue against my parted lips. I gasped against him, tugging sharply at the short strands of hair at the back of his neck. He bit down on my plump bottom lip in retaliation.

I knew my lips would be bruised later from the force of his kisses, but I didn't care.

His hips dug into mine, pushing me further into the plush cushion of the couch.

He grasped my neck, kissing over my breasts and heading lower.

"God I fucking want you again," he growled, slowly lifting my shirt up my stomach. "I always want you. The ache never goes away."

I breathed deeply, trying to steady my racing heart, but it wasn't working and I feared it might beat right out of my chest.

"I knew something was missing from my life, I just didn't think..." He paused, glancing up at me, his breath tickling my exposed stomach.

"You didn't think, what?" I prompted, needing to hear what he had to say.

"I didn't think it was you." He whispered the words, almost as if he didn't want to give voice to them.

He moved up my body and was about to press his lips to mine when we heard a high-pitched whining sound.

"Oh shit." He jumped away from me and off the couch.

Shiloh had eaten most of the popcorn on the floor.

Mathias looked at me with panic in his eyes. "I think I just killed my dog."

Shiloh laid on her side and let out a burp.

"She looks fine to me." I bent down, looking at her closer.

"I need to get her to the vet." Panic edged his voice. "This can't be good. I mean, she ate a shit ton of popcorn."

"She's probably only going to have a really bad stomach ache."

Mathias ignored me, instead running around the penthouse looking for his phone.

He called someone and paced back and forth. I ignored his portion of the conversation and kept an eye on Shiloh, just in case something bad did happen.

He hung up the phone and crouched down beside the puppy, lifting her into his arms, cradling her like a baby.

"The vet's coming over," he mumbled, rubbing the top of Shiloh's head.

"At one in the morning?" I gasped.

He glanced at me, his eyes flashing a silvery hue. "Yes.

Sometimes having money comes in handy."

"Of course," I sighed, sitting back and feeling like I was in his way. I stood up and looked around for my purse and jacket. I'd tossed them onto the floor on the way in, but they weren't by the entry. I finally found them sitting on a side table. Mathias must've picked them up. He'd always thrived on order while I needed chaos.

I shrugged into my coat and pushed the button for the elevator.

It pinged and I heard a rustling behind me.

I looked over my shoulder and found Mathias standing up with Shiloh in his arms. The look in his eyes reminded me of a lost little boy. He seemed hurt, confused, and desperation clung to his shoulders.

"Please, don't go," he begged.

A lump formed in my throat and I tried to swallow past it. "I thought you wanted me to go." The elevator doors opened behind me, but I made no move to step inside.

"I never said that."

"But you made me feel that way," I countered, crossing my arms over my chest. "You can't have it both ways—if you want me to stay you need to make me feel like I'm wanted, not like I'm a fucking inconvenience."

He sighed, glancing down at Shiloh in his arms. "I'm sorry for being an asshole, but that's me, Remy, and you know it. You've always known it. I can't be any other way."

I wanted to argue with him on the matter—because he'd certainly been sweet with the little girl at the restaurant tonight, and then again with his concern for the puppy. I wished he could see how thoughtful and caring he was, instead of only seeing the bad. Every person had good and bad traits, but Mathias thought he was bad through and through. He was so incredibly mistaken on that matter. He had more good in him than most.

When I stayed quiet, anger flashed in his gaze. "Fine, go. Leave. I don't give a fuck."

He stormed out of the living room and down a hallway. A moment later a door slammed.

I closed my eyes, warring internally. Did I go after him? Or leave? Neither seemed to be the right option, but I figured if I left he might never want to see me again and I *needed* him to want me around. So I set my purse down on the table again, and marched down the hall.

I pounded my fist against the closed door that led to his bedroom.

"I swear to God Mathias Wade if you don't let me in there right now I will throw something at this fucking door and break in. And once I do that, you'll be the one handcuffed to the fucking bed."

The door swung open and he waved me inside. "Oh look, you stayed," he sneered, "there's a first time for everything."

I winced, but turned away so that he didn't see the pain etched on my face.

"Maybe if you weren't always pushing me away, I wouldn't be leaving."

He growled something under his breath and sat down on the bed, laying Shiloh down beside him. He looked at her worriedly, his forehead wrinkling.

"She's going to be fine," I assured him, climbing on his massive bad and sitting so that the puppy was between us.

"She's so little," he whispered, rubbing her stomach as she slept, "this could be really bad."

"Well, the good news it's not chocolate. I read somewhere that, that's really deadly for dogs." I hoped the tidbit of information would make him feel better.

He jumped up from the bed and raced out the bedroom door.

I hurried after him, nearly tripping over my own feet in my haste to keep up. "What are you doing?" I hissed, finding him rummaging through every drawer and cabinet in the kitchen.

"Making sure I don't have any chocolate." He looked at me like *I* was the crazy one.

I rolled my eyes. "You can have chocolate in the house. Just don't give her any."

"But what if she finds it," he hissed, dropping to his knees to search one of the bottom drawers.

"She doesn't have thumbs. The chances of her opening a drawer or cabinet are impossible."

"What if she nudges it open with her nose?" He asked, making a huge mess as he tossed stuff out of a drawer. He found a Snickers bar in there and held it up triumphantly before throwing it away.

"I highly doubt that would happen." I pinched the bridge of my nose.

"But it *could* happen," he argued.

I sighed, crossing my arms over my chest. "I'm going back to check on Shiloh. I'll leave you to your raid."

He ignored me, continuing to tear apart his poor kitchen. All that stuff was going to be a pain in the ass to put away. Good thing I didn't live here.

Shiloh perked up a little when I entered the room, cracking her eyes open. I was sure she was fine, but Mathias' concern for her was adorable, although a bit annoying. He tended to go overboard with all things.

I made myself comfortable on his bed, grabbing the remote off the side table and turning the TV on. I lay down, flipping through channels, and Shiloh moved to lay curled up next me.

I stifled a yawn, my eyes growing heavy.

I was about to drift off to sleep when Mathias strolled into the room with a man trailing behind him.

The man introduced himself to me and then immediately checked on Shiloh.

He looked her over carefully and then turned to Mathias.

"She's fine," he declared. "She might have a stomach ache and nausea depending on how much she ate, but it's nothing to worry about."

Mathias let out a deep sigh of relief. "I'm happy to hear that. I was really worried."

"I know." The vet smiled. "But she's okay."

Mathias nodded and pulled out his wallet to pay the man. He led him out of the suite and returned, taking off his shirt and undoing the belt on his pants.

I sat up and moved to get off the bed, because clearly it was time to go home, but he stopped me.

"Stay the night, please. We don't have to do anything. Just sleep."

I stared at him like I didn't know him.

"I don't have any pajamas." It was the only excuse I had to leave. I *wanted* to stay. I *wanted* him to hold me in his arms. And that scared me like nothing else could, because wanting led to caring, and caring led to heartbreak.

He strolled to his dresser and opened the top drawer. He rummaged around and pulled out an old Willow Creek tour t-shirt. He tossed it at me and I caught it easily. "You can wear that. There are extra toothbrushes under the sink." He nodded his head towards the bathroom.

"Thanks," I mumbled.

I had no excuse now.

I padded into the bathroom and closed the door behind me. I

changed and brushed my teeth. Normally I would've left my clothes lying on the floor, but I knew Mathias hated that, and besides I'd need to put them on again in the morning and I didn't want them wrinkled.

Mathias was already in bed when I opened the door and even though the lights were now dimmed I could still feel his stormy gaze lingering on my body, particularly my legs.

I slipped into bed, Shiloh snoozing between us.

He reached up and turned the last light off, plunging us into complete darkness.

Neither of us said a word. The only sounds in the room were our breaths and Shiloh's light snores.

Back when we were young, our late night roof chats often led to him staying the night in my bed and sneaking out before my parent's woke up. I'd always felt comfortable then and safe in his arms.

But right now safe was the last thing I felt.

I knew I was in danger of falling in love with him all over again—because love is the one thing that can over power hate.

I was becoming tangled in the web of my own making, and I was afraid I might suffocate.

CHAPTER FOURTEEN

I WOKE UP with Mathias' body wrapped around mine, and his breath tickling the skin of my neck. Our legs were intertwined and he had my body hugged to his chest. I kind of felt like a human teddy bear.

I tried to pry his arm from around my torso but it wasn't working. He was too heavy.

"Mathias," I groaned, wiggling against him.

He tightened his hold and let out a soft growl. "You're not going anywhere."

"You're squishing me," I groaned, thrashing my body and trying to throw him off.

I squeaked when he moved lightning fast and pinned me to the bed, hovering on top of me.

"You're always so damn feisty." He blinked sleepy eyes at me and kissed my neck.

"I thought you liked that." I muttered, still fighting against him.

"Only when it's you." He cracked a small smile and rolled off of me. He grabbed a pair of black-framed glasses off of the night table and slipped them on, ruffling his brown hair further by running his fingers through it.

"Nice glasses Clark Kent."

He narrowed his eyes on me and glowered.

"What?" I shrugged. "It was a compliment. You can totally pull off the look." I left out the part where he could pull off anything... or nothing at all.

I slipped out of the bed and started towards the bathroom when I heard him hiss between his teeth. "Are you naked under my shirt?"

I looked back at him, quirking a brow. "Maybe," I said coyly.

"Fuck," he cursed.

Before I could make it to the bathroom he grabbed me around the waist and tugged me back into his bed. He lifted the shirt off, his eyes roaming over my body.

"I can't believe you slept in my bed all night practically naked. That's like torture." He pouted and I wanted to reach up and pull on his perfect bottom lip.

I shrugged. "You didn't know."

"I know now." His eyes skimmed over me again, and he bit his lip, looking pained.

"You can touch me, you know." I whispered conspiratorially.

"I'm enjoying the view." His eyes lifted to meet mine. So many different emotions flickered in eyes so fast that I couldn't even begin to decipher them.

His hand lightly grazed my sides and my blood roared in my veins with the simple touch. Goosebumps broke out over my skin and I closed my eyes as his lips met mine.

His kiss ignited a fire inside of me and I grasped onto his shoulders, wrapping my legs around his waist. Only his boxer-briefs separated us, and I wanted them gone.

"Mathias," I breathed his name against his lips, "please."

Oh God. I was *begging*. This was bad. He'd barely even

touched me and I already wanted his cock inside me.

He pressed light kisses down my neck, between my breasts, and over my stomach. He grabbed my legs and parted them. He rained kisses on my right thigh and I squirmed against his hold.

"Mathias." Again with the begging.

"Hmmm?" He hummed. "Do you want something?"

"Please."

"Please?" He questioned. "That doesn't tell me what you want." He looked at me with an evil smirk. I wanted to slap it right off his arrogant face for toying with me.

"You know what I want." I fisted the sheets tightly in my hands as he moved closer to the spot where I needed him most. He just hovered there, not moving and not touching. "Dammit Mathias!"

"I want to hear you say it." He took my chin between his fingers and angled my face to look at him. "Say it, Remy. Say it and you'll get exactly what you want."

"I want you to fuck me."

He grinned triumphantly. "Now that wasn't so hard was it?"

"You're hard."

He let out a bellowing laugh and pressed against me. I was tempted to rip his damn boxers off. "So it would seem."

"Would you please just shut up already?" I begged, grasping his hair and pulling his mouth to mine.

He resisted and my lips ached with the need to touch his. I think I let out a whimper.

Suddenly he pulled away and stood up, smirking at me as I lay naked on his bed. "You know what, I changed my mind."

"Wh-what?" I stuttered. No. He couldn't do this.

"Yeah," he shrugged, feigning that he was unaffected. "I think I'm just going to go make some breakfast." He grabbed a pair of sweatpants and pulled them on.

I stared at his bulge with narrowed eyes. "You realize that in punishing me you're also punishing yourself, right?"

He grinned, crossing his arms over his chest and I stared up at the ceiling so that I wouldn't drool over his abs. "I know," he said in a silky voice, "but it's the anticipation that always makes it so damn sweet with you."

With that he walked out of the room, closing the door behind him.

I couldn't believe this. I'd freaking begged him like a crazy person, giving in and telling him what he wanted to hear, and the asshole was still leaving me hanging.

I threw a pillow at the door and yelled, "You bastard!"

His only answer was to laugh at me.

I TOOK A shower, hoping that would help get rid of my aching desire.

No.

It made it worse.

Why?

Because I had to use his damn soap to wash with and now I could smell him all around me, it was the worst kind of torture imaginable. If he wanted me aching with want and desire he'd succeeded, but I wasn't going to ask him to fuck me. Nope. *He* was playing games, and I wasn't going to lose. I was going to make him so mad with desire that *he* lost his mind. He thought he held all the cards in his hands, but he was wrong.

I stepped into his bedroom with a towel wrapped around me and found him shrugging into a plain t-shirt. He wore khaki colored pants and sneakers. It was the most dressed down I'd seen him. He reminded me more of the Mathias I knew in high school when he was dressed like this.

"I got you some clothes."

"What?" I looked at him, confusion written plainly on my face.

"Clothes." He pointed to a shopping bag sitting on the floor.

"You left?" I didn't know why this tidbit of information was so important to me.

"No," he looked at me strangely, "I had someone pick it up and deliver it."

"Are you being sarcastic or serious?" I questioned, wrinkling my nose. "Because with you I can never really tell."

"Serious." He replied, grabbing a leather jacket. "I have to go meet up with the guys. Get dressed and we'll go."

"Wait... you want me to go with you?" I pointed at myself.

He rolled his eyes. "That's what I said."

And then he marched out of the bedroom, Shiloh at his heels.

I shook my head, baffled at his behavior.

I picked up the bag and dumped out the contents, finding a new pair of jeans, a red blouse—that was practically see-through—a black leather jacket, a pair of heels, and even lingerie.

I changed into the new clothes and found him in the kitchen, sliding a homemade waffle across the counter when I entered.

"You're a man of many talents," I said as I picked up the plate.

He merely pursed his lips in response and continued on with the task at hand. I sat down at the counter, glancing around. The penthouse was clearly decorated to his specifications, but it still seemed so cold. There were no personal photos or mementos. It was barren. I kind of wanted to go buy him some art for the walls and some colorful throw pillows. The white, black, and gray color scheme was so boring.

Mathias sat down beside me with a cup of coffee. He raised a brow when he noticed I wasn't eating. "Is something wrong?" He asked.

"No," I stuttered, "not at all."

He looked at me doubtfully.

"How long have you lived here?" I finally asked.

A wrinkle marred his forehead before he straightened out his features. "Almost two years. That seems like an odd question to ask."

I shrugged, getting up to pour my own cup of coffee. "It's just... I mean, this place is nice, don't get me wrong..."

"But?" He prompted, raising a brow. "There's always a but, so get to the point Remy."

"It's so boring," I frowned. "There's no color, or pictures. Not even personal photos." I sat down once more, watching him carefully.

He frowned, looking around. "I guess I never noticed. I like it."

"You like this?" I asked, sounding incredulous.

"I don't like clutter," he muttered.

I rolled my eyes. "Clutter is different."

He shrugged. God I hated it when he did that and looked at me like I was crazy.

"Would you like me to give you my credit card so you can go to Pier-Fucking-One and make the place all feminine and prissy?" He waved a hand wildly through the air.

I sucked my lips together, trying to contain my laughter. "I'm shocked you even know what Pier One is."

His lips quirked into a small smile. "Only because it's beside Petsmart and Target." He finished his waffle and stood to clean the plate. "Hurry up and finish eating," he growled when he saw that I'd barely made a dent in my plate of food, "or I'm leaving your ass here handcuffed to my fucking bed again."

"You wouldn't dare." I gave him a challenging look.

He leaned forward, resting his elbows on the counter and quirking his head to the side. "Want to try me?"

I scarfed down the waffle in record time and shoved the plate at him. "Happy?" I asked around a mouthful.

"Very." He suppressed a chuckle, washing the plate while I finished my coffee.

I put the empty cup in the sink and he huffed at me. "What am I, your fucking maid?"

I grinned evilly. "I'd love to see you in an apron."

"Only in your dreams." He rinsed out the cup.

I hopped up on the counter beside him, clucking my tongue. "Sorry, my dreams are a little more creative than that."

"Oh, really?" He chuckled, opening the dishwasher drawer. "I'd love to hear this."

"Hmm," I started, tapping my chin with my finger as I thought, "let's see, if I was dreaming about you, you'd probably be naked." He glanced at me, his lips twisting together as he fought a smile.

"Continue," he prompted, looking at me instead of focusing on the dishes.

"And then I'd get on my knees..."

"Remy," he growled.

"And wrap my mouth around you..."

"Fuck." His eyes widened.

"And then, just when you were about to come I'd stop, and then you'd slide inside me. I'd already be wet and aching for you and—"

One of the coffee mugs slipped from his hands and crashed to the floor.

"Shit," he cursed, bending down to pick up the pieces and

throwing them in the nearby trashcan.

I hopped off the counter and smirked. "I'll let you figure out the rest." I winked and he cursed again.

"You're mean."

"I'm not the one that stopped this morning." I crossed my arms over my chest.

He winced. "I'm beginning to really regret that idea."

"Too late to change your mind now," I clapped a hand on his shoulder as he stood, "we've got to go."

He stood in front of me, crowding my space until my back was pressed into the counter. "I should take you back to my room right now, tie you up, and show you what happens when you play with me."

"Sounds kinky." I grinned, sliding away from him and heading to the elevator. I glanced at him over my shoulder and gave him a coy smile. "Coming?"

"Oh we will be," he nodded, sauntering forward like a lion stalking his prey, "later."

CHAPTER FIFTEEN

"NICE HOUSE," I commented, when we pulled into the driveway of the large cape cod style home.

"Maddox, Ezra, and I bought it for our parents." He shrugged like it was no big deal. "It was the first big purchase we made once we signed our record deal."

Something in my heart warmed a bit.

"That was nice of you guys."

He glanced at me, seeming oblivious to his kindness. "Maddox and I owe Karen and Paul everything. They took us in instead of letting us get placed with some random family." Mathias had told me a long time ago how Karen and Paul had been their neighbors growing up, and the twins had become best friends with their son—Ezra, of course—so when Maddox and Mathias were put into foster care they stepped up to the plate and took in both boys. "They loved us when no one else did," he whispered, looking down and putting the car in park. He removed the key and sat back.

I wanted to tell Mathias that he was wrong—that I had loved him too.

But something told me that if I opened my mouth and uttered those words, they'd be nothing but a lie, because I *still* loved him. Against logic, against everything, I did and I think I always would. The kind of love we shared didn't go away easily—even when we crashed and burned, a lingering spark still burned. That's why, after seven years, I never stopped thinking about him. It was more than the fact that he hurt me, it was because he owned me. Mind, body, and soul. I was his. I didn't want to be, but I was.

When I didn't reply, he muttered, "Come on," and slipped out of the sports car.

He led me into the house—it was decorated with rich dark hardwood floors, pale gray walls, and comfortable looking furniture—and down a hall where he opened a door that revealed a set of steps.

He nodded his head for me to go first, so I did.

At the bottom of the steps we were met with an open living area set up for movie watching.

But that wasn't our destination.

He moved in front of me and I knew I was meant to follow.

Down another hall he opened a door and we stepped inside a fully functioning recording studio.

"Hey, Mattie Boy!" Ezra chimed from where he leaned back on a brown leather sofa. Even if I hadn't seen his picture in any magazines, I'd still recognize him. Although, he'd done a lot of growing up since we were sixteen. He was still thin and not as muscular as Mathias, but he had filled out more. His cheekbones were sharp, but softened by the heavy scruff on his cheeks. His black curls fell over his forehead and when he smiled a dimple pierced his cheek. "Nice of you to join us."

Mathias grunted in reply and sat down in a vacant chair.

The guys hadn't noticed me yet.

I spotted Maddox in the recording part, banging away at his drums. A girl around my age stood watching him with rapt attention. I recognized her from the magazines as his girlfriend Emma.

Ezra looked my way then and noticed me standing by the door, half in the room and half out.

"Remy?" He gasped my name, shaking his head and then rubbing his eyes like he couldn't believe what he was seeing.

I waved.

"It really is you." He stood up, moving towards me. I didn't know what to do when he wrapped his arms around me in a hug. I wasn't expecting that kind of reception at all. "I can't believe this."

"Remy?" Emma spoke. "Like, Remy *Remy?*"

My eyes widened in surprise. Had Mathias talked about me?

The girl spoke into some sort of mic and Maddox ceased drumming, looking up. His mouth fell open when he saw me.

He rushed out of the recording part and walked up to me.

"Remy?"

"That's my na—*ow!*" I rubbed my arm where he pinched me. "That was rude."

"Just making sure you're real."

"Shut up and leave her alone." Mathias growled, finally butting into the conversation. He grabbed me around my waist and pulled me onto his lap.

They all continued to stand there staring at me.

"I got the drinks!" A new voice joined us, the person it belonged to appearing in the doorway a moment later with a bunch of water bottles in his arm. "Why are y'all just standing there? I thought we were supposed to be working?"

Then the guy's eyes settled on me as he finally noticed that everyone was staring in my direction.

I recognized the tall blond guy as Hayes, the guitar player. He hadn't gone to school with us, so he definitely didn't know who I was.

"Uh... hello?" His eyes shifted around. I kind of felt bad for him. He was clearly out of the loop. "Who are you?"

"Remy." Everyone echoed.

"Nice to meet you, Remy," he muttered, setting the bottles of water down. "I'm Hayes."

"Oh, and I'm Emma." Maddox's girlfriend smiled apologetically. "I'm sorry I didn't introduce myself sooner, but I was taken off guard."

"I'm surprised you know who I am."

Emma's face wrinkled and she looked up at Maddox and then at Mathias. There was definitely a story there.

Mathias was still holding me, so I leaned my head back on his shoulder to look at him. "Talk about me often, darling?" I kept my tone light and playful, but I was really curious to know how Emma knew about me.

"No." He growled the single word, but his fingers curled possessively against my waist.

I raised a single brow, waiting for him to elaborate.

He huffed and glared at his twin brother. "If we're not going to work, I'm going to fucking leave."

Maddox crossed his arms over his chest. "And I've told you a thousand times that you don't need to use the word 'fuck' in every sentence."

"Sorry, but I fucking like it."

Maddox tossed his hands in the air, grabbed a water bottle, and headed back into the recording part. Emma glanced at me for a moment and left the room. Hayes and Ezra sat on the couch, and silence descended on us.

I'd often found silence to be more deafening than a roomful of people talking. There was something so heavy and oppressive about silence. It amplified everything and made you notice things you normally wouldn't. Like the way Mathias' forehead was wrinkled and his gray eyes were shadowed with thought.

I pulled my body from his hold and walked out of the room.

I thought he might follow me, but he didn't.

I found Emma sitting on the large couch in front of the massive TV in the basement. She was curled up with a book in her lap. I guessed the whole situation had made her feel awkward and she'd decided to retreat.

"Hi," I smiled, sitting down beside her.

She closed her book and glanced at me, looking sheepish. "Hi. I'm sorry we all kind of pounced on you. We were just shocked."

"I noticed." I let out a small laugh. "But I'm wondering how *you* know me?"

Emma winced. "By accident."

"That doesn't tell me much. Did... did Mathias tell you about me?" I closed my eyes and looked away so she couldn't see my face. I wanted so badly for her to tell me that he had, and that pissed me off. I wasn't allowed to want things like that.

"No," she shook her head. "Once... he... uh... walked in on Maddox and I making out and he made some smartass comment... I'm sure you know how he is. Then Maddox mentioned you and..." She trailed off, biting her lip and looking unsure with whether or not she should continue.

"And?" I prompted, needing to hear what she had to say.

"He threw a glass at us."

"He threw a glass at you?" I repeated. "*Why?*"

"Because he's Mathias," she shrugged, like it was no big deal. "A little while after that I asked Maddox about you and he said you guys had been together in high school and that Mathias—" She stopped herself and looked up.

That's when I glanced behind me and saw that Mathias had

joined us. He glared at the two of us and cleared his throat. "I think that's enough story time."

Emma gave me an apologetic look and said, "Excuse me," as she passed me.

"Care to join us?" Mathias asked, pointing over his shoulder back where the recording room lay.

"Yeah, sure," I mumbled.

I stood up and awkwardly followed him back to the room. I felt like a teenager again who'd just been caught doing something really bad. Only I hadn't done anything wrong.

Maddox and Emma were now sitting on the couch, along with Ezra. Hayes had moved to sit in front of the control panel and fiddled with some of the buttons there.

Mathias pointed a finger roughly at the chair, telling me to sit down.

Without saying a word he stepped into the recording space and the door closed behind him. I could still see him through the glass partition, but I couldn't tell if he was mad or irritated.

He stuck some earmuff looking things on his head and grabbed the microphone, sitting down on a stool.

"Are you guys recording new stuff?" I addressed all of them.

Maddox nodded. "Yeah, we're hoping to have a new album out by this time next year, but it might get pushed longer than that since we're going on tour from January until June."

I swallowed thickly, passed the lump in my throat. I'd forgotten about that—that in less than two months they'd be gone.

I glanced at Mathias through the glass, wondering why I suddenly felt so empty at the thought of him leaving me.

This was only supposed to be revenge.

But it was quickly becoming so much more.

My eyes never left him as he began to sing.

He looked so peaceful and content as he sang. He closed his eyes, feeling the words and the power of the song. He was so raw and real in this moment, and it was a beautiful thing to see.

I found myself leaving the chair and moving to stand in front of the glass.

I wanted to get closer to him. I wanted to sink inside him and feel everything that he felt.

I reached out, my fingers touching the glass the way I wished I could touch his voice.

He finished the song and his eyes opened. "How was that?"

Perfect.

"I think we're good, but do it one more time," Hayes told him.

His eyes met with mine briefly, giving me a small—almost shy—smile, before he started singing again.

I sat down once more in the chair and drew my legs up to my chest, wrapping my arms around them.

I felt Maddox's eyes on me, watching me carefully. I knew from the thin set of his lips that he wanted to say something but wasn't sure he should.

I looked in his direction. "Say it. I'm a big girl."

"What are you two doing?"

That hadn't been what I expected him to say.

"I don't know," I answered honestly. I knew what my motives were, but Mathias' were a complete mystery to me. He was always photographed with different women all the time, so I doubted I was special to him. On some of the nights I left him, I wouldn't have been surprised if he didn't go find someone else to keep his bed warm.

I wasn't special.

I wasn't special.

I. Wasn't. Special.

I repeated the mantra over and over again in my head, wondering why I wished the opposite to be true. I wasn't supposed to want a relationship. Not with anyone, but definitely not him. Not the guy that broke me in every way imaginable.

Maddox stood up slowly, shaking his head and his face twisted with indecision. He finally relaxed and let out a sigh. He looked at me dead on and said, "He still loves you, you know? I think you're the only girl he's ever loved, and the only one he will."

He nodded his head in goodbye and left the room, while I was left holding the ticking time bomb he'd planted in my hands.

This should have been good news for me.

After all, that had been my plan all along—to get him to fall in love with me.

Suddenly I hated my plan.

I hated myself.

I didn't want this bomb.

I didn't want it to blow up.

I didn't want to hurt him the way I had.

I didn't want him to feel the pain I'd experienced—because I might know all of Mathias' secrets, but he didn't know *mine*.

CHAPTER SIXTEEN

"WHY ARE YOU so quiet?" Mathias asked, parking his car in the garage attached to the hotel.

I shrugged. Apparently it was okay for *him* to be silent, but not me. I was consumed by my thoughts and the confusion I felt. Revenge had been my only goal and now... now I didn't know anything. I felt dirty and wrong and like the shittiest person on the planet. What kind of twisted person wants to hurt someone like that? Hadn't we both been through enough already? Why was I letting my demons rule my life?

"Remy," he growled my name. "Talk to me."

I shook my head back and forth.

It was amazing how quickly things could change. This morning I was begging him to fuck me and now I wanted to be as far away from him as possible. I needed to sort out my feelings and emotions.

Maddox claimed Mathias still loved me.

But how could you cheat on someone you loved?

None of it made any sense.

God, this was making my brain hurt.

I climbed out of the car and started walking away. I had no

idea where I was headed, but I didn't care as long as it was away from him.

Mathias clouded my thoughts. He confused me, and made me want things I wasn't allowed to have. He made me *like* him again. All I'd felt for seven years was hate, and then the last few weeks... that hate had gradually been leaching out of my body. Once Maddox said what he did, I knew I couldn't go through with this. I couldn't become someone so sick and twisted that they were willing to hurt someone else for revenge.

I wrapped my arms around my body and walked as fast as my feet could carry me in my heels.

"Remy!" He shouted my name, but I didn't stop. I didn't look. I didn't give him anything.

This time *I* was the one walking away from him.

"REMY!"

His voice was closer this time, and I could hear his feet slapping against the concrete.

I took my heels off and started to run, but not soon enough.

His hand closed around my arm and he yanked me against his chest.

"Why are you running away from me? What did I *do*?" Hurt leached into his words. He smoothed a thumb over my cheek. "You're crying."

I was. My cheeks were covered in wetness and I couldn't seem to stop it. I think I was finally crying for everything that had happened.

"Let me go." I wiggled in his grasp trying to get away.

"*No*. I let you walk away once before, but I won't do it again." He touched his forehead to mine.

"Stop it," I begged, pressing my forehead against his chest. My tears soaked his shirt, but he didn't push me away.

"Why are you crying?" He asked, awkwardly rubbing my back. Mathias didn't do comfort. "I don't think I've ever seen you cry." He whispered the last part.

I wanted to tell him that I might seem tough, but I wasn't. It was all an act. A mask I put on along with my red lipstick. It wasn't the real me. The real me was weak. The real me couldn't own up to the truth. The real me was just a scared little girl sitting alone in a hospital bed holding her stillborn daughter in her arms. I closed my eyes, clinging to him as the memory flooded me.

"What's happening?" I pleaded with them. "Where are you taking her? Is she okay? Why isn't she crying? Please, let me hold her!"

They told me nothing.

"Shh," my mom wiped a piece of sweaty hair off my forehead. Tears streamed down her cheeks.

"Mom?" My voice cracked on the single word. "Why won't they let me hold her?"

"I'm so sorry, honey." She held my hand, like she thought the simple gesture alone would hold me together.

"Let me see my daughter!" I screamed. I wanted to hold her, and kiss her, and tell her how beautiful she was. I wanted to see if she looked like Mathias or me. Even if I hated him now, I still wanted her to look like him. I hoped she had his dark hair and lips.

The doctor and nurses huddled around her small body, pressing her and poking her.

"Please," I begged, tears clinging to my lashes. "Please let me see her. Please. Please. Please."

"Remy," my mom said my name quietly, "she's gone."

"NO!" I shouted the word. "No, she's not! She's okay! She's okay! Just let me hold her and you'll see!"

"No, honey." She shook her head, tears clinging to her lashes.

My lower lip began to tremble with the threat of tears. "She's fine."

If I kept saying it, it had to be true, right?

"I'm sorry," she said again.

"Stop saying that!" I screamed at her. I shouldn't have been yelling at her right now. She was the only one that supported me when I wanted to keep my baby. My dad had been adamantly against it, and even my brother had sided with him. I guessed they were getting their wish now. I wasn't getting my baby.

The doctor carried my daughter over to me, a forlorn look on his face. "I'm sorry, there was nothing we could do. These things... they just happen sometimes and we don't know why."

He placed my stillborn daughter in my arms and they cleared out of the room, leaving my mom and me alone with her.

A gut-wrenching sob raked my body and I curled her tiny body into my neck. I never wanted to let her go. I wanted her to know that her mommy loved her. Her skin was still warm, but she was pale. Too pale. I cradled her in my arms. She didn't have Mathias' hair. She had mine. But she did get his lips and that made me smile through my tears. I'd thought I knew heartbreak before, but I was wrong. This was heartbreak. This was having my whole world ripped from my hands. It wasn't fair.

"Life never is," my mom whispered, and that was when I realized I'd said the last part out loud.

I wanted to know why this happened to me.

Why my daughter?

Why anybody's child?

This was the cruelest form of punishment that ever existed.

Her eyes were closed and I could almost pretend that she was sleeping. Almost.

I kissed her forehead. "Mommy loves you, Hope," I whispered.

"Hope?" My mom repeated.

"Hope," I said again.

She was my hope and now she was gone.

"Remy? Remy? Remy?"

My body was shaking.

Why was my body shaking?

"Why are you shaking me?" I asked.

He ceased the movements and stared down at me with confusion. "You just... zoned out. What's wrong with you?"

I closed my eyes, reaching up to wipe away the wetness on my cheeks.

I couldn't tell him.

Not because he didn't deserve to know, but because I wanted to spare him the *pain.*

That was comical really, since I'd spent the last few weeks planning to break his heart.

It was funny how quickly your thoughts and opinions of a person could change.

"I have to go." I tore out of his hold and this time he let me walk away.

I should've been happy about that, but I wasn't.

CHAPTER SEVENTEEN

"YOU REALLY SHOULD stop moping around the house." My grandma spoke up from the kitchen table.

I glanced at her, adding more sugar to my cup of coffee. "I'm not moping."

"You are." She declared, spreading out the newspaper on the table. "Want to tell me *why?*"

It had been a week since I left Mathias standing in the parking garage. He hadn't reached out to me, but I hadn't expected him to. It was better like this anyway. I didn't have to pretend anymore, and he could go back to his old ways. It was how it had been for the last seven years and it should stay that way.

Stupidly, I did miss him. He was my fucking kryptonite.

After that day in the garage, when I had to relive losing Hope, if I hadn't had my grandma to take care of I would've been on a plane out of here.

It was too much.

I tried not to think of Hope.

I tried to pretend she didn't exist.

But that was wrong of me. She was my daughter and her

brief existence should've been celebrated.

It was too hard though. The pain of losing her would never go away, I knew that now.

And I guess, when I came up with my game plan to seduce Mathias, I thought it would help if something crushed him the way I had been. I'd been a bitch and wanted someone else to lose something too.

And by doing that, I had let Hope down.

I think I let myself down too.

I didn't know who I was anymore since I lost her, and that scared me.

I needed to rediscover myself.

"Hey," she snapped her fingers, "I'm not getting any younger here. In fact, with every second I'm getting closer to death. So come here and tell your dear old grandma what's wrong, after all, chances are I'll take your secrets to my grave." She winked.

I laughed, for the first time in what felt like a while.

I pulled out a chair and sat down at the table. "It's Mathias," I started.

"That boy?" She glared. "The one that got you pregnant and left you all alone?"

I sighed. "He didn't know, grandma."

She rolled her eyes. "Well what is it about him that's been bothering you?"

"Everything," I muttered, doodling on the table with the edge of my fingernail. "I... I was seeing him again. And... I wanted to hurt him the way he hurt me..." I frowned, lifting the cup of coffee to my lips. "Isn't that awful?" I looked up at her. "I mean, what kind of sick twisted person does that?"

She stared at me, her expression sad. "You've been through a lot, Remy. You've handled it like a champ. But even the best of us crumble eventually."

I didn't feel like I'd ever handled anything at all. I'd closed myself off and pretended to be okay. Pretending was not reality. I'd done crazy, stupid things all because I was trying to feel *something*.

The only thing that made me feel anything—good or bad—was Mathias.

I felt like a part of my soul was tethered to him.

Maybe that was the real reason I came up with the game—as an excuse to get close to him.

I wanted to laugh at that stupid thought. I'd never been the girl to believe in fate and destiny and other mystical things.

"I don't know what I want anymore," I whispered, burying my head in my hands. "I still like him even though I shouldn't... even though I know he's bad for me. But I *can't* stop these feelings and that scares me. I don't think I can be with him again, because what if he hurts me?"

She looked at me seriously. "What if he doesn't?"

"You're not helping," I snapped, "you're only confusing me more."

"It's a legitimate question." She shrugged her thin shoulders.

"I don't think he wants me like that... he doesn't see a future for us." I nodded my head, agreeing with my own words.

"How do you know that?" She asked.

"Because he's Mathias," I answered simply. "He doesn't do commitment."

But he did with you. My conscience spoke up.

Until he cheated on you. I reminded myself.

She tapped her fingers against the table. "I think you're holding on too tightly to the past. It's done. It's over with. You can't change it. But you can change your future, because it's not set in stone. You're both adults now. Act like it."

She got up from the table then and waddled back to her

room, leaving me alone to ponder her words.

"Percy, life sucks." I mumbled to the cat that currently hogged my pillow. Always with the damn pillow. Couldn't he find a new spot?

Of course in typical cat fashion he ignored me. He didn't even crack one of his eyes open.

I didn't know what to make of my grandma's advice. It seemed too simple to let go of the past and move on.

The doorbell rang and I groaned. I didn't want to deal with anyone today.

"I've got it!" I yelled, just in case my grandma decided to get out of bed and go to the door.

I bound down the steps, ready to tell whoever was standing there to go to hell, but when I opened the door all the words died on my tongue.

"Mathias?"

He stood in front of me looking impeccably put together like always. His brown hair was swept away from his piercing gray eyes and he was dressed in a pair of jeans, a nice shirt, and jacket.

"Can I come in?" He asked, clearing his throat and pointing to the interior of the home.

"Uh... yeah. Sure." I was shocked and couldn't wrap my brain around the fact that he was here.

He took a seat on one of the couches in the living room and I took a few tentative steps toward him.

"I wanted to see you," he said the words slowly, "but I wanted to give you time to cool off."

"I'm fine," I grumbled.

"What happened that day?" He asked. "You just... you freaked out on me, Remy, and... you actually scared me."

I couldn't believe Mathias was admitting something like that to me. He might've shared things about his past with me, but he'd *always* guarded his feelings.

"Talk to me," he demanded when I stayed quiet. His features contorted with anger and I knew he was seconds away from blowing up.

"I don't know what to say," I admitted.

"Why does it always have to be a fucking rollercoaster with us?" He asked, staring up at the ceiling like it held all the answers in the world.

"Because that's how we are," I shrugged, sitting down in the chair across from him. "We're a hurricane raging."

He stared at me through hooded eyes. "Are you saying we're a catastrophe?"

"I guess so," I shrugged.

"You don't think there's more for us? You don't think there's a reason why we ran into each other again?"

"No," I said adamantly. If I believed there was a reason for us meeting again, then I would be forced to believe that there was a reason for Hope's death, and I'd never accept that.

"Who are *you*?" He asked. "Because this," he waved a hand at me, "this isn't the Remy I know. The Remy I know doesn't sit back so quiet and meek. The Remy I know shouts her feelings for the world to hear."

"Stop it."

"Come on, Remy, let it out." He stood up, stalking towards me. "Tell me what your problem is."

"My problem is you!" I yelled, shooting up into a standing position. If he wanted a reaction from me, I'd make sure he got one.

"Me?" He seemed confused.

"Yes, you!" I threw my hands in the air. "You're just... ugh! You're *you* and you confuse and frustrate me like nobody else can."

"I feel the same way about you." He said the words calmly, evenly.

"I don't know what you want from me," I whispered, "from this." I waved a hand between the two of us. "From us. Together."

Even though I had been playing a game, *real* feelings had developed again, because it was fucking impossible for me not to love Mathias Wade. He was planted into my DNA. He was my air. My life. Even though I didn't want him to be, he was. He always had been and he always would be. From the first moment he spoke to me, it was over then. For both of us. We were never going to be the same, because I was perfect for him and he was perfect for me. We were two pieces of a puzzle that fit together just right. That kind of love... it didn't go away. No, it only grew, even in the absence of each other it continued to blossom and grow into something stronger. Even my hate hadn't been strong enough to snuff it out. I'd been too blinded by revenge to see that.

He glowered down at me. "I think I've been pretty fucking clear, Remy."

"Nothing is ever clear with you!" I poked a finger against his chest. "You're so damn confusing and hard to read!"

"Me?!" He looked shocked. "What about *you?*"

"What about me?" I countered.

He groaned, shoving his fingers through his hair. "God, we are so fucked up. We can't even have a normal conversation." His jaw clenched and he shook his head back and forth. He scrubbed his hands over his face and let out a groan. "Why can't things ever be easy with us?"

"Because things that are easy aren't worth fighting for," I whispered.

One of his hands fell to my waist, his fingers tightening around one of the belt loops so I couldn't get away, and the other cupped my cheek. "Are you saying that *we're* worth fighting for?"

I swallowed thickly. "I don't know." And that was an honest answer. I loved Mathias when I was sixteen years old, but I wasn't sure if what I felt now was love, or a desire to hold on to the past. I also couldn't overlook the fuckedupness of the fact that a week ago I'd been set on destroying him. We were a disaster. Pure and simple.

He stared at me for a moment, his face void of any emotion. "If I walked out this door right now, and you never saw me again, how would you feel?"

I didn't even have to say anything, the flicker of pain that twisted my face spoke volumes.

"Tell me you want me, Remy." His fingers ghosted over my lips and my eyes closed.

"No."

"Tell me," he growled.

I shook my head. "I can't."

"Why?" His fingers skimmed down my neck and over my collarbone.

"You'll only hurt me." My eyes opened and I looked at him, letting him see the pain in my eyes that I always kept carefully hidden.

He pulled his bottom lip between his teeth and let it go. "I won't. Things are different now. Let me prove it to you."

My body unconsciously curled into his until I was tucked against him. I laid my cheek against his chest, my emotions raging.

"I'm not a kid anymore, Remy." The sound of his voice rumbled against my ear. "I won't fuck this up again. I swear. I know I'm not a good guy. I know I've done horrible things. But the only time I've ever felt halfway decent was when you were mine, and I was yours."

My heart stuttered in my chest and then began to beat more rapidly.

I took a step back and squared my shoulders. Jutting out my chin, I said, "Okay, but if you screw this up I'll hurt you. I don't know how yet, but I promise it'll be extremely painful."

He chuckled, reaching up to scratch his jaw. "I wouldn't expect anything less from you."

"Good." I nodded, wondering if I'd done the right thing—or if I'd just willingly handed over the last piece of my shattered heart for him to obliterate. I guessed the good news was if he completely destroyed my heart I really could be the heartless bitch I pretended to be.

"And now," he closed in on me once more, "I'm going to kiss you."

"Don't be so arrogant," I rolled my eyes, "maybe I don't want you to kiss me."

He chuckled, rubbing his thumb against my bottom lip. "I *know* you do."

"Oh, really?" I quirked a brow.

"Mhmm," he nodded, his eyes falling to my lips. His were only a breath away from mine when he let out a yelp and jumped away from me.

He swatted at something on his leg and I began to laugh manically. Percy was wrapped around his leg, trying to claw his way up his body.

"Jesus Fucking Christ, this thing is a demon!"

I probably should've helped him, but I was too busy wiping the tears of laughter from my eyes. "That's what you get for trying to kiss me."

"Remy," he groaned, his eyes pleading with me, "I think I'm bleeding."

"Alright, alright, you big baby," I chuckled, bending down to pry Percy off.

Percy did not release him easily. "Good kitty." I petted him on top of his head when I finally had him cradled in my arms.

"Your cat hates me."

"He does," I agreed, "I think he wants to be the only man in my life."

Mathias frowned, glaring at Percy. "He looks like he wants to eat me."

"Aw, he'd never eat you. He has better taste than that." I made a kissy face at the cat.

Mathias narrowed his eyes. "He's plotting to kill me. I can see it in his eyes."

"He truly is my soul-cat then," I joked.

He gave me a challenging look and I knew I was in trouble.

Feeling like a kid again I let out a squeal and ran for the stairs, running up them as fast as I could with Percy in my arms.

I dove into my room and tried to close the door, but Mathias caught it in his hand and pushed his way through.

Percy meowed and jumped out of my arms, running from the room.

"Oh, you're in trouble now." He stalked towards me.

The backs of my knees hit the bed and I fell down. He was quick to lower his body on top of mine, caging me in with his arms.

"Looks like you've got me right where you want me," I grinned.

He chuckled, kissing my neck. "Yeah, but you're not naked so that's kind of a bummer."

Then he covered my lips with his, kissing me deeply and reminding me how much I'd missed him this week—how much I'd *always* missed him. The thing about the heart is, once it's given itself completely to someone it's theirs forever, no matter the circumstances.

Once my lips were bruised with the imprint of his he pulled away. He lay on his back, staring at the ceiling, and I did the same. I was reminded of a time where things were simple and we were just Mathias and Remy. Now he was famous and I was keeping secrets. That right there was a lethal combination.

"I did come here for another reason," he said, reaching for my hand. He wound our fingers together and my whole body hummed with the touch.

"And what would that be?" I asked.

"I wanted to see if you and your grandma wanted to come to my parent's place for Thanksgiving tomorrow." He cleared his throat. "I mean, you don't *have* to, but I'd like you to be there. Never mind. You probably already have plans. Forget I said anything." He rambled in a very un-Mathias-like fashion.

I was shocked he was extending an invitation. When we... dated... before he *never* introduced me to his foster parents. Only his brother and Ezra knew about our relationship—and my parent's of course, who were never quiet about their disapproval of him.

"You didn't even give me a chance to respond." I laughed.

"Then do you want to go or not?"

"We would love to," I assured him. Sitting up I looked down at him. "But who am I going as? Your friend? Your fuck buddy? I want to be clear on how you're introducing me to your parent's. I don't want any surprises."

He glowered at me. "You're mine."

"Like I'm a toy to you?" I pushed, wanting to hear him say it.

"No, you're mine like you're my fucking girlfriend."

"So... I'm just your girlfriend that you only fuck?" Now I was messing with him.

I let out a small scream when he grasped my wrists and rolled me back onto the bed. He glared down at me. "You're my girlfriend. Although, that seems like too insignificant of a word for what you are to me."

"Are you okay with this?" I asked. "With us?" I didn't want to get my hopes up that there could be more for us, if this was only something casual and temporary for him. When I was young I never sat around and dreamed about a wedding, babies, and happily ever after's, but once I met Mathias I wanted all of that. He'd taken it away from me once, and I didn't think I could handle it if he did it again.

His tongue snaked out to moisten his lips. "Let's get one thing straight, Remy, and this is going to be the *last* time I say it. I want this. I want you. I want the good and the bad and whatever the hell else you throw at me. You're the only girl I've ever wanted and I refuse to let you get away from me again."

I wanted to tell him that he didn't let me get away, he *pushed* me away, but I kept my mouth shut. Some fights weren't worth it.

"I don't know what the future might hold for us," he continued, his hair brushing against my forehead, "so for now we take this one day at a time."

I nodded my head in agreement. "Okay."

"And if you ever freak out on me again, you have to *talk* to me." His lips brushed against my ear when he spoke. "Don't run away from me."

I closed my eyes, frowning. "You don't talk to me when you

have one of your... moments." I didn't know what else to call the times where he snapped.

He took my chin in his hand and forced me to look at him. "You know my darkest secrets, Rem. Don't ever say I don't talk to you."

"You don't talk to me *now*."

He sighed, rolling away from me, and pulled roughly at his hair. "We really are going to have to get to know each other all over again, aren't we?"

I shrugged.

He held out his hand to me, smiling boyishly. I liked this smile, and it wasn't one he wore often. "Mathias Wade. It's nice to meet you."

I shook my head, laughing under my breath. Taking his hand I said, "Remy Parker."

"Remy, how about we don't fuck this up this time?" He raised a brow, smiling crookedly.

But that's what we do.

"Sounds like a plan."

CHAPTER EIGHTEEN

"GRANDMA," I GROANED, "could you try not looking like you want to kill him?" I asked her, watching Mathias get out of a black SUV and head for the front door.

"No. He's bad. He hurt you," she snapped, "and if he doesn't keep his manner's in check I'll take him out at the knees." She waved her cane around for emphasis.

"I'm considering hiding that from you," I told her, crossing my arms over my chest.

"Oh, Remy, we both know you wouldn't take an old lady's cane from her." She smiled. "That would be far too cruel for even you."

"But you're not a lady," I laughed, heading to the door when I heard a knock. "Ow!" I turned back around hastily. "Did you poke me in the butt with that thing?"

She nodded, trying to hide a grin.

"You're bad," I narrowed my eyes. "I'm going to have a bruise from that."

"Well then, that young man can kiss your ass and make it better. Lord knows you should make him grovel," she muttered under her breath.

"Shh," I hissed.

I'd already swung the door open and Mathias stood there grinning. "What is this about your ass?"

"You both suck," I glared, stomping out the door and to the waiting SUV.

I then realized that I'd left my poor grandma alone to make her way to the car by herself, so I quickly did an about face to go back and get her.

Only Mathias was helping her.

Oh. My. God.

I think hell froze over.

Mathias Wade was helping a little old lady—but not just any little old lady, nope, he was helping my grandma... who hated him... and she wasn't even trying to hit him with her cane.

I grabbed my phone from my pocket and snapped a picture.

"What are you doing, missy?" My grandma asked, holding onto his arm as she climbed down the porch steps. "You know I hate having my picture taken."

"This is for blackmail," I joked, tucking my phone back into my pocket.

Mathias glared at me for that one and I simply laughed. I headed over to my grandma to take her from Mathias, but she swatted my arm with a loud smack. She might look little and frail, but that hurt.

"He's got me," she scolded, "and he's a lot better to look at than you."

"I thought you hated him," I snickered.

She glanced up at Mathias who shrugged in response, clearly not bothered by my statement.

"I might not like him, but that doesn't change his looks."

I snorted and Mathias' lips twitched with the threat of a smile. I wanted to tell him that it was okay to smile—that he didn't have to hide those things, but I left the words unsaid.

"Have you been working out?" My grandma asked him, reaching up to grasp his bicep through the material of his shirt.

"Grandma!" I scolded.

"It's like a rock." She rapped a fist against his arm.

Mathias looked at me, biting his bottom lip to hide his laughter. "Let's get her in the car before she gropes you some more," I shook my head, "she has wandering hands."

"Yeah, better stop her before she gets to the best part." He winked at me.

Grandma made a tsking sound and picked up her pace.

Mathias helped her into the back of the car and then opened the front passenger door for me. I looked at him like he'd grown three heads.

"What?" He asked innocently. "I can be nice."

I smirked and leaned forward so I could whisper in his ear. "Don't be."

There was nothing wrong with tender moment with Mathias, but I preferred him to be himself, which was raw, and smart-mouthed, and rough, and... I could go on forever.

Neither of us was perfect, and that's why we complimented each other so well.

He shook his head and stepped away. "Get in the fucking car, Remy." He paused, tilting his head. "Was that better?"

"Much," I nodded.

I climbed into the car and glanced back at my grandma. She sat watching me with a small smile on her lips. Something told me I was going to be listening to an epic speech later tonight.

"NICE SUSPENDERS," I commented, as I watched Mathias help my grandma out of the car—because she refused my help. I think she was testing him, to see if she could make him mad. So far it wasn't working.

He chuckled, shaking his head. "You love my suspenders."

"You can definitely pull them off," I assured him. He was dressed nicely in a pair of gray slacks, a white button down shirt, black tie, belt, and the suspenders. I was glad I'd worn a black dress and heels. "Although, I don't know where your obsession with them came from."

He closed the car door and started guiding my grandma forward. "They had me wear them during a photo shoot once, and I liked them," he shrugged.

When he brought up things like photo shoots it reminded me that he wasn't just Mathias anymore. Instead he was a world famous rock star.

I followed him up the front porch steps and he reached for the doorknob. He glanced at my grandma and then at me. "Be prepared for my mom to ask you five-hundred questions."

"Does she know I'm coming?" I asked, my eyes widening as I glanced at the door.

He nodded. "Did you really think I'd ask you to come and not tell my parents beforehand?"

"Well... yeah." I kept forgetting that things were different now, for the both of us, and we didn't have to hide our relationship.

He shook his head, laughing in a self-deprecating manner. "You have such little faith in me."

I frowned.

"I told them I was bringing my girlfriend, and they tried to ask me about you then, but I shut them up, so... they're chomping at the bit. Especially my mom."

"Great." I squared my shoulders.

I'd never met Mathias' foster parents since he'd always been secretive about our relationship. After him, I never dated again. Just a one night stand here and there, which meant I'd lived twenty-three years of my life without ever having to do the meet the parent's routine.

And to make it worse, it was Thanksgiving.

I needed a shot.

Something strong.

Where was the fucking tequila?

Oh dear God, he hadn't even opened the door yet and I already wished I was drunk. I hoped this wasn't an omen as to how the evening would go.

"Are you ready?" He asked me, and I realized he'd been giving me a moment to gather myself.

"Yeah." I smoothed my fingers through my straight hair and squared my shoulders as I plastered on my game face.

"Show time," he muttered, and pushed the door open.

Almost immediately I heard a high-pitched shriek and a woman say, "You must be Remy!"

I shot Mathias a scared look and he shrugged, letting me know I was on my own. Fucking Traitor.

His mom pulled me inside and enveloped me in a bone-crushing hug.

I was pretty sure my lungs were about to collapse.

"Can't. Breathe."

"Mom, let her go." Mathias groaned, passing by us as he toted my grandma along.

"I can't believe you brought a girl home." She pulled back, but kept her hands on my arms so that I couldn't go anywhere. "And she's real."

"Very real," I nodded.

"And pretty," she continued.

"Mom," Mathias pleaded, sounding very much like the teenage boy I remembered. "You're embarrassing me."

His mom grinned. "That's what mom's are for."

"Shit," he cursed, "this is only the beginning isn't it?" He waved a hand at his mom and me.

She nodded and he muttered something under his breath. Pushing a strand of hair from his eyes, he asked, "Should we get seated in the dining room or do you want to eat later?"

"Now," she nodded, "everybody else is seated."

Mathias tightened his hold on my grandma and the two left the foyer, leaving me completely alone with his mom.

I was going to kill him for this.

"I'm Karen," she smiled brightly. "You have no idea how nice it is to meet you."

"I'm Remy, but I guess you already knew that." I forced a smile, but I was afraid I looked like I was choking on something.

"Mathias has never even mentioned a girl around us, so when he said he was bringing his girlfriend to dinner I almost peed my pants with excitement." She danced on the balls of her feet.

"Uh…" I was at a loss for words.

Sobering, she grasped my hands. "My husband, Paul, and I have always worried about him more than the other boys. He's had a hard life, and we've been afraid he'd never find someone he trusted enough to let in."

I glanced down the hallway where Mathias had disappeared, her words having sparked a curiosity in me. I'd never once bothered to question what it was about me that made me different. When we were teenagers I figured we were drawn together because of our likeness, but he'd sought me out first and things escalated from there. So, what on earth did the enigmatic Mathias Wade see in *me?*

"I know he's not the nicest nor the easiest person to be around," she continued, turning my attention back to her, "but there's a goodness in him. He has a heart that's much kinder than he realizes."

"I know," I whispered. And I did know that, which only served to make me feel even guiltier for my previous intentions.

"I guess we should join them." She smiled politely and motioned for me to follow her.

When we reached an archway that led into the dining room Mathias was about ready to jump out of his seat. "Thank God." I heard him mutter.

There was an empty seat between Mathias and my grandma and he stood up hastily to pull out the chair for me. "Thanks." I shot a smile in his direction.

Maddox and Emma were seated across from us, along with another woman that I assumed was Emma's mother. They looked enough alike that they had to be related. Down on the other end sat Ezra, who seemed highly amused. I glanced down the other way and saw Karen take her seat beside her husband who sat at the head of the table.

He said a few words over the food and then stood to carve the turkey.

Underneath the table Mathias' hand landed on my knee, snaking slowly up my thigh and underneath my dress.

I jerked, nearly spilling the glass of water beside my plate.

Mathias let out a low chuckle and his hand came back to rest on my knee. He gave it a soft squeeze and then left his hand there.

My body heated at his touch, desire curling low in my belly.

Jesus Christ, the man could make me want him while sitting

at a table with his fucking parents. He was dangerous to be around.

I piled food onto my plate, but I'd lost my appetite. ...Unless wanting to lick Mathias counted as having an appetite, because in that case I was *starving*.

I nibbled at my food, pushing most of it around my plate. Everybody else chatted and I kept quiet until the attention was turned to me.

"What do you do Remy?" Karen asked.

I gulped down the rest of my wine—I was on my second glass, but unfortunately it would take a lot more than that to get me drunk.

"I'm working at a bar." I cringed once the words were out of my mouth. It sounded pretty bad. I was working at a bar, while her son was a famous rock star. She was definitely going to think I was using him. Fuck. I hastened to add, "I have a degree in marketing, but when I moved back here I needed to get a job and they hired me on the spot at the bar, so..." I trailed off and my grandma made a snickering sound beside me. She knew I was trying to impress them.

Mathias gave my knee a slight squeeze, as if he was telling me it was okay. He knew I didn't get nervous, like ever, so this was new for me. But this was also his *parent's* and dammit, I wanted them to like me. I wanted their approval. I wanted them to accept me the way my parent's never had with Mathias—and my poor father would bust a vein in his forehead if he knew where I was right now.

With his free hand he reached for the bottle of wine and poured me another glass.

"That's nice." His mother smiled.

I wanted to crawl under the table and hide, but since that wasn't in my nature I squared my shoulders and smiled instead. "Thanks."

"So you've lived here before?" Paul, Mathias' father, asked.

I nodded. "Yeah. Mathias and I..." I paused, not sure how to continue. Finally I settled on the safest thing to say. "We knew each other in high school."

"Oh," Karen's eyes widened in surprise. "He didn't tell us that."

I glanced at Mathias. "Of course he didn't."

He shrugged, tapping his fingers against the table. "I didn't think it was important."

"It's not," I snapped. It had been obvious that he hadn't told his parents about our past connection, and I'd been fine with that, but when he said it wasn't important that grated on my nerves. It made me feel like *I* wasn't important to him, which then made me wonder what the fuck I was doing here.

His hold on my knee tightened and I glared at him. He gave me a look that told me I needed to chill out. I resisted the urge to stab the heel of my shoe into his foot.

"They dated in high school." Maddox piped in.

"Oh fuck." Mathias dropped his head in his hands and for the first time through the whole meal my body was free of his touch.

"What?" Karen gasped, looking around at all of us.

I grabbed my glass of wine and chugged that sucker.

Paul looked like he was going to fall out of his chair.

This had officially turned into the most awkward Thanksgiving/Meet-The-Parent's dinner, ever. Seriously, I think we deserved an award for this.

"I didn't know you ever dated anyone." Karen fiddled with the napkin in her lap, a frown marring her pretty face. "I feel like we don't know you at all." Tears pooled in her eyes. "Why is it, that even after all this time, you feel like you can't talk to us?"

"Fuck, fuck, fuck," Mathias cursed, shaking his head, "here

we go again." He threw his hands up and said, "Please, for the love of God can we *not* turn this into a fucking therapy session where we all sit around and talk about How-To-Fix-Mathias. Frankly, I'm not in the fucking mood for it."

"Mathias," his mom scolded, "don't be like that."

"Then stop making me feel guilty." He leaned around me to glare at her. "And stop trying to fucking fix me."

Holy shit, I felt like I was sitting between a tennis match and any minute I was going to get pelted in the head with a ball.

Karen sighed. "Mathias, that's not what I'm trying to do. All we've ever wanted to do is help you, because we love you. You're blowing everything out of proportion."

"Like always," Maddox muttered from across the table.

Mathias sent a withering glare in the direction of his twin.

"Help me? You think you can help me?" He shook his head, letting out a breath. "There is no helping someone like me."

With that he stood up from the table and I half expected him to throw his plate or do something stupid, but instead he stalked out of the room, leaving us in silence.

We all stared around at one another, wondering what to do.

Grandma was the first to speak.

"Can we have desert now?"

We all laughed and she smiled at having succeeded in ridding the room of tension.

"Yes, I think it's time for desert." Karen pushed back her chair and left the room.

I stood too, and muttered, "I'll be right back."

Before I could leave the dining room, Maddox spoke. "He'll be in the guesthouse."

I stopped and looked at him over my shoulder. "Thanks."

I passed Karen in the kitchen and she smiled knowingly. "Are you looking for Mathias?"

I nodded.

"Come on." She ceased cutting the pumpkin pie and led me through the house and to a set of French doors. They opened into the backyard where a large pool sat—currently covered for the winter months. She pointed to the guesthouse, even though it was easy to see, and whispered, "Good luck."

I strode across the yard and paused in front of the door, taking a deep breath before pushing it open.

Immediately the light twinkling sounds of the piano floated through the air.

I paid no attention to my surroundings, instead striding up to Mathias and wrapping my arms around his wide shoulders. He instantly relaxed into my touch, but kept playing the piano. I didn't recognize the song, it was something soft and haunting sounding.

When he finished he sat still as a stone. He didn't even seem to be breathing. I didn't move either, and continued to stand with my arms wrapped around his neck. Eventually he turned and looked up at me. I swore tears shimmered in his gray eyes.

"What's wrong with me, Rem? Why do I do this? Why do I push everybody away?" He looked pained, and I hated that he hurt so much, and I hated even more that I had wanted to add to that pain. Mathias already hurt enough as it was. Now, I wanted nothing more than to make it all go away.

"I don't know," I whispered, rubbing his shoulders. "I guess maybe you're scared to let people in."

He took a shuddering breath. "I don't want to be like this. I don't want to be this guy, but I am." His hands quaked and he clenched them into fists, his knuckles turning white.

"Your family loves you, regardless," I told him. "You have to stop pushing them away."

"How could anyone ever love me?" He asked, his eyes

desperate for an answer.

"I loved you." My voice cracked and he wrapped an arm around my waist, pulling me down onto his lap.

He burrowed his head into my neck and I startled when his wet tears stung my skin. He pulled away slightly and grasped my cheeks, staring at me with an intensity that left me breathless. "Do you think you can ever love me again?"

"I don't know," I lied.

He nodded his head and swallowed thickly, like he expected that answer.

He smoothed his fingers through my hair and cupped the back of my neck. "I'm going to do whatever it takes to change that answer to yes, because," he whispered in my ear, "I never stopped loving *you*."

I closed my eyes, soaking in his words—basking in them. I wasn't sure I believed him, but I wanted it to be true. I wanted to believe his feelings for me never dimmed, the way mine hadn't for him. Even when I hated him with every fiber of my being I still loved him—because it was so much easier to hate someone you loved. And I loved him now, God did I ever. I'd believed I was over him, that my feelings had left, but if the last few weeks had proven anything it was that I was always going to love Mathias Wade, whether we were together or apart.

Despite our undeniable love and connection I still had a hard time believing we could make it. I *hoped*, but it seemed impossible.

He wrapped his arms around me and held me for a moment. It was a sweet gesture, and one I wasn't used to from him. I liked this side of him, but I still preferred the rougher, rawer Mathias. However, I knew right now he just wanted to hold me, so I offered him as much comfort as I could.

The door to the guesthouse opened, but Mathias didn't

move. I glanced over and saw Maddox standing in the doorway. "Your grandma is ready to go home."

I nodded. "Give us a minute."

"Sure thing." He gave me a small smile and closed the door.

Mathias had burrowed his head against my neck, but now he looked at me, tucking a piece of hair behind my ear. "Do you think we'll ever not be a fucked up mess?"

I smiled, letting out a small laugh. "I like our mess. Except..."

"Except what?" He prompted, his fingers skimming over my collarbone like they had a mind of their own.

"Except when you said you cheated on me. That was one mess I hated."

He swallowed thickly. "When you said you were leaving..." He looked away, his face contorting in pain. When he looked back at me his gray eyes were light and pleading with me. "It hurt so bad. *Nothing*, none of the shit I went through compared to the pain of knowing you were leaving, and you know how bad it was for me with my mom... you know what she did to me..." He closed his eyes and I knew he was thinking of his real mom, and all the evil things she'd done to him—like trying to drown him in a bathtub. Not to mention all the times he told me that she choked him, or hit him, or belittled him with harsh words. I hated that he'd had to go through that as a little kid and never got a normal childhood. By the time Maddox and he were put into foster care they were already older, and the damage had been done. "None of it was as bad as the thought of losing you. I didn't see how two fucked up kids like us could ever make it work, so I lied to you. I broke you the way you broke me."

A weight lifted off of my shoulders and I gasped.

"Say it," I pleaded, "I need to hear you say it."

He grasped my face in one hand, holding me tight enough that I couldn't move. Staring into my eyes he said, "I never cheated on you. When I was with you, I was only ever with you. You're the only girl I can say that to."

I closed my eyes, letting the truth of his words wash over me, and it felt so, so good.

"You're not lying now, are you?" I asked, hoping he couldn't hear the quiver in my voice.

He shook his head. "I was angry at you for a long time for leaving me, and since I'm such a selfish asshole the only thing that comforted me was knowing that you might be hurting as much as me... just for a different reason."

His reasoning for hurting me was twisted and sick, but that was Mathias.

His version of love was all kinds of fucked up thanks to his parents. He got the worst of it over his twin brother, and even today he still bore the scars of his past.

I clung to him, breathing harshly.

Despite the fact that he was telling me now that he had lied about Josie and the other girls it didn't erase the years of hurt I'd had to cope with. It didn't change what happened to our baby. His words had no magical powers to erase the past, but maybe they could help mend what was left of my heart. I hoped so anyway.

"You know I had no choice in leaving," I glowered, "how could you be so cruel?" I hit my fist against his chest, but he grabbed my hands to stop me before I could do anymore damage.

"Because that's what I do," his eyes were serious, "I destroy the things I love."

I swallowed thickly, damming back tears. I wouldn't cry. I refused.

"I'm so, so sorry for lying to you—for hurting you. I was... I wasn't in a good place, and I can acknowledge that what I did was wrong." He leaned his forehead against mine and his breath fanned across my lips. "I want to get better, for you, for me, for our future."

"For our future?" I whispered, my voice sounding awed.

He nodded, running his fingers reverently along my jaw.

"Do you really see a future for us?" I asked, grasping his hair between my fingers. It didn't matter how many times he told me, I still had a hard time believing he wanted more from me. "After all the shit we've been through, and put each other through, do you really think we can make it work?"

He nodded, placing his hand on my wrist and pulling my hand away from his hair to entwine our hands together. "Yeah, I think we can." He swallowed thickly, his face darkening with shadows. "If our years apart have taught me anything it's that my feelings for you are never going to go away. It doesn't matter how much I drink, or who I fuck, I only want you."

I winced at his words, hating the thought of him being with so many other women, but it wasn't like I'd been a saint either.

I knew that in order for us to truly work we'd have to put the past behind us and start anew. Which meant I needed to be honest. I could be honest about wanting to hurt him, but I couldn't tell him about the baby. Not now, maybe not ever. That was one hurt I wanted to spare him.

"Since we're being honest and all..." I started, glancing away and biting my lip.

He grabbed my chin and forced me to look at him. His eyes were steely. "What did you do, Remy?"

I squared my shoulders and jutted out my chin defiantly, refusing to cower. "After the first time I saw you at the bar I decided I wanted to hurt you the way you hurt me. I wanted to make you fall in love with me again, and break your heart like you did mine." I stroked my fingers against his slightly stubbled cheek. "It didn't take me long to realize that I couldn't do that to you." I took a shuddering breath.

He chuckled, shaking his head. "We're a fucked up pair, aren't we? Always trying to hurt each other." A small smile played on his lips and he cupped my cheek. "We really need to work on that."

I laughed, glad that he wasn't pissed. "Yeah we do. No more lying and no more games?"

He smiled crookedly. "That might be impossible for us." He smoothed his fingers through my hair and then the tips of his fingers grazed my collarbone. "But I think we can do it."

I hoped so. I really did.

MATHIAS HELPED MY grandma out of the car and inside. I took over from there and guided her to her bedroom. She lay down and reached for the remote.

"I'm ready for some trashy reality television," she declared.

"Of course you are," I sighed, reaching for her shoes. She swatted at my hand and I glared at her. "That hurt."

"Don't be a baby," she admonished me. She continued to push my hands away. "I can do this myself."

I rolled my eyes and stepped away from her. "Remind me again why I'm living here with you?"

"The free food?" She suggested.

I laughed, shaking my head as I walked to the door.

"Remy?" She stopped me.

I turned back to look at her, raising a brow as I waited for her to continue.

"He's not so bad." She shrugged her slender shoulders.

I laughed, smiling at her. "Are you going soft, grandma?"

She scoffed. "Hell no. If he hurts you again I won't hesitate to end him."

"Grandma!"

"I'm dead serious. If you see me in the backyard with a shovel don't come out. I don't want you to become an accessory in a murder charge."

I stared at her, fighting the urge to laugh. "I think you've been watching too much CSI."

"Oh no, I don't like that show. I watch Criminal Minds. That Morgan..." She licked her lips. "The things I'd like to let that man do to me."

"Oh my God," I gasped, this time unable to hide my laughter. "You're a piece of work."

She smiled widely. "That's why you love me." Sobering she said, "Go on. I'm sure he's still waiting for you and I doubt you want to spend your evening here with me. I'm *fine*." She waved her hand, shooing me on.

"Are you sure?" I asked, hesitant to leave her.

"I'm fine," she assured me yet again, "I was fine before you lived with me and I'm fine now."

"Okay, but if you need me call me." I pointed a finger at her warningly.

"Just go." Her attention was already focused on the TV.

I headed back down the hall and into the living room. Mathias still stood there waiting, his back turned to me as he appraised the photos on the wall. I noticed his eyes lingered on my high school graduation photo.

He heard me approach and turned, his hands shoved into the pockets of his pants. "Do you ever wonder what would have happened if you hadn't moved away?" His eyes were far away, remembering a time when things were simpler even though they'd seemed impossibly complicated.

My breath left me in a small gasp. "Every day," I admitted. For a long time that had been a question I'd obsessed over, especially when it came to Hope. If we hadn't left might I still have had my daughter? It was a question that was impossible to answer. "But the reality is, if we hadn't left I'm sure we would've ended eventually."

His eyes narrowed as he glared at me. "Why do you say that?"

"We were just kids." I shrugged. "Do you really think we would've lasted?"

His mouth twisted into a grimace. "Probably not."

"Exactly," I nodded, stepping closer to him. "At least now we have a chance to make it work. We're older and... I was going to say wiser, but I don't think either of us is very wise," I laughed.

He chuckled softly. "Definitely not." He brushed his fingers over my cheek and leaned in.

I closed my eyes in anticipation of his lips, but they never touched mine. Instead he nuzzled his head into my neck and his breath tickled my skin when he said, "Stay the night with me."

"Why?" I asked, keeping my voice steady.

"Because I want you to." This time his lips barely brushed mine. Tease.

One of his hands wound around my waist and he drew our bodies together. My hands moved to his chest, and I could feel the steady beat of his heart. I swallowed past the lump in my throat as I stared into his eyes. He made me crazy in the best way possible.

"I'll pack a bag," I whispered, leaning up to press my lips to his.

He pulled away before I could make contact and I glowered at him. He was trying to kill me. I was sure of it.

"Excellent. I'll wait here."

"You don't want to come upstairs?" I nodded my head at the stairs, surprise coloring my words.

He shook his head. "Nope. Your demon cat might attack me again."

"I'll hurry then." I swayed my hips as I headed for the stairs. I was on the third when I stopped and looked at him. "And Mathias?"

"Yes?" He prompted, a slight smirk lifting his lips as he tilted his head to the side.

"I swear to God if you don't fuck me tonight I will kill you in your sleep," I warned playfully.

He snorted, covering it with a cough. "Rem, I'm not much good to you if I'm dead," he winked.

Shaking my head I climbed the rest of the stairs and packed a small bag of clothes and checked on Percy, making sure to give him fresh food and water.

No more than five minutes later I was hurrying back down the steps, but with Mathias' glare you would've thought I'd taken an hour.

He took the bag from me and slung it over his wide shoulder as he reached for the door. I turned on the front porch light before following him out and locking the door.

Neither of us said much on the drive to the hotel, but sexual tension was thick in the air. He gripped the steering wheel so tight that his knuckles turned white, while I kept my eyes trained out the window—afraid that if I looked at him I might end up attacking him with my lips.

When Mathias parked the SUV in the parking garage beside his Corvette I nearly sighed in relief.

We stepped onto the elevator, keeping a careful distance between the two of us. My fingers itched to touch him so I clasped them together, refusing to be the first to give into temptation.

When the elevator opened he finally reached for me, taking my hand and pulling me into his arms.

Immediately I found my back pinned against the wall of the penthouse suite with my arms held above my head as his lips ravished mine.

It felt like it had been forever since he touched me this way, when in reality it had only been a week. I didn't know how I ever made it seven years without this... without *him*.

My legs wrapped around his waist and his hips pressed into mine. Our collective pants filled the air. I wiggled my fingers, itching to reach out and touch him, but for now my hands were held immobile above my head.

His tongue brushed against my lips and they parted with a gasp.

A low groan resounded in his throat and he bit lightly on my bottom lip, pulling it between his teeth and letting it go. His eyes were lust filled when they met mine.

A shaky breath left me, startled by the way he was looking at me—like I was his everything.

He ducked his head, kissing my neck and down over the tops of my breasts. Suddenly my dress felt too tight and restricting.

He finally let go of my hands and I wound my arms around his neck. He grasped my thighs, carrying me through the space.

He didn't put me down until we were in his bedroom.

He turned me around, sweeping my hair over my shoulder. He pressed a kiss to my neck and I relaxed against him as he eased the zipper down on my dress.

My dress started to fall and I pushed it off the rest of the way.

It fell into a pool of black fabric and I stepped out of it, kicking it and my heels away.

His eyes appraised me approvingly and my heart thundered in my chest.

I didn't get shy, but Mathias made me feel the closest thing to it.

He stalked forward, his moves lithe like a panther. He took my face between his large hands and slanted his lips over mine. I worked my fingers over the knot in his tie and removed it before starting in on the buttons of his shirt. I pushed the fabric over his shoulders along with the suspenders.

His chuckle vibrated against my lips. "Slow down, Rem."

"We have time for slow later." I stood on my tiptoes to whisper in his ear.

His chest rumbled with a low growl. "You'll be the end of me."

"Back at ya." I kissed him, slowly at first and then with more passion.

His fingers dug into my hips and I soon found myself flat on his bed.

His large body pressed into mine, making me feel incredibly small and protected in his embrace.

He pressed small kisses down my torso, reaching behind me to unsnap my bra.

My back arched off the bed as he tugged away the lacy fabric.

"Please," I begged.

He kissed me again, rolling his hips into mine. I gasped, my hands reaching for his pants.

"Remy," he warned with a low growl.

I took his face between my hands, rubbing my thumb over his lips. "I can't wait. Please, for the love of my sanity, don't draw this out."

He reached for my panties and tugged them down and I nearly did a victory dance—but it would've been in vain, because the bastard didn't listen to me.

His fingers pressed into me and a small scream escaped my throat as I fisted the sheets between my fingers.

"You like that?" He grinned.

I nodded, at a loss for words.

"See, slow is good."

"Shut up." My fingers tangled in his dark hair, drawing him to me for a kiss. I gasped against his lips when I felt my orgasm begin to build. "Oh, fuck. Right there. Keep doing that."

His fingers moved in and out of me, and he watched me with a look of awe on his face as I fell apart.

"You're so fucking beautiful," he whispered, sucking on my bottom lip.

I undid the button his pants, pushing them down.

He stepped back and removed the rest of his clothes, before grabbing a condom and rolling it on. He hovered over me, kissing me as he pushed inside me.

I let out a gasp, arching my neck and back as he pumped into me hard at first.

When I wrapped my legs around his waist he moved his hips slowly, drawing out every moment and savoring it.

We didn't normally do sweet, but this was exactly what this was and I kind of liked it. A lot.

He grasped my thigh, drawing one of my legs higher and I gasped at the sensation.

I panted, grasping his hair roughly between my fingers.

He growled, biting down on my lip in retaliation.

His hips continued to move in a tantalizingly slow rhythm.

He grasped the sheets roughly in his hands beside my head and his jaw was clenched tightly together. He was holding back and that was the last thing I wanted.

I grasped his chin in my hand, breathing, "Let go."

A look of pain flickered over his face and I knew he didn't want to. "Please," I begged, "let me see you."

"Fuck," he growled, and all restraint left him.

His hands and mouth were everywhere—nipping, biting, gripping.

The air was filled with our groans and pants.

I could feel myself building to another orgasm and I wrapped my arms around his neck, holding on for support.

He pushed deeper into me and a small scream left me.

The look on his face was full of satisfaction. God, he was beautiful and he didn't even know it. He looked at me with such honest trust and openness that I had a strange desire to cry. For some reason I was reminded of our first time together, and how closed off he'd been. He wasn't that way now, not at all. For once I could see all his emotions plainly on his face and I reveled in it.

I touched his cheek reverently; a part of me believing this might be a dream.

It didn't seem real that after all this time he was actually mine. I thought the book had been closed on our story a long time ago, but I'd been wrong. It had only been the beginning.

My back arched once more and he peppered kissed over my breasts as I came.

Sweat coated our skin as we moved together, always in sync.

His eyes closed and his teeth snapped together. I knew he was close. He buried his head against my neck, his breaths fanning across my shoulders.

"Oh, fuck." He growled softly and I felt him twitch inside me.

He held his weight above me as we both fought to catch our breaths.

His chest rose and fell sharply. He looked at me like I was a mirage beneath him and if he looked away I might disappear.

I reached up, pushing his hair away from his eyes before

grasping his face in my hands. "It's okay. I'm here."

The fear didn't leave his eyes as he rolled off of me and disposed of the condom. He climbed back onto the bed, and lying on his side he pulled me against his chest. His arms wrapped protectively around me and my eyes closed, a soft sigh escaping my parted lips.

Minutes passed and sleep threatened to overtake me. I was beginning to think he'd drifted off to sleep when he spoke.

"Don't go," he whispered, pressing a kiss to the back of my shoulder. "Don't leave me."

"I won't," I assured him.

I couldn't. Not even if I wanted to.

CHAPTER NINETEEN

"SHE LIKED TO hit me a lot," Mathias spoke, laying in my bed and staring up at the ceiling. "Maddox didn't get it as bad as I did... and I guess in a way I'm thankful for that. I could take the pain and the emotional toll, but he's got too much of a kind heart. It would've hurt him deeper than it has me."

I lay beside him, not touching. I wanted to reach out and wrap my hand around his, but I knew he wouldn't have wanted that, so I forced myself to keep still.

I wanted to argue with him and tell him that he was wrong, that he'd clearly been hurt by the abuse, but I knew that wasn't what he wanted to hear.

"Did you ever fight back?" I asked.

I heard the sheets ruffle as he shook his head. "No."

"Why?"

He was quiet for a moment and I worried I had pissed him off. That happened a lot—and he'd usually jump out of my bed and pull on his clothes, climbing out the window without a second glance at me.

But he didn't do that tonight.

Instead he seemed to be weighing his words carefully.

165

"I thought I deserved it," he finally whispered, his voice cracking. "I believed her when she said all those things about me."

I rolled over onto my side. This time I was unable to stop myself from touching him. I reached out, tracing my finger along his collarbone. He stiffened at first, but then relaxed into my touch. I laid my palm on his chest, right overtop of his racing heart. His hand came up to clasp mine. I thought he might push my hand away, but he held it there like he was afraid of me letting go.

"Nobody deserves to be treated like that. Definitely not you."

He stared into my eyes, a range of emotions warring on his face. "Haven't you met me? I'm not exactly the nicest fucking person to be around," he growled.

"No, not all the time," I agreed, ducking my head to avoid his intense stare. "But I see past that, and I know it's only a front. You're actually a pretty nice guy, Mathias."

The breath was knocked out of me when he rolled over suddenly, pinning me to the bed.

"I'm not a nice guy and you'd do well to remember that, sweetheart." He said the words with a sneer.

I wigged one of my arms free and reached up to cup his cheek. "You can try and scare me, but it won't work. I'm not afraid of you."

"You should be," he whispered.

I WOKE UP with my head resting on Mathias' bare chest as his fingers brushed softly through my hair. I wiggled closer to his warmth, blinking the sleep from my eyes.

"Hey," he murmured, his fingers stroking lower over my arm.

"Morning." I tilted my head back to look at him.

He gave me a small, adorable smile. "I was going to get up and make breakfast, but then I decided I'd rather lay here and wait for my girls to get up."

"Your girls?" I asked, putting a hand over my mouth to stifle a yawn.

He nodded his head to the bottom of the bed and that was when I saw Shiloh snoozing peacefully near his feet on her back with her paws in the air. She was honestly the cutest puppy ever.

He brushed his lips tenderly against my forehead and my eyes closed, a soft sigh escaping my lips at the sweet gesture.

"Now that you're up I'll take Shiloh out and make something."

"But I don't want to move," I whined, tightening my hold around his torso.

He chuckled, brushing my messy blonde hair away from my eyes. "Breakfast in bed then?"

I nodded. "That would be perfect. What time is it anyway?"

He glanced at the nightstand. "A little after eight."

"I have to go into work tonight." For the first time since I'd taken the job at the bar, it made me mad that I had to work. I wanted to stay in with Mathias.

He chuckled, playing with a strand of my hair. "At least I'll have you all to myself for most of the day." His voice lowered and he leaned down so his lips brushed my ear with his words. "And I'd really like to try out those handcuffs again, but for fun this time."

I tried to hide my smile. "Later."

He grinned, sliding out of bed and away from my hold.

The cold air hit my body and I immediately wrapped the

sheets around myself like a burrito.

Mathias laughed at me, pulling on a pair of low hanging sweatpants.

"Comfy?" He asked, his hands propped on his hips.

"Very," I nodded. "I'm not coming out of here, ever."

He climbed onto the bed and made like he was going to pry the covers off of me, but I rolled away, only tangling myself in them further.

"Nope," I warned him, "I'm not coming out, now go make me breakfast."

He chuckled and grabbed Shiloh, heading for the bedroom door. "You're so damn bossy."

"Says the bossiest man on the planet." I stuck my tongue out at him.

"Yeah, and you're even bossier than me." He stopped in the doorway.

"Just so you know, if I had use of my hands at this moment I'd throw a pillow at you."

He threw his head back and laughed. "Remy, Remy, Remy," he chanted my name, "you're in trouble for that one."

Before I could retort he closed the door and I was left alone.

I truly didn't feel like moving out of the bed, but I decided a shower would be nice.

I untangled myself from the sheets and grabbed my bag that sat by the bottom of the bed. I couldn't remember him bringing it in with us last night, since we'd been otherwise occupied. I figured he must've grabbed it when he got Shiloh.

I closed the bathroom door behind me and turned towards the walk-in shower.

"Holy shit," I muttered, taking in all the controls. The thing was like a spaceship. I opened the glass door and reached inside to turn the nobs. After a few minutes of messing with it, I finally got it set to my liking.

I took as quick of a shower as I could manage and changed into a pair of jeans and plain white t-shirt.

When I opened the bathroom door Mathias was stepping into the bedroom with a tray full of food. A girl could get spoiled to this.

"You showered?" He asked, setting the tray down on the bed.

"Obviously," I replied, gathering my damp hair up and securing it in a bun.

"Why?" He asked, arching a brow. "I'm only going to get you sweaty again." His voice lowered with promise.

"Then I guess I'll have to shower again." I shrugged, smiling playfully.

As much as I loved the aggressive side of Mathias, I was growing to love this side even more. I liked being able to laugh, and smile, and joke with him. It was a welcome difference.

We sat on the bed together, Shiloh between us.

He handed me a plate filled with scrambled eggs, toast, and bacon. "I can't eat all this," I told him, pinching a piece of bacon between my fingers.

"Hey, I made you a nice hot meal so you'll eat it and be happy about it."

I laughed, shaking my head. It was really good though, so I did end up eating it all.

"I think you should cook for me from now on." I put the plate down on the tray.

"Is that so?" He asked, raising a cup of coffee to his lips to hide his growing smile.

I nodded, rubbing my stomach. "You're a much better cook than me. Besides, I hate cooking."

"I think next time I'm going to make you help." His gray eyes flashed with amusement.

"If your kitchen burns down don't blame me." I shrugged.

"You're not going to burn the kitchen down." He rolled his eyes, standing and grabbing the tray. "I'll be right back."

He headed out of the room and my eyes zeroed in on a tattoo between his shoulder blades. I hadn't noticed it before, but then again my mind was usually otherwise occupied when I was around him. Shiloh jumped off the bed and trotted behind him like she was attached to his shadow.

I grabbed my phone from my bag and checked to see if I had any messages.

There was a text from my mom asking how I was.

Another was from my dad checking in on grandma.

There wasn't a message from anyone else, because honestly I didn't have anybody. Any friends I'd made in Arizona hadn't been true friends and we drifted apart. I'd known when I moved here that I would never talk to them again. I didn't have any desire to, and I think a part of me was kind of relieved to say goodbye.

I quickly typed back a response to each of my parents and by the time I was done Mathias was sauntering into the room in all his shirtless glory.

He sat down on the bed and bent over to pick Shiloh up.

Up this close there was no missing his tattoo. It was an intricate compass and beautifully designed.

I reached out to touch it, my fingers grazing his skin. He stiffened at my touch and I quickly withdrew my hand.

"When did you get this?" I asked.

"A while ago," he shrugged.

"Why a compass?" I asked curiously.

"Why so many damn questions?" He snapped.

"Don't get pissy about it," I muttered, "it was a simple question."

He sighed and mumbled, "Sorry."

I was taken aback by his quick and seemingly sincere apology.

With a sigh he ran his fingers through his hair and the brown ends stuck up wildly. It made him look younger and more vulnerable. He looked at me, his gaze steady. "I got it because I wanted something to remind me that no matter how rough the waters might be, I can always find my way back home. It's like my beacon of hope."

I closed my eyes, thinking briefly of my own *Hope* and how I lost her.

"That's a really beautiful reason," I finally replied.

He laughed. "Beautiful? Now you're making my tattoo sound girly."

I pushed his shoulder. "That's not what I meant and you know it."

His lips quirked with a small smile.

"Do you have any other tattoos?" I asked.

"One more," he answered. "But since you've been up close and personal with my body I'm shocked you haven't found it yet."

"Usually when we're naked you're kind of aggressive. It doesn't leave me a lot of time to... explore."

He snorted and I was glad that I could amuse him. "Well, we're not naked now so why don't you try to find it?" He smirked.

"Challenge accepted." I grinned gleefully.

I scooted over, closing the space between us and swung one of my legs over his lap so that I was straddling him.

Kissing his neck I murmured, "There's not one here." Moving lower I kissed his chest, right overtop of where his heart beat. "Not here either."

"Remy," he warned with a low growl, grasping my hips in his hands.

I grabbed his left arm, kissing his bicep and down his arm. "Nope, not there either."

He shifted restlessly and I smiled in satisfaction when I felt him harden beneath me.

I grabbed his other arm and kissed my way down, stopping when I reached his wrist. The tattoo was small, so small that I had to squint to make out the letters. When I read it a gasp escaped between my parted lips.

My head shot up, my eyes connecting with his.

"M-my name. You have my name tattooed on your body. Like permanently."

He huffed, rolling his eyes. "Yeah, that's kind of the point of a tattoo."

I held his wrist still and looked down at the tiny letters again.

R E M Y

"Why?" I asked, baffled. "After how things ended why would you have wanted this?"

I was lost and confused, and honestly very rattled—and it took a lot to unnerve me.

He shrugged, looking away.

"Mathias," I snapped, tightening my hold on his wrist, "tell me." In a softer tone I added, "Please?"

A muscle in his jaw twitched and he slowly returned his gaze to mine.

"Because I always knew you were the only girl I'd ever love." He smoothed his fingers over my cheek. "I wanted to immortalize that. I'm not ashamed of what I feel for you and I'm not going to hide it like a pussy. I made the mistake of pushing you away and thinking that our love wasn't strong enough to last, because I was an insecure kid with abandonment issues. It didn't take me long to realize my feelings were never going to go away and that I'd been a fucking idiot. A love like ours... it doesn't fade in absence, instead it keeps growing. It's all-consuming." He grabbed a piece of my hair, wrapping it around his finger. He leaned forward, pressing his forehead to mine. "It's a rare kind of love, and one that should be celebrated and embraced, so that's what I did, because trying to pretend it didn't exist was fucking impossible."

I closed my eyes, a wave of emotions threatening to drown me.

I took a deep breath and looked up at him. "How come you never tried to find me?" I traced my finger over his chest and down his stomach. "You could have found me if you wanted to," I said with surety.

He swallowed thickly, reaching up to rub his stubbled jaw. "Because I had convinced myself you would have moved on. I couldn't bear the thought of finding you, only to see you happy with some other guy—even though that's exactly what you deserved to have. So, me being the asshole that I am, drank and slept around." He sighed heavily. "I've done nothing but fuck up at every turn for the last twenty-three years of my life and I refuse to do it anymore, especially now that I have you back. I want to be worthy of you."

I wrapped my arms around his neck and laid my head on his chest. His arms wound around my body, hugging me to him.

"You're already worthy," I whispered.

A shaky sigh left him and when I tilted my head back to look at his face he seemed relieved.

He looked down at me, playing with my hair. "I know I can be harsh and an asshole most of the time and I'm not the most romantic guy, but I can promise you that I'll love you every day for as long as my heart beats. I want you to know that *this* is what I want." He lowered his mouth to my ear and whispered, "You. Here. In my bed. With me. Always."

I took a shuddering breath, soaking in his words.

Before I had a chance to respond I found myself roughly tossed onto the other side of the bed, and then he was on top of me, pinning me against the bed with his arms.

"Enough serious talk," his lips turned up into a smirk, "I'm going to fuck you now."

I smiled when his lips touched mine. The man could be deep one minute, and then an animal the next. I think that's why I loved him so much.

CHAPTER TWENTY

I PROPPED MY elbows on the bar and leveled Mathias with a glare.

"So, what are you going to do? Sit here the whole time I work like a bodyguard?" I raised a brow, waiting for his reply.

He lifted his glass of water to his lips, not saying a word.

"Mathias," I snapped. "This is my job. I don't need you to babysit me."

His eyes darkened and he set the glass down. "I've seen the way the men in here look at you. You're fucking insane if you think I'm not going to sit here and look out for you."

"I can protect myself," I sneered, hands on my hips. If there was one sure way to piss me off it was to treat me like some Barbie Princess.

"I'm not leaving." He leveled me with a glare, taking another drink of water, "but if you keep bitching at me I might need something stronger than this." A small smile lifted the corners of his lips so I knew he was joking.

"Whatever. Just don't cause any trouble," I warned, walking away to busy myself with actually working.

"When do I ever?" He chuckled.

I rolled my eyes, sighing at his response. "Hey Jeff, you're here early. It's only five," I remarked, noticing one of the regulars sidling up to the bar. "Are you lost?" I laughed.

"I've got a date," he grinned, pointing over his shoulder.

I peered around him and noticed a pretty brunette around his age sitting at a booth. "She's pretty," I smiled, "so what are you doing over here talking to me?"

"Uh..." He started and I noticed a sheen of sweat on his forehead. "I'm kind of nervous. I don't know what to say to her." He frowned. "I haven't been on a date in years, not since my wife left me. I'm too old for this."

"Aw, Jeff, you're not old."

"Fifty is old, Red."

I couldn't help smiling at the nickname—the one Tanner had given me, and all the regulars picked up on. I *hated* nicknames, but this one I liked. It wasn't condescending.

"No it's not." I shook my head. "Go back over there and talk to her. About anything... except the weather... or your dick. Don't do that."

He chuckled. "Thanks, Red."

"Anytime." I gave him a reassuring smile before he walked away.

I grabbed a rag and began wiping down the counter.

"Who was that?" I heard from behind me.

I stopped wiping and turned to glare at Mathias. "I'm working."

"You were talking and that wasn't working. Who was he?" His face was contorted in a grimace.

"Are you jealous?"

"No," he drew out the word, "that guy just seemed extra friendly."

I tucked the rag in the back pocket of my jeans and crossed my arms over my chest as I stared him down. "Jeff is a regular, and he's also practically as old as my dad. So, really not my type." Stepping forward I smiled coyly. "Besides, I already have a guy."

"You do?" He chuckled. "Tell me about him."

"Well," I started, clucking my tongue, "he can be kind of an asshole. But he's immeasurably sweet when he wants to be. He also has a huge heart, but he doesn't let many people in. He's smarter than he thinks he is and he's fiercely protective—so much so that apparently he has to come stand guard over me at work."

He chuckled, ducking his head. "He sounds like an incredible guy."

"He is," I agreed seriously. "I wish he could see that."

His fists clenched where they rested on the bar top and he looked away.

"Remy?" A new voice broke into my thoughts and I turned away from Mathias.

"Lana?" I questioned. "Are you sure you should be in a bar in your... state?" I asked, staring at her large stomach. Jesus, she looked like she was ready to give birth any second.

She laughed. "I'm not here to drink, obviously." She rubbed her stomach. "I remembered you mentioned you worked here, and I wanted to invite you to my baby shower." She held out an envelope for me. "I didn't have your address and I thought if I called you might forget about it. It's next Friday."

I held the envelope like it was a bomb that was going to explode in my hand. "Uh..." I didn't know what to say. Baby showers were not my thing. In fact, anything involving a baby wasn't my thing. It only served to remind me of what I didn't have.

"Please say you'll be there," she begged.

"I-I—" I stuttered, unable to form a coherent sentence.

"She'll be there," Mathias interrupted, "I'll make sure of it."

Lana's attention swiveled from me to Mathias and her eyes narrowed. "Mathias Wade? Wow. I haven't seen you since... well, since high school. Um... how are things? Like with the band? I just... oh my God, you're famous now and it's just... can I have your autograph?"

I snorted and Mathias glared at me for my rudeness—I don't know why he cared, since he normally acted like an asshat.

"It's good to see you, Lana," he said in an even tone.

"I... I can't believe someone we went to school with is famous..." She gasped, looking back at me. "And I mean, you *dated* him, like... whoa."

I rolled my eyes and reached into my pocket for the rag so I could return to cleaning.

"Lana, please pick up your jaw from the floor before you leave," I remarked.

Her eyes widened and her cheeks flamed with redness as she realized what a fool she was making of herself.

"I'm sorry," she blabbered, "please forget I said anything... wait," she looked from me to Mathias, waving a finger, "are you guys like... together again?"

"Yes.'"

"No."

I glared at Mathias.

"No," he repeated. "We're not together."

"Oh," Lana frowned, "my bad." She seemed to realize she'd stirred up something bad because she slowly backed away. "I'll see you at my baby shower, Remy!" She called, running out of the building.

I threw the rag down on the floor and stormed off towards the backroom. I didn't give a fuck if Tanner fired me again. Right then, if I didn't get away from Mathias, I might launch myself across the bar top and strangle him. I didn't want a murder on my hands, so I figured it was best to remove myself from the situation.

I was beyond livid that after everything he'd said he was now saying we weren't together. He was giving me fucking whiplash.

I sat down at the small table in the backroom and rested my head on the table. The cool surface helped to soothe me, but nothing could completely take away the anger raging inside me.

"Remy," Mathias growled my name as he stormed into the backroom, "don't fucking run away from me."

I turned my head away from him and mumbled to the wall, "I wasn't running away. I was removing myself from the situation."

"What are we, five? Let's talk about this like adults."

I snapped towards him and he backed a step away when he saw the anger on my face. "Adults? You want to talk about this like adults? Okay, how about you don't tell me we're together and then tell Lana we're not." I pushed at his shoulders and beat my fists against his solid chest.

He grabbed my hands and cradled them between his, holding on tight enough that I couldn't pull them away.

"Shh," he crooned, trying to calm me.

"Let me go!" I wiggled against his hold.

"No," he growled, wrapping his arms around my body and holding my back against his chest. I kicked him in the shin and he grunted, but didn't let go. "Rem, listen to me," he said in that silky voice that normally had me melting, but right now I was too mad for it to affect me. "Listen," he pleaded, tightening his hold against my struggles. His lips brushed my ear and I jerked away. "Remy," his voice rose with anger, "I only said that because she went all fan-girl and I didn't want her to go blabbing about it to someone else, who would tell someone else, who would then contact the media, and so on and so forth."

I stopped struggling, becoming dead weight in his arms. "So, what if she had?" I countered. "If we're together for real why would you give a fuck if the media found out?"

I felt his forehead press against my back. "I don't know," he mumbled. "I just... I hate the media. I hate what they do and say and how they misconstrue things. I don't want them to drag you into that. I was only trying to protect you."

"I can protect myself." I spat the words through clenched teeth.

"What's wrong with letting me take care of you? You don't have to do everything, you know."

"Let me go," I pleaded, trying to pry his hands off of me.

"Not until you listen to me."

"I am listening," I mumbled.

"No, you're not. You're fighting me. Please," he begged and I felt his teeth nip lightly at my shoulder, "believe me. I wasn't trying to hurt you, I was doing what I thought was best."

"So what? I'll always be your dirty little secret? Your whore on the side while some model is draped on your arm?" I panted, trying to catch my breath.

His hold loosened, but only enough so that he could turn me around to face him. He kept a tight hold on my wrists so that I couldn't get away.

"Don't you *ever* say that about yourself ever again." His eyes held a dangerous silvery glint.

"Why not? That's how I feel." I swallowed thickly, my mask slipping as my vulnerability shown. "That's how *you* made me feel."

He closed his eyes and his Adam's apple bobbed. "God, I'm sorry, Remy. I didn't mean it like that at all. My wanting to keep you away from the media has nothing to do with wanting to hide this. I promise you that."

"You know they'll find out eventually," I whispered, the fight leaving my body, "so why does it matter so much?"

His eyes popped open and his chest heaved with a heavy breath. "Because they ruin everything and I refuse to let them ruin this, the one good thing I have left."

I shuddered, folding into his arms and letting him hold me. "Okay," I said, resting my head on his chest, "I'm sorry for overreacting."

He laughed, his whole body shaking. "We wouldn't be Mathias and Remy if we didn't overreact."

"I guess you're right about that." I joined in with his laughter.

He took my chin between his thumb and index finger and lifted my head so I was forced to meet his gaze. "And you're going to her baby shower. Even if I have to kidnap you and throw you in the trunk of my car."

"Why?" I frowned. "I don't want to go." I pouted like a small child, panic rising inside me at the thought of being surrounded by all the baby things. I could handle being around pregnant women—and maybe that was because I hadn't had my pregnancy stolen from me—but babies and baby things sent me into a tailspin.

"Because you need friends."

"I have friends... I have you... and my grandma... and I kind of have Tanner," I rambled, "and we can't forget Percy."

"I don't count." He chuckled.

"Why not?"

"Because," his voice lowered with a sensual tone, "we have sex, therefore we're not friends."

"I'd say we are friends," I countered. "Look at all the

conversations we have. I know more about you than most people."

"You're not winning this argument, Remy," he glared. "And who the fuck is Percy?"

"My cat," I reminded him.

His face crinkled with disgust. "Fucking demon cat," he muttered under his breath.

"That's not his name. It's Percy. P. E. R. C. Y."

"Such a smartass," he mumbled and I fought a smile. "But don't think I haven't forgotten what you're trying to do. You're going to the party, Remy. Lana was your friend and she wants you there."

"Why do you even care?"

He frowned, my question having taken him off guard. "I don't know," he answered honestly, his brows furrowing together. "I guess I don't want your life to become consumed by mine."

"Wow, egotistical much?" I joked, biting my lip to contain my laughter. "Besides, *you're* the one sitting at the bar while I work."

He shook his head. "Fuck, I can never win with you."

"Nope." I grinned triumphantly.

"Hey, Red," Tanner poked his head into the backroom, "you have a job to do. Get out here."

"Fuck off, Tanner." I gave him the finger.

He shook his head and walked away. He was used to my antics by now.

I stepped away from Mathias and straightened my clothes. "I'm not going," I declared as I walked away—sure that I'd had the last word.

"Yes, you are," he sing-songed, and I knew he wasn't going to let this go.

Wonderful.

He sat down at the bar once more and feeling devilish I grabbed one of the kid's menus and crayons. I set them in front of him and he looked at me with a perplexed expression. "What the fuck is this for?" He waved a hand at the kid's stuff.

I smiled, but there was nothing nice about it. "If you're going to act like a child, I'll treat you like one."

"Now who's acting like a child." He waved a hand at me. "I don't see what the big fucking deal is. It's a baby shower. It's not like you're going to get pregnant by breathing the same air as her."

I sighed, closing my eyes. I took a deep breath and tried to center myself. I needed to let this go and give in. I couldn't tell him the truth behind why I didn't want to go. It was time to put my big girl panties on. "Fine, whatever, I'll go. This is stupid." I shrugged, turning away from him and getting back to work. Tanner really was going to fire me if I didn't get my shit together, and unfortunately I wouldn't even be able to blame him.

"And now you're mad at me." I heard him mumble behind me. I didn't bother responding. He'd already distracted me enough.

"You okay, darlin'?" One of the men at the bar asked.

"Yeah," I muttered, not even bothering to see who had spoken to me.

I hurried around taking new orders and refilling old ones—as well as tending to a few tabletops because one of the waitresses called in sick.

All the while Mathias sat at the bar—coloring that damn kids menu I'd put in front of him as a joke. His water was gone though, replaced by a glass full of scotch. I didn't know how he drank that stuff. It was lethal.

I shook my head as I passed him, heading over to one of the tables to take an order.

A good hour passed before I had a chance to catch a breath.

"Why don't you just quit?" Mathias asked while I fixed him another drink.

I raised a single brow, looking at him like he'd lost his mind. "Number one, I like working and number two I need the money. Most people aren't like you." I reminded him.

"I know," he took the glass from me, his eyes dark and serious, "but I would take care of you."

My mouth fell open and I stared at him, at a loss for words. There was no way I possibly heard him right.

"What?" I voiced.

"You heard me," he repeated, slowly raising the glass to his lips.

"You would take care of me?" I parroted his words back to him. I shook my head, laughing under my breath.

"I don't know why you're laughing. I'm serious." His brow wrinkled with frustration.

"I can't even get into this with you right now." I shook my head again, still mystified by what he said.

"Why not?" He asked. "I mean, I think I've made it pretty clear that I want you by my side for the rest of my life, therefore me wanting to take care of you shouldn't come as a shock."

My throat tightened up and I couldn't breathe. "Mathias, we've only been together for like... a month," I said, frazzled by his declaration. "You can't say stuff like that."

His teeth snapped together, a muscle in his jaw ticking. "So what? The fucking year we spent together means nothing to you?"

"I don't know," I cried, throwing my hands up in frustration. "It's just a lot for me to process when you say things like that.

I've taken care of myself for so long that I can't just become some trophy wife for you to have to prance around on your arm."

"You think that's what I fucking want?" He glared, his hand tightening around the glass. "That's not what I want at all. I love you for *you*. I'm not trying to change you, I'm just saying that... well, that I would take care of you. Isn't that what most girls want? To be taken care of? Fuck," he muttered, clutching his forehead, "you make my brain hurt."

I would have laughed at him if he didn't look so despaired.

"I'm sorry," I apologized, "I shouldn't have freaked out, but I'm happy here. I like doing something."

He nodded. "Yeah, I understand. I shouldn't have said it," he mumbled, raising the glass to his lips once more.

I reached out, placing my hand over his—suddenly feeling horrible for my behavior. He was only trying to be nice and I twisted that. "Don't feel bad," I pleaded with him, "what you said was a nice thing to say, but I'm not that girl. You should know I'm far too independent to sit back and do nothing," I winked.

He sighed heavily and looked up at the ceiling briefly—like maybe it held the answer to everything—and then his eyes lowered to mine. "We really fucking suck at this whole relationship thing."

I laughed, taking a step back. "That's because we're far from normal," I cracked a smile, "and I wouldn't have it any other way."

He smiled at that too, and reached into his pocket for his pack of cigarettes. He took one and stuck it between his lips.

"No smoking in here," I warned, pointing a finger at him like he was an unruly child.

A single brow arched as he raised the lighter to the tip. It caught and he sucked in the smoke before slowly blowing it out. Smiling crookedly he said, "I'm Mathias Fucking Wade and I can do whatever the fuck I want."

I turned my head away so he couldn't see me smile at his words.

For the rest of my shift I pretended he wasn't there, and when it ended we walked together back to his penthouse, where we both showered and collapsed in bed exhausted but happy.

CHAPTER TWENTY-ONE

"I CAN'T BELIEVE you're making me do this," I muttered, walking up and down the baby aisle in Target with Mathias. If I wasn't so mad it would be kind of funny to see him standing between all the baby stuff and looking like a fish out of water.

"She's your friend and you need to go," he stated, picking up a box. "What the fuck is this?" He asked, his brow wrinkling as he inspected the box.

I peered over his shoulder and laughed. "It's a breast pump for mother's that breast feed."

His eyes widened and he quickly returned the box. He ventured further down the aisle and picked up a blue stuffed elephant. "How about this?"

"Well, it's blue, and I don't know if the twins are boys so no. Let's keep this gender neutral."

He groaned, muttering under his breath about me being unreasonable.

"Don't complain," I lightly punched his shoulder as I passed him, "this was your idea."

"Ugh, whatever." He pinched the bridge of his nose. We headed down another aisle and he grabbed two gray blankets.

"How about these?"

I reached out, rubbing the soft knitted fabric between my fingers as a lump formed in my throat. I'd had a similar blanket for Hope, one I had planned to bring her home from the hospital in.

"No, not that one."

"It's a fucking blanket, how does it not work?" He snapped, replacing the blankets.

"I don't think she'll like it." I saw a pale yellow blanket with a bee design on it and grabbed two. "This one is cute."

"Great, then let's buy it and get out of here." He tossed a thumb over his shoulder.

"Allergic to baby stuff?" I joked, but was truly curious to know what he thought of kids.

He wrinkled his nose and looked around. "No, it's just weird. I mean, who knew babies needed all this stuff. They're so small."

I draped the blankets over my arm, heading towards the gift-wrapping aisle. He fell into step beside me, shortening his strides to match mine.

"So, would you want kids one day?" I ventured to ask. I didn't know why the question suddenly felt so important, but I needed to know. The doctors had assured me that what happened with Hope was random and that I wasn't defective—like I'd kept shouting in the hospital. They promised me that one day, when I was ready, I could have a baby. I knew it was silly, since we hadn't been back together long, but I couldn't stop myself from imagining a future that included more than the two of us.

He glanced at me, his eyes widening in surprise. "Uh…" He paused, scratching at the back of his head nervously. "Yeah, I guess so."

"You guess so?" I repeated, waiting for him to elaborate.

He frowned, his brows drawing together. "I *like* kids, but the thought of having a kid of my own is really fucking scary... what if... what if I'm a fucked up parent like mine were?"

I exhaled a breath I didn't know I was holding. Smiling, I grasped his forearm. "You would be an amazing dad." I meant those words wholeheartedly. I *knew* without a shadow of doubt that Mathias would be the best dad imaginable.

If things had been different and Hope had lived, I knew that once Mathias found out about her he would've been there for her in a heartbeat. He wouldn't have abandoned her the way he did me.

"You think?" He asked, his expression softening.

"I know."

He grinned and his smile made my stomach fill with a million butterflies. His smile was so rare, but one of the most beautiful things I had ever seen. Every time he graced me with its presence was a moment I cherished.

Sobering, he said, "What are we looking for now?"

Once more his steely mask fell into place.

"I was going to grab a gift bag and a card."

"Oh, right," he mumbled. "I'm going to go grab a coffee. I'll be at the front."

Without waiting for me to say anything he turned, shoving his hands into his pockets and walked away.

I turned down the gift bag aisle and grabbed one with zoo animals that was large enough for the two blankets. Stopping off at the cards I grabbed the first baby one I saw and headed to the checkout.

Lana's baby shower was starting soon, so I needed to hurry.

Mathias had insisted on driving me to Target for the gift, and then to the party, because he was convinced I was going to flake. Let's be honest, I probably would have.

I put the items on the conveyer belt and the cashier rang them up and put them in the plastic bag. He held the plastic bag out to me and I stared at him quizzically. "I haven't paid yet." I tried to hand him the cash in my hand but he dodged it.

"Mr. Wade has taken care of it."

"Mr—Oh fuck him. I can't fucking believe him. This is ridiculous. I can pay for my own damn stuff. Who the fuck does he think he is? *Mr. Wade.*" I mimed the cashier's tone, and snatched the bag from him. I probably should've felt bad for being so rude in front of the cashier, but I couldn't find it within myself to care.

I marched over to Starbucks and glared at Mathias who stood by the counter holding two cups of coffee, a smug smile on his lips.

"Seriously, Mathias?" I snapped. "I could've bought it."

He shrugged. "Too late."

"That's why you wanted to get coffee," I muttered, taking the cup he offered me, "so you could give the cashier money."

"You bet." He lifted the cup to his mouth.

"Did you also tell him to call you Mr. Wade?" I asked. I tried to sound angry, but I was really trying not to laugh.

He nodded. "Yep. It has a nice ring to it, doesn't it?"

I shook my head, trying to hide my smile at his antics.

"You know what else has a nice ring to it?"

"What?" I asked as we headed outside to his car.

"Remy Wade."

I spit out the coffee in my mouth all over the ground. I'm pretty sure a dribble got on my shirt too.

He stopped and looked at me, appearing slightly mad by my reaction. "Does the thought of marrying me make you gag?"

I wiped my mouth with the back of my hand. Shaking my head I said, "No, I was just surprised that you of all people would ever think about marriage." I might've had hopes for a future with him, but a huge part of me still doubted that he'd ever want that with me... or anyone.

His dark brows furrowed together. "Why is that so shocking?" He seemed truly confused.

I waved a hand at him, scoffing, "Because you're you."

"Oh come on, Remy, you can give me a better reason than that."

I sighed heavily and let it spill out. "It's just that you've never been Mister Commitment. Since you guys got famous you're *always* photographed with a different woman. You don't date so why would you ever want to get married?"

He took a step back and looked away, but not before I saw the hurt on his face. "I was committed to you," he said softly. "I *am* committed to you," he added with more force. "Is it so impossible to believe that I might see a future for us? I mean, I know I'm not the kind of guy who wears his heart on his sleeve," he waved his arms dramatically through the air. "I don't do romantic bullshit and I'm not going to give you some epic poem declaring my undying love, but I do—love you, I mean. I love you in the only way I know how and I'm sorry if it's not good enough and I'm sorry if it's flawed, but at least it's real."

The last thing I had ever expected was for Mathias to make a declaration like that.

I stood there, staring at him with an open mouth. I had no idea what to do or say. He'd officially stunned me into silence— which was kind of a miracle.

Finally I said the only thing that made any sort of sense to me.

"I love you *too*," I whispered, my voice cracking.

He lovingly stroked the side of my face with a sweep of his fingers before lowering his lips to mine.

Despite the cold temperature I suddenly felt like I was on fire.

His tongue swept against mine, drawing a moan from me. My fingers grasped at the soft material of his leather jacket as I angled myself against his body, wanting to get impossibly closer.

We startled apart a moment later when a car honked.

Mathias let out a low throaty laugh and stepped back.

He took the bag from my hands and wrapped an arm around my waist, pulling me along to his car since apparently I'd become immobile.

"Come on, Rem," he grinned, "there's a party for you to attend."

"Don't fucking remind me."

He laughed, opening the passenger door for me. "You sound like you're headed to the slaughter house."

"Might as well be," I muttered.

"It won't be that bad," he assured, handing me the bag.

The passenger door closed and he walked around the front with a lethal cat like grace. Everything he did was always done with such precision... at least when he wasn't pissed off about something. When he got mad he turned into a raging bull that took out everything in its path.

Once he was in the car I handed him the invitation with Lana's address and then I set about fixing the card and the blankets in the bag.

I had hoped the drive would take an hour, but it didn't take any more than ten minutes to reach her house.

This was going to be like walking into my own personal hell.

Mathias parked on the street and turned the car off.

I looked at him quizzically.

"I'll walk you to the door," he said in answer.

I knew that he was making sure I didn't make a mad dash for

it and hop over the fence.

Mathias met me at the side of the vehicle, laughing at the expression on my face. "You could try not to look so miserable."

I forced a smile and he grimaced.

"Never mind, smiling is worse."

"Thanks a lot," I mumbled. "You know, since you're my boyfriend you should really be nicer to me."

He shrugged, trying to hide a smile as he put a guiding hand at my waist—not so subtly pushing me up the fancy brick walkway.

"If I was nicer to you, you might start thinking there was something wrong with me."

"That's true," I agreed as we stopped in front of the door. It was painted a deep shade of red with a heavy knocker.

I took a deep breath, holding the air inside my lungs. Surely if I passed out Mathias would take mercy upon me and this whole debacle could be avoided.

The front door opened and with it the air rushed out of my lungs. Fuck. There went that plan.

"Remy! Mathias! Get in here you two!" Lana exclaimed in an overly bubbly manner as she wrapped her arms around my neck. I awkwardly hugged her back, silently counting how many minutes I needed to stay before I could leave without seeming like a party pooper.

Letting me go she hugged Mathias. His eyes just about bugged out of his head and he mouthed, "Help me."

I shook my head, smirking at him.

"Come on, come on." Lana grabbed each of our hands, pulling us inside. For being so pregnant she possessed an awful amount of energy.

"Oh, I was leaving," Mathias muttered, tossing his thumb over his shoulder. "I just gave her a ride."

"Oh, don't be silly," she giggled, closing the door and locking it. "All the husbands stayed."

Mathias paled and his eyes shifted to me and back to Lana. "But we're not married."

"Yeah, but you're friends, right?" She asked, clapping her hands together. My God she could give a cheerleading squad a run for their money with all this pep. She was never this happy when we were in high school. Had love seriously turned her into this creepily happy robot drone?

Mathias mumbled under his breath and pinched the bridge of his nose. "Whatever, I'll stay."

"Yay!" Lana did a little dance and I really hoped a baby didn't come flying out. "Follow me! The party is in the living room."

Mathias glanced at me, then at Lana's retreating form, and then back at the locked door. "Did you see how fast she locked that door? I feel like we just walked into the house of a serial killer and we're not getting out alive. If we make a mad dash for it, do you think she'll notice."

I smiled sweetly and started after Lana. "You're the one that was so insistent on me attending this baby shower, so we're staying."

"Fuck me." He cursed, tapping his fingers against his jeans. I knew he was itching to grab a cigarette but was trying to resist the urge.

I was a few steps in front of him now, so I stopped and smiled coyly. "Oh, I will later."

He grinned at my words and then seemed to remember where we were and mumbled, "This better be the fastest fucking baby shower ever."

"I think we should make a game out of this."

"What kind of game?" He whispered skeptically.

"Every time you complain I get to be on top for a minute."

"No fucking way," he shook his head. "I'm in charge. Always."

"Are you sure?" I asked, running my fingers along his chest. I hadn't even realized we'd stopped following Lana. "I think it could be fun."

He scrubbed his hands over his face and muttered, "Alright, but this better be worth it."

"It'll be the best sex of your life," I promised.

"Remy! Mathias!"

"Oh, shit," I muttered, hurrying after the sound of the voice. We stepped into an open living room with high-vaulted ceilings and beige walls. A large tan sectional took up most of the space, positioned in front of a gas fireplace with a TV over it. A few extra fold-up chairs were scattered throughout the room for the party, as well as a table for the cake and gifts.

I put my gift with the others and then Mathias and I took a seat.

He rubbed his hands against his jeans and glanced around like he was looking for the nearest exit.

This was going to be epic.

One of Lana's friends stood up, clapping her hands together to get everyone's attention. "First up we're going to play a game called Applesauce Never Tasted So Good. This'll be done in teams of two so we'll divide off as couples. I'll be handing out a trash bag for each of you to wear as a bib and the applesauce. Whoever eats their applesauce the fastest is the winner."

Mathias looked at me with a horrified expression. "This is barbaric."

"One," I coughed.

"Huh?" He looked at me, his brows furrowing together in a dark line.

"One. Minute."

"Fuck."

"Two."

"Shit."

"Three," I laughed.

He put a hand over his mouth.

The woman finished passing out the stuff and I felt bad that I didn't know her name. Hell, I didn't any of the people here. I figured Lana knew most of them through Clayton, her husband.

"You go first," I told Mathias, setting the bag and applesauce I'd been handed on the floor.

He glared at me, wringing the plastic trash bag between his hands.

"Come on, be a team player," I coaxed.

"This is fucking ridiculous," he spat, tying the bag around his neck.

"Four," I grinned.

He narrowed his eyes at me. "You're really enjoying my pain right now, aren't you?"

"Oh, I am." Plus, his utter contempt for the baby shower was distracting me from thinking about Hope.

"Oh, I forgot the blindfolds!" The woman that handed out the previous items jumped up from her seat with ties clutched in her hands.

"This keeps getting worse and worse." He rolled his eyes.

"Five."

"Hey!" He glared at me, snapping his fingers. "I wasn't complaining, I was merely stating a fact."

"Fine, four then." I shook my head, positioning my chair in front of him.

I took the tie from the woman and shielded Mathias' eyes, securing it in a knot.

"You know, this would have possibilities if you were the one blindfolded," he whispered under his breath.

I rolled my eyes even though he couldn't see me. "You wish," I muttered.

I sat back down and took the lid off the applesauce and grabbed the baby spoon.

"Is everybody ready?" She asked, holding up her phone to start a timer.

"Yes," everyone replied, except for Mathias and me that is.

"Annnnd Go."

I shoveled a spoonful of applesauce into his mouth and he turned away, covering his mouth with his hand. "Jesus Christ, Remy. I think you cracked one of my teeth."

"Don't be a baby," I laughed, attacking him with another spoonful.

He made a face much like a disgruntled small child would. "What the fuck is this? It tastes terrible."

"It's applesauce, remember?" I gathered another spoonful and prepared to attack him.

"It tastes fucking awf—"

I nailed him with the spoon and then he reached out, trying to push me away, which resulted in me losing my balance and falling out of my chair—which somehow made him fall over as well. Our legs ended up tangled together and we were covered in spilled applesauce.

"That didn't end well." I frowned, holding a piece of blonde hair that was sticky.

"This was a fucking terrible idea. Remind me never to force you to do something ever again." He chuckled, pulling the blindfold off. There was applesauce smeared across his cheek and I reached out, wiping it away with a swipe of my finger.

"We're kind of a mess." I bit my lip to stifle my laughter as I pointed to our clothes.

"Does this mean we can leave?" He asked, his eyes brightening.

"Ahem." Someone cleared their throat and I looked up to see the woman that was in charge of the game towering above us. "Do you think you two could compose yourselves long enough for us to finish the game?"

"Uh...?" I looked from her to Mathias. He held a hand over his mouth, trying to hide his laughter but his shaking shoulders gave him away.

She began to tap her foot.

"Yeah," I finally said, feeling like I was a child getting scolded by a parent.

Mathias and I both picked ourselves up off the floor and sat down—choosing to sit out the rest of this game.

I glanced at my phone, frowning when I saw that not even ten minutes had passed. This was going to end up being the longest day of my life.

The game finally ended and a winner was declared.

What did they win?

The satisfaction of being covered in applesauce.

I guess in that case we were all winners.

Mathias turned to me, his mouth parted as if he'd had some sudden realization. "Do you think they'll make us play pin the tail on the donkey?" He reached up trying to wipe applesauce from his hair, but his efforts were futile since it was already drying.

I snorted at his ridiculous question. "No, it's a baby shower not a kid's birthday party."

His eyes widened in horror. "They're not going to make us pin a tail on a baby are they? Because that's just wrong."

I stared at him for a moment, biting my lip to contain my laughter. Eventually I couldn't hold it in any longer and it burst forth, causing all the eyes in the room to draw our way, but I didn't care.

Mathias glared at me—daring me to keep laughing at him, but I couldn't help it.

Once I had control of myself, I held up a hand and said, "You may continue now."

And so they did, moving on to another ridiculous game—one where they'd melted chocolate onto diapers and you had to smell it and guess what chocolate bar it was. I thought it was disgusting. Mathias apparently did too, because after the second diaper he refused to play anymore.

After a few more ridiculous games we were finally rewarded with cake.

Mmm, cake.

That made this suckfest so much better.

The woman in charge of the games cut up the cake and dished out the plates.

Several of the attendees chose this time to approach Mathias, fawning over him and asking him for pictures. He took it in stride, even though I knew he hated the attention. It was a part of his job and he couldn't be too rude.

"Is this almost over?" Mathias hissed in my ear.

"I really hope so. I want to wash this applesauce out of my hair and I'm really looking forward to my sixteen minutes on top," I grinned triumphantly.

"We'll see about that, m'kay?"

I lifted a bite of cake to my lips, licking off the icing. "I'm not afraid to use your handcuffs against you." I warned him.

"Good luck finding them." He grinned.

I flicked icing at his face and it landed in a yellow blop on his cheek. He narrowed his eyes until they were nothing but thin slits and wiped the icing off. Holding out his finger to me he demanded, "Lick."

I did, not even caring that we were engaging in foreplay in front of a group of strangers.

His eyes darkened until they were nearly black.

"Now I just want to drag you out of here and fuck you in my car," he hissed under his breath.

"Presents first." I nodded my head towards the table of gifts.

He mumbled under his breath about not having the patience to wait.

"Seventeen," I sing-songed.

"Stop it," he growled. "I'm in pain over here and now you're mocking me. Don't kick me while I'm down."

I snickered, eyeing his jeans. "Looks like you're up to me."

"Shut up, Remy," he growled, wiggling uncomfortably in his seat.

Personally, I wanted to leave as badly—if not more than he did—but now that I was here I didn't want to be even ruder by walking out early.

We finished eating the cake and I took Mathias' plate, dropping both of ours in the waiting trash bag.

Everybody else had finished as well, which meant Lana and Clayton were about to start opening presents.

"Thank God," Mathias muttered when the first gift was handed to Lana, "it's about time."

It's almost over. I told myself.

Wrong.

They took their time, opening each gift slowly and carefully, then thanking the person who gifted it to them at least ten times.

I was pretty sure today was designed to be my own personal hell.

Not only was this boring as fuck, but all of the baby items

were a huge reminder of the fact that I didn't have my baby.

My chest felt raw and cut open as I remembered coming home from the hospital with empty arms, only to see Hope's crib still set up in my bedroom. When I'd cried out my mom had come running to me and then scolded my dad and brother for not doing away with it.

For a long time after that I was a shell of who I used to be. But gradually I went back to my wild ways. It wasn't the same though. It was like I was living someone else's life—acting the way I thought I was supposed to. I think a part of me had hoped that if I acted like I was fine eventually I would be. But I'd learned that the pain of losing Hope would never go away. It was something I would have to carry with me for the rest of my life and it was *okay* to *not* be *okay* all the time.

I closed my eyes, momentarily blocking out Lana and Clayton's smiling faces. I needed to regroup.

I'd been able to block out the memories while we'd been playing those ridiculous games and Mathias had been making me laugh, but now there were no distractions. It was all right there in front of me. Baby this and baby that. It was like being stabbed repeatedly in the chest while someone twisted the knife around.

"Are you okay?" Mathias asked, grasping my knee.

I nodded my head. "Mhmm."

He looked at me doubtfully, his brows drawn together. "You look like you're feeling sick."

"I'm fine. Honestly," I assured him—trying not to flinch when Lana held up a two tiny pink onesies.

"Rem—" He started, concern radiating off of him.

Sometimes it really sucked that Mathias was the only person that could read me so well. Most people probably didn't notice the stiffness in my posture or the way my lips tightened to hide my frown—but he did.

"I'm just getting antsy," I mumbled.

He looked at me doubtfully and shrugged before turning away. I knew he didn't believe me, but was letting it go. For now at least.

The next gift they opened was the one from Mathias and me.

"Aw, these blankets are lovely!" Lana chimed.

Lovely? Who in the their right mind used the word lovely?

"Thank you so much," she continued. "The girls will love them."

"Great," I forced a smile, "you're welcome."

Mathias glanced at me again, having noticed the slight waver in my voice. I had to get it together.

He didn't say anything this time. Instead he reached for my hand, entwining our fingers together. Mathias rarely ever held my hand and I let myself take a brief amount of comfort in his touch.

Once the last gift had been opened I stood hastily. I was leaving whether anybody else did or not.

I strode over to Lana—giving her a brief hug.

"We have to get together and have lunch soon." She grasped my hand, refusing to let go.

"Uh... yeah, sure." I agreed, in the hopes of getting away faster. "I really have to go."

"Oh, right, of course." She shook her head and let go of my hand. "See you soon. Bye, Mathias!" She called over my shoulder to Mathias who I was sure was leaning broodily against the wall and giving off a Stay-The-Fuck-Away-From-Me vibe.

When I turned around I saw Mathias saluting her with two fingers.

Before anyone could stop us we hurried to the front door and out to his car.

Finally in the safety of the Corvette I breathed a sigh of relief.

Mathias started the car and pulled away from the curb. I felt the heavy weight of his eyes every few seconds as he glanced in my direction.

"Rem, are you okay?" He asked again. Before I could respond, he continued, "You got kind of weird in there."

"I'm fine, honestly," I mumbled, looking out the window.

Mathias tapped the breaks and pulled off the side of the road. "What the fuck is going on with you? You were fine earlier and now you're..." He clenched his teeth and shoved a hand through his hair so that the dark brown strands stuck up wildly. "I don't know what you are, but something's wrong, and I know it. Talk to me."

I couldn't talk to him. Not about this. Not about Hope.

He stared at me and I was stuck, unable to look away no matter how hard I tried. Those strange gray eyes of his were pleading with me, begging me to open up.

My throat constricted as I remembered the boy who used to sneak in my bedroom window—who shared his darkest moments and deepest secrets with me, and now here we were back together again years later and I couldn't confide in him the way he had me. The difference was Mathias' secrets had never been something that might break me, but the one I was keeping from him would shatter him into a million pieces.

I couldn't hurt him like that.

I had to carry around the gut-wrenching loss of Hope *every single day*, but he didn't have to. If I never told him, he wouldn't have to experience the heartbreak of mourning a child.

"Rem," he pleaded, reaching up to cup my cheek. His palm was warm and rough. "What's going on?"

I swallowed past the lump in my throat and tried to clear my face of any emotion. "It's nothing."

"You're lying." The words came out in a harsh bite, a stark contrast to the way he lovingly stroked my cheek. "You keep getting weird on me, like that day in the garage. What is it, Remy? Do you owe someone money? Are you tangled up in something illegal? What the fuck is it? Tell me so I can help you."

I continued to stare at him, unable to form a coherent sentence.

He stroked his thumb in slow rhythmic circles against my cheek; like the small gesture alone could coax the words I refused to say from between my lips.

"I have a lot going on," I whispered after a minute. "It's all starting to catch up to me." That wasn't a complete lie. "I feel like I need a break—not from you, but from life," I hastened to add. "I wish for a moment I wouldn't have to deal with all of this and I could just... breathe."

He continued to stare at me, his eyes seeming to calculate something. His tongue flicked out to moisten his lips and I couldn't help the way my body responded by tightening all over.

"Come to L.A. with me."

I shook my head, my brows drawing together. I couldn't have possibly heard him right. My ears must've been broken. "What?" I croaked, my voice seeming to have left me.

"Come to L.A. with me," he repeated. "Next week. We have to take care of a few things before our tour so I have to go back for a few days, but let's make a trip out of it. We can get away, just you and me."

My mouth opened and closed as I tried to form words. "What about my grandma?" Was my intelligent response.

He chuckled, tangling his fingers in my hair. "I can have someone check on her."

"L.A.?" I repeated.

"That's what I said."

"I... I don't know," I frowned.

"You're the one that said you needed a break. Here's your break."

"What about the paparazzi?" I asked him. "They might photograph us together and then—"

He shut me up with his lips. Grinning like a mischievous little boy, he tucked a piece of hair behind my ear and said, "I'm done caring about them and the media. This is my life and they can fuck off." He took a shaky breath. "I know I told you a while ago that I couldn't promise you forever, but I was wrong to say that. I can't live my life without you," he whispered, his fingers gliding down my neck and lower where I was sure he felt how fast my heart was beating. "Those seven years without you were some of the worst of my life, and that's saying a lot considering all the shit I went through with my real parent's but it's the truth."

"Mathias—"

"Shh," he whispered, resting his forehead against mine. "Please say you'll go."

I contemplated for only a few seconds before saying, "Yes."

He kissed me again, this time his lips lingering longer against mine. He grasped my hand and pulled back onto the road.

I closed my eyes, knowing that right here beside him was where I had always belonged—and I only hoped that nothing would take us away from each other again.

CHAPTER TWENTY-TWO

I LET OUT a small squeak when the shower door opened. I had my towel thrown over the top of the glass and it was fogged up, so I hadn't noticed Mathias coming into the bathroom.

"I fucking hate applesauce now," he muttered.

"I have to agree." I leaned under the spray of water, trying to get the gunk out of my hair.

"Here," he batted my hands away, "let me do it."

I stood still, Goosebumps dimpling my skin as he worked his fingers gently through my hair. I closed my eyes, leaning my head back further.

I was glad to be away from the baby shower—and even happier at the thought of escaping to L.A. in a week with Mathias. I knew we had plenty of privacy here, but it would be nice to get away for a bit—to a place where the memories weren't quite as stifling.

"That feels good," I murmured as his fingers rubbed against my head.

He chuckled warmly and my eyes opened at the sound. He reached over and grabbed the bottle of shampoo, lathering it in his hands and then rubbing it into my hair.

A part of me still couldn't believe that I was here with him. I'd spent so many years hating him for abandoning me and the lies he'd told me, but despite all that I knew there was no place I'd rather be.

He rinsed the soap from my hair, kissing my shoulder before moving onto the conditioner.

It was nice to let him take care of me for a change. We were both always so stubborn, never wanting to let the other have more control that moments like this were rare for us.

"It's all gone now."

His voice startled me and I opened my eyes to find him grabbing the shower gel.

"But I think you're still dirty."

Oh, God.

He had a dangerous glint in his eye—one that had my throat constricting but my pulse racing at the same time.

"Is that so?" I asked, fighting a smile.

He nodded, stalking towards me until my back was pressed against the shower wall and the water cascaded down on top of us.

He lowered his head, the wet strands of his dark hair brushing against my forehead. His eyes flashed and his tongue flicked out to catch a drop of water on his lips.

"Are you afraid, Remy?"

My heart thundered in my chest, threatening to beat right out of the protection of my ribcage.

"Of you?" I asked, my voice barely above a whisper as my body arched towards him in anticipation. "Never."

He grinned at that, and then slammed his lips against mine in a bruising kiss. His hands braced against the shower wall beside my head, trapping me against him. When his chest brushed against my sensitized skin I cried out softly.

Heat soared through my body at his touch.

He bit my bottom lip and I whimpered as his lips moved down to my breasts.

All of my thoughts left me as his lips danced over my skin. The only thing that existed was him, the touch of his fingers, and the smooth feel of his lips.

I leaned my head back, letting the water pour down on my face as his hands ventured lower.

A small breathy gasp escaped me and his chest rumbled with a chuckle.

One finger slipped inside me and I moaned. "Mathias, please," I begged, even though I didn't know what I was begging for.

His body pressed into me—so close that I wasn't sure where I ended and he began. "I love hearing my name roll off of your lips," he murmured, taking my bottom lip between his fingers and letting it go.

"Is that so?" I asked, fighting to stay upright from the dizzying array of sensations rolling through my body.

He nodded, nuzzling my neck as his finger moved slowly in and out of me. The stubble on his cheeks scratched my skin, adding to the sensations.

It was all too easy for me to get lost in him and with a sudden clarity I realized what he was up to.

With a great deal of effort I pushed him away. Immediately I was overcome with a sense of loss.

"What?" He looked at me, confused.

"I know what you're trying to do." I glared daggers at him, trying not to let him see how much my body ached for his touch.

He ducked his head, trying to hide his smile. "You figured that out, huh?"

"I did," I nodded, moving around him so that I could reach

the door of the shower. I needed to get away from him before I gave in and told him to take me here and now. I looked at him over my shoulder and forced a smirk. "I'm getting my seventeen minutes."

He narrowed his eyes.

"Have fun getting the gunk out of your hair and thanks for washing me," I sing-songed, winking at him before stepping out of the shower and grabbing the towel to wrap around my body.

I heard him let out a low growl and then mutter, "This isn't over yet."

"You're right," I agreed, poking my head back inside the shower. "It's just getting started."

With that, I turned and left him to finish showering.

I brushed my teeth and then my tangled hair before padding into his spacious bedroom.

I heard the shower cut off and my heart began to race ten times faster.

It didn't matter how many times I was with Mathias—it always got better and I always wanted more.

I lay down on his bed, the fluffy white towel still wrapped around my body.

He appeared in the doorway of the bathroom a moment later. He'd forgone a towel and water still clung to his body.

"That wasn't nice, Remy," he glowered.

"Being nice is overrated."

He stalked towards me, his hands landed on my knees before skating up my thighs and beneath the towel. With one flick of his hand the towel fell from my body.

"Are you ready to finish what you started?" I asked, tracing my fingers over his full lips before trailing them down his neck and over his pecks before venturing even lower to his abs.

"Oh, I'm more than happy to finish it," he growled, claiming my hands and pinning them above my head.

"Nuh-huh, I don't think so." I broke his hold and pushed him down on top of the bed, straddling his hips. "A deal is a deal."

His lips twisted into a frown.

"You know," I smiled, rolling my hips against his and eliciting a groan from his throat, "I thought guys liked it when the girl was on top."

"I don't care what other guys might like. *I* like to be in control." His eyes darkened to a stormy gray.

I lowered until my chest was pressed against his and my lips grazed his ear. "Well, right now *I'm* in control."

He grasped my hips, his hold almost bruising.

Air hissed between his teeth and he growled, "And it'll be the last time."

My hair brushed against his chest as I sat up. "We'll see about that."

He started to say something else, but I cut off his response by kissing him. My tongue brushed against his and his fingers tangled in my hair, holding me to him.

I broke away from his lips and kissed down his neck and over his pecks, before circling my tongue around his nipple and blowing softly.

He hissed, his hips bucking. "Fuck, Remy," he groaned.

I smiled against his skin, and moved even lower as I kissed his abs.

His erection pressed against me and I rolled off of him so I could take his cock in my hand.

I circled my thumb around the tip and he closed his eyes as a low groan rumbled in his throat.

I smiled in satisfaction before lowering and wrapping my mouth around him.

"Fuuuuuck." He pulled my hair back and when my eyes

rolled in his direction he muttered, "Wanna watch."

I kept my eyes on his as I moved my mouth up and down. His stare was heated, sending tingles of anticipation all throughout my body.

"Stop." He pleaded after a few minutes. "Need to be inside you." He panted, gasping for breath.

I sat back, smirking at him. "So bossy."

"Damn right. You didn't think I'd give up *all* control, did you?" He looked at me like I was crazy. He opened the drawer beside the bed and grabbed a condom.

"Let me." I took the packet from his hand and tore it open, rolling the condom on.

"Fuck. You're really trying to kill me." His eyes were hooded with lust.

"Aw, Mathias, if I wanted to kill you that's what the knives in the kitchen are for."

He growled and grabbed my thigh, pulling me on top of him. "Now is not the time to tease me." His voice was low with warning.

I wanted to tell him that anytime was always the time to tease him, but in that moment he took matters into his own hands and slammed into me.

"Oh God." I wrapped my arms around his shoulders.

He chuckled, giving me a self-satisfied smirk. Jerk.

"You aren't allowed to do that," I hissed.

"Too late."

"I don't think so." I pushed my palms against his chest so that he lay on his back. I rolled my hips against his, going slow and enjoying the way his fingers tightened against my thighs as he fought his need for control. I leaned down, whispering in his ear, "Don't think, just feel."

He closed his eyes and when they opened they were

surprisingly calmer.

I leaned down and kissed him, long and slow.

He cupped my breasts, rubbing his thumbs against my nipples.

"Mmm," I hummed against his lips. His teeth lightly nipped my bottom lip before pulling it between his teeth.

I sat up, my palms flat on his chest as I worked my hips.

"At least the view is nice," he panted, his eyes glued to my breasts.

I wanted to laugh, but all I could do was focus on the different sensations rolling through me. I slowed down, wanting to enjoy every single second of this.

"Rem," he growled, fighting his desire to slam into me.

"No," I hissed, trailing a finger down his chest. He shivered beneath me. "So close," I breathed, rubbing my breasts before one of my hands skated down my stomach and below. His eyes followed the trail of my hand to where it disappeared between us.

His teeth clamped together and he mumbled a curse.

My pants grew louder until I was crying out in ecstasy. I collapsed against his solid chest and he wrapped his arms around me, holding me against him as our hearts raced in sync. He was still, but his body was taut as he fought his natural reaction. I guess he finally decided he didn't care what I wanted, because suddenly I was flat on my back as he braced his hands beside my head.

"Time's up." His voice was a husky growl as he began to move.

It felt so good that I couldn't find my voice to complain about him taking away my time on top.

He pushed into me with hard, deep thrusts that made me cry out with pleasure.

"You're mine, Rem," he hissed, biting the sensitive skin where my neck met my shoulder. "Don't ever forget that."

With every thrust he growled, "Mine. Mine. Mine."

And when he collapsed on top of me after finding his own release, I whispered in his ear, "Yours."

WE WERE STILL lying in the bed curled around each other when my phone rang.

"Ugh," I groaned, not moving to grab it.

"Shouldn't you get that?" He asked, drawing lazy circles on my arm.

"No," I groaned, closing my eyes and snuggling closer to him. It was nowhere near time to go to sleep, but I didn't want to move from this bed until tomorrow morning.

It stopped ringing, only to start up again a few seconds later.

"I think you need to get that." He released his hold on me and climbed out of bed, heading over to his closet. "It might be your grandma."

Shit. He was right. I was really sucking at this whole responsible adult thing.

I rolled out of bed and grabbed my phone out of my purse that lay haphazardly on the floor.

"Hello?" I answered, padding across the room to the dresser. I opened the top drawer, grabbing the first clothes I could find. Yes, I was keeping clothes at Mathias' place. It was weird, but with as much time as I'd been spending here it had become necessary.

"Charlene can't take me to bingo."

"Grandma?" I asked, putting the phone on speaker so I could get dressed.

"Yes, who else would it be?" She snapped.

Mathias snickered from the bathroom.

"Anyway," she continued, clucking her tongue at my stupidity, "I need you to drive me."

"Alright I'll be there in a few minutes." I shimmied into a pair of jeans.

"Good. Hurry. Bingo is important and I can't be late."

I sighed. "On my way."

I ended the call and finished getting dressed. Mathias emerged from the bathroom dressed in a pair of jeans, a black sweatshirt, with a baseball cap perched backwards on his head. It was strange to see him dressed so casually, but I kind of liked it. Although, those suspenders had certainly grown on me—but I'd never tell him that. He'd be too pleased with that information.

"So, we're going to bingo?" He asked, grabbing his wallet.

My eyes widened. "I was just going to take her and wait in the car."

He shook his head. "Where's the fun in that? Let's go too. Your grandma is hilarious."

"You like my grandma?" I tried to hide my smile.

"Of course. She's pretty cool for a grandma. I mean, she did read me the riot act the other day about how a gentleman should treat a lady."

"Oh God." I shook my head.

He fought a smile as he spoke. "To which I replied that I wasn't a gentleman and she smiled at me and said, 'Good.' I'm telling you that woman must've been something else in her day," he chuckled. "Now I know where you get it from."

I covered my face with my hands, my shoulders shaking with silent laughter.

It was kind of hysterical how my grandma used to hate

Mathias. Granted, she never met him when we were teenagers so her opinion had only been based on the bashing from my father, no doubt. And Mathias could come across as an arrogant jerk, but when he showed his true colors he was impossible to resist.

"I'll walk Shiloh while you finish getting ready." He leaned down and kissed my cheek. My skin warmed with the simple touch.

I hurried into the bathroom and tried to do something with my hair. It was a gigantic mess since it had been wet and then we ended up rolling around in the sheets. After a few minutes I deemed it a lost cause and pulled it back into a messy bun. I applied a minimal amount of makeup, topping it off with my red lipstick.

I slipped my feet into a pair of black-wedged boots as Mathias strode back into the bedroom. "Ready?" He asked.

"Yeah," I said, just as my phone rang again. I grabbed it out of my pocket and looked at the screen. "Crazy old lady," I muttered as I answered. "Yeah, grandma?"

"Where are you? It's been ten minutes and I need to be there in—"

I stood from the bed, following Mathias through the penthouse and into the elevator. I tried not to pay attention to how the sweatshirt pulled taut across his wide shoulders and how his jeans hugged his ass. Oh, fuck. I wanted to beg him to take me back to his room—or better yet, beg him to fuck me against the wall. Oh, yeah. That had possibilities.

Realizing that my grandma was still on the phone, I said, "We're getting in the car right now."

"Lies!" She cried.

I automatically looked around like the batty lady would be standing behind me, glaring, and pointing an accusing finger.

But of course she wasn't actually there.

"I would never lie to you, grandma," I assured her, even as I was lying to her. Granddaughter of the year right here.

She snorted and said, "Just get your ass here."

And then the line clicked off. I glared down at my phone and then looked at Mathias. "She hung up on me. How rude."

We stepped into the elevator and Mathias pushed the button to take us to the garage.

"She's sassy. I like it."

"Ew," I frowned, glaring at him, "it's like you have a crush on my grandma or something."

Mathias threw this head back and laughed. Like a real, genuine, body shaking laugh. I couldn't help the smile that lifted my lips at seeing him let loose. He was normally wound so tight that even when he laughed you could tell he was holding back.

"She is pretty cute." He finally replied with a shrug.

I shook my head, crossing my arms over my chest. "This conversation got weird really fast."

"You're the one that started it." He grinned.

I couldn't argue with that.

The elevator doors opened and Mathias pushed a button on his key, the brake lights on his SUV lighting up.

"How many cars do you have?"

He glanced down at me as he strode past. "Just the Range Rover, Corvette, and my motorcycle." He pointed to a sleek sporty looking bike.

"Jesus." I whistled in appreciation. "That's nice."

He smiled, his eyes lighting up like a little boy. "I have one just like it in L.A. We can take it out while we're there."

Me, Mathias, and a motorcycle... oh yeah, that sounded like a good time.

"We have to," I told him, still staring at the shiny red

motorcycle. It had been forever since I'd driven one, and if it hadn't been December with snow on the ground I might have begged him to let me drive it.

"Rem," he warned, "we've got to go."

"Oh, right. Grandma," I muttered, hurrying over to the SUV and away from the motorcycle.

I slipped into the sleek SUV and he started the engine. It was so quiet you could barely tell it was running.

He pulled out of the parking garage and we were immediately greeted with a red light.

And then another.

And then my phone started ringing again.

"I swear to God we're on our way," I said into the phone.

My grandma huffed over the line. "I'm about to walk there. I'm sure I'd beat you."

"Don't you dare," I warned, terrified that she might actually do it.

"I'll be waiting outside," she said.

"It's too cold," I protested.

"Then you better hurry."

She hung up on me... again.

"I'm pretty sure she's determined to worry me to death." I pinched the bridge of my nose and glanced over to see a smile curling his lips.

"She's probably just lonely since I've been monopolizing your time."

"Oh, please," I laughed, "she doesn't want me there. The other day I tried to talk to her for a while and she told she didn't have time to listen to me ramble because Pretty Little Liars was coming on."

He shook his head, turning into the neighborhood.

When we reached the house I saw the crazy old lady waiting

at the end of the driveway.

"She's going to get hypothermia," I muttered to myself, "and die, and it'll be all my fault and I'll never forgive myself."

Mathias put the car in park and undid his seatbelt, stepping out of the car before I could even blink.

My grandma smiled at him as he helped her into the car.

She sat down in the back and Mathias closed the door.

"At least one of you has some decency," she huffed, but when I glanced back at her she was smiling.

"Ha, ha," I rolled my eyes. "You didn't give me much of a heads up."

"Well, neither did Charlene—you know she normally picks me up," she rambled, clutching her purse in her slender age-spotted hands, "and she just didn't show. It was incredibly rude. Bingo night is my second favorite night of the week."

"What's the first?" I asked in wonder.

She gasped, like there was something seriously wrong with me for not knowing. "Vampire Diaries night, of course. Damon is delicious."

I snorted, turning it into a cough as Mathias got back in the car. My outburst didn't go unnoticed by him though.

"What did I miss?" He asked, clicking his seatbelt in place.

"Grandma has a crush on a vampire," I laughed, covering my mouth with my hand to stifle the sound. Oh God, this woman, she was seriously a hoot.

"What the fuck?" He looked at me and then back at my grandma. She must've glared at him because he paled and retracted his previous statement. "Sorry, I meant what the hell— HECK, what the *heck*."

Mathias trying not to curse was quite possibly the funniest thing I'd ever seen. His forehead was wrinkled with deep concentration and his fingers tapped restlessly against the steering wheel—although that nervous tick probably had more to do with him craving a cigarette.

After a minute of complete silence Mathias finally spoke. "Ladies, you do know I have absolutely no fuc—freaking—idea where I'm going, right?"

"Good catch," I laughed, reaching over and giving his knee a light squeeze. "You know where the old fire hall is?" I asked.

He nodded.

"That's where we're going."

"Easy enough," he muttered.

Five minutes later we pulled into the parking lot and my grandma was ready to jump out of the SUV.

"Whoa, slow down. Let me help you," I warned her.

"Oh please, you've helped me enough by making me late. I doubt I'll be able to get a seat near the front now."

I opened her door and held my hand out to help her. She reluctantly took it.

Mathias joined us and walked on the other side of her.

"Honestly, you two act like I'm going to fall over dead any second. I can certainly walk in here on my own."

"Grandma, there's snow on the ground. It's slippery, therefore we're helping you."

She muttered something about me being a pain in her ass, to which Mathias shot me look as if to say *why is it okay for her to cuss and not me?* Sorry bud, Grandma made the rules and the rest of us had to follow them—unfortunately she was usually exempt from her own rules.

We headed into the room that was blocked off for bingo and it was surprisingly full.

My grandma glared at me and mumbled, "You see, all the good seats are gone. Now I'm stuck sitting in the back."

"Why is this my fault?" I muttered, following her to a table.

"What are you doing?" She glanced at us, where we hovered behind her.

"Staying for bingo," I replied, pulling out a chair and urging her to sit—but not before removing her heavy winter coat.

"I don't need a babysitter," she pouted like a surly teenager. "Oh, hi Howard." She waved at the lone man sitting at the table.

"I'll get our boards," Mathias said, heading over to the side of the room.

"He does know he has to pay for them right?" Grandma asked, fixing her hair, which had been ruffled by the wind. "That's how they get their money for the prizes, you know."

"He knows," I assured her, taking my seat beside her.

Mathias returned a moment later with three boards. They hadn't started calling out numbers yet, so at least she couldn't bitch about missing that part.

"Y'all don't need to stay," she huffed. "I highly doubt you want to play bingo with a bunch of old farts."

Mathias snickered, covering his face with his hands.

"Stop your whining," I smiled at her, "we're here to spend time with you."

"Maybe I don't want to spend time with you," she huffed, squaring her shoulders and glaring daggers at us.

"So sassy." Mathias chuckled under his breath.

"We already paid for our boards," I told her, "so we're staying."

She sighed, exasperated. "You could always give them to me."

"Nuh-uh, not happening." I shook my head.

Before she could argue the matter further a man stepped up on a small podium, welcoming everybody, and got right down to business of calling out numbers.

I couldn't stop my smile when I glanced over at Mathias and

saw his lips pursed in concentration as he stared at his board, the little chips resting in his open palm.

Apparently bingo was serious business.

I tried my best to pay attention, but my mind began to wander.

I was truly excited at the idea of escaping to L.A. with Mathias. I knew the whole band was going, and he'd have work things to do, but it would still be nice to get away for a while.

Glancing towards my grandma, I frowned. I felt bad for leaving her on her own for a few days or a week—but the fact of the matter was, she'd made it pretty clear that she didn't need me around. It was my dad that had decided she needed supervision. While I was gone I'd definitely call her as often as I could—which would probably be only once a day, because on days where I stayed with Mathias she got mad if I called her more than that. She really was a stubborn lady, but I loved her for it. I hoped I could be just as badass as her when I reached that age.

Another letter and number was called and I scanned my page, groaning when there was no match. My grandma already had a few of the tokens on her board and Mathias had more than her.

Mine was blank.

That's what I got for not paying attention.

I forced myself to focus on the game and only had two chips down on the board when Mathias jerked beside me, shooting up into a standing position. "Bingo! What did I win?!"

I laughed at his adorable exuberance. I loved that these moments were becoming more commonplace with him. It was like he was finally letting his guard down.

The man on the stage came over to verify the board and then informed Mathias that he'd won fifty dollars.

"I don't need your money," Mathias scoffed—not rudely, "I should be giving you money."

"Uh..." The man looked at Mathias, studying his face. His eyes suddenly lit with recognition. "You're in that band, uh..." He snapped his fingers together. "Willow Creek! That's the one, right?"

"Yeah," he nodded. "I'm Mathias." He held out his hand.

"Wow, I can't believe you're here! Playing bingo of all things. Wow. Just wow." The man stammered, shaking his head as if he was in shock.

Mathias stood awkwardly with his hands shoved into the pockets of his pants. It seemed that when Mathias attended an event he put on his game face and acted a part—at least that was what I'd deduced from seeing photos in magazines—but in situations like this, where there were no cameras or roles to play, he became almost shy under the scrutiny.

Finally the man seemed to recover and said, "Since you don't want the money we can give you a shirt."

"Yeah, that's fine," Mathias shrugged.

Appearing almost sheepish the man asked, "Would you mind signing some?"

"Uh..." Mathias glanced at me and then around the room where all eyes were on him. "Sure. I can do that."

"Excellent," the man said. "I'll be right back."

Mathias sat back down beside me, his shoulders hunching as he glanced down at the table—like he thought if he didn't look at anyone then they couldn't look at him.

"Hey, it's okay." I reached over and squeezed his knee, trying to give him a reassuring smile.

He ignored me.

"You should sing us a song." I looked up, finding that the words belonged to the man sitting with us whom my grandma had called Howard.

"Yeah," someone else piped in, "we need some more fun around here. The most exciting thing to happen here was when Marvin peed his pants and that was more messy than exciting."

"Hey!" Yelled someone else—my guess being the man named Marvin.

Mathias finally looked at me. He didn't appear mad by the sudden recognition, but apologetic—like he was worried the attention bothered *me*.

"Yeah, I can do that," he said, standing. He removed the baseball cap he wore and set it on the table before shoving his hands in the pockets of his jeans and heading up to the podium area. Ignoring the microphone, he stood in the center of the small stage and asked, "What would you guys like to hear?"

Everyone shuffled their seats to see him better, a few people shouting out songs.

"That's a good one," Mathias smiled—a real smile—pointing to an older lady near the front. She blushed at the attention and ducked her head, her white hair fluttering around her face. It was pretty adorable.

"What's happening?"

At the sound of the voice I turned to find the man that had went in search of the shirts standing beside me.

"They wanted him to sing," I shrugged, smiling straight ahead at the man I loved even though he wasn't looking at me, "so he's going to sing."

"Oh," the man nodded, smiling slowly, "excellent. I'll leave these here then." He dropped a few black t-shirts with the fire hall logo on them onto the table.

"Do you have a stool?" Mathias asked suddenly.

The man beside me took off like a rocket, grabbing a stool from a closet and giving it to Mathias.

Mathias grabbed the microphone and took a seat on the stool.

He began to sing, and like every time I heard him sing a sweet feeling of calm washed over me. His voice was soft and husky with a raspy edge to it. He closed his eyes, feeling the song.

The people slowly began to clap along, but I was too enamored with watching Mathias to join in.

I'd seen clips of him performing on stage—and he always commanded the large space—but here, he was toned down and just letting himself love the music and the moment.

As the song came to a close he lifted his head, his eyes meeting mine. An invisible cord seemed to tie us together, and nothing—not time, or hate, or *anything*—could break it.

CHAPTER TWENTY-THREE

"YOU LOOK REALLY hot doing that," I commented, watching Mathias use the pull-up bar in the gym. He was shirtless and sweat glistened on his muscles while the loose shorts he wore hung low on his hips. I would not deny the fact that there were about a hundred naughty things running through my mind right now. Oh, the things I wanted to do to him.

"Stop. Looking. At. Me. Like. That." He huffed out between breaths.

"Like what?" I asked, watching the way the muscles in his arms flexed.

"Like. You. Want. To. Lick. Me."

"Oh," I nodded, wetting my suddenly parched lips, "I want to do much more than lick you. Trust me."

"Fuck," he groaned, dropping down. "I'm not coming to the gym with you anymore." He sucked in a lungful of air—and I was positive his sudden lack of oxygen had more to do with me than the pull-ups. "You're far too much of a distraction."

I grinned. "So are you."

He shook his head, grabbing a pair of boxing gloves. He nodded his head at a pair of pink ones. "For you."

I wrinkled my nose with distaste. "I might be a girl, but that doesn't mean I want everything under the sun in pink. Give me yours."

"Hell no," he said, the black gloves already fixed onto his hands.

I glared at the offending pair of pink boxing gloves. They were just so glaringly bright and attention grabbing. Why couldn't they be red? Red, I liked.

"Fine," I shrugged, taking a step back, "I'll just watch."

He turned around to glare at me. "I can't concentrate when you watch me."

"Too bad." I hopped up on a stack of mats, swinging my legs back and forth.

He turned back around, his shoulders visibly tense as he stepped up to the punching bag.

He slowly glanced over his shoulder and his eyes connected with mine. I gave him a winning smile. "Stop watching me," he growled lowly, a challenge in his eyes.

"Make me."

He stalked over towards me, his hands slamming down against the mats, one on either side of my legs. He leaned in until the tip of his nose touched mine and his full lips brushed my lips when he spoke. "Keep this up, Rem, and I will flip you over right here, right now, and fuck you so hard that everyone in this building will think my name is a prayer."

I licked my lips, nodding in appreciation. "I like the sound of that."

He ducked his head and his soft hair tickled my collarbone. His whole body visibly shuddered and when his gaze rose to mine his eyes were dark with lust. My insides stirred with delight at that look—the dangerous, promising glint shimmering in those stormy gray eyes.

His lips crashed against mine. I whimpered when his teeth sunk down on my bottom lip, pulling it into his mouth and letting it go with an audible pop.

I wound my legs around his waist and my arms around his neck, holding him close to me. If he wanted to get away he was going to have to physically pry me from his body.

A small sound escaped me before he swallowed it with another slam of his lips. His fingers wound into my hair at the base of my skull, tugging at the strands causing a gasp to emit from my throat.

God, he was fucking dangerous. I wondered if he had any idea the amount of power he yielded over me.

He pulled away roughly, taking two hefty steps back. Both of our chests rose and fell heavily with each labored breath. He looked absolutely delicious—yes, *delicious*—standing there with his lips roughened from our kisses and his hair tousled from my fingers.

With a cocky smile, he said, "I hope that'll hold you over for now."

I was tempted to launch my body at him and tackle him to the ground for that comment. I didn't though, because Drew, the owner of the gym, chose that moment to walk into the room.

"Behave." He smiled at me as he passed. To Mathias he said, "Are you ready for your lesson?"

Mathias nodded, putting the boxing gloves back on. I hadn't even realized he'd thrown them on the ground before attacking me with his lips.

Oh, his lips... I was positive that Mathias had the best lips on any man ever, and he definitely knew how to use them. And his tongue. And his—

"Remy!"

His sudden snarl jolted me from my thoughts as fast as being doused with ice-cold water.

"What?" I asked innocently.

"You know what." He stood in front of me with Drew hovering near the center of the room.

"I don't know."

"You were definitely undressing me with your eyes, and it's beyond distracting." His voice lowered and he growled lowly, "Be good and I promise to reward you later."

"Now you make me sound like a dog getting tossed a bone." I narrowed my eyes.

He chuckled, reaching out to skim the backs of his fingers across my cheeks. "Rem, you're going to get much more than a bone."

"Fine," I sighed, crossing my legs—trying to alleviate the pressure between them. "I'll sit here and be good."

He looked at me doubtfully, but backed away before jogging over to where Drew stood.

This was going to be fun to watch.

Drew gave Mathias some instructions and then they started throwing punches.

If I was a normal girlfriend I'd cheer for Mathias, but I definitely was as far as it got from normal. So, naturally, I cheered for Drew, which only served to piss off Mathias. He kept snarling—at Drew, or me, I wasn't sure, but I really enjoyed watching him get rowed.

Thirty minutes later the guys finished and I hopped off of the mats.

"Good job," I smiled at Mathias, kissing his cheek.

"Oh, so now you're nice to me." He rolled his eyes, trying not to smile.

I shrugged, following him out of the private room. "Normally I'd root for the underdog, but I wanted to piss you off so..." I left my sentence unsaid.

He stopped walking and grabbed my arm so that I was forced to stop too. "Whoa," he shook his head, "I'm no underdog."

I shrugged out of his hold. "I think Drew has a lot more experience than you, therefore you are the underdog." A playful smile quirked my lips and I crossed my arms over my chest.

His eyes narrowed and I let out a small squeal of surprise when he grabbed me and I suddenly found my back pushed up against the wall. He pressed his whole body against mine so that there was no room for me to wiggle away. My palms pressed flat against his sweat-dampened chest, waiting for what came next.

He lowered his head, brushing his lips against my ear and then grazing them along my chin. He repeated the same movements, going back up. His lips paused at my ear and he growled, "Baby, I'm no underdog." His hips ground into mine and I gasped.

Apparently, going to the gym was excellent foreplay. I didn't understand why people avoided it like it was the second coming of the plague.

"Mmm," I hummed as my eyes closed. I completely forgot about what he was saying.

He chuckled lowly and cold air blasted my suddenly heated skin when he stepped away.

Fuck.

He was so talented at starting something and then never finishing it.

Mathias Wade was the king of the tease.

"I'm going to shower," he called over his shoulder, heading over to the men's locker room.

I frowned at his retreating figure and tried to pretend that the deep-seated ache currently residing in my body was going to go away soon—ha, yeah right.

With a shake of my head I turned to the women's locker rooms. I needed to get to the bar for my shift, and then I'd be spending the evening packing before we left for L.A. in the morning.

I couldn't remember the last time I'd ever been this excited for anything. It was nice to finally have something to look forward to.

"JUST MAKE YOURSELF comfortable," I said sarcastically as Mathias sprawled out over my bed. He looked huge on the small bed. My queen-sized bed in no way compared to the massive one he owned.

"Is that sarcasm," he fake-gasped, wiggling around on my bed and adjusting the pillows. Percy hissed at him and Mathias—being such a nice guy—gave my cat the finger. I didn't bother to point out to him that the gesture was probably lost on Percy. "Demon cat," he muttered, glaring at my cat.

"Hey," I scolded, opening my closet door, "I don't say mean things about Shiloh, so don't say mean things about my cat."

"Shiloh is an angel," he rolled his eyes, crossing his arms behind his head, "therefore there is nothing mean you can say. Your cat is evil."

I rolled my eyes. "He's protective."

"Of you? Hardly," Mathias snorted. "He's more protective of this fucking pillow." He patted the one his head currently rested on.

"That's because you stole it from him," I reasoned, dragging my suitcase out of the closet. I stood with my hands on my hips, appraising my clothes and trying to decide what I wanted to take.

"We have plenty of room on the jet, take whatever you want," Mathias said, like he could read my thoughts.

I glanced at him over my shoulders. "You have your own jet?" I gaped.

He shrugged, reaching over to grab the picture frame I kept beside my bed. It was a photo of my family at Christmas years ago. We were all wearing these hideous sweaters and my brother and I were bickering in the photo, but it was one of my favorites. With his eyes perusing the photo he finally said, "It's the record company's but we have exclusive use."

"That's pretty cool," I said in awe. I knew Mathias and his band were famous, there was no denying that when the proof was everywhere, but having known him growing up I couldn't think of him any other way than as himself. I didn't see a famous rock star. I just saw the boy I'd always loved. Something told me though, that this trip to L.A., was about to show me exactly what Mathias' fame status meant for him and now for us.

"Yeah it's nice," he shrugged, setting the picture frame back on the end table. "It means I can bring Shiloh."

I perked up at that. "Does that mean I get to bring Percy?"

He glared at my cat, who sat on the end of the bed glaring right back. "The demon cat is staying."

"Nuh-uh," I shook my head, placing my hands on my hips, "if Shiloh is coming than Perce is too."

He pinched the bridge of his nose and muttered, "Fine, but keep that demon far, far away from me."

"Did you hear that, Perce? You're going to L.A.!"

Percy flicked his tail and turned his glowing orange eyes in my direction. He didn't seem to care that he was getting to go across the country. Cats could be so ungrateful.

I packed my stuff while Mathias meandered around my small

room. "This room doesn't really seem much like you," he commented, taking in the muted palate.

I was sure he was comparing it to my room I'd had as a teenager. The walls had been green with furniture in every color imaginable—because just to spite my mom I'd gone to yard sales every day all summer one year, buying the crappiest furniture I could find and then painting it a bright hue. I'd spent years balking my parents, especially my mom, but when I went through everything I did with Hope she was the one person that was there to pick me back up. I'd never thanked her though, and I guess that made me a crappy person, and an even crappier daughter.

"It's not really my style," I agreed, shrugging my shoulders as I zipped up my suitcase. "My grandma said I could redecorate and I had planned to, but then we started spending so much time together and I've been at your place most nights so it just felt sort of pointless."

He nodded, sitting down on the end of my bed. "Are you ready to go?" He asked.

"Our flight doesn't leave until morning." I glanced up at him, confusion wrinkling my brow.

"Yeah," he chuckled, "aren't you staying at my place, though? The car is picking us up at five in the morning."

"I thought I should stay with my grandma tonight." I frowned, standing up and brushing lint off my jeans.

"You're at my place most nights. What makes tonight different?"

"I feel bad," I admitted with a small shrug. "I'm supposed to be here looking out for her and now I'm off gallivanting around with you."

His lips twitched. "Did you just use the word gallivanting in a sentence?"

"I did."

He shook his head and reached out to pet Percy, but then realizing what he'd been about to do he quickly retracted his hand. Percy hissed at him and jumped off the bed while I tried not to laugh.

"I've got someone checking on her." He assured me. "She'll be fine. She knows how to call you and I even gave her my phone number."

"You gave my grandma your number?" I laughed. "You have met my grandma, right? She'll probably give it out to all her bingo friends."

"Nah," he waved a hand in dismissal, "she wouldn't do that. She says I'm too hot to share."

I snorted, covering my face with my hands. "The fact that my grandma has a crush on you is hysterical. She used to hate you, you know," I admitted, lowering my hands.

He shrugged his wide shoulders, completely unaffected. "Most people hate me before they love me."

I frowned at that, but his words were true. It was all too easy to hate Mathias. He came across as an asshole smart-mouth most of the time, but if you stuck around long enough and got to know him it was impossible not to love him.

I was glad I'd stuck around.

He stood, stretching his arms above his head. His white t-shirt rode up, exposing those delicious indents that disappeared beneath his jeans.

"You're staring, Remy." I could hear the smile in his words.

I raised my eyes to his. "You're my boyfriend, therefore I'm allowed to stare."

He suppressed a smile. "Good point." He reached for my suitcase and picked it up with ease—despite the fact that I was pretty sure it weighed a hundred pounds since I'd packed every single pair of shoes I owned. And clothes. Yeah, there were clothes in there somewhere. "Don't forget your demon cat."

I rolled my eyes. Percy was not a demon. I glanced at the cat and his glare was withering. Okay, so maybe he could be kind of demonic.

"Come on, Perce," I picked him up, tucking him under my arm.

When I reached the bottom of the stairs Mathias was already opening the front door to put my suitcase in the car.

"I'll be right there," I told him. "I have to say goodbye first."

I headed back to my grandma's room and found her absorbed in another show—this one they seemed to be dressed in period costumes.

"I'm heading out," I sat down on the end of the bed, "our flight leaves in the morning so I'm staying over there."

"Shh, it's just getting to the good part! I think Mary and Francis are about to kiss for the first time!"

"Huh?" I glanced from her to the television.

"Reign," she said, throwing up a hand to halt anything I might say, "this is my new addiction. God I love Netflix. If Netflix were a man I would so do him. Netflix brings me nothing but pleasure."

"Oh God, grandma!" I shrieked. "Keep your sexual comments to yourself!"

"I'm old, not dead. My lady bits still function you know."

If I hadn't been holding Percy I would've slapped my hands over my ears.

"*You* need your own show." I shook my head. "They can call it, *Grandma's Gone Wild*."

She rolled her eyes at me and finally paused the TV once the blond guy swooped in for a kiss. "Alright, give me a hug and get out of here. You're irritating me."

She held her thin arms out for a hug and I dove into her embrace. "I love you, you know that, right?"

She nodded against my shoulder. "Of course you do," she patted my back, "I'm impossible not to love."

I laughed, kissing the top of her head before pulling away. "You've got that right."

"Have fun, sweetie," she sobered. "I'll be fine, honestly."

"I know," I smiled.

I hated to leave her—not just because I was responsible for her, but because I loved her. However, she was the toughest person I knew and if she'd made it all these years by herself I knew one week wouldn't kill her.

"I'll see you soon." I stood up, switching Percy to my other arm. "Call if you need anything."

She waved her hand in dismissal and her show resumed once more.

I knew then that she was done talking.

Outside Mathias was waiting in his car. As he drove away from my grandma's home I couldn't help feeling like the next time I saw this place everything would be different. I only hoped things would be different in a good way, but something deep in my gut suggested otherwise.

CHAPTER TWENTY-FOUR

WARM LIPS PRESSED against the soft skin of my neck. I began to wiggle around and soon a laugh vibrated against me.

"Time to get up, Rem." Fingers tickled down my bareback.

"Don't want to," I mumbled, wrapping my arms tighter around the pillow.

"The car's waiting for us." Those same lips pressed against my ear. "We have to go."

I made some noise that was completely unintelligible.

"You never were a morning person," the voice mumbled.

Cold water prickled my skin and I groaned in protest.

"That's only a taste of what you'll get if you don't wake up."

I sat straight up. "I'm up. I'm up." I repeated, as if he didn't hear me the first time.

Mathias lounged in bed beside me, already dressed in a pair of tan colored pants, a white button down shirt, and a navy cardigan. He even wore his Clark Kent glasses. Normally I'd poke fun at him, just because I could, but I was too tired and he did look pretty hot so I couldn't complain.

"Do I at least have time to shower?" I pouted.

"No," he smacked my butt and stood. "We need to go. Like now."

After some more grumbling I managed to drag my sleepy self out of bed. I had planned to wear a sweatshirt and jeans, but then I began to panic, realizing we might be photographed together.

I decided to keep the jeans but chose a black peplum top with lace sleeves and my knee length red coat.

I brushed my straight hair and applied a minimum amount of makeup—and of course my red lipstick.

No woman could conquer the world until she'd put on her red lipstick.

"Remy!" Mathias yelled through the penthouse.

"I'm ready!" I yelled back.

My stuff was already waiting by the elevator since we left it there last night, so I had nothing else to grab. Except Percy—who had taken up residence on Mathias' pillow.

I slipped on a pair of heels and grabbed Percy.

Mathias was pacing in the kitchen. "God, woman," he groaned, "could you be any slower?"

"I guess you should have woken me up sooner," I reasoned, lifting my shoulders.

He mumbled under his breath and went to get Shiloh, returning a moment later with her on a leash.

Together we managed to get the animals and the suitcases into the elevator, but instead of taking it to the parking garage we stopped in the lobby and headed out front where an SUV was waiting for us. A big, burly driver in a black suit stood waiting.

"Is that your body guard?" I asked.

Mathias nodded. "Yeah. That's Hank. Hank, this is Remy. Remy, Hank."

We each said awkward hellos as he opened the car door for

us, before putting our bags in the trunk.

When we slipped inside the vehicle I was surprised to find Maddox and Emma sitting in the back. I mean, I knew from what Mathias said that the whole band would be going to L.A. but I just figured we'd be meeting up with them there. Silly me.

"Hi," I smiled at Maddox. Emma was currently passed out asleep with her head on his shoulder. On his other shoulder sat... "Is that a hedgehog?"

He smiled crookedly. "Yep. Sonic," he pointed to his shoulder, "Aquilla," he then pointed to his lap. Two hedgehogs. Wow.

"Uh..." I didn't know quite what to make of the spiky creatures. Percy finally seemed to notice them and hissed before scratching at me and jumping on the floor of the SUV. He glared up at me with disdain.

"I told you we should've left the demon," Mathias muttered, having witnessed the whole situation.

I rolled my eyes and relaxed into the seat.

"Ezra and Hayes are already on the plane." Maddox spoke from behind me.

"Of course they are," Mathias griped.

The trunk closed and Hank slid into the driver's seat, pulling away from the hotel.

The sudden jolting of the car caused Emma to momentarily wake up. I heard her mutter something before promptly falling back asleep cuddled against Maddox with her wild blonde hair hiding her face. I couldn't help watching as Maddox smiled lovingly down at her and kissed the top of her head. I quickly turned around before he could catch me watching them. Mathias didn't miss it though. He reached over, taking my hand in his. It wasn't much, but it was a simple gesture to show me that he cared. A smile touched my lips as I looked at our hands.

It was cute that Mathias thought he should show more affection—and even though I'd been admiring the sweetness of Maddox and Emma's relationship, I didn't need that. All I'd ever wanted and needed was Mathias, just the way he was.

I relaxed into the plush leather seat, settling in for the long drive to the airport. I was surprised though when Hank didn't get on the interstate.

"Where are we going?" I asked stupidly.

"To the airport." Mathias answered immediately with his usual sass.

I rolled my eyes. "I know that, but shouldn't we be going in that direction?" I pointed the opposite way.

He shook his head, glancing down at our joined hands like he wasn't quite sure what to make of them. "We're going to the airport here."

I racked my brain, trying to recall an airport here. "You mean that really small one?"

He nodded. "Yeah. It's easier for us to fly in and out of there. The private plane isn't that large and we can avoid getting mobbed by a crowd. Unfortunately," he winced, "we'll have to land at LAX so brace yourself. It's going to get crazy."

"Yeah." Maddox piped in from behind us.

"Great." I glanced out the window. I wasn't ready for this, but I had to be.

We arrived at the airport no more than ten minutes later. It was nice not having to go through security and then wait for the plane to be ready to board. Hank literally drove right up to the plane and we got out of the car, climbed up the steps, and took our seats.

Hayes nodded as we got on the plane. Ezra was already asleep in his chair with his headphones on.

Poor Emma was still half-asleep and Maddox had to

practically carry her to a seat.

"She really hates getting up early." He told me when he caught me staring.

"I'm with her," I agreed.

I took my seat and clicked the seatbelt into place. Percy sat in my lap and Shiloh snoozed peacefully on Mathias'.

"Go back to sleep," he urged.

I shook my head. "I don't think I can."

"Of course you can. I'll sing to you."

I looked up at him wide-eyed. "You're going to sing to me?"

"Sure," he shrugged, stretching his legs out. That was a major bonus of a private plane—lots of leg-room. Not to mention the seat was super plush and the interior was shiny and clean. I wouldn't feel the need to bathe in Germ-X like I normally did after traveling.

"Uh…" I didn't know what to make of that.

"Just get comfortable," he huffed.

"Alright, alright," I mumbled, trying to hide my smile.

I wiggled my butt around in the seat, trying not to jostle Percy too much, and then laid my head on his shoulder.

I was surprised when he laid his head on top of mine.

A smile of contentment lifted my lips and I scooted as close to him as I could get.

Closing my eyes, I waited for him to start singing.

When he did I immediately felt a flush of warmth in my body and tingles in my toes. I would never grow tired of hearing him sing at any time, but there was something I enjoyed infinitely more about having him sing only to *me*. I didn't recognize the song, but if it was one of Willow Creek's that wasn't surprising. I'd never let myself indulge in their music. It was too painful to hear Mathias' voice. But now I never wanted him to stop singing to me. I wanted to wrap myself up in the softness of his voice and stay there forever. His voice had a slight husky rasp to it that I loved. It made it rougher and more unique than everything else you heard on the radio. It was just as raw and beautiful as the man it belonged to. He'd hate it if he knew I thought everything about him was beautiful, but it was the only word to describe him. He was beautiful inside and out.

I closed my eyes, letting his warmth and voice envelope me.

Soon I found my eyes growing heavy and I was lulled into a deep sleep as his voice carried me into my dreams.

WE LANDED AT LAX and it was time to depart the plane. Mathias grabbed a black baseball cap and stuck it on his head, pulling the brim low before covering his eyes with a pair of dark sunglasses.

"You want one?" He asked, pointing to a stash of baseball caps and beanies kept in a basket on the plane.

"Uh..." I paused, debating. "Yeah." He handed me a red cap and I smiled. "Thanks."

I put it on and adjusted it so I wore it the way he did—hiding half of my face. The media didn't need to know who I was. I might've fought with him on that fact before, but that was only because I thought he was ashamed of me or something. In all honestly, I'd rather keep my anonymity for as long as possible.

"Show time," he muttered.

Taking my hand he led me off the plane and through the gate. We were the last to depart—the other band members having ditched us.

"Hank will bring our stuff and Shiloh and Percy to my place later. I thought it was best that they avoid this," he said to me, just before chaos erupted and I learned what *this* was.

High-pitched shrieks echoed around the airport as a group of teenage girls spotted Mathias.

"Fuck," he groaned.

He grudgingly posed for pictures and signed autographs before Hank and another large beefy guy showed up.

They ushered us out of the crowd and through the airport.

Outside I saw photographers lined up, their cameras flashing as they tried to snap photos through the glass.

Mathias wrapped an arm around me, holding me tight against his side, while Hank and beefy guy number two flanked us.

When we stepped outside the clicking of cameras and shouts from the photographers were nearly overwhelming.

"Mathias! Over here!"

"Mathias!"

"Who's the woman?"

"Mathias, are you dating now?"

"Is it serious?"

"Who is she?"

"Who are you?"

Oh, look, a question finally directed at me.

We reached the vehicle and Hank opened the back door. Mathias pushed at me, trying to get me to go in first, but a photographer chose that moment to practically shove a camera in my face and scare the crap out of me. The flash went off, momentarily blinding me and I covered my eyes.

A new arm came around me, and I started to scream when I realized the arm was so large it had to either belong to Hank or beefy guy number two.

I was lifted into the SUV and I immediately scurried to the other seat so Mathias could get in.

He sat down, letting out a hefty sigh as the door closed—

helping to drown out some of the noise. Beefy guy number two got in the driver's seat and Hank took the passenger's.

"How do you live with that?" I asked Mathias.

He shrugged, removing the baseball cap and ruffling his hair with a quick swipe of his fingers. "I don't like it, but it's part of the job."

"That was insane."

He nodded in agreement. "It was worse than I expected." His jaw clenched and he turned his gaze on me, his gray eyes so icy that I found myself shivering. "Does it scare you? Because if it does you should just leave now. This is one part of my life I can't change."

I gaped at him. My mouth opening and closing as I tried to form words.

"Do I like it? No. But it's not going to scare me away from you," I spoke fiercely. "I choose to be with you, because I love you, and nothing, not even this, can change that." I couldn't help muttering, "Don't be such a damn drama queen." I crossed my arms over my chest and glared out the window. I was slightly hurt that he thought that something as simple as a photographer snapping my picture would send me running. Sure, I didn't like it, but I expected it. I wished he'd have more faith in me.

"Rem," he started, and then grunted in annoyance before turning to look out the opposite window. In many ways we were far too much alike, one of those ways being our stubbornness. It always seemed to get us in trouble.

I noticed Hank reach up and turn the radio on to drown out the awkward silence. In that moment I was incredibly thankful for Hank... and you know, also when he saved me from some crazy photographers.

Despite the fact that it was cold back home, it still looked like it was summer here.

That was one thing I missed about Arizona, even though when I left to take care of my grandma I'd known I'd never go back there.

I hadn't planned to stay in Virginia either, but sometimes life had other plans for you. I turned to look at Mathias, taking in his steely posture and sharp jaw. I hadn't expected to find him again, once I did I'd wanted nothing but revenge, and now all I wanted was for us to finally get our happily ever after. We'd both been through hell and back—together and apart—and I felt we deserved to be happy, but dread slid like a thick serpent through my veins, because people like us didn't get a happy ending. In a movie we'd be the bad guys that everyone loved to hate, and secretly rooted for their demise. We didn't get to skip off into the sunset. No, we ended up alone and miserable—left questioning every decision we'd ever made and how it led to this... to nothing.

I didn't want to end up with nothing.

I wanted to end up with Mathias, but I *knew* that in order for that to happen I'd have to tell him about Hope and I... I just couldn't. Not only did I want to spare him the hurt, but I wanted to avoid the pain telling him would cause me.

Selfish? Yeah, I'd agree with that. I was a selfish person. So were most people, even though they didn't want to admit it.

But if being selfish meant that he'd never have to experience the hurt of losing our daughter then I would be selfish for the rest of my life and take my secret to the grave.

The car came to a stop in front of a set of wrought iron gates and I was jolted out of my less than happy thoughts.

The gate swung open and we drove through a slightly overgrown tree line before they parted to show a large white, rectangular home with a balcony wrapping around the second level. The entire home was covered with wall-to-wall windows.

"This is home when I'm here." He shrugged, finally speaking.

"It's gorgeous." There was no denying that fact.

"Let me show you around," he said as the car came to a stop.

Hank opened the door for us and said they'd return soon with our luggage and the animals. I really hoped Percy and Shiloh were okay.

Mathias guided me to the heavy wood front door with a hand at my waist. He dug a pair of keys out of his pocket and slid it into the lock.

A gasp escaped my parted lips.

While the penthouse at the hotel was muted colors and decorated sparsely this house was the complete opposite. Despite the fact that all the outside walls had windows the house was relatively warm looking, with rich woods and brown hues decorating the space. It was definitely masculine, but I loved it. Due to the style of the home I expected it to be decorated like the penthouse, but I was pleased I'd been wrong.

He led me into the family room where a tan suede sectional was positioned in front of a fireplace with a flat screen TV mounted above.

Decorative burnt orange pillows and a throw blanket decorated the couch.

"I hired an interior designer," he admitted with a sheepish shrug. "There was no way I could do this on my own, let alone ever have the time. I think you're right, I should do something else with the penthouse. When I moved in there…" He turned away from me, his jaw clenched tight. "I guess I wanted it to reflect me—to be just as empty as I was on the inside. I'm not so empty anymore." His gray eyes flooded with love and I swallowed thickly.

I couldn't stop myself from wrapping my arms around him.

He was slow to do the same, but eventually he did. I rested my ear against his chest and closed my eyes as I memorized the steady *thump, thump, thump* that was the beat of his heart.

He rested his head on top of mine and we stood there silently as minutes passed, neither of us willing to let go.

"I love you," I finally whispered. "I know I never say it, but I do. I love you so much that it scares me." My voice cracked and I clung tightly to his shirt.

"I love you too." He pulled away just enough to press a tender kiss to my forehead. I sighed softly and my eyes closed at the sweet feel of his lips.

I knew I needed to release him so I did just that, instantly missing the warmth his body provided.

Reaching for my hand he flashed me a small half-smile. "Let me show you the rest of my place."

The floor plan was open so I could practically see the whole downstairs from where we stood, but I wasn't going to complain.

He led me from the family room into the dining room. It was decorated with a dark wood table and beige fabric covered chairs. I doubted the room had ever been used.

From there he guided me into the kitchen. Like the rest of the house the walls were a light golden hue with espresso colored cabinets and gold-flecked granite countertops. It was gorgeous and I couldn't help picturing the two of us cooking in here together—you know, after I learned how to cook. I was turning into a sap, so sue me.

I was too busy looking around the kitchen in awe to notice him approach. He grasped my hip, turning me around to face him, and pressed me against the edge of the center island.

His eyes were dark with lust and he lowered his forehead to mine.

"I think we need christen every room."

I tossed my head back, laughing. "Oh, do you now?"

He nodded, skimming his lips along my jaw before nipping my chin lightly with his teeth. "Definitely. I want a different memory for every room."

"Mmm," I hummed as his lips captured mine.

His tongue slid against mine, eliciting a moan from my throat.

"I. Thought. You. Were. Going. To. Give. Me. A. Tour." I panted in-between kisses.

"Fuck the tour."

I was okay with that.

His hand skimmed up my thigh, cupping my butt, and then he lifted me onto the countertop. My legs parted and he stepped into the space between, never breaking his lips from mine. He reached up, cupping my face in his large hands and holding me prisoner.

In the small space between us I began to undo the buttons of his cardigan, pushing it off his wide shoulders. Next went his white button down shirt. Then he removed my coat and shirt.

Bra.

Jeans.

Panties.

Gone.

Gone.

Gone.

I lay down with my back pressed flat against the countertop. The cold surface made me shiver and my nipples tightened in response.

"Fuck, you're beautiful." He growled lowly as his eyes raked over my body.

I bit my lip, watching as he rolled on the condom.

Once it was in place he grabbed my hips and pulled me over.

He slammed inside me and I let out a small cry.

"I didn't hurt you, did I?" He asked, suddenly stilling.

"Please, for the love of God," I reached forward, my fingers grazing his abs, "don't fucking stop."

A small smile touched his lips and he began to move.

I let out a small moan, clenching around him.

He palmed my breast, rolling his thumb over my swollen nipple while his other hand roamed lower. When his fingers found my clit I gasped, my back arching off the countertop.

"Oh God," I whimpered.

He lowered his head, sucking on my other nipple.

I was a goner.

He continued to pump into me at a vicious pace and I found myself coming a second time with him.

He collapsed with his chest on top of mine, our sweaty skin sticking together. I wrapped my legs around his waist as we both tried to even our breaths.

He was the first to recover. He pulled out of me and removed the condom, tying it off before tossing it in the trashcan.

I was too tired to move, but luckily I didn't have to. He reached for me and pulled me off the counter and into his arms.

"Next room," he growled.

I nodded, more than happy to indulge his fantasy.

AFTER HAVING SEX in every room downstairs we finally were too tried to continue. We got redressed and collapsed on the couch in the family room. He turned the TV on and I laid down with my head resting on his thigh. I paid no attention to the TV as my eyelids grew heavy.

Just as I was about to doze off asleep there was a knock at the door.

Mathias groaned and tapped my shoulder so I'd sit up.

"That'll be Hank with our stuff."

"Percy!" I cried with sudden renewed energy.

I tumbled off the couch and hurried after Mathias, reaching him just as he swung the door open.

Shiloh immediately bound inside, tearing her leash out of Hank's hand.

Poor Hank let out a curse and that's when I noticed Percy clawing at the large bear of a man.

"I'm so sorry!" I cried, rushing forward to grab Percy from his hands.

"It didn't hurt," Hank shrugged, but the claw marks on his arms and neck told a different story.

Percy wasn't too pleased with me either and scratched at me so I'd put him down. As soon as I did he promptly ran into the dining room and hid under the table.

"Demon cat," Mathias muttered.

For once I agreed with him.

He took the bags from Hank and they said their goodbyes.

"I'm hungry," Mathias announced.

"Okay," I said slowly. "Do you want to go out, or—"

"Let's make frozen pizza."

I nodded my head in approval. "So fancy. I like it."

He chuckled, shaking his head as he started in the direction of the kitchen. "You're lucky I like your sarcasm."

I padded after him, rolling my eyes despite the fact that he couldn't see me. "And you're lucky I tolerate you."

"Good point," he shrugged.

In the kitchen he opened the freezer and pulled out a box of pizza with practically every topping on it. I had no idea where anything was located so I hopped up on the counter while he fixed everything. Besides, watching him was way more fun than helping.

Shiloh joined us shortly, sniffing every surface.

For kicks I almost reminded Mathias to get rid of any chocolate, but I decided that would be too mean even for me considering the panic attack he'd nearly had the last time.

He finally slid the pizza into the oven and set the timer.

He turned to me, placing his hands on the counter beside my legs. "So," he started, lowering his head so he could peer into my eyes, "do you like it here?"

I let out a small laugh. "I haven't seen much, you know, besides your cock. But it was pretty nice. I quite like it actually."

He ducked his head to hide a smile. Raising his eyes to mine he brushed his thumb against my bottom lip. "You and your dirty mouth."

My eyes dropped to his lips. "That wasn't even dirty."

He tucked his head into the crook of my neck and I felt him smile.

I expected him to say or do something else but after a pause he took a step back and held out his hand for me.

"Come with me."

I tucked my hand into his and hopped off the counter.

He led me to a wall of windows and I gasped. I'd been too preoccupied by thc opulent inside to notice the beauty that lay beyond the windows.

The house was nestled high on a hill over looking a barren, private beach. Directly outside the windows sat a large swimming pool with shimmering blue water. Lounge chairs were set up by the pool, and off to a corner was an area sectioned off with rocks and chairs surrounding a fire pit.

He slid open a door—that I'd actually believed was a window

since it blended in so effortlessly—and guided me outside.

The air was warm with a slight breeze.

I released his hand and started removing my clothes.

"What are you doing?" He asked, watching my movements.

"What does it look like I'm doing?" I raised a brow as my fingers found the button on my jeans. I left my bra and panties on just to mess with him.

He shook his head, looking at me like I'd lost my mind as all my clothes fell in a heap on the grass.

I dove into the water and found that it was actually warm. I guessed he kept it heated.

I rose to the surface, pushing my wet hair away from my face.

"Aren't you coming?" I asked, treading water.

He shook his head yet again, as if he couldn't believe he was about to do this. He stripped down to his boxer-briefs and dove into the water. He surfaced in front of me and shook his head, sending water droplets flying all over the place.

"You're crazy, you know that, right?"

I smiled, wrapping my arms around his strong shoulders. "I know," I agreed, watching a droplet of water cascade down his cheek and over his lips. "But life is pretty boring without the crazy moments."

He chuckled. "You've got that right."

Before he could say anything else I leaned in and kissed him, stealing away that drop of water.

He swallowed thickly, his eyes growing serious. The strands of his wet hair brushed against my forehead as he spoke. "To think, we almost missed out on this. On us." He brushed his fingers lightly over my cheek. "I never thought I was the kind of person who had good luck or got second chances, but here I am, defeating the odds—living my dream, and getting my girl back."

My girl.

I didn't know what to say to that. I was so overcome by his words that for once in my life I was actually speechless. "I guess some things are meant to be," I whispered when I realized he was still waiting for a reply.

His tongue slid out to wet his lips and his forehead wrinkled with thought.

I didn't know what he was going to say, and nothing could've prepared me for the words that left his mouth.

"Marry me."

I choked on a gasp. "What?"

"Marry me," he repeated, dead serious. "Not right this second, but soon. Like this week. We're playing a show in Vegas while we're on the west coast. While we're there let's get married."

"Are you insane?" If he wasn't holding onto me I was pretty sure his words would've sent me sinking straight to the bottom of the pool.

"On the contrary, I think this is the most sane I've ever been." He cracked a smile. "Now, please, don't make me ask again."

"I-I—" I stuttered, shaking my head back and forth as every reason why I should say no flitted through my mind. Unfortunately, one word outweighed every negative thought I had. "Yes." Tears pricked my eyes. I never thought I'd be one of those girls that cried when she got engaged—in fact, I'd rarely even imagined this moment. "Yes," I said again, loving the sound of that word. "Yes. Yes. Yes."

His lips smothered mine in a bruising kiss as I continued to whisper, "Yes," over and over again. Now that I'd said it, it was my new favorite word and I never, ever wanted to stop saying it.

CHAPTER TWENTY-FIVE

AFTER MATHIAS' SURPRISE proposal we'd gotten out of the pool and dried off. The pizza had finished baking, and although it was a little burnt, I still declared that it was the best thing I'd ever eaten.

Now, Mathias guided me up the staircase with a twinkle in his eyes.

My heart thumped steadily in my chest. Each beat seemed to say, *He wants to marry you.* I was still in shock. The last thing I had ever expected was for Mathias to ask me to marry him. Even if someone had asked me where I thought we'd be in five years I definitely wouldn't have answered with married. I never thought it was something he'd want, and I'd always been okay with that. Now, though, as his warm hand enveloped mine, I couldn't help smiling with glee at the thought of calling him my husband. I had to admit, I really liked the sound of that.

He paused in front of a door, glancing back at me with an almost shy smile.

Pushing the door open he stepped back and let me step inside the room first.

I let out a small gasp and spun around, trying to take in all the details.

The bed took up most of the space. It had four posts that soared high and was a deep rich brown. The wall behind the bed was covered in what looked like wood flooring. It sounded strange but it actually worked. Two of the other walls were painted a deep burnt orange color, while the last wall was a solid window over looking the pool and the beach below. The bed was covered in a thick brown comforter with orange pillows. Surprisingly this room had carpet. It was thick and plush and for some reason I had the urge to kick my shoes off and dig my toes into it, so I did just that.

Mathias chuckled as he stood watching me. He leaned casually against the wall with his hands in his pockets. He hadn't bothered to put his shirt or cardigan back on so his chest was left bare. I never knew a body could be a work of art, but his was. With soft skin and hard planes of muscle, he was nothing less than magnificent—and mine.

"Like what you see?" He grinned, while his own eyes scoured my body.

I licked my lips and nodded. I glanced at his bed and back at him, frowning.

He noticed the downturn of my lips and strode forward, taking my face between his hands. "What is it?" He asked, his eyes scanning my face for any explanation of my sudden sadness. "What's wrong?"

"It's stupid," I winced, refusing to speak the words aloud.

"Tell me," he coaxed, his eyes pleading.

"I..." I gaped at him open-mouthed like a fish. "It's just that... Fuck." I cursed, wishing he'd release me so I could escape the intrusiveness of his gaze.

"Remy," he warned, "tell me what's wrong so I can fix it."

I swallowed past the lump in my throat. I felt silly and oh-so girly in this moment. "It's so dumb," I frowned, biting my lower lip in the hopes that I could stop the tumble of words, "but I *hate* the thought of you fucking me in this bed where you've brought countless other women." I'd never had that worry at his penthouse because he was never photographed with women at home—then again, the paparazzi didn't seem to want to bother hanging around our small town. But I *had* seen countless photos in magazines of him with different women in L.A. and the thought of him bringing them back here, to this bed, literally made me sick to my stomach.

He stroked his fingers lightly over the curve of my cheek, his eyes darkening. "One, I've never brought any woman back here. This is my home and I don't want it tainted with meaningless hookups. Two," his voice lowered and his lips pressed against my neck, right over the spot where my pulse raced wildly, "I'm not going to fuck you in this bed."

"You're not?" My voice came out sounding surprisingly strong despite how weak I suddenly felt.

I felt him shake his head and I shivered as his hair tickled my neck. He pulled back, looking into my eyes. His Adam's apple bobbed and his eyes flicked down to my lips and then back up. "No," his voice was barely above a whisper, "I'm going to make love to you."

That was the last thing I'd ever expected him to say.

My heart raced in anticipation at the promising glint in his eyes.

"No one's ever made love to me before," I whispered, my chest heaving with each breath as I struggled to get enough air.

He pushed forward and I was forced to take a step back, and then another, until the backs of my knees hit the bed and I was forced to lie down.

"I've never done it," he admitted, his fingers skimming down my neck, all the way to the bottom of my shirt. His fingers wrapped around the end of it and he slowly tugged it upward, stopping when he reached the bottom of my bra. My skin felt heated all over and when he kissed my stomach I was sure his lips would be burned. He lifted his head, his eyes connecting with mine yet again—and my body clenched all over from the intensity of his gaze. "But something tells me I'm going to enjoy this."

My heart beat so fast that it sounded like thunder in my ears—a steady roar promising more.

He sprinkled kisses all over my stomach and small little sounds escaped my throat.

I was used to hard and fast with us, and this was anything but that.

His fingers dipped beneath the edge of my jeans, teasing me as he went no further and made no move to remove them. I covered my mouth with my hand to resist the urge to beg him for more.

He kissed his way up my stomach, this time lifting my shirt off and gently removing it. My blonde hair tumbled forward and he pushed it away, his eyes feasting upon my breasts, which were barely contained in a lacy black bra.

"I never thought I'd get you *back*." His voice cracked. "I believed I was nothing but a sick bastard that didn't deserve you. I was wrong though. I do deserve you. I deserve happiness and you bring me that." His lips skimmed down my neck and over my breasts. "I'm done punishing myself for things that were out of my control." His eyes met mine and it was like he was peering straight down into my soul. "My parent's might've been bad people, but I realize now that it doesn't mean I am just because their blood runs through my veins. Loving you has shown me that."

I closed my eyes, soaking in his words and the beauty of

them. "You were never a bad person," I whispered after a moment.

He looked at me doubtfully, his chest shaking with a silent chuckle.

"Misunderstood, yes," I continued, "but you've never been a bad person. Beneath all your... assholishness," I said for lack of a better word, "you have a heart of gold." I placed my hand over his heart, feeling it thump steadily in time with mine.

"If I had a heart of gold I wouldn't have lied to you when you left," he growled. "I wouldn't have done half the shit that I have."

I swallowed thickly, remembering back to that day and everything that happened after. "Even good people make mistakes."

He shook his head, but instead of arguing with me he simply said, "I'm done talking now."

In an achingly slow manner he removed the last of my clothes and proceeded to kiss every inch of my body.

My whole body tensed with the desire to connect with his.

Grazing my fingers down his bare chest until I reached his pants, I said, "I think you're wearing too many clothes."

"Slow, Rem," he growled, nipping my earlobe.

"This is slow," I argued.

He merely chuckled, sweeping his lips over my breasts.

He would be the death of me, but at least I'd die happy.

While he kissed my neck his fingers slipped inside me. I gasped at the same time he groaned.

"Christ, your pussy is always so wet for me."

I wanted to come back with some witty response, but my brain had shut down for the moment. Words fled my mind and all I could focus on was the touch of his fingers and the feel of his weight resting on top of my body.

His fingers rubbed against me, working me into an orgasm. As I came, panting his name, his eyes never left mine and his contained a gleam of satisfaction.

"I like it when you say my name like that," he growled, undoing the button of his pants.

Sweat dotted my skin and I struggled to catch my breath. "Like what?"

"Like I'm everything to you."

Before I had time to process his words he'd stepped out of his pants and he gave his cock a light stroke before slipping on a condom and covering my body with his.

Pushing my hair from my eyes he whispered, "I love you," before slowly sinking inside me.

My breath caught on a gasp as my whole body shook with his intrusion.

I wrapped my legs around his waist, my fingernails digging into his back as he rolled his hips against mine in a leisurely pace.

He rested his forehead against mine, peering into my eyes as he made love to me—and he was right, this was definitely making love, not fucking, and I loved it. I never knew sex could be like this. So powerful. It was like we were connecting not only physically, but spiritually as well. It was a beautiful thing and I never wanted it to end, and I realized it didn't have too, because I was going to be his wife.

Tears pricked my eyes and one slid down my cheek.

His eyes followed the trail of the tear. "Why are you crying?" He asked, still pushing into me at that deliciously slow pace.

"I don't know," I whispered, taking his chin between my thumb and forefinger. The light stubble on his chin scratched my fingers, but I didn't mind the roughness.

He wiped away the wetness with a swipe of his large thumb.

"I don't want you to be sad," he frowned.

"I'm not," I shook my head, "I'm so undeniably *happy*."

Confusion marred his brow, but he let it drop. His pace picked up slightly, but was still slower than our normal frantic coupling.

He sucked at the skin on my neck, no doubt leaving behind a mark, before trailing his lips over the valley between my breasts.

I could feel another orgasm approaching and my whole body clenched.

"Fuck," he groaned, kissing me.

I gasped beneath him when my orgasm hit and cried out his name. My nails dug sharply into his back and he hissed. I shook all over and sweat dampened my skin. I'd never had an orgasm that powerful before.

He wasn't far behind me, growling lowly as he found his own release.

We stayed connected and he was careful to hold his weight so that he didn't hurt me. When he caught his breath he slipped out of me and disposed of the condom. Returning to the bed he lay down beside me, pulling me against his side.

"Fucking hell," he muttered, staring up at the ceiling while I still struggled to get enough air into my lungs, "if I had known it would be that good I would've made love to you a long time ago."

Despite my lack of oxygen I still managed to laugh. "Well, there's always next time."

"Hell yeah."

And then he proceeded to show me over and over again why making love was better than fucking.

THE EARLY MORNING sun filtered in through the open windows, bathing our bodies in a golden glow. I trailed my fingers lightly over his chest, watching the way his muscles clenched and danced at my touch. Neither of us had gotten much sleep, maybe two hours at the most, having spent the entire night wrapped in each other's arms.

"Why do you want to marry me?" I asked. My breath tickled his chest and his nipple tightened at the sensation.

"Why would you ask that?" He sounded mad.

I tilted my head back to peer up at him. His dark brows were pulled together and his forehead was wrinkled with irritation. "I was just wondering. I mean... I never thought you'd want that."

"I didn't," he admitted on a sigh, "but with you I want it all."

My heart skipped a beat at that. "*Why?*"

"Because I love you." He answered simply, his fingers resuming their slow rake through my hair before stopping at my neck. He began to massage the stiff muscle and I nearly moaned. His fingers stilled once more and his whole body went rigid against me. "Have you changed your mind?" The fist on his free hand clenched. "Do you not want to marry me?"

I sat up, my blonde hair forming a silky sheet around us. "That's not what I was getting at, at all." I reached forward, stroking my fingers along his cheek. He sighed happily at my touch and began to relax. "I want this, I want *you*, more than anything. It's just hard for me to see why you would want me. You talk about how you're a bad person, but what about me?"

I was pretty sure it was a safe bet that my sins were far worse than his. After all, I was hiding a massive secret from him. Yeah, I was trying to protect him, but that didn't make the fact that I was keeping a secret from him okay.

He sat up too, clasping my hands in his like he was afraid I might run away and he needed to keep a tight hold on me.

"What's going on Remy?"

"Nothing," I lied, hoping he couldn't see the tears shimmering in my eyes. "I just wanted to know why."

"Fuck," he growled, looking away. A muscle in his jaw ticked. Looking back at me he said, "I want to marry you, because you're my best friend. I want to marry you, because I love waking up beside you. I want to marry you, because I love seeing you strut around in my shirts. I want to marry you, because I love having you in my house, in my space and I love knowing you've been there and that you're coming back. I want to marry you, because without you my life feels incomplete." He paused, taking a deep breath. "But most importantly, I want to marry you because I love you—I have since I was sixteen years old— and I'll never stop."

Happy tears pricked my eyes for the second time in a matter of hours. Clearly I was turning into a sap.

I wrapped my arms around his neck and kissed him long and deep. "I love you too," I said on a breath.

He smiled against my lips. "So, you're really going to marry me?"

I nodded and was rewarded with one of his rare blindingly bright smiles that made my insides dance and sing.

He kissed me quickly, his lips a bruising pressure against mine.

His fingers curled against the nape of my neck and his smile never wavered.

"Did you really think I had changed my mind?" I asked.

He shrugged, laying back down and pulling me with him so I was once again lying in the same position with my head cradled on his chest. "You looked so upset..." He trailed off. "So, yeah, I guess I did think that."

"I'm sorry, I didn't mean to scare you like that. But I

wondered why, because I know I'm not always the nicest person."

He laughed, his whole body shaking with it, which in turn made mine shake. "And neither am I. That, my dear Remy," he kissed my forehead, "is why we work."

I closed my eyes, breathing in his scent.

"Get some sleep," he whispered, brushing his lips against the top of my head, "I have to film a commercial in a few hours."

"A commercial?" I questioned.

"Yep," he grabbed the edge of the sheet and brought it over our bodies, "for Pepsi."

"You're so cool," I yawned, "and you're going to be my husband."

"Just go to sleep, Rem," he growled.

I didn't think I'd be able to fall asleep, but like on the plane he began to sing softly and in a matter of minutes I slept peacefully.

CHAPTER TWENTY-SIX

WE STEPPED INTO the garage and I followed Mathias over to a sleek cobalt blue Honda motorcycle. It looked fast, and that fact made me excited.

"Are we taking this?" I asked, practically dancing on the balls of my feet.

He looked at me like he didn't even recognize me, which was understandable since I rarely got excited over anything.

"Yeah," he nodded, heading over to a row of silver lockers that lined the back of the garage. He also owned a sleek silver car that looked like nothing I'd ever seen before. Something told me I didn't want to know how much it cost.

Opening one of the locker doors he grabbed two helmets. I was already wearing a black leather jacket while he wore a brown one.

"So..." I reached out, taking the offered helmet, "are you going to let me drive it?"

"Fuck no." He pushed a button to open one of the garage doors before slipping the helmet on his head.

He tossed his leg over the side of the bike and a moment later the engine roared to life.

I had to admit he looked mighty sexy straddling the sleek

motorcycle. Downright lickable.

"Hurry up, Rem," he growled over the motor. "We're going to be late."

"Oh, right," I muttered to myself, getting into place behind him. My hands lightly grasped his sides and when he knew that I was comfortable we shot out of the garage. The bike was crazy fast and my hair whipped around me as the air stung my skin even through my layers of clothes.

I was enjoying every moment of it though.

The L.A. traffic was insane and we got stuck in traffic before arriving at a building that looked like a rundown warehouse. I spotted several cars in the parking lot and figured the rest of the band was already here.

We dismounted from the bike and removed our helmets. I pulled my hair back into a ponytail to help tame the strands.

Taking my hand Mathias led me through a backdoor and down several hallways.

The space opened up and a whole set was in front of us along with cameras. Off to the side sat a rack of clothes and a makeup team.

"They're going to put makeup on you?" I tried, and failed, to suppress a laugh.

"Yes," he growled.

Maddox approached us from off to the side. He was dressed simply in a pair of loose jeans and a white t-shirt that molded to his chest. His drumsticks rested in his back pocket. "Emma's over there," he nodded his head in the direction of another doorway. "Free food," he whispered conspiratorially, "and lots of Diet Pepsi. It's like heaven."

Mathias released my hand. "Go on." He nodded as well. "I have to go get ready anyway."

I watched as he strutted over to the wardrobe like he owned

the damn place. He oozed effortless confidence.

Maddox cleared his throat, forcing my attention back to him. "So," he started, "how are things?"

"Uh... Good?" I didn't know why it came out sounding like a question. He'd caught me off guard though and I had no idea how to respond. I had no knowledge of how much Mathias shared with his twin, and I definitely didn't know if he wanted to tell his brother we were planning to get married or if he wanted to keep it between us for now.

Maddox nodded, looking over at where Mathias argued with the stylist about the wardrobe. "That's good." He stuck his hands in his pockets as his silver eyes swiveled back in my direction. "I can tell he's happy."

I nodded too, feeling extremely awkward. I didn't know Maddox very well. When we were teenagers we only hung out a few times, and it wasn't like we'd ever been friends.

"Are you happy too?" He asked, reaching up to sweep his dark hair away from his eyes.

A small smile touched my lips as I watched Mathias. "Yeah, I am. The happiest I've ever been."

Maddox grinned. "It's crazy how after so many years apart you guys still connected. What you have is special. Anyone can see that."

I nodded, smiling at Maddox. "Yeah, it is."

Just then Mathias voice raised and we looked over to see him yelling at the poor stylist. It looked like a vein was about to burst in his forehead and his face had turned red.

"I better go calm him down," Maddox groaned. "Emma's in there," he repeated, "she'd love to see you so feel free to say hi."

I nodded as he took off to calm down his twin and I went in search of Emma.

I found her just where he'd promised. This room was

sectioned off with a long table covered in various food items, and a couch and chair set. Emma sat in the chair and Ezra and Hayes occupied the couch.

When Emma saw me she instantly brightened, waving me over. "Grab a muffin!" She cried, pointing to the table overflowing with food. "They're delicious. This is my third." She held a half-eaten blueberry muffin aloft.

I grabbed a muffin, my mouth already watering. Mathias had let me sleep in, which meant once he did wake me up there'd been no time for breakfast, so I was starved now.

"It's so nice to not be the only girl around here anymore," Emma said when I dropped into the chair beside her.

Hayes turned his attention in our direction and mock-glared at her. "You know you love us."

She sighed, smiling. "Yeah, I suppose I do. You guys are like the annoying over protective brothers I never had."

Hayes chuckled, leveling his eyes on me. "Joshua Hayes," he stuck his hand out for me to shake, "better known as Hayes or The-Greatest-Member-Of-The-Band." His smile made his eyes crinkle at the corners. "I'm sorry I didn't properly introduce myself to you the first time we met. I was in quite a bit of shock that Mathias brought a girl to the studio. He's never done that, but these guys filled me in," he waved his hand around, "and now I understand. So, anyway," he rambled, "I wanted to apologize. I hope I didn't come across as rude, I was just shocked."

I cracked a smile, peeling the wrapper off the bottom of the muffin. "If I'd been in your position I would've been just as shocked and confused, so I understand."

"So, you guys were like high school sweethearts I hear?" He pried.

I coughed on the bite of muffin I'd taken, the small crumbs

tickling the back of my throat. I grabbed a water bottle, and after a moment managed to compose myself. "We were hardly high school sweethearts."

His lips turned down. "But you dated?"

I shrugged. "I suppose." It was nearly impossible to define what our relationship had been. "I mean, we were *together*, but... it was complicated."

Hayes scratched the top of his head, his blond brows pulled together. "God, this is making my brain hurt."

I laughed, setting my half-eaten muffin aside. "We were together in high school, and we're together now. The rest is..." I shrugged, letting my sentence drop.

Hayes shook his head and glanced at Ezra with a wry smile. "What the fuck is wrong with the world that Mathias would get a girl before us?" Grinning at me, he said, "I honestly thought the fucker was going to be alone and miserable his whole life. He's not exactly the easiest person to deal with."

"Neither am I," I countered.

Hayes sat back, tapping his fingers along the armrest of the couch. "Mhmm, I can tell," he smirked. "I think I can see why you two work so well."

"We need you two out here." A woman called, poking her head through the doorway.

Ezra sighed and stood up, stretching his arms above his head before heading out of the room. He hadn't spoken at all since I'd entered the room and from the dark circles beneath his eyes and the pale hue to his skin, I thought the guy might be sick—and yet here he was, showing up to work.

Standing, Hayes smiled down at me. I had to crane my head back to see his face. The dude was a giant. "I'm looking forward to getting to know you, Remy."

I smiled in return and he ducked out of the room. Seriously, he literally *ducked* so his head wouldn't hit the doorway.

I grabbed my muffin up once more, hoping this time I might actually get it eaten.

"I know they can be weird sometimes, and rather nosy, but they're all great guys. We're a family. You included."

I laughed, wiping the crumbs off my jeans. "What an unconventional family."

"I suppose so," she smiled, her shoulders shaking with soft laughter, "but a loving one." Sobering, she turned towards me, tucking her legs behind her on the chair. "When Maddox told me about you and Mathias I always hoped that maybe you guys would find your way back to each other."

"Like fate?" I asked, quirking a brow.

"Yeah, or like soul mates or something."

My lips twitched with the threat of laughter. "I don't believe those things exist."

"How can you say that?" She asked, seeming confused by my easy dismissal of her notion. "You don't think it's possible that there's some cosmic force out there and that nothing, not time nor distance could've prevented you two from ending up together?" Before I could respond she let out a soft curse and covered her mouth. "Shit, I sound like my mom."

I laughed at her, shaking my head. Despite the fact that I didn't really know Emma I still felt comfortable around her. She had one of those easy-going personalities that instantly made you fall in love with her. She was adorably irresistible.

She joined in with my laughter. "This is what I get for being raised by a hippy."

I grinned at that. "Your mom sounds awesome."

"Oh, she is," Emma agreed, "but she's a little out there. I love her for it though."

"What does your mom think of you dating a rock star?" I

asked. If my mom knew I was dating Mathias again she'd probably pass out and my dad would grab a gun. I didn't even want to guess at what their reaction to marriage would be.

Emma smiled, wiggling around in the leather chair. "My mom loves Maddox. I think she might love him more than she loves me," she giggled. "He's quite the charmer."

"It's good that your mom likes him."

"Definitely," she nodded. "I really lucked out." She glanced wistfully at the doorway like Maddox might appear any second. "He was my first boyfriend, my first everything. I also know he'll be my last and I wouldn't have it any other way. I know some people think it's crazy to only ever be with one person and that you're living in a fairytale to think it'll ever last, but I know it will with us."

"I think that's pretty beautiful," I said, and meant it.

She smiled bashfully, her cheeks coloring. "I'm lucky."

"So is he."

She tucked her hair behind her ear and pointed to the doorway. "I guess we should go watch them in action."

I nodded in agreement, throwing away the muffin wrapper and empty bottle of water.

The guys all stood on the stage set up. Well, except for Maddox—he sat behind his drum kit.

Mathias had changed into a pair of gray pants, a button down white shirt tucked into them, with a black belt and tie. His hair was styled away from his face, making his unique gray eyes stand out.

Music pumped out from a pair of speakers and the guys went through the motions of actually performing.

Emma stood beside me, watching them with love in her eyes. To me, she said, "Maddox is obsessed with Diet Pepsi so he was thrilled when Pepsi wanted them to do a commercial. I think this is honestly the highlight of his career," she laughed, shaking her head.

"It's crazy isn't it?" I nodded towards the guys on the stage.

She glanced at me, raising her brow in question.

"I knew them—except for Hayes—way before they were a band. I mean, they still played and Mathias sang some, but it was just something they did. I never imagined it would become who they are. I knew they jokingly talked about trying to make something happen with it, but I guess... I never imagined it would actually happen."

In high school I'd been to a few of their gigs, mostly performances in small venues around our hometown, and I never believed then that it would turn into something more— that they would actually make something out of it. I felt bad for that—for not believing in them more.

Emma shrugged. "Some dreams do come true."

My gaze rose to Mathias and I took a deep breath as his eyes connected with mine and a slow smile graced his lips as he continued to mouth the words to the song. "Yeah," I agreed, "some do."

AFTER THE COMMERCIAL ended we all decided to grab a bite of lunch together before heading over to the recording studio.

The recording studio was located in a plain looking building on the outskirts of L.A. I was sure it had been purposefully designed to look non-descript.

We were the first to arrive and I climbed off the motorcycle, removing the helmet and trying to tame my hair. Mathias stood and took off his helmet as well. He grabbed mine and secured both to the bike.

I startled when he took my face between his hands and placed a soft, chaste kiss on my lips.

"What was that for?" I asked, sounding breathless despite the simple kiss.

He shrugged. "It was because I can."

I let out soft laugh. I should've expected that answer, it was so very Mathias.

Before the others showed up I hastened to ask, "Are you going to tell them? That we're getting married?"

He took my hand, leading me towards the entrance of the studio. I glanced down at our hands. I still wasn't quite used to his new displays of affection, but I was enjoying them.

"I haven't decided yet," he replied, holding the door open for me. I slipped into the darkened space and then followed him down a plain hallway. He opened another door that opened into a private recording studio.

"I don't care," I whispered to his turned back and he glanced at me over his shoulder. "Either way, I'll be happy, but I do think you should say something to your brother. I think he'd be hurt if we excluded him."

Mathias winced and nodded his head. I figured he was agreeing with me, but he still didn't confirm whether or not he'd tell them so I decided to let it drop.

A few minutes later a man entered the studio. He was tall and slender, older—probably in his fifties—with a shiny baldhead.

"This is Julian, our manager." Mathias introduced me with a groan. He was clearly irritated by the man's sudden appearance.

"Hi." I took his outstretched hand. "I'm Remy."

He smiled, his grip firm. His dark eyes shifted from me to Mathias. "Can I talk to you for a moment? Alone," he added, as if his tone hadn't already suggested that I wasn't welcome for this conversation.

Mathias gave me an apologetic look before ducking out of the room behind Julian.

I sighed heavily, taking a seat on the plush leather couch.

A moment later the muffled sound of raised voices could be heard through the door. They sounded like they were arguing and I felt like it might be about me.

A minute later Mathias strode back into the room, slamming the door closed behind him. His hair was mused like he'd been tugging on it.

"Is everything okay?" I asked.

He dropped down onto the seat beside me. "Yeah."

"No, it's not. I can tell." My hand rested on his thigh as I leaned towards him. He slowly turned to look at me and I could see the frustration in his eyes. "What's going on?"

"Just Julian being an ass," he grumbled, his jaw tight with tension. "He needs to mind his own fucking business."

"Was it about me?" I whispered the words, afraid of his answer.

He didn't need to speak though. His eyes said it all.

I let out a disgusted laugh. "Why?"

He shrugged, picking at an invisible piece of lint on his pants. "Julian hates me. I never bring the right kind of attention to the band and I guess he assumes that the same will be true of you."

I narrowed my eyes. "But you never even told him that we were together."

He chuckled, scratching at his lightly stubbled jaw. "Julian is very... perceptive. It's why he's good at his job."

"I'm sorry," I mumbled.

He looked at me quizzically. "Why are you apologizing?"

"I don't know. I just don't want you to be on the outs with

your manager because of me."

He snorted. "I'm always on the outs with Julian. He hates me and I hate him, but I can't deny what he's done for the band."

Before the conversation could go any further the rest of the band joined us along with a few other people.

In no time they were taking turns in the booth.

"Why are you recording a new song?" I asked curiously. "I thought you guys were focused on the tour."

Hayes answered me, but his eyes were trained on the sound booth where Mathias was currently singing. "We're always working on new music. There's never any down time for us."

I processed his answer and sat back against the plush couch. I was beginning to see that all the time I'd been spending with Mathias was rare. More often than not the guys were busy doing something music related. That would be hard to adjust to, but watching Mathias sing and seeing how much he truly did love it, I knew I'd put up with anything for him.

That's what love did to you.

It made you willing to sacrifice your happiness for someone else's.

CHAPTER TWENTY-SEVEN

I STOOD BY the wall of windows in the family room. My arms were crossed over my chest as I watched the sunset. It was a beautiful kaleidoscope of reds, oranges, pinks, and even purple. It was made even more stunning by the way it reflected off of the ocean.

I felt Mathias walk up behind me. His warmth and solid body was a steady presence.

I leaned against him and his hand settled on my waist.

"I got you something," he whispered, his lips ghosting along the shell of my ear.

"You did?" I asked, turning in his arms so that the view was now behind me.

He nodded, reaching into the pocket of his black pants. He pulled out a navy colored jewelry box. Cracking a smile he said, "Don't expect me to get down on my knee. I'm not romantic enough for that."

I tossed my head back, my hair swishing around my shoulders as I laughed. "And yet you bought a ring."

"Arguably, you don't know it's a ring yet, but that is, in fact, the case." He opened the lid, showing me the stunning ring inside.

I stared at the ring with a look of awe. The center was some sort of amber colored jewel, square cut, with small diamonds surrounding it. It was unique and different—beyond anything I could've imagined for myself.

"I didn't think you'd get me a ring." I don't know why those were the first words out of my mouth.

He chuckled, shaking his head and smiled wryly. "I'll admit, I got it for entirely selfish reasons."

"Mhmm, I see." I clucked my tongue.

He took the ring out of the box and reached for my hand. I gave it to him willingly and he slid the ring over my finger. It was a perfect fit. "You're mine, Parker," he smiled triumphantly, "and now everybody else will know too."

I wrapped my arms around his neck and leaned up to kiss him. "Such a caveman," I murmured against his lips, "and for the record, I'm not yours yet, Wade."

He lifted my hand, kissing my fingers just below the ring. "You've always been mine." His eyes were filled with desire and I felt my belly dip with excitement. Cupping my cheeks between his large hands he lowered his head. His voice was nothing more than a soft growl. "Don't deny it."

A sound that could only be described as half-moan, half-sob bubbled out of my throat. I swayed against him, clutching the fabric of his cotton t-shirt between my fingers.

His fingers slid down to my chin and he grasped it between his fingers. I saw a million different thoughts and emotions flicker through his eyes. To anyone else, his eyes were nothing but liquid steel. However, with me, he was never able to mask them so easily.

I waited with baited breath for what he would say.

"Tomorrow."

"Huh?" My brows rose with confusion at his single word.

"Tomorrow. We're leaving for Vegas in the morning, and by this time tomorrow night you'll be my wife."

Before I had a chance to respond he lowered his mouth to mine, stealing all my thoughts, my breath, and maybe even a piece of my soul.

THE AIRPORT IN Vegas had been just as insane as L.A. if not more so, probably brought on by the fact that Willow Creek was playing a show there tonight.

The craziness had followed us all the way to the hotel, where security had to form a barricade for us to reach the door. Emma and I dashed inside while the guys signed autographs and took pictures.

Now, the group of us poured into an elevator, heading up to the penthouse suite of The Mirage. I was wondering how it would work with the group of us sharing a suite, but when the doors opened revealing the massive space I knew it wouldn't be a problem.

"We get the biggest room." Mathias grabbed my arm, rushing around to find it.

Nobody bothered to object and I figured none of them really cared.

When Mathias finally found the room he deemed the biggest he pulled me inside and closed the door.

The room was decorated in muted grays and whites with a bed low to the floor.

I figured his urgency was due to a desire to get naked, but I was wrong.

He paced the length of the room, steepling his fingers

beneath his chin.

"Mathias—" I started and he stopped in front of me. He looked worried, little wrinkles turning down the corners of his mouth.

"I don't know how to tell Maddox."

"Oh," I mumbled, sitting down on the bed. "Uh... I guess that is a problem."

Still frowning, he added, "He might try to talk us out of it."

I shrugged, unaffected. "So? When have we ever listened to anybody else? This is what we want."

"Right," he nodded, resuming his pacing. "It's just... He's my brother. My *twin*. No matter how much I might act like I don't care, I *do*."

"Sit down," I told him, patting the space beside me on the bed. After a few more paces he did. "Stop worrying. We'll go out there and tell him together."

"He's going to be pissed," he warned. "Especially over the fact that mom and dad aren't here."

"We can wait," I whispered, that thought filling me with sadness. "If that's what you want."

"No, absolutely not." He shook his head roughly, rubbing his hands on his jeans. He reached up and removed the baseball cap he wore, spinning it around in his hands before putting it back on, but backwards this time. "This is what I want. I want you to be my wife and I think I might die if I have to wait."

I rolled my eyes, bumping my shoulder against his in jest. "Don't be so dramatic."

He wrinkled his nose and grumbled, "I'm not being dramatic."

I wanted to argue that matter further, but before I could speak he was standing up and heading for the door with a purposeful stride. I guessed he'd made up his mind that it was now or never.

I hurried after him and we found Maddox, Emma, Ezra, and Hayes all hanging out in the living room part of the suite watching TV.

Mathias stood directly in front of the TV, diverting their attention.

"I have something I need to talk to you about." He looked right at Maddox when he spoke. "All of you," he added, his gaze landing on each one of them.

I stepped forward and wrapped my arms around in his, leaning against him.

"What's going on?" Maddox turned the TV off and gave us his full attention.

Mathias wrapped his arm around my waist and cleared his throat. Taking a deep breath the words tumbled out. "A few days ago I asked Remy to marry me and she said yes."

Everybody looked shocked. Seriously, all of their mouths fell open and they looked at us like we were some exotic species they'd never seen before.

Maddox recovered first. "Uh... Wow." He shook his head. "Congratulations guys, that's awesome." He stood, as if to come towards us.

"That's not all." Mathias held up a hand.

"You're having a baby too?!" Emma shrieked so loud that my ears began to ring.

At the word baby I flinched and felt Mathias stiffen against me. "Uh... no. No babies."

"Oh." Emma frowned, looking devastated.

"We're getting married."

Maddox's lips twitched and then he began to laugh. "That's typically what an engagement means." He glanced towards Emma with a wistful look, as if he was imagining what it would be like to be married to her.

"No," Mathias shook his head, "what I mean is, we're getting married today."

He held his head high, his shoulders squared as he braced himself for whatever his twin might say. Mathias didn't care what many people thought of him, but his brother's opinion was one that mattered.

Maddox looked shocked, as did the others—even more shocked than when Mathias said we were engaged.

"But mom and dad aren't here," Maddox argued. "You know mom will be devastated if she misses this."

"I'm doing this for me, not mom and dad."

"Dammit Mathias!" Maddox roared, standing up with his fists clasped at his sides. Emma looked flabbergasted at his sudden outburst and I got the impression that Maddox didn't get mad about much. "Sometimes you have to think about other people besides yourself!"

Mathias grasped my hand and positioned his body slightly in front of me, like he was protecting me. "I don't expect you to understand our decision, but this is what we're doing. We're getting married today whether you like it or not."

Maddox glared at his twin, anger rolling off of him in waves. "You are the most stubborn, arrogant, asshole I've ever met."

Mathias shrugged. "You're not telling me anything I don't know." Despite his carefree attitude I could tell his brother's words had upset him.

"I can't believe you." Maddox's jaw was clenched so tight I was surprised we couldn't hear the grinding of his teeth. Glancing at his watch, he muttered, "Call mom. Before you do this. Call her. And I really hope to God that she makes you feel guilty as fuck."

I watched Mathias' lips twitch. "You never say fuck."

"Yeah well, I'm really fucking pissed off and I guess you're rubbing off on me."

Mathias shook his head. "I'll call her," he promised, turning to leave the room with a tight hold on my hand. Glancing back at his brother, he added, "I don't expect you, or any of you," he added to the rest of the group, "to come but I..." He cleared his throat. "I'd really like for you to be there."

With a nod he ducked out of the room, dragging me along behind him.

Once we were safely in the bedroom he collapsed on the bed. He reached into his back pocket, his fingers fumbling as he pulled out a pack of cigarettes and a lighter.

"I don't think you're allowed to do that in here," I warned.

He glared at me, the cigarette dangling between his pursed lips. "I'm Mathias Fucking Wade and—"

"'I can do whatever the fuck I want,'" I mimed his tone.

He cracked a smile before lighting the cigarette and taking a drag. Blowing out the smoke he watched it circle up to the ceiling before disappearing. "Well, that went about as well as I thought it would."

"Maddox is right, you know," I whispered, fearing his wrath—and sure enough his eyes were cold as ice when they landed on mine. "Your parents should be here. Hell, so should my grandma and my parents... although my dad would probably try to kill you," I mused, shrugging apologetically.

"Are you saying we should wait?" His words were laced with anger.

"No," I shook my head. "I'm just as ready as you are. All I'm saying is, I get where Maddox is coming from and our family is going to be pissed at us."

Mathias shrugged, propping his head up on a pile of fluffy pillows. "Most people are always mad at me for something. I'm used to it."

"Yeah, but your mom and dad also love you."

He turned his head towards me and rolled his eyes. "I've been nothing but a pain in their ass."

"So? You're a pain in mine too, but I still love you."

He stared at me for a moment. "I also fuck you. There's a difference."

I snorted. "Are you saying I love you for the sex?"

"Well, no," he frowned. "I don't really know what I'm saying."

"Obviously," I muttered.

Putting out the cigarette in a decorative vase on the side table he then crossed his arms behind his head. "What time is it?" He asked.

"Ten," I replied.

"Would you be opposed to getting married tomorrow evening instead of tonight?"

"Uh..." My brows furrowed. "What are you thinking?"

"Postponing would give me enough time to get my mom and dad on a plane—your grandma too."

I smiled at that, nodding eagerly. I would be fine with it only being the two of us standing in a chapel somewhere, but it felt *right* having our family there. It made it more real.

"What about your mom and dad?" He asked.

I frowned, thinking of them and my brother. I shook my head, hoping he didn't notice how much my next words bothered me. "They wouldn't understand."

"Rem." His voice deepened as he reached for me. He pulled me down onto the bed beside him. I tossed one of my legs over his and he wrapped his arms around me. My hand rested on his chest as I curled against him. His heat warmed me, instantly filling my body with calmness. "I'm sorry."

"Don't be," I whispered. "I love you and that's all that matters."

He kissed the top of my head and my eyes closed as a happy sigh escaped my parted lips. "I'm one lucky bastard."

I poked his side, grinning. "And don't you ever forget it."

"Never." He pressed closer to me, lowering his lips to mine. The kiss was slow and deep, making my toes curl. Kissing my forehead he pulled away and sat up, grabbing his phone. "I have some phone calls to make."

I nodded, my heart beginning to race with anticipation. Be it today, or tomorrow, the thought of marrying him filled me with the kind of excitement I so very rarely felt. I knew that if this was any other person I wouldn't feel this way.

This was once in a lifetime—and I got it twice, because I got a second chance.

"You can stop glaring at me like you want to kill me." Mathias snapped at his twin when we joined the others at the hotel restaurant for dinner.

After making all the arrangements for his mom, dad, and my grandma to fly out to Vegas we'd emerged from the bedroom to find that everyone else had left. I knew that pissed Mathias off, but he managed to keep his anger tamped down. I saw now that it might still be unleashed.

"We're getting married *tomorrow*," he emphasized the word, "and mom and dad will be here *tonight*."

"They're coming?" Maddox asked, brightening with this news.

Mathias nodded and looked at me before speaking. "We agreed that it would be best to have them here."

"Good." Maddox plucked at the collar of his shirt like it was suddenly too tight.

Mathias sighed, grabbing my hand beneath the table. I knew he wouldn't say it, but he was relieved to have Maddox back on his side.

A waiter appeared to take our orders and I picked the first thing I saw on the menu. I wasn't very hungry. I was nervous to see them perform tonight. I knew it would be a vastly different experience seeing them on a concert stage versus hanging around in the recording studio. But I was actually the most nervous for the questions I might be asked.

On our way to the restaurant I saw someone reading a magazine.

My face was on the cover, with the caption *Who is she?*

I'd known going into this that my life was going to change, but imagining it and seeing it were two different things.

"Are you okay?" Mathias whispered in my ear, picking up on my distress.

"Yeah," I nodded. I didn't want to worry him with my silly fears. I was strong and I'd get through this. Nothing knocked me down for long, not even my own self-doubt.

He looked at me doubtfully, but since the others were around he didn't press the issue.

Emma waved her hand, trying to catch my attention. I raised my chin in her direction to let her know I was listening.

"Since y'all are postponing until tomorrow this means we can get you a wedding dress."

I blanched. "Uh... I was just going to wear jeans."

Emma looked like she'd been shot she was so shocked. Her eyes threatened to bug out of her head. "Jeans? You can't wear jeans to your wedding! I mean, I'm all for non-traditional but there has to be some sort of dress."

I hung my head. Shit.

I glanced at Mathias. "Are you wearing a tux?"

"Yes," he replied.

"Of course," I sighed. I shouldn't have expected any less since he was always dressed impeccably.

"We might be getting married in Vegas," he tapped his chin, "but this won't be a typical Vegas wedding. We're definitely not getting married by an Elvis impersonator."

"Does that mean we're going to the drive-thru chapel?"

He snorted. "I love that you sound excited by that idea, but no. I have something else in mind."

"What is this 'something else' you have in mind?" I coaxed, rubbing my hand up his thigh.

He grabbed my roaming hand and put it back in my lap. I pouted—not even caring if someone noticed my downturned lip.

"This might be a last minute wedding, but it's still going to be a wedding," he promised.

"You're making my brain hurt," I grumbled.

Everybody else was watching the volley of our conversation with rapt attention.

"Just don't worry about it. I have it taken care of."

Of course he did—and I wasn't surprised he wasn't going to tell me more than that. Typical Mathias. I was secretly glad that I didn't have to be a part of whatever he was planning. He was better at that kind of stuff than me. All I wanted to do was show up—and I guess now wear a dress.

Talk of our wedding ceased and the guys lapsed into conversation about the concert and what songs they were performing.

Mathias chatted easily with them, even throwing in a smile or two. Based on the reactions from the other three guys it was easy to guess that this was a new development. I knew Mathias was usually extremely quiet around others—and when he did open his mouth it was usually to say something rude.

Emma asked me questions about which kind of dress I thought I'd like. I tried to answer as best as I could, but when I proved useless she finally smiled and said, "We'll go to a store and take a look around. You can try on a few and we can even Facetime my best friend. She's a stylist and has her own store now, so she might be able to help us. She's better at this kind of thing than I am."

After we finished our dinner we were ushered out of the restaurant by a group of body guards, through the lobby, and out into a waiting limo.

"A limo?" I asked Mathias, arching a brow as I climbed inside. Lights flashed around us and the roar of the crowd was deafening—and I knew it was only going to get worse once we arrived at the venue.

"It was the only thing large enough so that we didn't have to take separate vehicles."

He was right about that, but I still found the massive machine to be obnoxious.

"What's this concert for?" I asked him.

We sat at the end of the limo in front of the divider that separated us from the driver. Hayes sat to our left, Ezra to our right, and Emma and Maddox occupied the seats in front of us. There was still enough room for a few more people.

"It's a benefit concert so there are a few more artists here. We're all playing two songs," he replied, adjusting his bow tie. I *really* liked that bow tie. I hoped he wore it tomorrow too.

"So what's the cause this is for?" I was prepared for him to snap and tell me I was asking too many questions, but he didn't.

"Kids with cancer."

I snorted. Why did they pick Vegas for this? Also, I couldn't help thinking of the little girl at the restaurant who he'd been so kind too. So many kids had to suffer and it was heartbreaking.

As if answering my unspoken question, he said, "I think they chose Vegas because so many people are here on break for Christmas and New Year's. Drunk people like to spend money."

I snorted at his serious tone. Sobering, I said, "I can't believe it's almost Christmas. Wasn't it just Thanksgiving?"

He chuckled, leaning over to graze his fingers along my collarbone, and eliciting a shiver from me. "Feels that way, but we've been a little too wrapped up in each other."

I guessed that did explain it.

The limo came to a stop and a moment later the door opened.

Before we even got out of the car the flashes and clicks of cameras was nearly overwhelming—not to mention the screaming.

Mathias held tightly to my hand like he was afraid I might get sucked into the crowd and lost forever.

People screamed the guys' names, thrusting out scraps of paper and boobs for them to sign. Ezra and Maddox stopped to sign a few autographs, Mathias ignored everyone like they didn't even exist, and Hayes dove after the boobs with a grin on his face like he'd just one the lottery. Maybe he had. The Boob Lottery.

We were ushered through a backdoor and then into a large waiting area. Willow Creek was written on a piece of paper and taped to the door.

"Who are the other artists?" I asked anyone that would answer me.

Hayes began naming different bands, ticking each one off on his finger. There were four other bands besides Willow Creek performing and each one was a big name.

There was still an hour before they went out so everybody settled into the room. Maddox sat in the corner knitting—yes, knitting—Hayes tuned his guitar, Ezra napped on the couch, and Mathias was busy fixing his hair.

I joined Emma in the corner where she sat on the floor.

"I can't believe I'm getting married," I admitted to her. "I never thought I would."

Her smile was kind. "There are a lot of things we all think we'll never do, and then life throws you a curveball and you see that the things you didn't want are exactly what you need." Clearing her throat, she added, "As long as you're happy that's all that matters."

"I am happy," I nodded, rubbing my suddenly sweaty palms on my ripped jeans. "So," I turned to her, "what was your curveball?"

She sighed dreamily and smiled at Maddox. "Him."

I liked her answer.

Because mine was the same.

Just a different guy.

It wasn't long until a man walked by the door and said, "Thirty minutes." Then, "Fifteen."

When it was five minutes until Willow Creek went on stage they were ushered out of the room. Maddox stopped to give Emma a kiss and I was surprised when Mathias did the same with me.

His hand was a steady weight against my waist. He lowered his voice to a whisper. "It makes me happy to know that you're going to be standing out there watching me."

With those words he pulled away and hurried after the guys.

Emma and I lagged behind talking while the guys got wired up or whatever it was they were doing.

I gave Mathias a smile and thumbs up before he stepped out

on the stage. It was an awkward gesture, but he grinned and tipped his head in my direction, so at least he seemed to appreciate it.

Emma and I stood off to the side of the stage, against the wall so that we weren't in the way of the people working.

I watched Mathias walk up to the microphone and the others took their places as well.

He spoke to the crowd for a moment, working them into a frenzy.

Mathias might not have been the best people pleaser, but when it came to the band he knew how to put his game face on and make people fall in love with him.

The crowd chanted, "Willow Creek!" over and over again to the point that when he started to sing I doubted they even heard him.

Where Emma and I stood the view of the stage was rather awkward, but I wasn't going to complain. We were incredibly close to the stage, but positioned to the left and a little behind them.

"They're breathtaking, aren't they?" She asked, swaying to the music. The purple hue of the stage lights made her face glow with an ethereal light.

"That they are." I agreed wholeheartedly.

In the blink of an eye their set came to a close and they drifted off the stage.

Their clothes and hair were damp with sweat, but they all smiled victoriously like they'd just run a marathon and come in first place.

Mathias brushed his hair away from his eyes with a sweep of his long fingers. "So, what did you think?" He asked, looking down at me.

"You were amazing. So you think you can sing to me all of

the time?" I joked. "Our life can be one big cheesy musical."

He tossed his head back and his laughter echoed around us. It didn't escape my notice how his brother, Emma, Hayes, and Ezra looked at him like he was a stranger when they saw him laugh. Slinging his arm over my shoulder he guided me back to the room we'd been in before. "How about I stick to singing you to sleep?"

"He sings her to sleep?" I heard Ezra whisper under his breath behind us. I snorted and hastily tried to turn the noise into a cough.

"Yes, I do," Mathias chimed, having heard his band mate.

"Who the fuck are you?" Ezra asked, shaking his head so that his black curls bounced.

"The new and improved Mathias," he joked, releasing me from his hold.

They had some clean clothes stashed in a duffel bag so each of the guys took the time to change.

There was nothing left for us to do there so we headed outside and into the waiting limo. There was still a crowd but it had thinned out a lot.

"I think we should go dress shopping," Emma announced.

I looked at her like she was crazy. "It's after midnight."

Now it was her turn to look at me like I was the crazy person. "This is Vegas. It only comes to life at night."

Across from me Maddox frowned and when I looked at Mathias he had the same look on his face. They both spoke at the same time, saying the same thing. "I don't want you out at night by yourselves."

Emma and I looked at each other, both breaking out into laughter.

"Stop laughing," Mathias groaned.

Maddox shook his head, rubbing his chin to hide his smile.

"Ezra will go with us." Emma pointed to the bass player currently sprawled out on three seats.

"Me?" He pointed at his t-shirt clad chest. "Why me?"

"Because I know you're just going to go back to the hotel and do nothing," she reasoned.

"What about Hayes?" He swung his arm in the direction of the giant guitar player. The guy had to be well over six-foot-four, but he was thin and lean.

"I'm sure Hayes wants to go out."

"Mhmm," Ezra hummed in agreement, "therefore he can go out with you. I'm tired."

"And awfully cranky," she added on. "What's wrong with you?"

"Nothing," he grumbled, looking away.

She clearly didn't believe him, but let it go. "I think Hayes' idea of going out is to a club, not wedding dress shopping."

"You've got that right." Hayes finally piped in.

"Maddox and I can go with you," Mathias added.

"No!" Emma cried, leaning forward like she was ready to lunge at him. "You're the groom, therefore you can't see the dress beforehand. Besides, you two can have some twin bonding time or whatever."

Mathias rolled his eyes and huffed a sigh. "I don't see what difference it makes. I'm going to see the dress at some point, and then I'm going to rip it off of her later."

"We don't need the details." Maddox held up a warning hand, but was fighting a smile.

Mathias shrugged. "Don't be such a fucking priss. Everybody knows what happens after the wedding and it isn't playing Scrabble."

I laughed, burying my face into the curve of his shoulder to muffle the sound.

"Fine, fine, fine." Ezra sat up, his messy black hair sticking up wildly around his head. "I'll go with them so you two don't have to worry and you," he pointed at Hayes, "can go have fun."

"Thanks, Ez." Maddox reached forward, clapping Ezra on the shoulder.

Ezra finally cracked a smile, his dark brown eyes lightening. "Yeah, well, you guys are right. They shouldn't be out on the streets alone. Not here."

The limo came to a stop at the hotel and after a quick kiss Mathias ducked out along with Hayes and Maddox.

Emma spoke to the driver, telling him where we wanted to go. A moment later we pulled away from the hotel.

Ezra stretched out once more on the seat, crooking his arm over his eyes. "I could be sleeping right now. Instead, I'm going to look at wedding dresses. Remind me, how did I get talked into this?"

"Because you love me." Emma laughed, kicking his knee with her foot.

He grumbled, but smiled in her direction. Yeah, yeah. I guess I do."

"I'm extremely lovable," she agreed.

The two bickered back and forth for a while like siblings.

It didn't take us long to arrive at the dress shop. I could tell from the outside alone that this place was going to be crazy expensive. Before I could tell Emma we needed to find another store she held out a shiny black credit card.

"Mathias gave me his card. Don't worry about it."

I still didn't breathe a sigh of relief. It seemed unfair for Mathias to be spending a ridiculous amount of money on a dress I'd wear once. Not to mention the expensive ring he'd already put on my finger, and there was no telling what he had planned for tomorrow.

"Don't worry about it," Emma repeated as Ezra headed for the door of the building. "Seriously. He just wants you to be happy and..." She blushed. "He also said the dress was for him too—he told me to make sure you got something sexy so that all he can think about is... uh... all the ways he... uh..." Her cheeks went from pink to red. "...wants to fuck you... His words. Not mine."

I laughed at poor Emma, following behind her and Ezra.

Emma pulled out her phone and glanced at me over her shoulder. "Do you mind if I Facetime Sadie?"

"Sadie?" I asked, confused.

"Yeah, my best friend. The stylist."

"Oh, yeah. Sounds good." I shook my head, noticing the way Ezra's whole body tensed at the mention of Sadie's name.

"What's wrong with him?" I asked, pointing to where Ezra stood broodingly against the wall with his arms crossed over his lean chest.

She followed my gaze and frowned. "He's not normally so forlorn," she shrugged, "but..." She paused, as if she wasn't sure how much she should say. Finally she sighed and seemed to decide to tell me the whole thing. "He became really good friends with Sadie after Maddox and I started dating—I guess you could almost say they're best friends. They bonded over their interests and then Maddox and I kind of ditched them a lot, which forced them together. Anyway," she took a deep breath before pushing forward, "Sadie's been dating this one guy, Braden, and he's kind of an asshole. I don't like him and Ezra definitely hates him. He's just a jerk and he doesn't treat her very well, but he asked her to marry him over Thanksgiving and she said yes. Ezra thinks she's absolutely stupid, and said as much, so she's not speaking to him right now. I think she's being dumb too, but Sadie always does what Sadie wants." She shrugged, trying to act like she didn't care, but I could tell she did.

"Well, that sucks," I said, for lack of anything else to say.

She nodded, and her eyes looked haunted. The guy must've been a real tool. I really hoped her friend got away from him before she ended up married with a kid.

"Enough of that." She waved her phone around. "Sadie will want to help."

"Isn't it like four in the morning there?" I asked before she could call her friend.

"Crap," she put her phone away, "you're right. Sadie will be pissed if I wake her up. I guess you're stuck with only my help. I'm really not good at this kind of stuff, but I can pass my opinion."

"Sounds good," I agreed.

A woman approached to help us and proceeded to ask me a million questions about what kind of dress I wanted. She very quickly learned I had no idea.

The only word I could give her was, "Sexy." It was what Mathias wanted and me too. I didn't want the typical wedding dress. I wanted something daring.

She nodded and said, "I think I know just the dress."

She dashed off through a door, mumbling that she'd be back in a minute.

"We need a dress for you too," I told Emma.

"Me?" She pointed at herself, looking shocked.

"Yeah, you," I laughed. "You're going to be my bridesmaid."

"Me?" She repeated. "Are you sure?"

"Absolutely."

I didn't know Emma well, but I really liked her. And now that Mathias and I were tying the knot Emma and I would be spending a lot of time together. I felt that given enough time we could become really good friends. Maybe even best friends. I'd never had a best friend before. Yeah, Lana and I had been friends in high school, but I'd never confided in her the way best friends did. I wasn't a very trusting person, but there was something about Emma that made me feel instantly at ease. I knew I could tell her something personal and she wouldn't go blabbing to anyone, not even Maddox.

"Wow," she smiled. "I'm honored."

"You can pick whatever you like," I told her, waving my hand to encompass the store. "It's not like I have anything in mind."

"But it's your wedding."

I shook my head, smiling. "That might be true, but I don't care about the details. All I care about is the fact that the man I love will be waiting for me at the end of the aisle."

Her smile lit her whole face. "That is the important part. A lot of people seem to lose sight of that."

I nodded in agreement.

The sales lady returned a few minutes later with three dresses in garment bags tossed over her arm.

"Dressing rooms are back here," she nodded, "follow me."

Ezra grunted, looking extremely uncomfortable. "I'll stay here."

Emma followed me back to the dressing area and took a seat while the woman ushered me into one of the closed off rooms.

I undressed and she helped me into the first gown. I glanced at it in the mirror, my eyes widening.

"Do you like it?" She asked.

"I love it," I breathed. I ran my fingers along the lacey fabric, admiring my reflection in the mirror.

The dress was stunning. But it was also daring and sexy, just like I had asked for. The top was done in an intricate lacey design with a nude colored background. It had short-sleeves, but somehow it didn't look stuffy and added to the sexiness of the dress. It dipped down low in the chest area, showing off my cleavage, but not enough to be trashy.

It was then accented with a thick gold belt.

The bottom of the dress was a loose tulle-like fabric with a high slit on the side. In the back there was a short train.

I also liked that it was cream colored instead of stark white.

I spun around, looking at the dress from all angles.

I could tell the saleslady was pleased that I loved it.

"Would you like to show your friend?" She asked.

I nodded, unable to form words at the moment.

She opened the door and I stepped out so that Emma could see.

She gasped, her hands flying up to cover her mouth. "Oh my God," she gasped. "Please tell me you love it. It's... Wow."

I stood up on the podium, looking in the mirrors once more. "I think I'm in love."

Emma squealed, clapping her hands together.

I turned towards her and frowned. "Do you think it's wrong to fall in love with the first one?"

"Sometimes the first one is the right one."

Her words hit me hard as I realized how true they were.

Mathias was the first guy I ever loved, and he'd be the last.

The same was true for her and Maddox.

Any worries I had about choosing the first dress I tried on evaporated.

"I'll take it." I told the saleslady.

"Excellent."

She took me back into the room and helped me out of the dress.

"We'll have this dry cleaned and sent to your hotel by tomorrow afternoon. Just leave us with your information."

I nodded. "I'd also like to get a bridesmaid dress for my friend.

"Of course," she smiled. "What do you have in mind?"

"Something gold or champagne colored."

I hadn't had anything in mind for Emma's dress before, but since my dress had the gold belt I thought it would be nice to have her dress in that color tone.

"I'll be back with a few options."

She took my dress and slipped out of the room while I finished putting my clothes back on.

"She's going to grab some dresses for you." I told Emma when I emerged from the room.

"This is so exciting! I can't believe Mathias is going to be the first to get married."

I laughed. "Yeah, I'm pretty sure everyone thought that would be you and Maddox."

She smiled, giving a slight shrug. "He would've married me years ago if I let him, but I wanted to wait. We met so young and I wanted us to have fun being a couple before we put such a heavy label on our relationship."

"That's wise," I agreed.

"I think I'm ready now, though," she added.

"Have you told him that?" I asked, sitting down beside her.

Her nose crinkled. "No."

The saleslady breezed up to us with a selection of dresses. I immediately vetoed a few, but one in particular caught my eye. "This one," I said.

It was an elegant gold sequined dress that shimmered when the light hit it. It was in a similar style as my gown, with slightly longer sleeves and no slit. I thought it would be gorgeous on Emma, with her fair complexion, freckles, and wild blonde hair.

"That one is my favorite too," Emma whispered.

This time it was her turn to be ushered into one of the closed off dressing rooms. I sat waiting patiently.

When she stepped out of the room I gasped.

"You like it?" She asked, spinning in a circle.

"It's perfect!" I couldn't hide my smile or the excitement I felt.

This was really happening.

And while I wouldn't have minded it just being Mathias and I, it was even better knowing the ones we'd love would be there.

I knew it wouldn't be a lavish wedding, and that was fine by me, because it was still going to be perfect for us.

After paying for the dresses, and leaving the information for the hotel so they could deliver, we headed out.

"That was surprisingly fast." Ezra commented, as we walked down the street to where the limo was parked waiting for us. "I thought we'd be there for a few hours."

"I'm not like most girls," I quipped.

He chuckled, flashing me a genuine smile. Bumping my shoulder playfully, he said, "I know. You couldn't be like most girls in order to deal with all of Mathias' bullshit."

I laughed in agreement.

"I want you to know that all of us think you're really good for him," Ezra confessed, his voice dropping low. "I don't think any of us have ever seen him so happy. So... uh... well, thanks."

We slipped into the limo and I stared at Ezra, not knowing what to say.

He stretched out on the seat and closed his eyes, saving me from having to reply. "I'm going to sleep," he announced.

"We'll be back at the hotel in like ten minutes," Emma cried.

Ezra yawned. "And that's ten minutes of sleep I can have. Now shush."

Emma shook her head and mouthed, "Boys," to me.

I was with Ezra though. I suddenly felt absolutely exhausted and all I wanted to do was go to bed.

When we arrived at the hotel the three of us made our way clumsily to the elevator. It seemed the need to sleep had finally caught up to Emma as well.

I swore Ezra fell back to sleep standing in the elevator, but when the door slid open he promptly strode off towards his room.

"Goodnight," Emma chimed, waving at me before walking in the direction of the room she shared with Maddox.

I stopped off in the kitchen and grabbed a bottle of water.

The bedroom was dark when I opened the door, but the sheets rustled and a light soon flicked on.

"Hey," Mathias greeted me, his voice thick with sleep. "You're back. Did you find a dress?"

"I did," I smiled, leaning over to kiss him. He groaned low in his throat at the feel of my lips and cupped the nape of neck, deepening the kiss. "You're going to love it." I told him when he finally released me.

He looked me up and down, his eyes darkening to the color of storm clouds. "Not as much as I love what's underneath."

"Pig," I scolded, taking my shirt off and throwing it at him.

He deflected it easily, his eyes roaming my body hungrily as I changed into my pajamas.

"Don't get any ideas, Wade," I warned, peeking at him over my shoulder. "I'm exhausted."

He pouted like a five year old, and instead of it making him look silly he was made even more irresistible. Damn him.

I padded into the bathroom to brush my teeth and returned to bed.

He lifted the sheet up and I slipped in beside him. I was instantly cradled against his large body.

"I missed you." He whispered the words so low it was like he didn't want me to hear them. "It's the craziest thing, even when I know you're coming back and won't be gone long, I still miss you. While you're gone there's this ache in my chest that won't go away." Kissing the top of my head, he murmured, "I ached like that for seven whole years, Remy. Seven. It was like my own personal hell."

Tears pricked my eyes at his confession. "It was hell for me too."

In those seven years my hatred had tried to overshadow my love for him. I'd still missed him though, against all logic. I'd ached and pined for him. I'd tried so hard to extinguish the flame that burned bright inside me for him, but I never could— and if I had succeeded we wouldn't be here right now. Nothing would've been able to stop me from my plan to hurt him. But love is a funny thing, once it's given you can't take it back. It's forever, no matter what happens. You might move on, but at the end of the day you can't change the fact that you loved someone and they'll always own a piece of your heart. Mathias owned all of my pieces.

"Let's never hurt each other again." His voice was a soft sigh in the dark. "Deal?"

"Deal."

CRAZINESS ENSUED FROM the moment I woke up. Mathias and the guys bowed out, citing that they were working to get everything set up for the wedding.

That left Emma and me alone.

"I hope you don't want help with your hair or makeup," she told me over breakfast, "because I suck at that."

I assured her I could manage. I didn't bother telling her that Mathias had already offered to hire a hair and makeup artist, but I refused. I didn't want today to turn into a circus.

Time passed in a blur and before I could blink it was evening and time to finish getting ready.

Emma had already helped me into my dress and I now stood freshening my makeup.

She poked her head into the doorway of the bathroom.

"Maddox just texted me and said to meet them in the ballroom. There will be bodyguards waiting for us when we get off the elevator."

I frowned. "Is it crazy down there or something?"

She sighed. "Someone from the hotel tipped off the media that there was going to be a high profile wedding here tonight, so they've swarmed the hotel like the vultures they are. Apparently they're camped out in the lobby." She rolled her eyes and glanced down at her phone. Looking back up at me, she said, "You'd think they'd have something better to do than stalk famous people."

I added a pale pink gloss to my lips and another swipe of mascara. My makeup was understated, but I didn't want an overly dramatic look. My hair was simple too. I'd curled the normally straight strands into loose waves.

"You look gorgeous," Emma smiled, leaning against the doorjamb.

"Thank you."

"Are you ready?" She asked, checking her phone again.

I took a deep breath and smiled at my reflection. "Yes."

I was nervous, but also incredibly excited.

I followed her out of the suite and into the elevator.

My heart thumped so loud that I heard every beat ringing clearly in my ears like it was counting down the seconds until

Mathias became my husband.

I never thought I would be the kind of person to get emotional over this sort of thing but I was seconds away from bursting into tears—happy ones and some sad ones too, because Hope wasn't here to see this.

Emma and I were silent on the ride down in the elevator. I think she knew that I didn't want to talk.

As soon as the elevator doors opened the two hulking bodyguards turned and spotted us. They managed to block us with their large bodies as paparazzi scrambled to take a photo and hotel management yelled at them to get off the property.

We were quickly ushered out of the space and down a hallway.

Tall wooden double doors came into view and my heart raced impossibly faster.

I knew that Mathias was behind that door.

Waiting for me.

This was it.

A woman I'd never seen before handed Emma and me a bouquet of flowers.

"Ready?" The woman asked.

Emma looked to me for confirmation.

"Yes." The word was barely a breath.

The doors swung open and Emma stepped forward, gliding down the aisle.

Then the music changed and that was my cue.

I took a step and halted, taking in the magnificent room.

The ballroom had been sectioned of with thick sheets of gold hued fabric, creating a more intimate space.

The only guests seated were Hayes, Ezra, Karen, Paul, and my grandma.

I knew to most people that was hardly an appropriate

amount of guests to have at a wedding, but for us it was just right.

The lights were dimmed and the aisle was covered in white rose petals. For someone that claimed to be so unromantic Mathias was actually quite good at it.

At that moment my eyes landed on him and everything else—the room, the music, and even the people—ceased to exist.

It was only the two us tethered together by a connection so intense that even if we lived a hundred years we'd never understand it.

I felt weightless as my feet carried me up to the altar where he stood waiting for me.

I knew people always talked about the bride taking away the breath of the groom, but right now I'd say we were equally breathless.

His broad shoulders were accentuated by the cut of the black tuxedo. It was adorned with a bow tie—which made me smile—and I was pretty sure he was probably hiding some suspenders under there. He was right, while I might make fun of him, I really did love those suspenders.

Emma took the bouquet of flowers from me and Mathias clasped our hands together.

Somehow over the pounding of my heart I managed to hear the words the minister—or whoever he was—spoke. We took our turns saying our vows and when he slipped the simple silver band on my finger I knew I'd never felt more complete than I did right now.

My whole life, the good and the bad, had all been leading to this one single moment.

I knew, in Mathias, I had found my home.

Emma handed me my ring for Mathias and I shook my head, beaming at him.

He truly had thought of everything.

He didn't think he was a Prince, or a knight in shining armor, or anything worthy of a title or praise.

But he was all those things and more to me.

I slid the ring onto his finger, staring at the thick band that symbolized our love and commitment to each other.

I was filled with such joy that I thought I might burst. I never knew it was possible to be this inexplicably happy.

Something was said about kissing the bride and then Mathias took my face between his hands, lowering his lips to mine. I clutched at his arms to keep myself upright. I really thought I might pass out.

His lips glided against mine and I moaned into his mouth.

With a chuckle he broke the kiss, placing one last tender kiss to the end of my nose.

He leaned his forehead against mine, his hands still cupping my face tenderly.

"Hello, wife."

"Hello, husband," I replied breathlessly.

His tongue flicked out to moisten his lips and he kissed me softly once more.

He took a step back and his hand slid down to hold my mine.

Facing our family and friends we were introduced as, "Mr. and Mrs. Wade."

I smiled, happiness fluttering through my body. Normally I'd argue that it was archaic for the woman to have to take the man's name, but I didn't care.

I was proud to be a Wade now and even prouder to be his.

CHAPTER TWENTY-EIGHT

SINCE THERE WERE so few of us Mathias arranged for all of us to have a nice dinner versus a reception.

"I can't believe you were really going to do this without me here." Grandma glared at me from across the table.

"I'm sorry," I shrugged, leaning against Mathias. Since the moment we'd said 'I do' we had yet to cease touching one another in some way. "You're here, that's what matters."

"And I have him to thank for that." She pointed her fork at Mathias.

Mathias smiled at her. In fact, he hadn't stopped smiling since his eyes landed on me when I stepped into the ballroom. I couldn't recall a time I had ever seen him this happy.

"Yes, ma'am." He tipped his head in her direction.

"See, he's a good boy, and you're just a disgrace."

I sighed. My grandma was always going to love to poke fun at me.

"Not that we're not thrilled," Paul, Mathias' foster dad, spoke up, "but what made you guys decide to do this?"

I looked at Mathias and he looked at me.

Shrugging, Mathias said, "It was going to happen one day. Why wait?"

Paul nodded, absorbing Mathias' words.

After chatting for at least an hour everybody stood to head off to their rooms.

Mathias grasped my wrist, brushing my hair away from my ear so that he could whisper, "I got us our own room."

"Why?" I asked. "We have plenty of space in the penthouse."

He shook his head and his breath fanned across my cheek, making me shiver. "I plan on hearing you scream my name all night long and nobody but me is going to hear that."

I shivered again. I nodded, having momentarily lost my voice.

Before we could head off in the direction of our own room my grandma cleared her throat. "Can I talk to you?" She asked me.

I glanced at Mathias and he waved his hand in her direction and walked off to give us some space.

"What's wrong?" I asked.

She stared at Mathias over my shoulder and then back at me. "Does he know?"

My heart stopped beating in my chest.

It was one thing knowing in my heart that it was wrong to keep Hope a secret, it was another hearing the complete disapproval in my grandma's voice. She looked at me with angry, accusing eyes.

"He has a right to know, Remy."

I didn't know how my grandma could possibly know that I'd never told Mathias about Hope. But then again, she always did seem to have some kind of freaky telepathy.

I swallowed past the lump now lodged deep in my throat. "I know." My voice cracked. "Fuck, I know," I groaned. I buried my face in my hands, trying to force back the sting in my eyes.

"That baby was his too." She reached up and pulled my

hands from my face, her grip surprisingly strong despite her frail frame. Her eyes were now filled with sadness. "I know it killed you, pretty girl, but this is the kind of secret that can destroy a relationship and now..." She trailed off.

"A marriage," I supplied for her.

She nodded, patting my cheek. "Tell him. Keeping this a secret will tear you apart. You're a strong woman Remy, but there are some things not even the strongest person can bear to live with. He can handle it. I have faith in the both of you."

I took a deep breath and nodded. "I will. I just... I need some more time." I bent down and wrapped my arms around her. She hugged me back fiercely—like she was trying to infuse her strength into me so that I would be strong enough to do this.

"I love you," she whispered, kissing my cheek. "And I'm so proud of the person you've become."

"Thank you." I hastily wiped away a tear. "I love you too."

She headed off in the direction of the elevators and I turned to Mathias. He'd long ago removed his jacket and was left in a crisp white shirt and, no surprise, suspenders.

"What was that about?" He asked, meeting me halfway.

"She just wanted to give me some marriage advice," I lied.

He chuckled, not picking up on the note of falsity in my tone. "I'm sure that was some epic advice."

"Yeah, it was great," I mumbled, following him to the elevators.

I needed to get my emotions under control before he noticed something was wrong with me. The last thing I wanted to do was ruin tonight for us.

"Care to share?" He asked as the elevator doors slid open. We stepped inside and he pushed the correct floor number, spinning the room keycard between his fingers.

"Oh, um, she'd probably kill me if I told you. It's a secret."

He stared at me, his eyes flitting over my features. His lips turned down into a frown. "Are you okay?"

"Yeah," I assured him quickly. "I'm a little emotional, but okay." That sounded believable, right?

He reached out, brushing his fingers lightly down my cheek. His touch sent little sparks zinging through my body and I closed my eyes, inhaling a ragged breath. I hoped that my body never stopped reacting to him like that.

I absorbed the feeling of his fingers on my face and leaned into his body, my palms flat on his chest.

I feared that when I told him about Hope he'd hate me. That it would truly be the end of us and I would never be touched, held, or loved by him again. I'd lived without him once and it had been the worst kind of torture imaginable. I wasn't sure I could go through that again.

But I also knew that this secret would strangle me from the inside out if I kept it much longer.

Soon, I chanted in my head. *I'll tell him soon.*

The elevator doors slid open and he took my hand, leading me down the hallway. He looked at me over his shoulder, a small smile curving his full lips.

He quickly opened the door to the room and yanked me inside. As soon as the door was shut he pushed me against it, his lips coming down to cover my own. A little hum worked its way out of his throat and I gasped when his fingers dug into my thighs, lifting me up. My legs wound around his waist and my fingers grasped at the short strands of his brown hair, holding him to me.

His tongue slid past the seam of my lips and I moaned, my hips rolling against his.

He carried me away from the door and a moment later I found myself sprawled on the bed.

He gazed down at me with dark eyes, licking his lips.

"God, that fucking dress couldn't have been more perfect."

"You like it?" The words came out as a gasp as I struggled to get enough air into my lungs.

"I fucking love it."

He pulled at his bow tie and it dropped to the floor, then the suspenders, and his shirt.

"What? I don't get the whole striptease?" I pouted as he stalked towards me.

He chuckled huskily and leaned down, kissing the spot on my neck where my pulse fluttered like a frightened bird. "I want this to last as long as possible, and if my pants come off now it'll be over before it even starts, and that would be embarrassing." He rose up and winked at me.

I took his face between my hands, the light stubble scratching the palms of my hands. I ran my finger along his bottom lip and his eyes closed as he sighed.

"Fuck," he groaned, his eyes liquid fire when they opened. "This doesn't feel real."

"I know what you mean," I whispered.

He swallowed thickly and kissed me, his hands roaming down my body. One hand landed on my bare thigh and snaked up through the open slit in the dress.

"I've never seen anything more beautiful than you in this dress, standing in front of me, saying 'I do.'" He whispered against my lips before kissing his way down my neck and over the exposed curves of my breasts.

"I t-thought you said you w-weren't romantic," I panted, trying to catch my breath.

His chuckle vibrated against my chest. "I'm not, but I'm working on it. I find that you make me want to do and say things I would normally find repulsive."

"Uh... thanks?"

He stared down at me with a contemplative expression. "It's a good thing, Rem."

"Just shut up." I grabbed his hair between my fingers and hooked a leg around his waist, pushing so that he fell with his back on the bed and I was on top.

Oh, yes.

I covered his mouth with mine, kissing him so deeply that the texture of his lips would be imprinted on mine for days.

My hands snaked down his hard chest and over his abs.

When my lips and tongue followed the journey of my hands he groaned. "Oh, fuck."

I reached for the button on his pants and he grabbed my hand.

"No," he growled, his eyes darkened with desire.

"Yes," I countered, but before I could move any further I found myself flat on my back once more. "That's not fair," I pouted.

"Do I look like I care?" He growled.

He flipped me again, this time so he could undo the zipper on the back of my dress. He slid the dress off and hissed between his teeth when he realized I was only wearing panties and no bra.

"Thank God I didn't know you were wearing practically nothing under this dress or I would've pulled you into a closet and fucked you until you passed out."

"Why don't you just fuck me now?" I asked, rising up on my knees with my hands on the bed. I glanced back at where he stood and gave him a coy smile.

He pursed his lips, running his fingers languidly down my bare back. "Oh, I will, trust me. But first I'm going to make love to you the way a man should his wife."

Oh fuck me. Sweet words from Mathias were better than his dirty talk.

He placed soft kisses down my back and Goosebumps broke out across my skin.

He flipped me over onto my back again, much more gentle with me this time.

He cupped my breasts in his warm hands and my body ached with the desire for more.

He rubbed his thumbs over my nipples before his lips replaced them.

His hands skimmed down my sides, hooking into my underwear and tossing them into a far corner of the room.

Kissing his way down my stomach his lips found my core and my back arched at the feel of his tongue. My fingers wound into his hair and I wasn't sure if my objective was to hold him to me or push him away.

Sweat dampened my skin and little sounds kept escaping between my parted lips.

I gripped the bed covers in my fists so tightly that I was surprised they didn't rip in half.

When I came I screamed his name so loud that I put a hand over my mouth to muffle the sounds.

He rose up, giving me a self-satisfied smile.

I tried to catch my breath, but something told me it was gone for good.

He undid the button on his pants and ever so slowly slid the zipper down.

My eyes followed his movements and my tongue flitted out to wet my lips.

His pants dropped to the floor and my whole body tightened with anticipation of what was to come.

He grabbed a condom and put it on and I nearly cried out

with impatience at having to wait a second longer.

I thought he might truly be trying to kill me.

He lowered on top of me, carefully holding his weight above me as he gazed down at me. I pulled him closer to me so that his chest was pressed against mine. I didn't want there to be one inch of my skin not covered by his.

One of my hands rested on his chest, over his steadily beating heart, while the other cupped his neck and I played with the short strands of his hair.

"I love you," I whispered as he pushed inside me.

"I love you more," he breathed.

With every thrust and every breath we continued to whisper *'I love you'*, as if neither one of us wanted to stop hearing the words.

We came together and he held me in his arms before taking me again even slower and sweeter than the first time.

Eventually we passed out from exhaustion, our limbs and hearts tangled together.

Forever intertwined.

"MORNING, WIFE." MATHIAS smiled, stepping into the bathroom and wrapping his arms around me from behind.

"Husband," I replied, rolling the foreign word around on my tongue.

It seemed strange that we were both so at ease with those words, but I guess when you marry the right person for you they don't seem so scary.

His hands rose and he tugged at the top of the towel I had wrapped around my body from my shower.

"Again?" I asked, looking at him behind me in the mirror and raising a brow. We'd had sex so many times since stepping into our hotel room last night that I had lost count. My body was tired, but when the towel fell from around my body and he cupped my breasts in his hands I couldn't stop the moan that passed through my lips.

His voice was a husky growl in my ear. "I haven't *fucked* my wife yet."

"Ohhh." The word came out as one long moan.

"Bend over," he commanded.

Fuck. Yes.

I did as he asked, my tender breasts pressing against the cool granite countertop. My hands planted on the counter and my feet stayed firmly on the ground.

His fingers skimmed over my ass and his eyes connected with mine in the mirror. "I want you to keep your eyes on the mirror and watch everything I do to you."

My fingers flexed at his words and I spread my legs wider.

I watched with baited breath as he grabbed a condom from his pocket and then dropped his low-slung basketball shorts.

Despite the stiffness in my muscles I still yearned for the feeling of his body connecting with mine.

He thrust inside of me and I cried out. My fingers flexed, reaching for something to hold onto but there was nothing.

"Look at me," he growled, and his hand connected sharply with my ass. He then smoothed his hand over the spot that stung.

I opened my eyes, I hadn't even realized that I closed them, and kept my focus on his in the reflection of the mirror.

I didn't think I'd ever seen anything more erotic than watching him fuck me.

He held my hips in a bruising grip and the veins in his arms stood out against his skin.

He lowered his torso and skimmed his lips over my back.

"Please," I begged.

He reached between us, his fingers rubbing against my clit. Between the sensation of him pounding into me, his roving fingers, and watching him in the mirror, I was a goner within minutes.

He wasn't far behind.

"Remy." He growled my name over and over again. His sweat-dampened body stuck to mine as we sunk to floor, clinging to each other. My legs rested on either side of his and my arms wound around his neck.

I didn't see how I'd find the strength to move.

Mathias rested his head against my neck, his heavy breath tickling the skin of my chest.

He cupped my cheek and lifted my lips to his, kissing me long and deep. When our mouths parted, he whispered, "We have to go."

"Now?" I asked, not caring that there was a slight whining tone to my voice.

"Now," he repeated.

"I don't think I can move," I warned him. "Possibly for the next five years."

He ran his fingers through my slightly damp hair. I was sure it was a wild mess after what we did.

"I can carry you."

"Uh-huh," I muttered.

"Don't doubt me, baby." He growled lowly.

"Never," I said sarcastically.

He pinched my side and I yelped.

"Jerk," I snapped.

"But I'm *your* jerk," he grinned, kissing the end of my nose.

"That's right." I laid my head against his chest and my eyes began to drift closed. We'd been up most of the night, with only a few hours of sleep in-between our love making, so I had no idea how he expected me to get ready to head back to L.A.

I let out a small squeal when my equilibrium shifted and I opened my eyes to see that he was standing up with me cradled in his arms.

"Put me down." I smacked his chest.

"You said you needed to be carried." His gray eyes were lit with laughter.

"I was joking."

"Well, I was serious when I said I'd carry you."

"Are you going to dress me too?" I asked when he sat me down on the bed.

He grabbed a pair of jeans from his suitcase—he'd had all our stuff transferred to this room yesterday without me knowing.

Stepping into the jeans he pulled them up and secured the button and zipper. The knowledge that he was boxer-less beneath those jeans was going to kill me today.

"Stop staring at me," he said, but smiled cockily so I knew he liked the attention.

With a groan I stood from the bed and got dressed. I pulled my messy hair back into a bun and within minutes we were packed and ready to head down to the lobby.

Two bodyguards waited outside our hotel room door.

That was something that would take me a while to get used to.

They grabbed our luggage and flanked us on each side as we headed into the elevators.

"Are you ready?" Mathias asked me, taking my hand and squeezing it tight.

He didn't wear a baseball cap this time, and he didn't offer one to me.

There was no hiding anymore.

I nodded and he pushed the button for the lobby.

With each floor we descended my heart lurched a little.

Everything was about to change.

DESPITE THE FACT that it took us no more than three hours to finally reach the front door of Mathias' L.A. home I felt absolutely exhausted.

I dove for the couch, landing flat on my stomach and wrapped my arms around a throw pillow. Shiloh and Percy trotted over and I laughed when they both jumped up on the couch, snuggled together.

"Look who made friends," I called to Mathias, as he strode through the house turning on lights and staring angrily at his phone. "What's wrong?" I asked, not liking the wrinkle marring his brow.

"Fucking Julian," he cursed.

"What happened?" I asked, sitting up.

I pulled my hair out of the bun and let the blonde strands flow around my shoulders.

"It's all over the internet that I married a mystery girl," he rolled his eyes at the title, "and apparently it's creating a shit-ton of trouble for him, but I don't really give a fuck."

"Mathias—" I frowned.

"Don't," he hushed me, pinching the bridge of his nose. He let out a loud groan and sunk down onto the couch with his head in his hands. Leaning back, he growled, "Julian's on his way over, and I really don't want to have to deal with his bullshit."

"What's wrong with us getting married?" I whispered, reaching over to pet Percy since I needed the comfort at the

315

moment. The cat glared at me first, but then gave in to my touch. I figured he was pissed that we'd gone off and left him with a stranger to pet sit.

Mathias glanced at me sadly. "My reputation."

"Oh," was all I said.

He nodded. "The media is assuming the wedding was a drunken mistake and they've already confirmed that you're the same woman I showed up at LAX with, so now... now they're digging around trying to find your name and any information on you that they can."

"Oh," I said again. It seemed to be the only word my brain could produce at the moment.

"Fuck, I'm so sorry, Rem."

"Why are you apologizing?" I finally seemed to snap out of my haze. I stood and made my way over to him on the opposite side of the couch. I sat down beside him and wrapped my arms around him, laying my head on his shoulder.

"You shouldn't have to deal with this kind of shit."

"Mathias," I said his name sternly, "I knew that things would be this way. You can't change the fact that you're famous and people want to know every detail of your life, which includes me if we're together."

He sighed heavily and his fingers stroked my knee. "I love that I get to live my dream, but I really fucking hate the baggage that comes with it. Having the whole world want to know all about you makes it hard to keep something to yourself. Something to hold onto that's real."

"I'm real," I whispered.

He swallowed thickly and looked into my eyes. "You're right."

He kissed me slow and sweet, sucking on my bottom lip like it was his favorite candy.

We jumped when there was a loud banging at the front door, accompanied by the ringing of the doorbell.

"Julian," he muttered. "That was fast. He must've been in the area already."

He untangled from my hold and went to get the door.

"You might want to go upstairs," he warned.

I steeled my shoulders as he reached for the doorknob. "I'm not going anywhere."

It was going to take a lot more than a psychotic manager to scare me.

Julian burst inside as soon as the door opened. His face was red and a vein in his forehead bulged.

He was speaking so fast and so loudly that I couldn't understand a thing he said at first.

"What the fuck were you thinking?!" He roared, pacing the floor. "Did you have another one of your drunken binges and think it would be a great idea to marry some redneck hick from your hometown?!"

"Hey!" Mathias yelled back, shoving a finger into Julian's chest. "Don't you ever fucking talk about her like that!"

"Do you have any idea what kind of PR nightmare you've pulled with your little stunt?!" Julian gesticulated his arms around the room in a wild manner.

"Stunt?" Mathias pointed at his chest. "This is my life! And *that*," he pointed at me, "is my future! So get that through you're thick fucking skull or you're fired!"

"You can't fire me!" Julian spat. "We have a contract!"

"You can fucking sue me, because if you don't learn to accept that Remy is my *wife* then I refuse to work with you!"

Julian stood in front of Mathias, breathing deeply as his nostrils flared like a bull's.

"What the hell am I supposed to say to the press about this?"

Julian asked, his tone much calmer than before, but from the clenching in his jaw I knew he was trying hard to hold back.

"How about the truth?" Mathias spread his arms wide. "That I reconnected with my high school sweetheart recently and we decided to get married." He shrugged. "It's that simple."

Julian shook his head. "Do you really expect people to believe that of *you*? The bad boy of the band? Suddenly you're some romantic guy falling back in love with some girl from your past."

"It's the fucking truth," Mathias spat.

Julian shook his head. "And no one will believe it."

"Then you figure something out, that's why you're our manager."

Julian stood for a moment longer, shaking his head like he was debating with himself on whether or not to say anything more.

After a minute he spoke. "I want you two to pack your shit and get back to Virginia while I deal with this. Just stay out of the spotlight for a few weeks, okay?"

"Sure thing." Mathias saluted Julian mockingly.

With a shake of his head Julian headed for the door.

It slammed behind him—Mathias' doing, not his.

"So..." I started, smiling sheepishly. "Now what?"

Mathias ran his fingers through his hair and then crossed his arms over his chest. "We do what he said. We go home."

Home. I liked the sound of that.

CHAPTER TWENTY-NINE

TIME SEEMED TO pass in the blink of an eye.

Christmas came and went without much pomp and circumstance. Mathias and I exchanged gifts and set up a tree in his penthouse. We spent the day watching movies before having dinner at his parent's house—grandma tagged along, of course.

My parent's hadn't been happy when they found out about us getting married. I had expected that, and frankly that's why I hadn't bothered to tell them. They saw it on TV and I couldn't even feel bad about it since my dad acted like a raging dickwad when he called. My mom took it much better—after telling me how disappointed she was that I was doing this to myself *again,* she finally sighed and said it was my life and she'd support my decisions even if she didn't like them. My brother never called. Shocker. We were just one big happy family. Not.

I still hadn't told Mathias about Hope yet. Each time I opened my mouth ready to tell him, it was like my throat closed up and I couldn't form a single word.

I knew I had to, and soon, but it seemed impossible.

"Where is this party again?" I asked, adding another layer of red lipstick to my lips. My dress was also the same shade of red, falling all the way to the floor. The top was a sweetheart neckline with sleeves that swept down to my elbows. It was backless as well. When Mathias first saw it on me his eyes had flashed with lust.

"It's at the Wentworth's mansion," Mathias said, stepping into the bathroom and glancing at his reflection in the mirror so that he could straighten his bow tie. "They have a fancy New Year's Eve party every year and they asked us to play. We said yes since Hayes is Lily's nephew." I shook my head and at my noticeable confusion, he added, "I'll introduce you to everybody and explain the dynamics, don't worry."

"I still don't see why we're leaving so early. It's barely five o' clock." I fluffed my curled hair one last time and padded into the bedroom to slip on my heels.

"There's someone I want you to meet." He said vaguely.

"And you're not going to tell me who this someone is?" I placed a hand on my cocked hip, staring him down.

"Nope." He smiled boyishly and grabbed a black bag so I couldn't see what was in it. "But he's important to me, so I want you to meet him."

I sighed, grabbing my black sparkly clutch. "Okay."

If he wanted it to be a surprise I'd keep my mouth shut... for now.

Instead of hiring a driver for the evening Mathias chose to drive his Range Rover. I was glad for that. I didn't really like having a driver. It was so foreign to me.

The sky was already growing dark, and since it was a cloudy night you could barely see the crescent shaped moon.

Mathias drove a few towns over, turning into a neighborhood. The homes were small, and mostly rundown with paint peeling off of the siding and broken shutters.

He pulled into a gravel driveway of a home that appeared to be in better shape than most.

I didn't recognize the house, or even the neighborhood, so I honestly had no idea who he could be bringing me to meet.

He unbuckled his seatbelt and his sigh echoed through the car. "This is it."

"I deduced that."

His lips twitched. "Don't get sassy with me."

He slipped out of the car, grabbing the black bag from the backseat.

I followed him to the front door and after he knocked we waited for a moment.

The door opened to reveal a frazzled looking woman that appeared to be in her early thirties. Her brown hair was frizzing out of its ponytail and her clothes hung loosely on her thin frame. She smiled pleasantly at Mathias and opened the door wider.

"Collin will be happy to see you. He's been asking when you're coming to see him for weeks."

As if summoned by her words a little boy of about six came running towards us, his brown hair blowing with the speed.

He jumped into Mathias' arms, and Mathias caught him easily.

"Mattie you're here! You're finally here!" The little boy wrapped his arms around Mathias' wide shoulders.

"I told you I'd be back to visit soon." Mathias hugged him back just as fiercely.

I stood mystified, watching them. I couldn't figure out who the little boy was and how Mathias knew him.

"I know I'm late," Mathias set the boy down, "but I brought you some Christmas presents."

"Presents?" The little boy beamed. "Gimme!" He reached up and Mathias handed him the bag that had fallen on the floor.

Once the bag was in his grasp Collin took off running once more.

"Who is this?" The woman asked, eyeing me warily.

Mathias grasped my waist, pulling me firmly against his side. "This is Remy, my wife."

"Oh, right," the woman shook her head. "I remember seeing that on TV. I'm sorry. I tend to tune that stuff out."

"Might as well," Mathias muttered, "all they do is tell lies."

I gave his hand a squeeze and he looked down at me. "I'm so confused," I frowned. "Who is Collin?"

"My Little Brother," he replied.

I opened my mouth to retort that Maddox was his brother and he didn't have any others, but he beat me to it.

"I'm his Big Brother—you know, the Big Brothers Big Sisters club."

"Oh," I drew out the word. "Now I get it."

"This is Laura, Collin's mom," Mathias introduced me to the woman.

"Hi," she gave a small wave. "I'll be back there if you need me," she pointed towards a bedroom. "I know Collin doesn't want me around right now." She rolled her eyes, but laughed and you could tell she was happy Mathias was there.

"So... explain this to me?" I asked in a hushed voice.

"I decided to get into the program because I wanted to help children in a small way. You know I didn't grow up with the best parent's and get the support I needed, so I wanted to be that mentor I never had." He shrugged like it was no big deal, but it *was*. He had the biggest heart, bigger than anybody else I knew. "I got paired with Collin, and it's really been perfect. His dad walked out a few years ago and he barely remembers him, so I'm proud that I can help fill that role with him." Mathias' chest swelled with pride as he spoke. "He has dyslexia like me too, and so I'm working with him on things to help him learn to read that *I've* learned over the years. I don't ever want someone to tell him he's stupid, just because he has a learning disability. It might take him longer, but he *will* learn how to read."

"Mathias..." I started, and then didn't know what else to say. He was the most remarkable man that I had ever met.

"You don't need to say anything," he whispered, caressing my cheek.

"Mattie!" We heard yelled from the other room. "Get in here so I can open my presents!"

Mathias chuckled. "That's our cue."

I followed him into the small living room that also doubled as a dining room. The carpet was new and the furniture looked new as well.

Collin sat beside the tree that glowed with colored lights and was covered in more tinsel and ornaments than it looked like it could hold.

He'd dumped out the contents of the bag, revealing four wrapped presents.

"Come on, open them, bud." Mathias coaxed, sitting down on the floor beside Collin.

I took a seat on the couch.

"Who is she?" Collin asked, reaching for a present—the largest one.

Mathias chuckled and ruffled the boy's hair. "My wife."

"Wife?" Collin wrinkled his nose. "Does that mean you're going to have babies? That's what mommy says husbands and wifes do."

"Wives," Mathias corrected automatically. "And yes, one day we'll have babies."

"Will I be their big brother?" Collin asked with wide eyes.

"Of course," Mathias grinned.

"Good," Collin beamed, and then began to tear into his presents.

The first one turned out to be a remote controlled car. The second a remote controlled airplane. The third a remote controlled train set. Clearly the kid had an obsession and Mathias knew it. Collin gushed over the presents, throwing them at Mathias with cries for him to get them out of their boxes.

"Sure thing," Mathias said, standing up and heading over to the small kitchen to grab a knife. "You've got one more present."

"Oh, right." Collin clapped and grabbed the present. "What is this?" He asked, holding up the box that contained an iPad.

Mathias sat down beside him once more, and began cutting at the tape on the box for the plane. "It's an iPad, so you can Facetime me and we can see each other even when I'm gone."

And my heart just melted.

That's right, Remy Parker's—correction, *Wade's*—heart just melted into a pile of goo at the cuteness.

"So I can see you anytime?" Collin asked, joy lighting his little face.

Mathias grinned and nodded. "Pretty much. Unless I'm working."

"Cool!" Collin cried, diving into Mathias arms—thank God Mathias had set the knife on the floor on his other side.

He held the little boy tight, like he never wanted to let go.

"I love you," Collin said into Mathias' neck.

"I love you too, bud."

Tears pricked my eyes.

I wished he could see himself right now. If he could he wouldn't think he was a monster. He would see himself for the beautifully broken, tormented, but kind soul that he is.

Collin let go of him and Mathias finished unboxing the gifts.

Soon the plane buzzed around our heads, crashing into walls. Collin's giggles became infectious.

Watching Mathias with Collin was bittersweet, because I couldn't help thinking of Hope who would've been the same age had she not been stillborn

Mathias let go of Collin and the little boy grabbed the control for his plane once more. While the plane zipped around, Mathias picked up the control for the car, racing it around the coffee table.

"My plane is going to beat your car!" Collin cried, racing his plane around the table above the car.

"No way," Mathias chuckled. "I'm going to win."

"No, me!" Collin's tongue stuck out between his teeth as he concentrated on making a turn. "I won! Did you see, Mattie? I won!"

Mathias grabbed the little boy, tickling his stomach. "Yeah, yeah. I saw."

"Stop tickling me!" The boy wiggled, tears of laughter tracking his cheeks.

Mathias let him go and Collin ran off. A moment later Christmas music began to play.

Bursting back into the room with energy that never seemed to wane Collin cried, "Let's dance! You too!" He grabbed my hand, yanking on my arm. I stood up and he pointed to Mathias. "With Mattie."

Mathias smiled boyishly and held out his hand to me. "You heard the kid. Dance with me."

I smiled and placed my hand in his. He pulled me against him and murmured, "Closer," when I kept a respectable amount of distance between us.

I shook my head, prepared to tell him no when I saw that Collin had disappeared once more.

325

One of his hands rested on the small of my waist while the other held my hand firmly.

He sang the words of the song softly under his breath, swaying us back and forth.

Soon the giggles of Collin returned and I looked over Mathias' shoulder to see the little boy plugging in a set of Christmas lights.

Before I could ask him what he was doing he grabbed the string of lights and started running around us.

Soon our legs were tangled together with the lights and I grasped Mathias' shoulders to stay up right.

"Whoa, careful, Collin." Mathias warned.

"Mommy! Come help me!" The little boy called, jumping up so he could try to get the lights higher.

Laura appeared in the doorway and shook her head when she saw what her son was up to. "Collin, take those off of them. Now."

"It's okay," Mathias told her, "let him finish."

She sighed, looking weary. "Are you sure?"

"Of course," Mathias replied, and I figured he'd do pretty much anything to make sure Collin was happy.

Laura helped Collin finish wrapping us in lights and then he demanded that we pose for a picture.

"Grab my phone." Mathias nodded to where he'd left it on the coffee table.

Collin picked it up and handed it to Laura. Cupping his hands around his mouth, he whispered, "I don't know how to work it. Will you do it for me?"

She laughed at her son and ruffled his hair. "Sure."

"Smile you two. One, two, three."

The flash on the phone went off.

"Another!" Collin clapped his hands.

This time Mathias leaned in and kissed me, which made Collin cry, "Ew, gross!"

"Alright, one more," Mathias said. "You better get in this one, bud, since this was your idea."

Collin bounced over to us eagerly and stood in front of us with his arms crossed over his chest. Based on Laura's laugh I assumed he made a funny face.

"Okay, you have to undo us now," Mathias said.

"Does this mean you have to leave?" Collin frowned.

Mathias nodded and the little boy's head hung limply. "How long will you be gone?"

"A while," Mathias' Adam's apple bobbed. Laura began to undo the lights from our bodies. "I'm going on tour with my band. You might see me on TV. And remember, I got you the iPad so we can Facetime. We're still going to see each other."

"You promise?" Collin asked, wrapping his arms around his small body. "You're not going to leave forever like my daddy are you?"

The lights fell on the floor and Mathias stepped over them, bending down in front of Collin. "I would never leave you forever."

"You didn't promise," Collin pouted, tears falling from his eyes.

"I promise, bud."

"Okay," Collin's voice cracked, and he reached his small arms up to wrap them around Mathias' neck.

When I looked over at Laura I saw that she had tears in her eyes just like I did.

I could tell it was breaking both of their hearts to say goodbye.

The tour didn't start up until mid-January, but I knew Mathias would be busy working on other things and probably wouldn't have a chance to see Collin again before we departed.

Mathias finally let go and kissed Collin on his forehead.

Holding out his fist Collin bumped his smaller one against it. "See you later, right?" Mathias asked.

Collin nodded, reaching up to wipe away his tears.

"I love you," Mathias told him. "And whenever you miss me, just place your hand over your heart like this," Mathias held his fist against his chest, "and know that I'm missing you too."

Collin nodded and mimed the gesture, hugging Mathias one last time.

We hurried outside then and into the car. As we drove away I turned to look at him. "You give me a new reason to love you every day."

He took my hand, entwining our fingers together and lifted our joined hands to his lips so that he could kiss mine. "I guess that means you'll never fall out of love with me then." His eyes were serious.

"Never," I vowed.

He nodded, his eyes on the road.

Tomorrow, I told myself.

Tomorrow I would tell him about Hope. No excuses.

Even if *he* might fall out of love with *me*.

"WHOA," I GASPED as I stepped out of the car. "They *live* here?"

Mathias closed the car door, locked it, and took my hand. A cigarette dangled precariously between his lips.

"Yep," he nodded.

"How do they not get lost?" I hissed as we walked up to the large front doors. I kept looking around with my mouth hanging open. It was completely dark now, but the whole front of the house was lit brightly with strategically placed spotlights.

Mathias shrugged in answer to my question and reached up to grab the cigarette. He blew out a string of smoke and dropped the finished cigarette on the ground, crushing the lit tip with the edge of his shoe.

He reached out and opened the front door.

We stepped inside a massive foyer and people stood around mingling.

My head swiveled around, trying to take in every elegant detail of the home.

"This way," he tugged on my hand, leading me away, "we need to go to the ballroom."

"They have a ballroom?!" I shrieked. "In their house?"

Mathias merely chuckled at me, but I couldn't believe that someone had a ballroom in their house—although, it was a mansion, not a house, so I guessed they could have whatever they wanted.

We followed the sounds of music and chatter, soon stepping into a room that was the size of the whole house I grew up in.

I spotted Emma and Maddox speaking with Hayes and a few other people. Ezra was there too, with his back turned to us.

We joined them and I immediately complimented Emma on her dress. It was a beautiful floor length gown in a deep blue color with a beaded top. It made her blue eyes seem even bluer and her hair was pinned back elegantly.

"Thank you," she smiled, "yours is amazing too."

Squeezing my hand to get my attention, Mathias began to introduce everybody. "This is Trace Wentworth and his wife Olivia," he pointed to a couple. The man was tall with the greenest eyes I'd ever seen and an easy smile. His brown hair flopped over his forehead into his eyes. Olivia looked like a small little pixie next to him. She was dressed in a pretty pale pink dress, her dark hair curled down her back, and she held a baby boy in her arms. He couldn't be more than a few months old, with dark hair like his parents. He was dressed in a tiny suit, with a small pair of converse on his feet.

He began to fuss and Trace reached for the baby. "Dean wants his daddy."

Olivia sighed good-naturedly and smiled at her husband as she handed over the baby. "He really needs to go to bed."

"I can do that," Trace smiled lovingly at his wife and lowered to kiss her cheek. "It was nice to meet you," he turned his attention to me. To the rest of the group, he said, "I'll be back soon."

Mathias took the interruption in stride and moved on to the next person. "This is Trenton Wentworth."

This guy was just as tall as Trace, with the same facial features and build, but blue eyes instead of green.

"I'm the rude one's brother," Trent winked playfully, eliciting a growl from Mathias.

I gave his hand a small squeeze and he quieted.

"This is..." Mathias paused and frowned. "I don't know who the fuck you are."

The girl rolled her eyes and her plump lips pulled down in a pout. Flipping her fiery red hair over her shoulder, she said, "Just because you're famous doesn't mean you're allowed to be rude. I'm Avery, Olivia's best friend—also know as the life of the party and all around greatest person alive. This is my boyfriend Luca." She pointed to the big bear of a man beside her. He grunted in response and looked like he'd rather be anywhere but here. Poor guy.

"Avery," Mathias repeated, trying to repress a laugh.

"And don't you forget it." She rolled her eyes.

Moving on to the last person standing there, he said, "This is

Lily Wentworth, Hayes' aunt."

Hayes stood beside the woman with his arm thrown over her shoulder, smiling widely. "I'm her favorite nephew," he boasted.

"You're my *only* nephew," she countered, shaking her head. I could tell she was fighting not to laugh.

"Same difference," Hayes chimed. "So, anyway, in case that got really confusing for you, Lily is my aunt and this is her house. Trace and Trent are my cousins."

I laughed. "Thanks for the repeat, but I think I got it."

He tipped his head in my direction with a smile.

"Well, that's everyone you need to know," Mathias said, releasing my hand and placing his at the small of my back instead.

"Not everyone," Emma interrupted, her eyes near the entrance of the ballroom.

A moment later we heard a high-pitched shriek and Emma was nearly tackled to the ground. If Maddox hadn't grabbed Emma around the waist, both girls would've went falling to the floor.

After the girls recovered, both laughing, Emma turned to me. "This is Sadie, my best friend that I was telling you about."

"Hi," Sadie smiled, stepping forward to hug me. I was surprised by the gesture, but quickly returned it. She was gorgeous, with sun-kissed skin like she'd just been to the beach, and brown hair curling halfway down her back. Her brown eyes were sweet, but twinkled with mischief. "You must be Remy."

I nodded.

"Emma's been telling me a lot about you. I'm starting to get jealous. I think she's replacing me," the girl jested.

A loud clearing of a throat had all of us turning in the direction of the man standing behind Sadie. He was tall and wide, like a football player, with short blond hair. There was something about him I instantly didn't like.

"Oh, right," Sadie's face turned red, "this is my fiancé Braden."

Even after being introduced the guy said nothing, just glared at all of us.

"Excuse me," Ezra muttered, breaking through the group. He strode up to Braden and clapped him on the shoulder. Ezra was a little bit taller, but definitely not wider, than the guy and used that to his advantage by looking down on him. "I think we should have a little chat."

"Stop it," Sadie hissed under her breath.

Ezra glanced at her and shook his head. His look said she was stupid to think he was going to drop whatever this was.

"I don't have anything to say to you." Braden finally spoke, his voice booming around us and drawing the attention of those near us. He crossed his arms over his massive chest, his feet planted firmly apart.

"Really? That's great, because I have some things to say to you, so you can stand there and listen."

Braden rolled his eyes. "Is this because I told her she couldn't hang out with you? As her fiancé it's my right to decide who she's *friends* with," he sneered the word, "and I don't want her to be friend's with any man. Especially one I'm pretty sure she's fucked."

Sadie gasped, her whole body flushing with embarrassment.

Ezra clenched his teeth, his hands fisted at his side. "What the fuck did you just say?"

Braden didn't back down. "Are you deaf? I said I'm pretty sure you fucked my girl, so as long as I'm in the picture, you won't be."

Ezra cocked his fist back and punched Braden in the face. Braden then threw a fist into Ezra's side.

As the guy's scuffled we all looked on in horror.

No one seemed to know what to do.

Maddox and Mathias were the first to move. Each one grabbed a different guy and tried to get them off of each other. Neither Ezra nor Braden was willing to back down from the fight which made things even more difficult for the twins.

Tears streaked down Sadie's cheeks and I felt so sorry for her. I could see the confliction on her face.

The guys finally broke apart and Lily came scuttling forward. "I'm sorry, but you two need to leave." She pointed to Sadie and Braden.

Sadie nodded, like she had expected as much.

Braden threw a fit about how he hadn't done anything, blah, blah, blah. But Sadie simply grabbed him by the arm and quietly towed him from the room.

You could feel the shame rolling off of her shoulders, and I wondered how she'd ever gotten involved in a guy like that.

"I hate him," Emma spoke up, glaring at Braden's back until he disappeared.

"Me too," Ezra said, clutching his side. There was a small cut on his upper lip that trickled blood.

Emma sighed when she saw him. "We have to respect her decision. It's her life."

"Well, she's making the worst mistake of her life," he seethed, reaching up to wipe away the blood from his lip.

"I know that, and you know that, but she doesn't. The more we balk her on this, the closer it will drive her too him," Emma reasoned.

Ezra tugged at his hair and let out a growl.

Emma stepped forward and grabbed his hand, forcing him to look at her.

"I know you love her—" Ezra opened his mouth to argue with

her, but she held up a hand and he shut up. "—like a friend and want what's best for her, but she's stubborn. Nothing you do or say is going to make her change her mind about him. You have to let his go."

Ezra closed his eyes and his whole body shook with a breath. "I'll try, but she deserves better."

"I know," Emma agreed.

Taking a step away Ezra mumbled, "I'm going to the bathroom. I'll be back in time for our set."

Emma frowned at his retreating form.

"Dinner is going to be served in a few minutes if you'd like to take a seat." Lily swept her hands in the direction of the tables scattered around the space.

Mathias steered me towards one and Hayes, Trenton, Maddox, and Emma joined us. Olivia, her friend, and her friend's boyfriend sat at the table beside us since there was no longer enough room at ours.

Ezra didn't return for dinner, and his absence weighed heavily upon all of us. When Maddox and Emma excused themselves from the table and left the room I knew they were going to look for him.

The tables were soon cleared of dirty plates and it was time for Willow Creek to perform on the stage setup in the corner of the ballroom.

Maddox, Emma, and Ezra returned just in time. The guys immediately climbed on stage. Maddox pulled his drumsticks out of his back pocket and sat down behind his kit, banging out a beat.

Mathias took his place in front of the microphone and winked when he caught me looking at him.

Emma stood beside me, swaying to the music as they played. Despite the fact that she'd probably seen them perform hundreds of time she still looked on with awe.

Mathias' eyes connected with mine as he sang, and to me it felt like we were the only two people present. He had this way about him that made me forget anything else even existed.

The first song ended and they moved into another one, this one a little more fast-paced.

Emma grabbed my hands and cried, "You have to dance, Remy!"

At first I was hesitant—mostly because this dress was tight and the last thing I wanted was for it to split up the sides—but Emma was impossible to resist. Soon the two of us were laughing and dancing, not caring if we looked like complete and utter goofballs.

The guys played a few songs and then there was some more entertainment before we were all ushered outside.

"What's going on?" I asked Mathias.

"You'll see," he smiled, shrugging out of his tux jacket and draping it over my shoulders so that I wouldn't be cold.

Somewhere, someone began to countdown to midnight and we all joined in.

"Ten, nine, eight, seven, six, five, four, three, two, one!"

Mathias leaned down and kissed me, murmuring, "Happy New Year," against my lips.

Fireworks went off all around us and now I knew why we'd all been dragged out into the cold air.

"Happy New Year." I mimed him as a heavy weight settled on my chest.

Off to our right a gasp had us turning to look.

"Oh my God," I smiled, lifting a hand to my mouth.

Maddox kneeled on one knee in front of Emma. From where we stood we couldn't hear anything that Maddox was saying, but tears shimmered in Emma's eyes. She nodded her head yes and he slipped the ring onto her finger. She dove into his arms and he spun her around, their lips pressed firmly together.

Even though I feared that my life might be falling apart, I was still happy for them. I eventually looked away, wanting to give them any amount of privacy that I could offer.

I turned my face towards the sky, watching it explode in a fiery cascade of silver and gold.

Mathias' fingers tapped against my waist and I rested my head on his shoulder.

Each bang of the fireworks sounded like a bullet lodging itself into the beating heart of our relationship. Nothing would be the same once I told him, and I only hoped we could make it through this. I believed our love was strong enough to overcome anything, especially as hard as we fought to get to where we were now, but this might be one sin that not even that love could overcome. That thought left me bereft and empty inside.

CHAPTER THIRTY

I WOKE UP the next morning with what felt like a fifty-pound weight on my chest. I knew today was the day. I couldn't keep this a secret any longer. I still had no clear idea on how to tell him. This wasn't exactly easy news to break to someone, and knowing Mathias he would snap at me and not let me finish explaining.

I slipped out of the bed and went over different scenarios in my head, wondering how would be the best way to tell him.

My heart clenched with fear.

I didn't want to do this.

But I had no choice.

I thought I might throw up.

Nope. No. I was good.

I could do this.

I padded out of the bedroom, heading towards the kitchen for coffee.

"Remy."

I stopped in my tracks at the icy tone. He didn't shout my name, but the single word was lined with steel.

I closed my eyes.

He knew.

I didn't know how he knew—unless I'd been talking to myself out loud and didn't realize it—but somehow he did.

I rounded the corner and came face to face with him.

I thought I'd seen Mathias angry before, but nothing, and I mean *nothing* compared to his anger now.

He was pale, his skin a ghostly white. A vein in his forehead pulsed and his hands were scrunched into fists.

"What the fuck is this?" His voice was still that deadly calm before the storm.

"What?" I was surprised by how strong the single word sounded. On the inside I was freaking out.

He grabbed my arm and pulled. I nearly tripped over my feet.

"Ow, Mathias, you're hurting me," I cried, prying my arm from his hold.

He didn't say he was sorry, but his eyes appeared to be slightly apologetic.

"Tell me they're lying." He pointed at the TV and I looked to see some celebrity gossip show on TV. There was a picture of the two of us, and they were talking about how it was so romantic that we'd gotten back together all these years later after the death of our daughter. They were saying some other things too, but all I could focus on was the daughter part.

I sunk to my knees, tears rolling down my cheeks.

That was answer enough for him.

"Fuck!" He screamed, grabbing the coffee table and turning it over with a crash that I was sure was heard through the whole hotel.

I tried to get oxygen into my lungs, but it was like I had forgotten how to breathe.

I knew it was going to be bad telling him, but this was the worst way possible for him to find out.

You should've told him a long time ago, my conscience piped in. I told her to take a fucking hike. There was nothing I could do now to change my decisions. All I could do was explain my side and hope he saw that I'd meant well.

He paced around the room, cursing and throwing things when he felt like it.

"Mathias, please—" I started.

He stopped with his hands on his hips and glared at me like I was the most disgusting thing he'd ever laid his eyes on. I felt so small beneath that gaze.

"Explain!" He shouted. "Fucking explain this to me!"

"I don't know where to *start*." My voice cracked.

"How about at the fucking beginning? You..." He stopped, his breath coming out in ragged pants. "You were pregnant?"

I nodded, tears stinging my cheeks. "Yes. When I left. I was going t-to tell you that d-day in the parking lot and then..." I trailed off, he knew what happened, what *he* said to me, so there was no point in continuing.

"And then you never fucking thought to give me a call and say, 'Oh, hey, Mathias, I thought I should let you know I'm pregnant and the baby is yours.'"

"I was a kid!" I yelled, rising to my feet. "I was a kid and so were you! I was a kid that was madly in love with you and you *broke* my fucking heart! You crushed me! Excuse me for thinking you wouldn't want anything to do with me or our daughter!" My chest rose and fell with rapid breaths.

"I had a right to know!"

"I would've told you eventually had she..." A sob raked my body and I bit down on my fist to stifle the sound. "...Had she lived." I finally managed to get the words out.

"What the fuck happened?!" He asked. "I want to know everything! I deserve to know!" He thrust a finger against his chest and I swore there were tears in his own eyes.

I wrapped my arms around myself, sniffling as I fought more tears. "I don't *know*." My voice cracked yet again. I could see that he was about to argue with that statement, so I quickly continued. "Everything was fine. I did everything right, Mathias! You have to believe me! I stopped smoking, I ate healthy, I did everything the doctors told me to do, but then she stopped moving as much and... and they induced labor, but it was too late." My lip trembled with my tears. "She was already gone."

I buried my face in my hands, crying harder than I had let myself cry since the day the doctors took her from my arms.

Mathias stared at me, his mouth moving back and forth, but no words came out. He seemed at a loss as to what to say.

"After that... it didn't seem important to tell you. She was gone, and even though I thought I hated you, I still loved you. And because of that love, I wanted to spare you the pain I had to live with." More tears flowed down my cheeks. I was drowning in them. "Every single day since then I've had to live with the fact that I'll never see her grow up. I'll never get to hear her call me mommy. Or take her to her first day of school. I'll never get to teach her how to ride her bike. I'll never get to brush her hair, or tuck her into bed at night. I'll never get to tell her I love her, and that kills me a little inside every day. Can you blame me for wanting to spare you that torment?" I wiped at my face, struggling to breathe.

"You still had no right to take that choice away from me!" He yelled, a muscle in his jaw twitching.

"I know. I can see that now, and I'm sorry. But *please* understand where I was coming from. I was going to tell you, today actually, but I... I didn't get the chance." That was taken away from me like so many other things.

"Fuck," he cursed, pulling at his hair, "I want to believe this is a fucking nightmare." His voice was suddenly soft and defeated sounding.

"It feels like it sometimes," I whispered.

"What was her name?" He asked, startling me.

"Hope," I whispered. "Hope Wade. I didn't give her a middle name."

His shoulders hunched forward, as if by having a name she suddenly became even more real to him.

With a growl he picked up his phone and slammed it into a wall. A dent was left behind and the phone shattered.

"It's not fair!" He screamed, losing all control.

He destroyed everything in sight—shattering lamps, ripping the couch cushions off. The whole room soon looked like a disaster zone.

I stood there, unable to move.

I didn't know what to do or say to calm him, and something told me there was *nothing* I could do.

When he finally stopped raging he returned to his icy calm. He pointed a finger at me and hissed, "I hate you and I will *never* forgive you for this."

I nodded, and my tears began to flow at a faster rate.

I had expected his words, but they still hurt.

Numbness spread through my limbs and I sunk to the floor, my back against the wall.

He glared at me for a long moment, before shaking his head and storming away.

I heard the sound of the elevator doors opening and then he was gone.

I knew that this very well might be the last time I ever saw him.

I couldn't blame him for hating me.

This really was my fault.

My decisions led to this moment.

And I would have to live with that regret for the rest of my life.

WHEN I FINALLY pried my body off the floor I tried to clean up the space, but I soon felt far too tried to deal with anything.

Sluggishly I made my way back to our bedroom and immediately fell asleep.

I was pretty sure I could sleep for a thousand years.

Anything to avoid having to deal with the mess my life had become.

I STARED AT the plate of food I had warmed, but I wasn't hungry.

Mathias hadn't come home yesterday, and today was a new day with still no sign of him.

I was supposed to work at the bar today.

I called in and quit.

I figured Mathias was done with me—he was probably getting divorce papers drawn up already—and I would be moving back to Arizona. There was no way I could stay here after this and I had no place else to go. My parent's would say, 'I told you so,' but I honestly couldn't fault them for that. They had every right to rub it in my face that I'd screwed up yet again.

I threw the food away and cleaned the plate, before sitting down with my laptop and playing the video once more. The one brief news clip that ruined my life.

Over and over again, I watched it.

So much for staying out of the spotlight. I was sure Julian was about to have a heart attack trying to deal with this.

It was clear that the so-called journalists had been digging into my past, trying to find out anything they could about Mathias' mystery girl. I guess they were trying to find a reason for why Mathias would choose me to settle down with. I knew it wouldn't have taken much sleuthing for anyone to find Hope's death certificate. Coupled with all the hospital visits and timing, it was easy to put two and two together.

He shouldn't have found out like that, though, and it was nothing but my own fault for not having the guts to tell him.

There wasn't much I feared, but losing him was number one.

That didn't matter now, because regardless, I had lost him.

I wished he could see where I'd been coming from, though. My intention had *never* been to hurt him. It had been the complete opposite.

The elevator dinged and hope soared in my chest.

Disappointment quickly replaced it when Emma stepped out of the elevator and not Mathias.

She winced when she looked around and saw the mess.

Her eyes landed on me and she frowned. I was sure I looked scary. I hadn't showered yesterday or this morning. I hadn't even bothered to brush my hair or change my clothes. I didn't have the energy to do anything.

"Hey," she smiled.

I closed the laptop and set it beside me on the couch.

"Are you here to kick me out?" I asked.

I expected Mathias to show up for that part, but maybe he was still so angry that he couldn't bear to look at me, even to tell me to get the fuck out of his place.

"No," she shook her head, her brows furrowing together as

she navigated the mess and sat down beside me. "Why would I do that?"

I turned red-rimmed eyes in her direction. "Because I'm sure Mathias doesn't want me here anymore."

She shrugged.

"Have you seen him?" I asked, swallowing past the lump in my throat.

She nodded. "He showed up at the guesthouse. We'd already seen the news and Maddox didn't think Mathias knew about the baby. Maddox said Mathias might not be the most open person, but that he'd never keep that a secret from him." She sighed, tapping her fingers along the back of the couch.

"Do you think I'm a horrible person for not telling him?" I knew she'd be honest with me.

"No, I don't think you're horrible. Do I think it was wrong? Yes. But I can also understand why you did it. You were young and you lost your baby. You probably thought you'd never see him again, so what difference would it have even made? But when you reconnected with him now... you should've been honest."

"I didn't want him to have to grieve every day for the rest of his life like I do. I didn't want him to ask himself the endless amount of questions that I ask myself. I wanted him to be able to live his life without asking *what if.*" I reached up, swiping away a tear. You would've thought I would have run out of tears by now, but somehow they kept flowing.

"I think he knows that, but he's still..."

"Mad?" I supplied for her and she nodded.

"You should've told him, Remy, instead of letting it get this far. It wasn't fair to him to find out like this. I know, because I've been in a similar position." She reached forward, grabbing my hand and holding it in comfort.

"You have?" I asked.

"When I met Maddox, Willow Creek was already gaining popularity, but I had no idea who they were. I'm kind of aloof like that," she rolled her eyes and laughed, "anyway, he never told me that he was in the band, and I found out by accident when Sadie saw a picture of Maddox and me in a magazine." She shook her head, letting out another small laugh. "I was so mad at him for not telling me—for not trusting me. I was so angry that I found out who he was in a magazine. *He* should've told *me* just like *you* should've told *Mathias*. When you're in the spotlight like they are... there are no secrets. Everything comes out eventually." She frowned.

"I don't know what to do," I whispered. "He probably wants nothing to do with me. He has every right to hate me." I bit down on my bottom lip to stop the trembling and turned the bands around and around on my ring finger. "But I can't imagine my life without him."

"Then don't," she said, placing her hand on my knee. "Don't give up on him. Fight for him the way Maddox fought for me. Love isn't easy. In fact, it's downright painful sometimes. But when you find the right person for you, those bad moments are worth it."

"I can't expect him to forgive me for this." I shook my head.

"You have to make him understand," she argued.

"How?" I pleaded.

"Be honest."

"I've already told him why and I don't think he cared." I picked at a loose thread on one of the throw pillows, needing to do something to keep my hands busy.

"Then tell him again. He was angry before, but after he's cooled off he might be more willing to listen to you."

I didn't believe her. "He's never going to get over this."

"He will." She assured me. "He's just in shock right now. In the span of a few minutes he learned not only that he had a daughter, but that she was gone too."

I wiped away my tears and reached to grab a tissue to blow my nose.

I nodded, processing her words. "I want to make this work."

"You're a fighter, Remy," she gave my hand a squeeze, "so just keep on fighting for a little longer."

"I think I can do that."

"Good." She reached out and hugged me. "You two will work it out. I know it."

Her words made me feel better, even if I didn't quite believe them.

CHAPTER THIRTY-ONE

JUST KEEP FIGHTING. Emma's voice echoed in my mind.

I didn't know how much longer I could.

I stepped into the bar and took a seat. "Give me something strong. I want to be so drunk that you have to drag me out of here covered in my own vomit."

Tanner stared at me with disbelief. "You quit."

"Yes, I quit my job. That does not mean I quit drinking... I mean, I never really drink, but right now I need to get shit-faced."

Yep, getting shit-faced sounded like the best idea ever right now.

After tucking me into bed with a cup of tea Emma had left me alone. I'd tried to go to sleep, but it was fucking useless.

So here I was.

At the bar.

Three o' fucking clock in the afternoon.

But it's always five o' clock somewhere, right? Isn't that how the saying went?

"What's going on, Red?" Tanner braced his hands on the bar in front of me. His lips were turned down in true concern. "Is this about what they're saying on TV about a baby?"

"You would be right." I snapped my fingers.

He narrowed his eyes. "Are you already drunk?"

"Possibly," I admitted.

"Shit." He scrubbed his hands over his face. "Okay, okay," he muttered, "so why are you so upset about this?"

"He didn't know," I mumbled.

Tanner's eyes widened. "Well, fuck." He reached for a bottle beneath the bar, grabbed two shot glasses, and poured the drinks. He shoved one in front of me and held the other.

"Are you supposed to drink on the job?" I raised a brow.

He lifted it to his lips. "I'm the manager," was his response.

I took mine and he refilled both.

"I can understand your desire to get drunk now," he admitted.

I glanced down at the second shot with a frown.

Getting drunk wasn't solving anything.

Instead it was making me feel worse.

"I miss him," I whined. "He hates me now and I can't even blame him." I hiccupped, and covered my mouth. "Excuse me."

Tanner stared at me for a moment. "That was a big secret, Red."

"I know," I agreed, laying my head on the counter. "This is so bad."

My tears began to dampen the bar and Tanner poked my shoulder.

I sat back up and glared at him. "That wasn't nice."

"You're getting your germs all over my clean bar. Now take your shot." He thrust the shot in my direction.

I downed it, wincing at the aftertaste.

"Listen, I like you, Red," he started, "but that's some bad shit not telling a guy about his kid and then..." He trailed off, having heard about her death on the news. I fucking hated that the details surrounding Hope were out there for the world to hear and know.

"I know, I know." I agreed with him, burying my face in my hands. "I fucked up so bad. That's what I do. It's what *we* do," I mumbled, lumping Mathias into my equation, "we fuck up everything."

I laid my head back down on the counter. Tanner scolded me again, to which I gave him the finger. Some guy at the bar laughed so I gave him the finger too.

Tanner sighed heavily. "This doesn't seem like you, Red. Sitting here sniveling."

"I'm *wallowing* not sniveling. There's a fucking difference. Get it right, doucheknozzle." I sat back up, waving my arms wildly through the air.

He snorted. "Wow, you're highly entertaining when you're drunk."

"I'm not drunk I'm..." I paused. "Okay, yeah, I'm totally drunk."

Tanner shook his head, crossing his arms over his chest. "I'd like to think we're friends..." He waited for me to nod in agreement, before continuing. "So, I'm going to be straightforward with you."

"Oh, great." I rolled my eyes. "You better give me another shot for this."

He did, forgoing one for himself.

His elbows rested on the bar and he leaned towards me. "This is some bad shit you've got yourself into."

"Yeah, I know. I didn't come here to hear you tell me that. Trust me, I've been telling myself that plenty."

He glared at me to shut up and I mimed zipping my lips and tossing away the key.

"But as your friend, I'm here to tell you it's not irreparable."

I snorted.

"I'm serious," he continued. "I've known Mathias for a few years now since he started coming in here, and let me tell you, there's been a huge change in him during the time he's been with you. Trust me, that guy isn't going to walk away from this— and by this, I mean you."

My lips flattened into a thin line. "You think?" I asked, daring to let myself feel a smidgen of hope.

He nodded. "I'd be shocked if I was wrong. Wanna bet on it?"

I shook my head. "I'm too drunk to bet. You'd take advantage of me."

His body trembled with laughter. "God, I love you, Red. Best thing that ever happened to this bar was you walking in here and demanding a job."

"I am pretty fucking awesome," I agreed.

He chuckled, grabbing the glasses off the counter and dropping them into the sink. "Why don't you go rest up in the back?" He suggested. "You look like you're dead on your feet. I'll get you home after my shift ends."

I stood up, ready to disagree with him, but my legs began to shake and I knew there was no way I was walking out of here and all the way down the street back to the hotel.

"Okay," I agreed.

When I didn't move and he noticed the shakiness in my legs he sighed and came around the bar. He put a hand around my waist and guided me to the backroom and onto the couch.

"Stay." He pointed at me like I was a disobedient dog.

"Yes, dad," I sassed.

He shook his head and left me alone.

I might not have been able to sleep earlier, but with all of the alcohol in my system I soon passed out.

"FUCK, RED," TANNER groaned, "I think you just clawed the shit out of my arm. Trim your nails or something."

I flopped onto the couch, and out of his arms, feeling like I was going to throw up.

I told Tanner such and he promptly said, "Oh, hell no, Red. Hold it in."

Yeah, that so wasn't happening.

I jumped up from the couch and nearly tripped over something that was broken. It was anybody's guess as to what the object was since most things in the suite were broken now.

"Fuck," Tanner said.

He grabbed for me, trying to help me.

"Tanner, no—" I tried to warn him, but it was useless. He was in the way and my vomit wasn't staying down a second longer.

His shirt got splattered and he made a face of pure disgust.

"Ew," his nose wrinkled, "you owe me a new shirt for this and like fifty bucks, because I don't get paid to deal with drunk people. I just supply them with the liquor."

"Sorry." I put a hand over my mouth. I did feel bad. I hadn't meant to get sick all over the guy, or show up at the bar for an impromptu therapy session.

"It's okay," he grumbled, removing his shirt.

I lay down on the couch once more and Tanner went to the kitchen to dispose of his shirt in the trashcan.

"Is there someone I can call to come sit with you?" He asked, his footsteps coming closer. Suddenly he peered at me over the top of the couch.

"No," I answered with a sad lilt to my voice, "I don't have anybody."

That was the sad truth.

I was all alone in the world.

Shit. There came the tears again.

"Fuck, Red," he frowned, "I didn't mean to make you cry."

"S'okay," I muttered, "it keeps happening."

He swallowed thickly and stepped around the couch, taking a seat near my feet. Percy hissed and Tanner reared back, not having realized the cat was on the couch. Percy was sneaky like that.

"What're you doing?" I mumbled, hoping my words weren't slurred together.

"You said you didn't have anybody to sit with you, so this is me babysitting you so that you don't choke and die on your own vomit. I don't want your death on my hands," he rambled, trying to hide a smile, "mostly because I'm afraid your husband might kill me."

"He's not my husband anymore," I muttered, staring up at the ceiling.

"Says who?" He countered.

"Trust me," I turned my head in his direction, "he doesn't want to be. Not after this."

"You don't know that, Red. Give him a chance."

It grew quiet between us, but after a while I couldn't stop myself from saying, "I think we're out of chances."

"There's *always* a chance."

I wanted to believe him.

Oh, God, how I wanted to.

CHAPTER THIRTY-TWO

IT HAD BEEN a week since Mathias walked out. A week since I'd seen his face or heard his voice. A week of nothingness. And in another week he would be gone on tour.

He didn't even come back for Shiloh and the poor thing kept moping around as pathetically as me.

Emma kept me updated by sending random texts here and there on how he was doing.

It didn't matter though.

Because *he* wasn't the one telling me.

All I wanted was some sign of communication from him.

But I got nothing.

Nothing but the fear that he really might be planning to divorce me.

The pain of that thought nearly ripped my heart out of my chest.

I had no idea how to fix this.

And maybe that was the point—that there was no way to fix it.

I just had to live with it.

But I didn't want to have to live with this.

I *wanted* to get my happy ending.

I used to think that girls like me didn't deserve a happy ending, but I was wrong. I deserved to be happy just as much as the next person, and despite my choices I deserved to have Mathias in my life. If he still wanted me, that is.

I just didn't know how to make him understand.

I finally made myself shower and get dressed.

Tanner called to check on me. He'd done that three times a day, every day, since I got drunk and he had to drag my sorry ass home. I had to admit, he was a pretty nice guy.

"How are you feeling, Red?" He asked.

I grabbed a water bottle from the refrigerator, the phone cradled between my ear and shoulder.

"Not drunk," I replied.

He chuckled. "That's a good thing."

"We'll have to agree to disagree," I muttered, lifting the water to my lips and taking a sip.

"Seriously, though, how are you feeling today?" He pestered.

I leaned a hip against the counter. "The same as yesterday and the day before that and—"

"So, basically like shit," he interrupted.

"Yep," I mumbled. "At least I showered."

"Thatta girl."

"Shut up."

"Hey, don't be mean to your best friend."

"You're *not* my best friend."

"You threw up on me," he countered, "that's practically a blood bond."

I rolled my eyes. "Whatever. I think I'm going to go see my grandma."

"That sounds like a good idea," he agreed. "Talk to you later."

"M'kay," I said, and frowned. Jesus, I sounded like Mathias. "Bye."

I set my phone on the counter and buried my head in my hands. I had made such a fucking mess of things. I'd spent most of the week crying, gorging myself on ice cream, and avoiding alcohol because that turned into such a mess the first time.

But enough was enough. I had to get out of here and return to the real world. Life went on whether or not I was present for it.

I headed over to my grandma's like I told Tanner I was going to. My grandma was the only person I had here and I hoped she could make me feel better. Then again, she'd probably be too busy watching some trashy reality TV show to talk to me.

Since I didn't have my car I took Mathias' Range Rover. I figured he was already so mad at me that using his car wouldn't matter much.

I parked in the driveway and clenched the steering wheel in my hands, banging my head against the headrest.

Why?

Why me?

Why did my life always have to get crapped on?

Why couldn't I be allowed to be happy?

My eyes burned with the threat of tears, but they'd dried up a few days ago so none spilled over.

With a sigh I turned off the car and walked up to the front door.

I still had my key, but suddenly I felt like I didn't belong here.

Like I didn't belong anywhere.

Fuck, this had been a bad idea.

I doubted she wanted to see me.

She'd probably take one look at me and say, "Remy, you really fucked things up this time."

She wouldn't be lying. I had.

I knocked loudly on the door so she would hear me.

I stood with my hands clasped together, praying that she didn't turn me away.

A few moments later I heard her grumbling on the other side.

When the door opened she glared up at me. "Oh, it's you."

I flinched at that. I deserved it, but her tone still stung.

"Can I come in?" I asked hesitantly.

"If you must," she huffed.

The door closed and I followed her into the kitchen, sitting across from her at the table.

She proceeded to glare at me.

Neither one of us would speak.

I began to wonder why I even came here, but I made no move to leave.

Minutes passed and finally she was the first to break the silence. "He came over here you know."

I perked up at this information. "He did?"

She nodded. "I saw on the TV that they were talking about the baby, but I hoped you told him beforehand."

"I was going to tell him that day," I whispered, tracing the edge of my fingernail around a ring on the table.

"You should've told him a while ago, Remy."

"Fuck," I buried my face into my hands. "I know. Okay." I let my hands drop. "I know I fucked up."

"Yes you did," she nodded. Sobering, she added, "But everybody makes mistakes."

"Not mistakes this big," I countered, hanging my head in shame.

"A mistake is a mistake. Some *are* bigger than others," she agreed, "but any mistake can be forgiven," she spoke wisely.

"I don't know how to ask him to forgive me."

"You just *do*." She took my hand. Hers looked so small against mine, but right now she was the stronger of the two of us. "Life is full of hardships. You act as if what you did was unforgivable, but Remy, you didn't do anything wrong."

"But I did!" I cried. "I didn't tell him about Hope! How can he ever trust me again?!"

"Shhh," she patted my cheek, "calm yourself."

I took a few hiccupping breaths and seemed to gain control of myself once more.

"I'm not saying what you did wasn't bad, all I'm saying is it wasn't *wrong*. You did the right thing for you and him at the time. You lost your daughter and honey," tears shimmered in her eyes, "from the things your parent's told me... it sounds like we lost you too for a while." I watched as she began to cry. "You were so young and you made the only decision you knew how to make. No one can blame you for protecting yourself."

"*I* blame *me*." My voice cracked.

She shook her head. "There's no point. Instead, you need to tell yourself how strong you are. You should be proud of the person you are today. I know your daughter would be proud of you."

"Don't say that," I begged, my eyes stinging with tears. They began to cascade down my cheeks and dripped onto my shirt. I guessed they hadn't dried up after all.

"It's the truth, honey."

I began to sob, because she was wrong. So, so wrong. There was no way my daughter would be proud of me, of the things I'd done, and the way I had hurt Mathias. I was a shameful excuse for a human being.

"Do I think you should've told him back then?" She started in again. "Yes, yes I do. But I've also never been in the position where I lost a child, and thank God for that, so there's no telling what I might've done in your shoes. We all make decisions in life, and we have to own them."

I wiped my face on the sleeve of my shirt, not even caring that I was smearing mascara all over it.

"Why are you being so nice to me?" I whispered. "You seemed awfully pissed off when I showed up."

She shrugged. "I wanted to be mad at you, but frankly I can't. Not because I'm your grandma, but because you look miserable. Seriously, you look awful," she reiterated.

I began to laugh—the first time in a week—and it felt so good.

I hugged my grandma, kissing the top of her head. She might've been batshit crazy, but I loved her to death.

"Thank you."

"For what?" She asked, returning the hug.

"For making me feel better."

"Yeah, yeah," she patted my back and let go, "but if you don't work things out with him then I'm disowning you."

I snorted. "You used to hate him based off everything mom and dad told you about him. What made you change your mind with him? And be honest. Don't give me one of your bullshit answers." I warned her with a smile.

"I saw the way he looked at you."

My brows pulled together.

"He loves you, Remy," she said, "a strong, fierce kind of love—one that's rare and doesn't go away."

I nodded at her words and took a deep breath. "Thanks for the talk. I'm going to head out."

"Okay," she nodded. "I love you, but you seriously need to do something about all of that." She waved a hand at me.

It was then that I noticed my jeans were dirty, my shirt was on inside out, and my shoes didn't even match.

And here I thought I'd been doing so well this morning.

Leaving my grandma's I headed to the gym—thankful that not only did I have gym clothes stashed in my locker, but regular clothes as well. You know, since I dressed like a bum this morning.

Once there I took out my aggression on the punching bag.

I kicked and hit it until my arms were sore. Every single piece of sadness, anger, and resentment that had been bottling up inside me for the last six years poured out of me as I hit it.

When I was finished I showered and changed into fresh clothes.

I was torn between heading to Maddox and Emma's—where I was sure Mathias was still holed up—and going back to his place.

I finally settled for the former.

This girl that kept sitting around moping, and crying, wasn't me. I wasn't weak. I was loud mouthed and I fought for what I wanted. I didn't sit back and wait for somebody else to take action first.

I took charge.

I was the hero of my own fucking story.

I BEAT ON the door of the guesthouse with the side of my fist. I didn't care if I had to stand there all day knocking. I wasn't leaving until I saw Mathias and had a chance to talk to him. I wasn't wallowing anymore. I was taking charge and doing what I wanted.

The door finally swung open and I nearly fell inside, but I quickly righted myself, squaring my shoulders.

Emma stood in front of me. She didn't look too happy.

"He's not here."

"What?" I gasped, and suddenly it felt like the ground had disappeared from beneath my feet.

"He left a few hours ago and I don't think he's coming back."

Air rushed in and out of my lungs as I processed her words.

"Did he say where he was going?" I pleaded with her.

She shook her head. "No, he's just gone."

Gone.

Just gone.

This was what I deserved, but it didn't make it hurt any less.

"I... uh... better go then."

I turned away hastily and hurried back to the car.

I kept my head held high.

I would not break.

I drove slowly back to the penthouse, silently inventorying everything of mine at his house that I would need to pack. Sadly, it was mostly clothes and Percy. Not that I would pack Percy in a box, that would be cruel even if cats did love boxes.

I pulled into the parking garage and slammed on the brakes when I saw the Corvette parked in its usual spot.

For the first time since he said my name so icily a week ago, my heart began to beat at a steady pace.

He was here.

He was really here.

I parked the car and all but ran to the elevator.

As it soared to the top floor I willed it to go faster.

When the doors opened I called out, "Mathias!"

I rushed forward and heard the sound of his footsteps approaching.

The air was sucked out of my lungs when he appeared.

We stood, staring at each other, separated by our own pain and suffering.

I couldn't move or speak for a moment. My eyes roamed over

his body, as if I was looking for some significant change that had happened in the last week. He did look rather tired, with purple rings beneath his eyes.

"I'm sorry," he spoke. "I'm sorry I told you I hated you. I don't. I fucking hate myself." He scrubbed his hands over his face. I took a tentative step forward. "I've had a lot of time to think and I'm sorry for my reaction, but most of all I'm sorry for lying to you that day in the parking lot so long ago. It's my fault. I set this whole thing in motion," he rambled, barely able to catch a breath.

"No—"

"I pushed you away! I hurt you and I abandoned you when you needed me most!"

I took another step forward, and then another, until he was so close I could reach up and touch him if I wanted to.

I tilted my head back and looked up at him. "It was no one's fault. Trust me, I know. I wanted to blame myself for a long time. I even blamed you. I blamed everybody, to be honest. But I was wrong to do that. These things... they just happen."

"Why did it have to happen to *us?*" He countered, his eyes two dark storm clouds.

"Because," I placed my hands over his chest, comforted by the familiar beating of his heart, "we're stronger than most people."

"I don't feel very strong right now." His voice lowered to a soft whisper. "All I can think about is this tiny baby that needed her daddy and I wasn't fucking there. I wasn't there, because I pushed you away. I broke you and I broke her. I broke us all. I keep feeling like if I had been there this wouldn't have happened." Tears filled his eyes, one spilling over and rolling down his cheek. I wiped it away and his breath caught in his throat.

Shaking my head, I said, "You're wrong. There was nothing you or I, or anyone, could've done to prevent this."

He swallowed thickly and stared down at me, fighting his emotions. "I was with Collin yesterday and..." He closed his eyes. "Every time I looked at him I kept thinking about the fact that if she were alive she would be his age. And then I thought about all the things you said you'd never get to do with her, which made think of all the things I wouldn't get to do with her and fuck I *want* those things." He wet his lips, pulling in a lungful of air. "I know we were just kids ourselves and would've had no business raising a child, but it's unfair that we didn't even get a chance." This time it was his turn to wipe a tear away from my cheek. "I don't even know who she *looked* like." His voice cracked and more tears filled his eyes.

I closed my eyes, steeling myself. Recalling those final moments with Hope was always painful. "She had blonde hair, so light it almost looked white." A wistful smile touched my lips. "And she had your lips. She was so tiny and perfect. I kept looking at her, trying to find something wrong with her. Some outwardly proof as to why this happened to her. But she was honestly perfect. The most beautiful thing I had ever seen."

Mathias scrubbed his hands over his face. "I can't believe you had to go through that by yourself."

"Now do you see why I didn't want to tell you? I *love* you and I never wanted you to have to hurt like this."

He took my face between his large hands and we breathed the same air for a moment. "Remy, this was always our hurt. It was never your burden to bear alone."

I let out a small cry and clung to his shirt, burying my face in his chest. I wanted to hold on to him forever. I didn't want to ever have a fight like this again or to have to watch him walk out and leave me.

"Shh," he murmured, stroking his fingers lightly through my hair. "I'm so sorry. For everything."

"Me too," I whispered.

He reached down and grabbed my chin, forcing me to look at him. "I forgive you."

At those three words I breathed a sigh of relief and a weight lifted off of my shoulders.

He stroked his fingers down my back.

"I was so mad, but I realized I was more mad at myself than you. I was being stupid to walk out. This is just another part of our story, right?"

"One of the worst parts." I laughed, releasing him from my hold.

"It's not too late for us, is it?"

I wiped away the last of my tears and shook my head. "It's never too late."

"Thank God for that," he growled, taking my face between his hands and lowering his mouth to mine.

Mathias and I had been through a lot at a young age, and we'd always have our ups and downs, but no matter what we would always work it out, because our love was forever.

He pulled away and smiled down at me. "No more secrets?" He asked.

"No more secrets," I vowed.

"Good." He pressed his forehead to mine.

Wrapping my arms around him, I said, "I'm so happy you came back."

"Me too," he murmured, holding on to me too.

"I expected you to divorce me," I admitted.

He chuckled. "I'd be lying if I didn't say there was a moment of weakness where I considered it. But in the end, the thought of my life without you in it was far too painful. I've changed a lot,

Remy. I'm not that same guy I used to be. I'm working on thinking things through and not being so impulsive. My impulsivity tends to ruin things," he frowned, stroking my cheek. "Think of me as the new and improved Mature Mathias."

I laughed. "I still liked the old Mathias."

"How about a happy medium?" He suggested, guiding me over to the couch.

He collapsed onto the cushions, pulling me down with him. I landed with a thud on his hard chest and he grunted from the impact.

"Sorry," I mumbled.

He put a pillow behind his head and soon Shiloh and Percy joined us on the couch. He wrapped his arms around me and we lay there together, breathing in each other's presence and reveling in what we could've lost again if one or both of us chose to be stupid.

Mathias was right. He had changed, but so had I.

Both of us for the better.

We were both stronger, happier people now.

He smiled and laughed more. He listened to his heart instead of running away.

And me?

I didn't hide behind the persona of my red lipstick anymore.

I was just Remy and he was just Mathias.

Things might not have been perfect, but I knew they never would be with us.

All that mattered was that we had each other.

EPILOGUE
—FIVE MONTHS LATER

"IT'S THIS WAY." I held tightly to Mathias' hand, guiding him around the grassy area.

His hand was slightly sweaty in mine and I knew he was nervous.

I was too.

I'd been shocked when he told me he wanted to visit Hope's grave after the tour ended, but I didn't object.

I might've gotten my closure with her death, but he never did.

The sun shined down us, bathing us in a warm golden glow. I was excited for the summer, especially since the tour was finally over and we'd have a chance to relax.

"It's this one." I stopped in front of the small grave with her name, birth and death date. It broke my heart that the dates were the same. It still seemed unfair, but I'd long ago stopped questioning it. Sometimes things happen in our life that are out of our control, and you either let it make you or break you.

Mathias' hand slipped from mine and he let out a ragged breath, dropping to his knees in front of the stone. He ran the tips of his fingers over the indented letters that formed her name.

A dark gray splotch landed on the headstone and I looked up, expecting to see that the sky had darkened and it was starting to rain, but no, that wasn't the case.

Mathias was crying.

The kind of cry that made his whole body shake from the force.

I reached out, placing my hand on his shoulder.

I didn't say anything. I gave him his moment.

"It never really seemed real before," he whispered.

He slowly raised his head and his tear-rimmed eyes met mine. I stroked my fingers over his cheek and then his lips.

"I wish it wasn't," I murmured.

He stared down at her grave once more and I startled when he began to sing a lullaby.

Now I was the one crying.

Damn him.

I hurriedly wiped the tears away before he could see.

When he finished singing the song, he whispered, "Daddy loves you."

He rose to his feet, drying his face with the back of his hand. "How did two fuck-ups like us get lucky enough to have a second chance?" His hands fell onto my rounded stomach. We hadn't been trying to get pregnant, and we'd both been shocked over the news, but also incredibly happy.

"I don't know. I guess maybe it was fate." I smiled at him as he lovingly stroked my stomach.

"Or maybe," he kissed my forehead, then my cheeks, and finally my lips before murmuring, "it was Hope."

THE END

BONUS CONTENT

INTERVIEWER: Thanks for sitting down with us today. Every celebrity news station has been vying for this interview and we're honored you chose us. You don't normally do interviews, correct Mathias?

MATHIAS: No, I fucking don't. And I'm only doing this one because my manager made me. He's a real prick.

INTERVIEWER: <clears throat> Alright, then... <shuffles notes> Everybody has been looking forward to hearing from you both about your sudden decision to get married and now the news that you're having a baby. Congratulations, by the way.

REMY: Well—

MATHIAS: I wouldn't call it sudden. Not when you've been in love with the person for seven years. <rolls eyes> This is why I fucking hate interviews. None of you do any fucking research.

INTERVIEWER: Uh... moving on then... are you enjoying being married? Remy, how are you adjusting to life in the spotlight?

MATHIAS: Being married is just like dating. Except the sex gets better. Don't ask me how. But it does.

REMY: I guess I'm adjusting fine. <shrugs> It's just a part of his life, and mine now. So I roll with it. I also wear lots of hats now.

INTERVIEWER: <chuckles> How was life on the road with the *Coming Home Tour*?

REMY: That was hard. I missed being home and relaxing on the couch, watching movies. Whatever.

INTERVIEWER: Now that the tour is over what are your plans?

MATHIAS: Baby proofing the fucking house.

REMY: <laughs> And working on Mathias not cussing so much.

MATHIAS: Good fucking luck. <mumbles> I need a cigarette.

INTERVIEWER: Do you know if the baby is a boy or girl?

MATHIAS: We do and it's none of your fucking business.

INTERVIEWER: You lost your first child together when you were only teenagers, does that leave you with any fears this time around?

REMY: \<looks at Mathias\> Yeah, of course. I mean, there's *always* the possibility that something could go wrong. We see the doctor regularly and he assures us that everything looks as good as it can.

INTERVIEWER: Mathias, I heard that you actually didn't know about your first child, is that true?

MATHIAS: \<glares\> I'm not answering that.

INTERVIEWER: \<shrugs\> It seems that if it were true, that would be something difficult to work through? Yet, you both seem incredibly happy and you're having another baby together.

MATHIAS: Look, people make mistakes. I've made a hell of a lot them myself. We've made a lot of mistakes together. \<reaches for Remy's hand\> And we'll continue to make mistakes, because we're far from fucking perfect. But when you love someone as much as we love each other, and you've fought as hard as we have to get to where we are, you don't fucking let go of that. \<kisses Remy\>

INTERVIEWER: Well, I think that's all the questions we have time for today. Thank you for joining us.

REMY: Thanks for having us.

MATHIAS: Thank God this nightmare is over. See you never, asshole.

IN YOUR HEART

Coming June 2015

- A WILLOW CREEK NOVEL -

I thought I had found love.
I thought I had found my forever.
I'd never been more wrong in all my life.

Sadie Westbrook's seemingly perfect life comes to a screeching halt when she catches her fiancé in bed with another woman. Suddenly, everything she believed in is tested and there's only one person she can turn to—the guy who has been by her side ever since their best friend's fell in love and became inseparable.

Ezra Collins—the bassist for the band Willow Creek—has only ever had one weakness, and her name is Sadie. When he receives a frantic call he rushes to her aid, helping to pick up the pieces of her crumbling life—even if that means letting Sadie live with him.

The close proximity tests the limits of their friendship and as the lines between friends and lovers blur they'll have to decide if falling in love with your best friend is worth the risk of losing them.

ACKNOWLEDGEMENTS

Wow. I can't believe I'm writing *The End* on my eighteenth book. Seriously, when did that happen? Writing this book has been an experience unlike any other. I was terrified to write Mathias' book. It's such a departure from *Last To Know* and I'm sure it was nothing like what you all expected. This book pushed me to be a stronger writer and for that I'm thankful. And to be honest, this book also kind of wrecked me. I'm not the kind of author that gets emotional when they write, but with this book? I cried. And I cried. And I cried some more. I was overcome by the emotions, hardships, and beauty that was Mathias and Remy's story and I'm thankful that they chose me to tell it.

Thank you so much to my beta readers Becca, Haley, and Stefanie. You truly have kept me sane through all my books and have helped calm the negative thoughts. Thank you for loving this story as much as me. It's meant so much hearing your positive notes. And I love you for the critiques too.

Grammy... if you can see this, then you shouldn't have read this book. You've really got to stop doing that. Kidding. I love you!

Regina Bartley, I don't know what I would do without you! For realz! You are my writing soul twin. Haha.

Regina Wamba, no book is complete without thanking you! You always give me the most beautiful covers. And I can't forget one of the most important aspects you helped me with—naming Remy!

Eric and Jen, I can't thank you enough for bringing my characters to life. You both did an incredible job at truly capturing the essence of the characters and I couldn't be happier!

Angela, Angela, Angela. Thank you for formatting my books and making them pretty. You're the best!

ABOUT THE AUTHOR

Micalea Smeltzer is a bestselling Young and New Adult author from Winchester, Virginia. She's always working on her next book, and when she has spare time she loves to read and spend time with her family.

Follow on Facebook:
https://www.facebook.com/MicaleaSmeltzerfanpage
Twitter: @msmeltzer9793
Instagram: micaleasmeltzer
Pinterest: http://www.pinterest.com/micaleasmeltzer/

Made in the USA
Middletown, DE
07 August 2015